THE PAPER MARRIAGE

Susan Kay Law

B

BERKLEY BOOKS, NEW YORK

THE BERKLEY PUBLISHING GROUP
Published by the Penguin Group
Penguin Group (USA) Inc.
375 Hudson Street, New York, New York 10014, USA
Penguin Group (Canada), 90 Eglinton Avenue East, Suite 700, Toronto, Ontario M4P 2Y3, Canada
(a division of Pearson Penguin Canada Inc.)
Penguin Books Ltd., 80 Strand, London WC2R 0RL, England
Penguin Group Ireland, 25 St. Stephen's Green, Dublin 2, Ireland (a division of Penguin Books Ltd.)
Penguin Group (Australia), 250 Camberwell Road, Camberwell, Victoria 3124, Australia
(a division of Pearson Australia Group Pty. Ltd.)
Penguin Books India Pvt. Ltd., 11 Community Centre, Panchsheel Park, New Delhi—110 017, India
Penguin Group (NZ), 67 Apollo Drive, Rosedale, North Shore 0632, New Zealand
(a division of Pearson New Zealand Ltd.)
Penguin Books (South Africa) (Pty.) Ltd., 24 Sturdee Avenue, Rosebank, Johannesburg 2196,
South Africa

Penguin Books Ltd., Registered Offices: 80 Strand, London WC2R 0RL, England

This is an original publication of The Berkley Publishing Group.

First edition: March 2008

Library of Congress Cataloging-in-Publication Data

Law, Susan Kay.
    The paper marriage / Susan Kay Law.—1st ed.
      p. cm.
    ISBN 978-0-425-21935-5
      1. Married women—Fiction.   2. Single fathers—Fiction.   I. Title.

PS3562.A8612P37 2008
813'.54—dc22

                                          2007046576

PRINTED IN THE UNITED STATES OF AMERICA

10 9 8 7 6 5 4 3 2 1

THE PAPER MARRIAGE

ONE

Sometimes your life changes on a perfectly ordinary day.

It seems like it shouldn't. Such momentous events should be accompanied by great rolling black clouds and brutal claps of thunder, a sign from above that *here* is the moment that your life stops being one thing and becomes another.

The first time Ann McCrary's life changed, she knew it the instant they told her.

The second time, it snuck up on her. The day slid by, mundane, almost unnoticed, and it was only later that it hit her: yes, that was the day, almost twelve years after the first one, when it all started.

It was a brilliant spring afternoon, the third of May. Ann turned her neat, gray Camry into her neat, green street, in a neighborhood that was everybody's fantasy of coming home. It was lined with the kind of Dutch Colonials and Cape Cods and four squares that were nice houses eighty or ninety years ago and now were wildly expensive to buy, even more insanely pricey to build new. People coughed up the money anyway, trying to acquire the kind of life that existed on old TV shows and in babyboomer fantasies.

There should have been huge, old trees arching over the street to complete the picture, a Norman Rockwell canopy that fell to Dutch elm disease years ago. New maples and slender ashes speared along the curb, trying to take their place, a thin green echo of what used to be.

She headed for her modest, shingled saltbox, deep-breathing through the mix of anticipation and grief that always met her as she approached her house. She kept waiting to get past it, waiting for the day when coming home after work would be just that, an everyday occurrence that didn't hold any expectations or any regrets.

Not yet, apparently. But she couldn't sell. She just couldn't.

A beast of a Harley-Davidson, all snarling black and chrome with a beat-up black leather jacket draped over the back, sat in front of the house next door. A Gabberts delivery truck was parked half-in, half-out of the driveway. She couldn't help but be a bit curious about her new neighbors; the neighborhood grapevine had failed utterly to find out who'd bought it, which was just odd. Usually by a new family's move-in day, the whole street knew name, rank, and marital status.

When Mrs. Hillerman moved into assisted living, her house had sold in less than a day. Not unusual; houses around here often sold even before they went officially on the market, frequently to a friend of a current resident who'd been waiting to swoop.

But Mrs. Hillerman hadn't updated so much as a tile in her Tudor in the forty-five years she'd lived there, and so Ann figured it might take a little longer to sell.

Ann turned into her driveway and rolled into her garage. A tall cedar fence separated her property from Mrs. Hillerman's. She peered through the hedge of lilacs that cloaked the fence, a few heady, purple blooms just starting to open. Two hulking delivery guys, grimy baseball caps on their heads and burly biceps exposed by their sweaty T-shirts, lugged a mahogany breakfront up the back staircase.

Likely the motorcycle belonged to one of them. At worst, a grown kid of the new owners who'd be gone soon enough. There were a couple of guys in the neighborhood who had Harleys, fifty-year-olds who'd sprung for cycles instead of convertibles. But they didn't park them on the street; they were inside the garages, admired more than ridden, treated with the reverence of the symbols they were.

She assumed the new neighbors would be nice; most people who lived here were. But she'd miss Mrs. Hillerman, who was always grateful for a little company, the only other woman living alone in the entire neighborhood.

Cleo was whining by the back door. Ann let her out to do her business while she changed. The dog was waiting by the back door, nose nudging her leash impatiently, by the time Ann'd gotten into her workout clothes.

She hooked the leash to Cleo's red leather collar, rechecked the laces on her Asics, and started to run.

Ann walked into Cedar Ridge on the dot of six thirty, Cleo trotting by her side. The smell of the place assaulted her, as it always did. Thankfully it didn't reek of the urine and decay that pervaded the small nursing home her grandmother had died in, but the odors were strong just the same, a burning wave of antiseptic and the stench of an industrial kitchen. It didn't seem to matter if it was chicken or beef for dinner; the odor never changed.

"Must be six thirty." Ashia, Ann's favorite nurse, was at the nurse's station tonight. She checked her watch and flashed her sunshine smile, as bright as her yellow and red headcloth. "I don't know why we even bother with clocks."

"Someday I'm coming at seven, just to mess you all up."

"No you're not," Ashia said confidently, leaning over the counter to wiggle her fingers at Cleo.

If anyone would know Ann's habits, it'd be Ashia, who'd been here since the start. Then, she'd been scrubbing floors and barely able to speak English. She'd put herself through nursing school since then, but unlike most, she hadn't fled for easier, happier jobs.

"How was his day?" Ann asked, her regular question, though she'd given up hope of getting a different answer to it a decade ago. She wondered why she bothered to ask; maybe because if she didn't have her routines, she wasn't sure what she'd have left.

"Quiet." She beamed when Ann slid a foil-covered pan on the white laminate counter. "What did you bring us tonight?"

"Cinnamon rolls. Maple glazed."

Ashia poked beneath the foil. "Aayee, you are going to be the death of my figure one of these days."

"Got to keep you around somehow," Ann said.

"And where else would I go?"

A million other places, Ann thought. *Any other place.* If she had a choice, she'd be out of here in a hot second.

She headed off down the long, narrow hallway, lined with flat white doors, most of them gaping open, as if welcoming visitors who rarely came. Her shoes squeaked on the industrial gray linoleum, Cleo's claws clicking in rhythm. The murmur of muted televisions leaked from every room: *Wheel of Fortune, Eyewitness News,* reruns of *Andy Griffith* and *Seinfeld.* Sometimes there was a groan, the heavy bass rumble of a snore.

A woman in a faded blue housecoat, her back curved into a harsh C, pushed her walker down the hall, shuffling in her pink crocheted slippers. Mr. Landen sat in his wheelchair in his doorway, his head nodding. She'd never seen him anywhere else.

When Cleo was at her side, no one ever noticed Ann walking down the hall. Cleo nudged the twisted claw of Mr. Landen's hand, and Mr. Landen roused briefly, resting his palm on the dog's head, the skin on the back of his hand thin as gauze, clotted with purple brown liver spots. Cleo waited until he dropped off again before continuing her rounds.

She wandered in and out of rooms, accepting her due. Ann let her take her time. Putting off the inevitable; she recognized what she was doing, felt the nagging prod of guilt that came along with it. And yet she couldn't bring herself to hurry.

But they reached the end of the hall anyway. This door was closed and, like the rest, it was decorated with a paper lavender Easter egg and a couple of cardboard tulips. They'd stay until they were replaced with flags for Memorial Day, along with gold foil stars on the doors of the old men who'd served.

After all these years, she knew Cedar Ridge's routines.

And her own, as well. She took a deep breath and pushed open the door.

Ann looked at Mary first. Avoiding the inevitable again. She was such a chicken. It wasn't as if she didn't know what she'd see if she looked at the bed first. Wasn't as if it would ever be different if she put it off long enough. It didn't seem to matter.

Mary McCrary glanced up, her fingers never pausing as she poked her knitting needles in and out of fuzzy pink yarn.

Ann's mother-in-law was a handsome woman. In all the years she'd known her, not once, even after hours at the hospital, had Ann ever seen Mary anything but impeccably put together, her hair in a neat, smooth style, discreet but lovely diamonds in her ears, her makeup tastefully present but never overdone. When Ann was a teenager and routinely enthusiastically embarrassed by her mother, who wandered around in skirts that belonged in dustbins, her graying hair flying to her waist, and not a smudge of makeup, Ann had longed for a mother like Mary. Someone who looked like a mother was supposed to look. Someone *normal*.

Mary's gaze fell on Cleo, and her mouth thinned to a narrow slice of Estée Lauder rose. Mary thought that a "rehabilitation facility"—Cedar Ridge was not a nursing home to her, never would be—was no place for a dog. Ann had gotten Cleo certified as a therapy dog shortly after she'd brought her home, just so she could bring her here. Cleo was left alone enough.

"How was he today?"

"Excellent." She jabbed at the pink yarn, the steel needles glittering. "He was very alert today. I think because Melissa was on duty. You know he likes her better than that Carmelita woman."

Ann sighed, biting back the argument. It did no good to insist that John had no more sense of who cared for him than the potted geranium on the windowsill did. Twelve years, at least a dozen doctors, and Mary still expected John to wake up at any moment.

Ann wasn't sure that it wasn't better that way. Hope, however impossible and misguided, had to be better than . . . nothing.

Mary stood. She still had good posture, her back straight in its pale blue twinset, her hips narrow in pressed gray wool. There were lines on her elegantly boned face now, a lot of them, deep circles under the eyes. At fifty, she'd looked a decade younger, but she'd aged thirty years in the last ten.

She gathered up her knitting and reached for her bag, rose tapestry with shiny brass buckles.

"It's pretty," Ann said. "What are you making?"

Mary shoved the yarn away and tucked it firmly under her arm. "Baby blanket. Lori's expecting again, a girl this time."

"Oh. That'll be nice." After three boys, no doubt Mary's niece was thrilled to find out she was having a girl. "How many greats does that make for you?"

Mary gathered up her purse and rummaged through it for her car keys, giving the task far more attention than it required. Her mother-in-law always put them away in the same place, a tiny pocket just below the handle.

Mary always put everything in its place.

"Seven," she said briskly. "Five nephews, two nieces."

Stupid, stupid, stupid. Ann knew better than to ask, but it was such a polite question, asking after someone's family.

But it only reminded them both that there weren't any other *greats* in Mary's life. Not the ones she longed for.

Ann had never said the right thing around Mary. It had always been perfectly clear that Mary did not consider her good enough for her son. She'd been too polite to mention it, though not everyone in Mill Valley had had the same manners, and

Ann had heard more than a few comments in that vein over the years.

They'd gotten used to it, though, both the town and the McCrarys. Maybe because, after a while, it became obvious the relationship was going to last. Or because anyone with half a brain cell could tell that Ann was madly, completely in love.

It had just gotten to the point where Ann was starting to hope that Mary might like her someday. Maybe, just maybe, even love her a little, because she'd finally recognized that Ann made her son happy.

Their almost relationship was just one more casualty.

Mary passed her on the way to the door, giving her a quick, obligatory hug.

"Drive safe," Ann said. It was thirty-seven miles back to Mill Valley, a round trip Mary had made nearly every day for the past twelve years. A blizzard had stopped her once or twice, but mostly the post office had nothing on her.

"Of course." Of course she was careful. Ann sometimes wondered if Mary was ever tempted to not be, to just aim her Lincoln at a telephone pole and floor it.

Except that would be far too messy and dramatic for Mary McCrary.

Mary allowed herself one glance back at the bed, the muscles of her face tense, as if they'd been frozen into a careful mask, one that would never give anything away.

"Would you like me to walk you to your car?" Ann offered.

"Don't be silly." Mary waved away the suggestion. "If all these old geezers can totter around here without hurting themselves, I imagine I can make it to the parking lot in one piece."

"I didn't mean—"

"I know what you meant." Mary met her eyes, a moment of sympathy, and then her expression hardened. *If I can do this, so can you, and you're not getting out of a second of it by escorting me to my car.*

Ann watched Mary make her way down the hall, nodding politely to everyone she passed but never pausing. What was she thinking? Could she not wait to leave, or wished she could stay? Was she wondering how long it would be before she lived in a place like this herself, rather than simply visiting someone there?

Okay, she'd stalled enough. Ann steeled herself for it, forcing a fake smile, wondering as she did so why she even bothered, and walked quickly to the bed.

"Hello, sweetheart," she said, and bent to kiss her husband.

TWO

"So when you turn into Ward-fuckin'-Cleaver?" Boom shoved a six-pack of Summit into Tom's hands the instant he opened the door and shouldered his way into the entry.

Boom stood in the arch of the living room, taking in the deep, flowered sofas, the rocking chair with its frilled seat in the corner, and the gauzy painting of a garden over the cream marble mantel. He shook his head sadly. "Christ. Didn't know the old lady left her furniture here for you."

"She didn't," Tom said.

"Don't tell me you *paid* for this shit."

"I sure did." He hadn't actually seen it before he'd bought it, however, which was one more mistake in a long line of them. But what the hell did he know, or care, about furniture? He'd told the decorator he wanted it to look pretty, something a girl would like, and let her have at it. He hadn't figured she'd design something for a girl in 1957.

He should have warned her that the girl in question was a teenager now, and the last time he'd seen her she had a ring in her nose, black hair, black lips, and a snarl worthy of a bad-tempered badger.

"It's not that bad." He took a gander over Boom's shoulder and winced. "Okay, maybe it is."

"How much this run you?"

"How the *h* should I know?"

Despite the fact that the diamond in Boom's left ear would have paid for any house in the neighborhood, Boom could account for every single one of the many, many cents he'd earned. Tom, however, just had his business manager automatically transfer some money every time the balance in his account dropped below 50K. In his opinion, the best thing about having money was not having to think about it anymore.

"Well, at least it should be a decent investment," Boom said glumly. "Maybe it'll look better after we start drinking."

"Maybe." Tom didn't think so, though. In fact, he figured if they drank enough, the place might start looking downright scary. But since he was only going to be here until September, it really didn't matter. He figured you couldn't lose your manhood by living on the set of *Driving Miss Daisy* for just three and a half months.

Boom clomped his way through the living room, swearing as he banged into a little mahogany table that held a collection of silver boxes. He crushed a delicate swath of lace curtain in his meat hook of a fist and peered intently out the window. "Yup," he said. "She's still there."

"Please tell me there's somebody hot in this neighborhood."

"Probably. The question is whether any of 'em are over twenty," Boom said. "But definitely not that one."

A lady stood in the yard of the neat white Colonial across the street, her fists on her substantial hips. She'd been gardening, by the looks of the big yellow gloves on her hands and the ovals of mud on her knees. She was staring at Tom's front door, her mouth open, gray hairs straggling from the loose knot at the back of her head.

"You think she's staring 'cause she doesn't know who you are?" Tom asked. "Or because she does?"

Six-foot-four-inch, two-hundred-and-eighty-pound bald black men were probably a rare enough sight in this neighborhood to attract some wary attention. In most places, however, what Boom attracted was out-and-out awe.

"You kiddin'?" Boom asked. "Everybody in this state knows who I am."

"Yeah, you don't exactly blend in." Tom chuckled. "You want a beer?"

"'Course I want a beer. You didn't think I brought those for you, didja?"

Tom led Boom down the hallway with its gold-framed mirrors and an arrangement of fake tulips claiming space on a dark-wood table. The kitchen was at the back of the house, a narrow space with bright fluorescent lights and a small arch that led to a tiny nook with built-in benches. Quaint, the real estate agent had said. He'd told her he wanted something homey, something that looked like Grandma's house. She hadn't believed him at first, showing him a contemporary box on Lowry Hill and a white and steel townhouse that overlooked the river. Once he'd convinced her that was really what he wanted, however, she'd done exactly that: found him a grandma's house.

Boom stopped dead on the checkered linoleum. "Dude," he said. "You got fruit on your wall."

"I know," Tom said sadly, already missing his black granite counters and stainless-steel appliances. Not that he'd ever cooked in it, but the place had *looked* badass. There weren't many cars at Metro Maserati that were sleeker than his stove.

The Formica in this kitchen was lemonade yellow, edged with dented metal. The fridge had round corners and looked small enough for Boom to pick up with one arm.

"You got a stove like Rachael Ray!"

"Rachael Ray?"

"Food Network, Nash. Food Network."

"Since when do you watch the Food Network?"

"You can only watch porn so long, and there ain't much else in those hotel rooms but TV." Boom shrugged, not the least bit embarrassed. When you were Jerome "Boom" Bonderman, being secure in your place in the world and your essential guy-hood came with the territory, and neither porn nor cooking shows could shake it. "Food TV's better. Chicks who can cook. Good as it gets."

"Yeah." Tom gave Boom's stomach a punch. He thought he'd put enough juice in it to at least earn a flinch. No such luck. "It's starting to show, Boom."

Boom had been a rangy first baseman when he'd first broken into the league. He'd put on ten pounds per year his first six seasons, but since his home run production had gone up five a year as well, the team'd shut up about his weight. They'd moved him to right field, and finally DH, and only a couple of sportswriters had dared to comment about his expanding waistline.

Boom didn't care. Thank God for the American League, he'd laughed. Let him have a good five years more than he otherwise would have.

"You better call an exterminator," he said. "Coulda swore I just felt a bug brush by my belly." He took another sorrowful look around the kitchen. "The things we do for females."

"Yeah," Tom agreed. "The things we do." He ignored the jibe at the weakness of his punch. Boom'd never let him win that argument. "Come on."

He headed down the narrow staircase, Boom clomping behind him. "You're gonna break the damn stairs, you keep stamping like that."

"If you hadn't up and moved into Barbie's great-grandma's house, wouldn't be a problem," he said. "You coulda taken her to the condo."

"No, I couldn't." His beautiful condo, he thought with warm nostalgia. Two floors perched high on the top of a building smack in the middle of downtown. He had a pool table instead of a dining table, a basketball hoop on the wall of the two-story living room, and a television screen bigger than half the movie theaters in town. Everything a guy needed. "It's not the right place for her."

"You're giving this thing a good try, I'll give you that," Boom said. "You're bleepin' nuts for doing it, but you're trying."

"You're not helping, Boom." He already knew he was nuts for trying it, too, and he didn't need Boom's opinion reinforcing it. But there simply wasn't anything else he could do, not and be able to sleep at night.

"Now *that's* what I'm talking about!" Boom said when he reached the bottom of the stairs.

The basement was the one room in the house where Tom had chosen everything himself, every last stick of it. The room was dark as a dance club, with glass block windows no bigger than a tackle box set high in the walls and the kind of paneling that had been in half of his friends' basements when he was in junior high. He'd gotten his first kiss and copped his first good feel in a room a lot like this one.

But there the resemblance ended. A projection TV dropped down from the ceiling, aiming at a white screen that took up one entire end of the room. In front of it sat massive black leather theater seats in two rows, the second raised on a foot-high platform. They reclined, had two cup holders apiece, and were hooked into the stereo system so they shook when something blew up on-screen.

The other end of the room had its own smaller plasma screen, mounted above a big cherry bar with two refrigerators behind it and a brass rail running the length of the front. A pool table occupied the middle of the room, a sleek nickel fixture above it. Pinball machines flanked the table, blaring with colored light, neon bikini babes pouting sexily above. There was even a race simulator, a climb-in machine in sizzling red with a black seat and a stick shift the size of a baseball bat.

He'd had to tip the guys a grand apiece to get them to bring everything down those narrow stairs, and even then they'd beat the hell out of the walls in the process. But it had been worth it.

"This is more like it." Boom dropped into one of the leather seats and kicked it back into full recline. "Give me one of those."

Tom handed him a bottle, took one himself, and stuck the

rest of the six-pack on the floor between them, figuring there was no point in putting it in the fridge. They weren't going to last long enough to get warm, anyway.

Boom twisted off the cap and downed the whole bottle before Tom settled himself in his own chair.

Dispensing with the niceties, Boom grabbed two more.

"Thought you brought those for me," Tom said.

"I brought them to christen the house. Doesn't matter who drinks them."

"Don't drink 'em all. Don't want you sleepin' on my sofa tonight." He wasn't really worried. Boom could go through triple that six-pack and still be cold sober; Tom had seen him do it more than once. It was his metabolism, Boom claimed. Which was also why he didn't weigh twice as much as he did, considering he regularly put away enough food for an entire offensive line.

"You should be so lucky so's I'd sleep here," he said. "You miss me, and you know it." They'd been roommates at training camp the first year they'd been called up.

"You could always get married again. I'd let you move in after you got kicked out this time, too." Boom had spent six months in Tom's guest room when his first marriage had ended, which was four months longer than the marriage itself had lasted, to the relief of everyone involved, including Boom.

Tamara, Boom's ex, was a former Miss Alabama, a Stanford law grad, and—then, and now—both the most beautiful and meanest woman Tom had ever met. Last he heard she was headed for D.C., which Tom figured were the natural waters for gorgeous and lethal sharks like her.

"You promised," Boom said. "You promised if I ever started mumblin' about gettin' married again, you'd shoot me first. I'm countin' on you, man."

"It's a deal." They clinked bottles. Boom took another long swallow while Tom reached for the universal remote, which controlled nearly everything in the room and which he figured, if need be, could probably be programmed to maneuver the space shuttle home.

"Better drink up, Nash, while you can." Boom handed him another bottle. "So when's she comin'?"

"Saturday. I'm picking her up at the airport on Saturday." Just thinking about it had him slugging the beer almost as fast as Boom.

"Hmm." Boom settled back, resting the bottle on his stomach. "Well, call me when you need me."

"What makes you so sure that I'm gonna need you?"

Boom gave him a long, pitying look. "Oh, you're gonna need me."

———

The motorcycle was gone by the time Ann got home. The furniture truck, too, and all the movers. There was a gleaming charcoal Bentley parked in the street and a low glow from one of the basement windows. Guess her new neighbors had rich friends.

Her nighttime routine required no more thought than the rest of her day. Let Cleo out one last time. She'd be coming into heat soon, and Ann had the right stud all picked out. A new batch of puppies, their fourth. She'd miss her running partner for a while, and her life would get a lot more complicated with a houseful of wriggling puppies, but she looked forward to it. They'd bring life to the place, shake things up in a way she would enjoy.

While Cleo settled in, she rinsed out the Tupperware container she'd used to carry her supper to Cedar Ridge; she always ate dinner with her husband. Shut off the porch lights, check the locks on the door—it had taken her years to get used to the fact that she had to lock up at night, because her mother hadn't locked a door in her entire life. Anybody who wanted to get in that bad, would, Judy had said; anybody else was welcome to come in anyway.

But despite the fact that the neighborhood looked like

Pleasantville come to life, and was flanked on two sides by golf courses—an extremely tony private one, and a nice egalitarian public one—the fact remained that there were busy streets nearby bordered by a cluster of fast-food restaurants and inexpensive apartments.

It was a strange neighborhood, all told, a pocket that claimed the narrow ground between the urban and suburban. She and her neighbors had their own little park, at the end of a dead-end street, with bright-colored playground equipment and an ice rink in the winter. Block parties in the summer, including a bang-up Fourth of July celebration with kids running through the streets with melting bomb pops and hissing sparklers. A Halloween parade, the children marching up and down in their costumes while their parents cheered from the sidewalks, camcorders whirring away.

A perfect neighborhood for a family, she and John decided when they bought the house, though it hadn't been updated in thirty years and, even so, it was a huge financial stretch for them. But they had a clear vision for their future, had had it since they were fifteen, and this house and neighborhood were part of it. So even though it meant they had to put off having a baby for a few more years, it would all be worth it in the end.

But they'd waited too long. Oh, damn, they'd waited too long.

She crawled into her bed, a beautiful, sleek, dark-wood piece with leather insets in the headboard. It had been bought in celebration after their firm had turned its first profit.

Moonlight sifted through the delicate curtains. Cleo thumped her tail on the floor, waiting politely for permission, until Ann patted the bed beside her.

Insomnia rarely troubled her anymore. There had been months—really, a couple of years—where she walked around in perpetual exhaustion because she couldn't sleep at night in her empty, lonely bed, couldn't stay asleep if she did drop off.

But Cleo had helped, and so had the running, and eventually she'd slept in that bed longer alone than with her husband, and, well, she'd just gotten used to it.

Not tonight, though. She tried designing in her head. The Erickson project was giving her fits; they wanted four bathrooms, and a big tub in two of them, but they didn't want to ruin the lines and the feel of their turn-of-the-century four square just two blocks from Lake Harriet.

She heard the low rumble of male voices outside; must be from next door. A boom of laughter, hearty and substantial.

No more old ladies for neighbors, she thought, unless it's an old lady that's got a lot of sons who come visit her.

Or an old lady who had a lot more fun than she did.

The car roared away, a door slammed, and everything went quiet.

Around three, she gave up. She tugged on a robe, went down to the kitchen, turned the lights on full, and plugged in her KitchenAid.

Brownies tonight, she decided. Brownies made everything better.

THREE

"Ann. Ann!"

She considered ignoring the voice, then sighed, paused in her tracks, and turned. Lorraine Kozlowski was already halfway across the street, trowel in hand, her eyes bright with anticipation.

Lorraine already lived there when John and Ann moved in, and Ann had learned early the only things that mattered about her. She loved two things: her garden, which put every other yard in the neighborhood to shame, and gossip. She knew the names of all the people in every house, the age of their children, the health of their parents, and whether they were getting divorced—probably before they did.

"You goin' over there?" she asked when she reached Ann's side, her voice an excited stage whisper.

Ann shifted the plate of brownies from one hand to the other, scrambling for a graceful exit line. "Yup. Welcome the new neighbors, you know." She took a quick, hopeful step in that direction.

Lorraine grabbed her arm, holding her in place. "You don't want to do that."

Ann sighed. Okay, there was no getting away, not without hurting Lorraine's feelings. And when it came right down to it, Ann felt a little sorry for her. Since he'd retired, Lorraine's husband spent every spare moment on a boat or in a tree stand. Escaping, Ann privately figured. Her children—two daughters, one son—had moved out of state, made the obligatory once-a-year visit, and that was that.

But Ann still didn't want to spend the morning hearing every detail she'd dug up about who'd moved in, not to mention the latest misdoings of the Bensons' delinquent seventeen-year-old son.

"You don't want to go over there!" Lorraine said.

"I'm just going to bring them some brownies," she said. "Take no time at all."

Lorraine looked up and down the street, squinting, as if making sure there was no one spying on them. Then she leaned closer. "I think they're drug dealers."

"Drug dealers?" She bit down on the inside of her cheek to hold back the smile. "Here?"

"I saw it on the news," she said with absolute conviction. "Those meth labs, they put them in the most ordinary houses they can find, where nobody would think of looking for them."

"Well, nobody would think of looking for them here, that's for sure." Drug dealers next door. That was a new one, even for Lorraine. She'd speculated about Helen Mortimer having an affair with her female Pilates instructor, which had been almost as surprising. Of course that one had turned out to be true.

"Did you see that car here last night?"

"Well, yes, I did."

"It was here really late."

"Was it? I didn't notice."

"And—" Her grip got more urgent, her voice more insistent. "You should have seen the man who went in there!"

"Lorraine, I'm sure that—"

"He looked like that rapper," she said. "You know the one. Bald, with all the tattoos and the muscles, who likes to run around with his shirt off?"

"Lorraine, you noticed his muscles?"

"Well, not really, I—" She paused, pink flushing her soft, sagging cheeks before she returned to the matter at hand. "My grandson's got a poster. This guy had all those chains around his neck, too, and that *car*, except he was *bigger*. Bigger than Barbara Longley's grandson. You know, the one who plays for the Gophers?"

"Really." Lorraine had gotten caught up in her story, and so her grip had relaxed, and Ann took the opportunity to shift away and start sliding down the sidewalk.

"I looked it up on the Internet. That car goes for at least a hundred and fifty thousand dollars. How else could a guy like that make all that money except drugs?"

"How else, indeed." Freedom. She was four steps away and gaining. "I tell you what, Lorraine. You keep watch. If I don't come out in twenty minutes, you call the police."

———

Well, well, well, Tom thought when he opened his door. Guess there were a few hot ones in the neighborhood after all.

A long, rangy body and the legs to go with it, nicely shown off in baggy running shorts. Streaky brown hair with a definite curl, pulled carelessly back. Her T-shirt was too loose for him to tell what was underneath—too bad, that. No makeup at all, an angular, serious face.

He was rather proud of himself that he'd finally gotten to the point that he could appreciate a woman like her. He'd been dazzled by flash early on, paid the price for it, and had been immensely relieved when he'd grown out of it.

She had a plate in one hand and a puzzled expression on her face.

"I—" She wrinkled her brow. Trying to place him, he figured, and glanced at his watch.

She shook her head. "Oh, sorry. Well. I'm Ann McCrary. Next door." She poked the plate in the direction of the neatly kept shingled house. He'd worried about who lived next door, in a place that well-groomed. The last thing he wanted for a neighbor was the kind of guy who measured his dick by who had the best grass. Living next to a guy like that was a risk you took by moving into a neighborhood like this.

But whoever the guy was next door, he obviously had better things to do than work on his lawn, if this was his wife.

"I . . ." She frowned again. "Have we met?"

"Don't think so."

"Huh." She stuck the plate in his direction. "I brought you brownies."

"Brownies." Oh, yeah. That's what you did out here, wasn't it? Bring offerings of food to new neighbors.

The suburbs. Goddamn it, he was living in the suburbs, even if it was just barely.

He peeled back the tinfoil. They were still warm, as dark brown as strong espresso, and a chunk of chocolate oozed from one.

He picked one up and chomped half in one gulp.

Jeez. Maybe the suburbs weren't so bad after all.

He chewed, swallowed. "You make these yourself?"

"I—" She was still trying to puzzle it out, looking him up and down, a faint frown marking her brow. "Of course I made them," she said, offended.

Guess you didn't question a lady's brownies.

"From scratch?"

"Yes." Her frown deepened. "Where are you from?"

"South Dakota."

"Oh. Couldn't be that, then. Do you go to St. Joe's?"

Church. She went to church. Was he supposed to go to church now? He hadn't set foot in one since his mother's funeral. He'd forgotten that people—save Big Al Thompson, their Holy Roller left fielder who was constantly trying to convert the rest of the locker room, and who was about as annoying a man as he'd ever played with—went to church.

"Nope."

He swallowed the rest of the brownie. Yup, it was really that good. He glanced at her left hand, found the telltale glint of platinum, and sighed.

Of course she was married. Legs and homemade brownies; single was out of the question.

"Where do you work?"

"What's this? You're the advance guard sent to find out all about me and report back to the neighbors?"

She flushed immediately, red as a teenager caught parking. "I'm sorry, I . . . You just look so very familiar."

"Got that kind of a face."

"No, you don't, I—" Her expression cleared. "You're the man in black!"

He looked down, making a show of checking his clothes. T-shirt, jeans, sneakers. "Guess I am." The press had liked that one, the man in black thing. Dubbed him that right after he'd been called up to the bigs, a tall, skinny twenty-year-old with a fastball that approached 100 mph. He'd spent two years in the pen, made starter early in '91. In the World Series against Atlanta, he'd given up only two runs in twenty innings. He'd had another five good years before he blew out his shoulder. Four All-Star appearances, one Cy Young. And then a lousy two years, trying to come back. Washed up by thirty.

"No . . . you know. What was your real name? Nash. Tom Nash."

He wiped brownie crumbs off on his thigh and checked his watch. "Got it in one." It had taken two minutes, forty-five seconds to recognize him this time, which was a full minute longer than average. He stuck out his hand. "Still is my real name."

"Oh, shoot. My manners." She put out her own. "Ann McCrary. I live next door." She peered behind him. "Are your . . . parents here?"

"Now there's something I haven't heard in a while. Don't I look old enough to buy a place on my own?"

"Sorry." Ann knew she was gawking; she couldn't seem to stop. She remembered him now. They'd actually been at one of the games he'd pitched during the playoffs that year, and she'd watched the rest on TV. He was taller than everyone else on the field; cold, pale blue eyes glowering beneath the brim of his cap;

whipping the ball at the plate as if it were hurled from a sling-shot. The press loved him, young and handsome enough to be on a magazine cover, a relentless monster on the mound but off it, a Midwestern kid made good.

If Ann had ever thought about it, she would have been sure that she was not the type of person susceptible to being star-struck. She never read *Us* except at the salon, couldn't have picked Paris Hilton out from a lineup of blondes.

But she was just so surprised to see him here. And she couldn't reconcile it, a millionaire jock—no longer that young, but still tall and gorgeous and mysteriously sexy—showing up next door.

"Your . . . wife?" Too nosy. But the questions kept popping out, because he didn't belong *here*. He belonged someplace hip and sleek, with girls on each arm who looked like they'd walked out of a music video. Not in Mrs. Hillerman's old house, with its rosebushes on either side of the brick steps and window boxes already planted with petunias.

"Don't have one of those." He didn't seemed disturbed by her questions, just leaned against the doorjamb and broke off another corner of brownie. She supposed he was used to questions, and to openmouthed women staring at him.

What was he *doing* here? She wouldn't have been any more surprised if the president had opened the door. Maybe less; politicians liked to pretend they were common people. Tom Nash had never been common, at least not since somebody figured out just how fast he could throw a baseball.

"I'll just go home now," she said and turned to scurry away and leave the poor man alone.

"Hey."

She turned at his call.

"Are there kids around here?" he asked.

Kids. Why would he care about kids?

"Are you a pervert?" The words came out before she thought about it. *Shit.*

But what did it matter? she thought a second later.

If he was a pervert—and that made more sense than anything else, about why somebody like him would move in next door— he'd be on notice that she'd be watching. That *everybody'd* be watching, though that would have happened anyway, and he'd have to be a complete idiot not to realize that. Tom Nash didn't just slip into a neighborhood unnoticed.

And if he wasn't . . . Well, he'd hate her forever. Which didn't matter, either. Wasn't as if they were going to be best friends, anyway.

But he laughed, so hard he had to juggle the brownies. He held up a hand to hold her in place while he gathered enough air to talk.

"Do I *look* like a pervert?"

And now he was making fun of her. Heck, she was pretty sure he'd once been one of *People*'s Fifty Most Beautifuls. "Of course not. Which is kind of the point, isn't it? If a pervert *looked* like a pervert, he'd never get close to anybody."

"He? It's always a he?"

Okay, so now he was making her out to be a sexist. And there was no way she was getting out of this looking good.

"My dog needs me," she said—*Coward!*—and turned for home.

"Hey! I'm not a pervert!"

He was loud enough to have her looking up and down the street to see if anybody was watching. And laughing.

"I've got a daughter. She's coming to live with me for the summer, and I was hoping . . . Well, I want her to like it here."

"Oh. A daughter." That made more sense. She still couldn't put him together with this place, but at least there was a reason. "Of course, there are kids. This place is kid central." The pang was so mild she barely noticed it. It had been stronger once, enough that sometimes, on gorgeous summer days, she'd had to stay inside rather than see all those beautiful children. But the hurt had gotten scabbed over, or just lost among all the other scars. "Mortimers, over there. They have five-year-old twins, a girl and a boy, and a three-year-old. Andersons, down

the block, have school-age kids . . . first and third. I think."
She frowned. There were always kids running around, bright
eyed, happy, enough of them that she couldn't always keep
them straight.

But he was shaking his head. "No, no, she's sixteen. I don't
know what to do with her. What do sixteen-year-old girls *do?*"

"Well, assuming they're anything like what my friends
and I were when we were sixteen, you probably don't want
to know."

He looked stricken. Worried, as if it hadn't occurred to him
that his daughter might get in trouble.

"What does she like?" Ann asked.

"She likes . . ." He stopped, frowning fiercely. He used to
glare at batters like that, right before he unleashed his fastball.
She was half-surprised they hadn't just dropped their bats and
taken the strikes, because there was no way they were hitting him
when he was in his prime, anyway. "Aw, hell, I don't know."

"Hmm." A divorced dad, then, who didn't know his daughter well enough to know what she'd like. Ann understood that,
didn't she? A father who couldn't be bothered?

She wondered what had possessed him to bring his daughter
here for the summer. All she'd gotten since her father left had
been postcards. Certainly no invitations.

"I should know, shouldn't I?" he said glumly. "I used to
know. When she was little, it was easy. Send her a doll, a book,
whatever she asked for. But then she got older, and she—"

Oh boy, Ann thought. He was in trouble. The girl wasn't even
here, and it was obvious the man was in trouble.

No doubt he deserved every bit of it. She didn't have much
sympathy for men who thought fatherhood meant shooting out
swimmers and maybe signing a check now and then. She only
hoped the girl wouldn't have to suffer for it.

"Teenagers. Right. Well, right on your other side—" she nodded in that direction, at the yellow stucco two-story with a big
silver maple in the front—"Kozlaks, there. They have a boy, I'm
pretty sure he's sixteen."

"No boys!"

"Ooo-kay," she said, thinking: *Man, you have no idea, do you?*

"I'm sure there are some," she went on. "Enjoy the brownies." She could hear Cleo whining on the other side of the fence, unhappy to have been left behind, and she seized on the excuse. "Have to go. And good luck!" *You're gonna need it.*

FOUR

It was a beautiful Saturday afternoon. The window to John's room was open, and Ann could smell spring. Cleo had her nose over the windowsill, ever hopeful.

"We'll go out. Soon enough." She checked her watch; she'd been here two hours, not quite enough. But oh, it was so lovely, and who knew how long it would last? It wasn't as if he would know . . .

Guilt niggled at her. It was still a far shorter visit than in the early days, when she'd spent every waking hour at John's bedside.

She glanced over at him. He was pale, much thinner than he'd been. He'd been a linebacker in high school, with shoulders far wider than any other tenth grader, when she'd sat behind him every day in algebra and admired them. He wouldn't have noticed her, not John McCrary, the golden boy of Mill Valley. The best family, the best-looking boy in the class, not to mention smartest and just plain *nicest*.

Certainly, he wouldn't notice Ann Baranski, not with anything more than his innate kindness and a certain amount of pity, not with her mousy ways and her homemade clothes and her weird family. What were they out there on that farm, anyway, hippies? Didn't they know that *no one* was a hippie anymore?

But he had. To the dismay of his parents and the bewilderment of the rest of the sophomore girls.

Wouldn't last, they'd all whispered. She was probably putting out to hang on to him. He'd tire of her soon enough.

They'd been right about one thing. She had been putting out. Not to keep him—she had never believed she'd ever be able to keep him—but because she wanted at least a little bit of him to keep. She'd be his first, he'd be hers, and at least he'd always remember her.

But his muscles were gone now, his limbs atrophied and twisted. The shine was off his new-penny hair, what there was left of it; they clipped it very short, for ease of care. His eyes were open a bare slit, the irises darting from side to side; it had taken years before she'd accepted that he wasn't seeing anything, that there was no control or intent in those spastic motions, any more than there was a smile in the random twitches of his lips.

John. Her John. She blinked against the burn. She didn't usually cry anymore; she'd used it all up, grieved as much as there was to grieve. Now it was simply her life, a routine of work to home and John's room. No time for anything else, no room for anyone else. This was what it was.

She reopened their book, flipping through to find the last page they'd read. She used to try to talk to him as she sat there. Trying to get through to him, hoping her voice would somehow reach whatever consciousness was there. But she'd run out of things to talk about early on; one could only spew for so long about work and the weather and the news. But it seemed . . . rude somehow, and futile, to sit there quietly by his side, watch TV or read as if he weren't there at all or was just another inert piece of furniture in the room.

So she'd taken to reading aloud. Mysteries, mostly, which she figured they both could enjoy. Though she had accepted sometime over the years that he wasn't hearing her, she'd kept up the habit.

"'The weight of the gun in my hand suddenly doubled, as if responsibility weighed it down. I heard something scrabble in the alley ahead, too big to be a rat, and—'"

The door to John's room was open, and a whistle pierced the air, somewhere down the hall, the kind of wolf whistle they used in old cartoons. She heard the rumble of conversation, rusty old male voices cracking into flirtation.

Laughter echoed through the hallway, female and raucous, powerful enough to be heard blocks away.

Ann winced. *Crap,* she thought, and braced herself.

The laugh burst forth again, unselfconscious, brazenly flirtatious for all that it was forceful as a foghorn. All through her teenage years the sound of that laughter had made her blush as surely as getting shoved into the boys' locker room, because it meant her mother was coming. And where Judy Baranski was— though at the time she'd been going by Reflection, a moniker she'd mercifully finally surrendered in '85, when she decided she needed to get in touch with her roots—Ann's mortification soon followed.

That laughter still had the same effect. There was nothing polite about it, no avoiding it, a joyful bray. And Ann wasn't entirely sure if it was simply its volume, a bludgeoning of amusement, that embarrassed her, or if some tiny part of her was just a little bit jealous, for she wasn't sure if she had ever enjoyed anything as much as Judy enjoyed damn near everything.

It didn't even seem real to Ann. Nobody had that much fun. Even lying on the cold marble capital steps with fake blood streaming over her, shouting *"murderer"* at visiting presidents— something she'd done to at least three of them—she was having fun. To listen to Judy, being hauled away by the "fuzz" was just this side of a trip to Disneyland.

"Hi, honey!" Judy breezed in, the scraps of her multicolored patchwork skirt fluttering around her sturdy legs. There was a stain on one knee—just dirt, Ann devoutly hoped—and her waffle-knit shirt was a dark, unevenly dyed purple that did nothing to hide the fact that she wasn't wearing a bra, and that she really needed one. A loopy-knitted scarf in a glittering green hung around her neck, and her hair, long and center parted and nearly all gray now, streamed down her back.

She wore no makeup, and beat-up Birkenstocks, and Ann had never been able to figure out why, despite all that, and despite the fact that she'd passed sixty-two several years earlier, Judy still claimed as much male attention as Sophia Loren in her prime.

She stamped a quick kiss on her daughter's cheek, bringing with her a drift of lavender and sandalwood, the soap she made herself and sold through a gift shop in downtown Mill Valley, mixed with the acrid bitterness of cigarette smoke.

"Hello, handsome." She bent over John, giving him a hearty smack on his forehead. Her voice, her actions, were completely casual, as if she were simply greeting John as he walked into her kitchen like he had a thousand times before.

She dropped the bulging tan hemp sack on the nearest chair, olive green vinyl with a slit in the seat exposing a curl of pale stuffing. She pulled out a small nosegay of lilacs and laid it on John's chest, right over the thin gray cotton of his hospital gown.

"Mom—"

"The sense of smell is our most primeval," Judy said. "It calls up memories, emotions."

"But you know he can't smell. The doctors—"

"Doctors." Judy made a sound of disgust. She had little use for medical professionals. Acupuncturists, herbalists, absolutely. The midwife who'd delivered Ann at home, fine. But doctors— they were lumped with politicians, policeman, and businessmen in the *not to be trusted* category. "What do they know?"

Ann opened her mouth, then snapped it shut. What was the point? She'd never been able to change her mother's mind about anything.

Judy was just lucky, cushioned by her robust good health. When she got sick enough that her tisanes and teas didn't help, she'd change her tune.

Judy laid her hands on John's side and closed her eyes. Communing. Ann had seen her do the same thing with a tree, with an ailing horse, the crumbling wall of Fort Snelling.

She opened her eyes and nodded.

"He's still here, honey."

"Sure," Ann agreed. It didn't even upset her anymore. If John's spirit were floating around, surely he'd be communicating with Ann. Or his mother. Not Judy, who he'd always regarded with bemused and befuddled affection. She wasn't *his* mother, so her eccentricities, her *weirdness*, didn't bother him the way they did Ann. It wasn't his mother, his lovely, mannered mother, who'd gotten caught dancing in the town park naked under the full moon. He could just be amused by her.

Judy tugged a chair over by her daughter and contemplated her seriously. She had beautiful eyes, a smoky green with lashes thick as her pet goat Hermione's.

It was the one feature Ann had gotten from her mother. Everything else—her height, her lanky frame, her hair—she'd gotten her from her father.

"Ann, you're holding him here. He's not going to be released until you tell him it's okay." Judy took her hand, patting it comfortingly. "You need to let him go, honey."

"Sure," Ann said. "Hey, John! You can go. I release you. You're free!"

"Now, now." Judy patted her hand, her expression disapproving. "There's no need to be flippant."

She might have sounded flippant. But it felt anything but, her stomach lurching as if she'd just swallowed something that didn't sit right. She *knew* John couldn't hear her, knew that nothing she said or did made any difference. If it would have, something would have happened a long time ago.

He would have come back to her. God knew she'd begged him long enough.

Changing the subject seemed the simplest approach.

"So what are you doing here?"

She didn't see her mother often, not as much as the brief forty-mile distance between them should have allowed. But as much as Ann didn't understand her mother, didn't know how anyone could live in the shifting, cheerful chaos of Judy's life, Judy didn't understand her daughter, either. Couldn't see how she could have grown into such a pragmatic and conventional creature.

"Came to take you out for your birthday, of course."

"Oh. Of course." They'd had a small cake at the office on Friday, an appropriate celebration for the workplace, and then Ann had promptly, and quite deliberately, forgotten about it. *Thirty-nine*. One more until she was technically middle-aged.

And yet half the time she felt like she was still waiting for her life to get started.

"Because if I'd told you, you would have found a way to get out of it."

"I would't—"

"Don't you lie to me, Annie. I can always tell when you're lying to me."

"You lie to me all the time."

"That's not lying. That's just creativity." Judy never let trivial details like reality mess up her life. Even as a child, Ann had never been able to buy into the glimmering visions her mother spun, fairies and rainbows and—the biggest fantasy of all—a peaceful world without pain and strife.

She'd tried. Who wouldn't want to live in Judy's fantasies? They were pretty and gentle and entertaining. But Ann kept getting bogged down in the details, in noticing that the wind rattled the cracked windows of her bedroom, that a big water stain the color of dried blood took up half her ceiling, that critters skittered up and down the walls at night.

"Besides," Judy said. "I'm good at it. You're not. Until you learn to lie with a little flair, you might just as well not try."

"Why don't you go pick something up for dinner," Ann suggested. "We can eat here."

"It's all going to end up tasting like antiseptic." Her expression grew serious, which was rare enough for Ann to take notice of it, because she was used to being the serious one in the family. "You need to get out of here, honey. Please. It's beautiful out, it's your birthday, and this is no place to spend it."

It *was* lovely out. Ann could smell it through the open window. Spring was finally catching a good hold, making way for summer. There was an ornamental plum on the property, which bloomed for only about three days every May, three glorious days, a smell so sweet and heady that every year she wondered, after it was all over, if it could have possibly smelled that good. It was blooming now; hints of it came through the window on the warm breeze.

"Too nice to stay inside," Judy coaxed. "How many days like this do we get?"

The Minnesotan in Ann responded automatically, a reflex inbred in anyone who'd spurted from the womb within state borders: one must always appreciate each nice day, wring the fullest from it, because one never knew when one would be blessed with another. It was what spurred pasty-legged joggers to swarm trails in their shorts anytime the thermometer rose past forty, what made throngs of schoolgirls lie out in their bikinis in April and golfers pull out their clubs the instant the fairways cleared of snow—all in temperatures that would have the rest of the country pulling out their parkas.

"I'll even buy you meat," Judy cajoled.

"Well that does it, then."

She slipped a bookmark into her book and tucked it away on the shelf. The TV was still on—a golf tournament, someplace warm and gloriously sunny—and debated snapping it off. But it made the room so quiet, empty. Unbearably lonely, and so she left it on.

There were always people in the hallway at Cedar Ridge. She supposed they found their rooms too quiet, too. She'd learned a few names over the years: Mrs. Halloren, a retired teacher, the little sign by her room proclaimed. Sometimes she seemed to know exactly what was going on, and sometimes she just stood in her doorway, silent but grinning her wide, gummy smile at anyone who glanced her way.

Mr. Schultz, with a face with more wrinkles and folds than features, not a hair on his head, who wheeled his chair up and down the hallway with fierce determination, ready to run down anyone who dared to get in his way. And Owen MacEvoy, who was Pine Wing's pervert.

It was the odd thing about aging, Ann had discovered. It stripped away inhibitions and tact and other niceties of society, baring what people were like underneath. Some sweet, kind people got even sweeter. Some who'd faked kindness for most of their life settled into out-and-out mean. And it seemed like a good one in four men turned into hopeless and perpetually hopeful sex fiends.

It had shocked Ann at first, three weeks after John had been transferred from the hospital to the nursing home. She'd been looking for a pop machine—okay, she hadn't been able to stay in that room one more minute—and had careened around a corner, her eyes blurring with tears, and been confronted with a pink, dangling penis, two wrinkled, loose-skinned testicles hanging low beneath, all surrounded by flaccid skin and the limp sides of a threadbare terry robe.

She'd just stood there, her mouth open, too surprised to move. And then she'd turned and fled, running to the nurse's station to report her, ah, sighting. The nurse had blown out a long-suffering sigh, said, "Not again," and ambled off in the direction Ann indicated.

By the time men ended up in Cedar Ridge, she had figured sex was the last thing on their minds. But apparently not. If some of the fellows there were any indication, the fact that they no longer had anything else to claim their attention—jobs or families or any hobbies beyond the weekly sing-alongs—had freed them to revert to an adolescent state of constant rut. Their flesh might not respond quite the same way as it had back then, but they were every bit as single-minded.

Mr. MacEvoy was particularly persistent. He lived two doors down from John, with a roommate that Ann had never seen awake, and she'd learned long ago to avert her eyes every time she passed his door, just in case he was showcasing something she would really rather not see.

If she ever started really missing sex, she figured all she'd have to do was take a good gander at Mr. MacEvoy's desiccated bits, and she'd be so traumatized she'd never think of it again.

"Hey, lady!" he called as Judy swung by.

"Hello!" she said cheerily.

"Come on, Mom." Ann took her arm to hurry her along.

"Wait." Judy stopped in her tracks and spun to Mr. MacEvoy. His burgundy velvet robe was mercifully closed, and it swallowed up his fragile frame like a young boy wearing his dad's coat, making him look as if there was nothing left of him but bones. As he leaned on his walker, his baggy, thin blue pajama bottoms sagged beneath the raggedy hem. What remained of his hair stood straight up on his head, pale and delicate as dandelion fuzz.

"Mom, we gotta go." Now that she'd made the decision to leave, Ann was anxious to escape. Not to mention that Judy's interactions with other people always held the potential for embarrassment.

At least, she thought, Mr. MacEvoy wouldn't remember it afterward.

"Don't be rude." Judy beamed.

Great. Her mother was lecturing *her* on manners. Judy, who'd had a poster that said, "Tact is the enemy of truth" over their kitchen table, which had held piles of wool and quilt scraps far more often than food. Ann had had to check out a book on table etiquette the first time she'd been invited to John's for dinner, because Judy had believed set mealtimes were too rigid, and that one should eat according to one's hunger, so food, to the shifting cast of residents of the farm, was a matter of scavenging what you could when your stomach told you, not a meal to be eaten with your family.

"Hello." Ann grinned at Mr. MacEvoy and stuck out her hand. His daughter came to see him one Sunday a month, but Ann had never seen anyone else visit.

He licked his dry lips as his faded blue eyes behind lenses thick as bulletproof glass focused with unerring accuracy on Judy's chest. "Show me your tits."

"What?" Judy blinked and took a step back.

"See? Can we go now, Mom?"

Judy shook her head. "Why, now, nobody's said that to me since . . . It must have been the Dead concert in Milwaukee." Her smile was full of nostalgia. "They carried me above the crowds like Cleopatra, and—"

"*Mom,*" Ann said, hoping to head her off.

"Please?" Mr. MacEvoy's voice quavered hopefully.

"Well, now, I—"

"*Please.*"

"Well, sir, I'm sure I've never been asked quite that politely before," she said matter-of-factly, as if the request were nothing out of the ordinary.

His arms trembled as he pushed himself straighter, not even blinking, as if he were afraid he might miss his only chance.

"Oh, what the hell." Judy grabbed the bottom of her grubby sweater in both hands and lifted, giving a little jiggle as she did so.

"*Mom!*" Horrified, Ann grabbed her arm, yanking on it so that Judy had to release the sweater on that side. It fell down, but the other side caught on her substantial breast, so one remained exposed, making her resemble an overaged, overweight Aphrodite.

Ann tugged on the sweater hem until her mother was as decent as she was ever going to be and started dragging her down the hall. She didn't dare look around. If there were witnesses, she didn't want to know about it. She already knew what her nightmares were going to be about tonight.

"Hey!"

She glanced back over her shoulder.

"Thank you." Mr. MacEvoy's faded eyes were watering, his expression as fervently grateful as a devout Catholic who'd just been blessed by the pope. "*Thank you.*"

FIVE

Ann had hustled her mother into her car, slammed the door behind her, peeled out of the parking lot, and was two blocks away before she could breathe normally again.

"Annie? What about my car?"

Damn it. "We'll get it towed."

"Towed?"

"I don't dare let you back there. God knows what'll happen."

Judy chuckled. "I'm not going to jump him, if that's what you're worried about. My charity only extends so far."

"Charity? Is that what it is?" Her fingers were cramping around the steering wheel, her stomach twisting just as tight. It was a common affliction in her mother's presence. "My mother, the flasher."

"Oh, come on. You saw how grateful he was."

"You're going to get arrested."

"It won't be the first time."

"Don't remind me," Ann said grimly. "I'm not bailing you out this time."

"For what?"

"Contributing to the delinquency of a septuagenarian."

"Is there such a thing?" Judy shifted in her seat and regarded her daughter curiously. "Maybe there should be. It's ageism, isn't it, that one can corrupt a child, and not the elderly? But then, that implies that they can no longer make decisions on their own behavior, and one mustn't assume—"

"Mom," Ann cut in, knowing that the speech could go on for hours if she didn't. No doubt in a few days she'd open the *Tribune* and find her mother's name in the "Letters to the Editor." At last count, she was the most frequent contributor, holding first place by a full dozen letters over a man named Chuck Carlson, who apparently held extremely passionate opinions about eminent domain, gun laws, and cat hunting. "It's indecent exposure, at the very least."

"Humph." Judy tsked. "Let them try. I'm a registered nudist. I'm sure the ACLU would be happy to help. Besides, it was an act of kindness."

"He'll probably have a heart attack. If he dies, I'm giving you up. Don't think I won't."

"Then he'll die happy, won't he?"

Ann lifted one hand off the steering wheel to rub at her temples. "I'm adopted, aren't I?"

"No, you're not. Though if I didn't know for sure, I'd wonder myself, because I can't imagine how you got such unnatural inhibitions about such a beautiful thing as the human body. But you're mine all the way. Only three hours of hard labor, my dear, and—"

"And completely natural, too, no drugs at all," Ann finished. "Though why childbirth was the exception to the rest of your life, I'll never know."

"Would you rather I'd lied about it?" Judy asked in genuine curiosity.

"Yes," Ann said flatly. About her mother's recreational chemical use, and her adventurous sex life, and everything else that had Ann thinking *eeewww*, even now, when she should have grown immune.

"I refuse to believe that you do not value honesty and individual freedom above society's artificial rules and boundaries," her mother said. "In fact—"

In desperation, Ann turned to the one thing that she knew would shock her mother into silence. "I want McDonald's for my birthday dinner."

———

"Thank you," Judy said as the waitress showed her to her seat. "It is good to know that you still have some appreciation for thinking about where your food's coming from."

"I just didn't think I'd enjoy my burger if I had to listen to a recitation of the evils of factory farming and corporate greed with every bite."

"I wouldn't," Judy said. "It's your birthday, I said you could choose whatever you wanted."

"Uh-huh." Ann was unconvinced.

"But—" She accepted a menu from their waitress, a small woman with limited English, graying hair, and an unlined face who could have been anywhere from thirty to sixty. At Ann's skeptical look, she admitted: "I wouldn't have *said* anything, though I can't say it wouldn't have been difficult. But I couldn't be held responsible if I turned green from the smell of the grease. One can't always control one's revulsion."

"Isn't that a lovely image to begin dinner with?" They'd settled on Vietnamese, because the small, family-run restaurant didn't offend Judy's ethics, and because she was fond of mock duck. As soon as Ann had stopped home to drop Cleo off, they'd headed here.

The place had white walls and tiny tables covered with white paper. There were red place mats with the Chinese zodiac on them, and a small altar in a far corner holding a bronze, big-bellied Buddha, surrounded with strips of gold-printed red paper and flanked with incense spearing up from porcelain containers. A whiteboard displayed hand-scrawled specials: crab with ginger, whole steamed walleye, salt-crusted shrimp.

They both waited, holding their tongues, until there was

food on the table in front of them. Steam spiraled up from the little, handleless china cup as Ann poured her tea; Judy had hot water for herself, pulling from her bag an herbal blend she mixed herself.

There were spring rolls for both: vegetable for Judy, shrimp for Ann, with tart-sweet nuoc-nam dipping sauce the color of a sunset.

"So," Judy said, "who's going first?"

"We have to talk about something?" Ann asked innocently. She took a huge bite of her roll, tasting the brisk green of cilantro, feeling the spring of the rice noodles.

"Well, you can skip your turn if you want." Judy's tea smelled like a meadow, grassy and floral, and she added a squirt of honey. Her own honey, from the bees they kept in the orchard. If her mother had to, Ann thought, she could live from the contents of her bag for a week.

"Oh, no." Judy was big on talking things out. Even—*especially*—things her daughter would rather not discuss. In high school her friends thought it was great that her mother had taken her to the gynecologist before her fourteenth birthday. That she could tell her mom that she'd slept with John, when most of them lived in mortal fear both of pregnancy and their parents finding out.

But Ann had never wanted to talk about it. No one should have to listen to sex advice from parents. Particularly when accompanied by illustrative anecdotes.

What happened between her and John was between her and John. Period. It was a vow, a promise; Judy would never have understood that. She considered sex a natural biological function. Interesting, enjoyable, but not to be cluttered up by unnecessary artifices such as ceremony and emotion.

So they *were* going to discuss it, no matter what. And since they were, she was getting her say in, too.

"You just can't *do* stuff like that, Mom."

"Why not?" Judy asked, sounding genuinely curious.

"Because it's . . . it's . . ." Ann frowned, unable to come up with a neat, clean reason. "Because some things you just don't do."

"But why?" Judy slid her plate aside and folded her hands on the table. Her hands were rough, the nails clipped ruthlessly short, the skin reddened. They were strong hands, hands that had picked Ann up when she'd fallen, that had kneaded bread, milked goats, pulled weeds.

"I don't understand why you can't understand this." Exasperation pitched her voice higher. "If we all did exactly what we wanted, if there were no rules, things would be such a mess."

"You're so certain of that. I'm not." Judy sipped her tea, her hands steady, eyes calm. "Rules are mostly designed to keep things the way they are. Keep the people in charge in charge; that's why they make them. I have more faith in the rest of us than you do, darling."

More faith. Her mother lived by faith and philosophy; Ann lived by order and reality. They could have inhabited different planets.

She looked at her own hands. They had the same shape as her mother's, the same long fingers and wide, sturdy palms. Her nails were short, too. But hers were neatly trimmed, the skin pale and smooth.

And she was simply too tired to *discuss* anything with her mother anymore. Judy spent half her life "discussing" things. Ann was never going to win, and if she had half a brain she would have given up trying long ago.

"Have you heard from your father?" Judy asked quietly.

"I got a postcard three months ago. He was in Panama." *Been floating in the ocean, my girl. Sun's warm, fruit's ripe. You could come. Be good for you. Life's too short not to enjoy it.*

That was Bruce in a nutshell. It'd be cool if Ann came and played with him—as long as she didn't lecture him too much, and she made all the arrangements—but it was simply too much trouble for him to come see her.

"Oh. I thought maybe for your birthday . . ." Lines scored deep around Judy's mouth; she spent a lot of time in the sun, and it took its toll. But the weathering didn't detract from her looks; the lines that you noticed were merry crinkles at the corners of her eyes, her smile. "I'm sorry, honey."

Sorry about what? That her father couldn't be bothered to remember her birthday, or that she'd chosen Bruce for Ann's father in the first place?

They'd never married. They hadn't had to: Bruce had a bum knee, so he was medically ineligible for the draft, anyway, so what was the point? Ann had a few memories of them as a family, just the three of them. A picnic, somewhere sunny, her mother's hair long and the color of a deer's coat, her father laughing as Ann tried to catch the butterflies swooping by. Curling up in a bed, in a very cold room, all three of them together, with an old quilt over them, and feeling her parents' warmth on each side of her, as safe as she'd ever felt. A tent—she was pretty sure they'd lived in a tent one summer; she could remember the light through the yellowing canvas.

But by the time her memories were more than brief, disconnected images, they already lived in the farmhouse, and George and Marybelle Maloney had moved in. She was too young to understand why Marybelle slept with Bruce and George slept with her mother. It was just how it was. And then George left, and there were others, in and out, men with long hair and torn blue jeans, women with soft, dreamy smiles who smelled like flowers. They were all nice to her; she was the only child, and it wasn't until she was older, until she started to understand what the other kids at school said, why their parents wouldn't let them come out to her house to play, that she started to realize it was weird, unusual. *Wrong.*

She'd been seven when her father left with a woman whose name Ann could no longer remember. The woman had a necklace, long and twinkling with purple crystals that she let Ann wear sometimes, and she'd play the guitar for them all, her voice sad and smoky.

There were letters at first, lots of them, with bits of leaves pressed into them, or a sketch Bruce had made of something he'd seen: a cactus, a black-and-white magpie, a great big sailboat heading out to sea. They'd gotten less frequent as she'd gotten older, and finally she realized that the woman probably had very little to do with her father's leaving. The desirable ethics of subsistence farming weren't enough to keep him there when the romance got buried under the work, and apparently his daughter hadn't been enough, either.

"Why didn't you ever leave?" Ann asked Judy suddenly. Why hadn't it ever occurred to her before to wonder? Judy didn't fit into Mill Valley any more than Bruce had. She'd grown up there and had fled at sixteen. She hadn't returned until her father was dead and her mother already lost to Alzheimer's, so it wasn't that she thought Ann deserved grandparents.

She had few friends in town, except the travelers who moved in and out. To the residents of Mill Valley, even the people she'd grown up with, she was just too . . . odd to bother with.

She didn't dress like them, think like them. Didn't bother to go to church, wasn't even a C & E Lutheran. She could have a cult out there, for all they knew.

"Where would I go?" Judy leaned back, allowing their server to place their plates in front of them, and the strong aroma of onions and lemongrass drifted up from Ann's imperial chicken. "Mom and Dad left the land to me. You know that's how I want to live, close to the land, growing my own food."

"But you could do that anywhere. Someplace where there are more—" Ann tried to think of a more polite way to say it, then wondered why she was bothering. Judy believed in true kindness and appreciation, but she couldn't care less about the formalities of tact. "Someplace where there were other people like you."

"And why would I care if there were people like me?" she asked in genuine curiosity. "It's good land. I couldn't sell it and buy any nearly as good in California or Oregon; it's too expensive. And somewhere else in the Midwest, where I could afford it . . . What difference would that make?"

"That's awfully practical of you."

"Besides," Judy said. "I'm making too much money to move."

"You what?" Ann couldn't have heard her right.

"Yup." She tucked a piece of pressed tofu into her mouth and chewed enthusiastically. "Turns out chefs just *love* to buy goat cheese and heirloom tomatoes from old hippies. Seems more 'authentic' to them somehow."

"Chefs?"

"The worse I look, the more they'll pay. I let the dirt stay under my nails the last time, got an extra eighty cents a pound for the cheese."

"Money." Ann pictured the farm with its rusted tractor that hadn't moved in two decades beside the rutted gravel drive and the buildings that looked as if they'd been abandoned for years, and she couldn't put it together with money. "But the place . . ."

"I could care less about the house, you know that. But you should see my new milking parlor." Judy's eyes shone. "I know you don't understand it, honey, but I'm happy."

"Happy." Happy in a broken-down farmhouse with peeling paint and shattered windows, in a town that would never accept her, and the longest-lasting relationship in her life—besides her daughter—was with her goat Hermione?

"Yes, happy," Judy said firmly. "I wish I could say the same about you."

"About me?" Ann put down her fork, smoothed her napkin in her lap. *Happy* wasn't something she gave much thought to. *Not miserable, not bawling* was about as good as most days got. Happy was beyond her. Had been beyond her since the day that a car had plowed into John's on his way to a job site, three days before their sixth wedding anniversary. "Happy's asking a lot, Mom. Too much."

"But *why*?"

"You know why."

"No, I don't." Skin wobbled beneath her chin as Judy shook her head. Her shoulders were broad beneath the gray cardigan she'd knitted herself, sturdy enough to take on the world, and Ann wished, just for once, she could go lay her head on that shoulder and that would make it okay. But it didn't work that way.

Her mother loved her; Ann knew that. She just didn't understand her at all.

"I know it's a cliché, Ann. But truly, John wouldn't want this for you. You know that."

Ann didn't cry anymore. She *didn't*. But her eyes burned now, because the last thing she ever wanted was for John to be disappointed in her.

She focused on the wall, forcing her lids to stay open until her eyes dried, staring at a photo of a rice paddy, green and curving.

"Now there," Judy said briskly. She might be fond of Native American ceremonies and pagan dances, but she also had a strong streak of practicality. She had to, or she would have lost the farm to taxes years ago. "It's time to move on, Annie."

"I've moved on. As much as I can."

"Moved on?" She poured more hot water into her cup, the china clinking. "You live in the same house. You work in the same firm."

"I like my house. Just like you said you like the farm." *God help her.* "And as for the firm—it's my firm, too. I'm supposed to give it up because it was ours? We do different kinds of work now than what John and I did together."

"Because you chose to, or because you had to?"

Ann took a big bite of chicken so she didn't have to answer. She'd never told her mother about all the jobs she'd lost, all the proposals she'd sweated over that they hadn't won, for the kinds of buildings that had been John's dream: a new bank, a residential tower, a couple of substantial, architecturally progressive infill houses in Kenwood, a small jewel box of a museum. They'd wanted the kind of buildings that won awards, got spreads in architecture magazines, structures that were sleek and innovative and all about the form.

She'd tried. She had. But she didn't like the buildings, and the clients hadn't liked her. "Too conventional," one had said. "Unimaginative."

That had stung. But then she'd gone to see one of the houses designed by a rival firm, once it was completed. It was beautiful, glass, steel, and concrete angled into dramatic light and shadow, but it was also, she thought, cold and uncomfortable, and then she'd felt better.

So she'd changed what kind of architecture the firm focused on. If she hadn't, she would have lost the business, and that was a far bigger dream of theirs than what kind of buildings they would design.

"You've never even taken a vacation," her mother said.

"What happened to all your theories about discovering your own path in life?"

"I might have my theories, honey, but I'm also still a mother." She hadn't touched her mock duck in at least five minutes, which proved exactly how serious about this conversation she was. Judy was a hearty eater, if somewhat limited by her beliefs, and she believed the sensual pleasures of the plate were as much a gift as any other kind. "It's been twelve years, Ann. If you haven't found your path on your own by now, I figure you can use a little nudging."

"This is nudging?" Pushing, maybe. Ann suspected an out-and-out shove was hovering. "I can't take a vacation. I've got a business to run."

"Annie." Judy took Ann's hand, gave it a sympathetic squeeze. "He's not going to wake up while you're gone. You won't miss it."

"I know. I'm not afraid he's going to wake up," Ann snapped. She'd accepted that a long time ago. Mary triumphantly bore every newspaper article she could find about long-comatose patients who woke up and she still may have clung to the idea that someday her son would open his eyes, but Ann had given up. Or been used up. "I'm afraid he'll die while I'm gone."

There. She'd admitted it.

"Oh, Annie." Judy hopped to her feet, bangles jangling and

unbound breasts swaying. She came around the table, threw her arms around her daughter, and hung on.

Judy was a physical woman. Comfort, grief, celebration—they were all better expressed with a hug than words, she'd always believed. Ann had she spent half her childhood cuddled up in her arms, against her soft torso that smelled of dirt and sunshine.

"Mom. Mom! We're in a restaurant."

"Huh?" Under her mother's grip, she could see the young men at the next table, neat in their khakis and polos—a quick dinner before hitting the bars—shifting uncomfortably, glancing suspiciously at the scene in the making next to them.

Emotional women, the quick flicker of their eyes seemed to say. God forbid some of that scene would spill their way.

"Who cares?" Judy said. But she gave her daughter one last pat and slid back into her chair. "He wouldn't mind, though. And it wouldn't change anything."

"I would mind." Ann knew what she could live with and what she couldn't. And she couldn't live with that. "Besides, I've done what I can. I got Cleo."

"Wow. You got a dog. Shaking up your world, all right."

Oh, here it came. Ann felt the muscles of her shoulders knot up. "I love my dog."

"Of course you do. Humans need animals in their life. But she's not going to keep you warm at night."

"She does a lovely job of keeping me warm at night."

"Now you're being purposely obtuse."

"No, I just don't want to hear it." If she shoved a spoonful of rice in her mother's mouth, Ann wondered, would it shut her up?

"You need a lover."

"There it is." Ann threw down her chopsticks. They clattered off the edge of the table, spun across the concrete floor. The men at the next table were looking at her again, wary, ready to bolt. "I'm married, Mom."

"Well, technically, of course." She waved her hand as if shooing away a fly, dismissing an institution that was generally regarded as the foundation of modern society as if it were no more important than an inconvenient bug. "I've never understood . . . But that's not really the point, is it? No one, and I mean *no one*, including John, would fault you for not wanting to go through your entire life without ever having sex again!" Her voice was getting louder.

"I took a vow." She was getting louder, too, the words coming fast, but she couldn't help it. "I know that's alien to you, but I did. And just because you took another lover every time you got a whim, every time your life got a little stale or you were the least bit unhappy, doesn't mean that it's right for me!"

Shoot. By now Ann was nearly shouting, and her face had grown hot. She'd never been able to hide her blush. The guys at the next table had put down their chopsticks and were staring at her mother, openmouthed. Neither of them could have been more than twenty-five, handsome enough in a bland way. Obviously they were up-and-comers working their butts off at their first job who had never, ever, considered a woman over sixty a sexual being. They were half-intrigued, half-horrified by the idea.

She didn't understand how this kept happening, how her mother could pull her into situations like this despite her earnest efforts to avoid them, drag her into mortifying conversations, even when she'd promised herself she'd remain calm and unaffected.

She grabbed another pair of chopsticks and pulled them apart until the connection snapped, sending a sliver of wood flying. She bent over her plate, fixing her gaze on the yellow tangle of slivered onions and chicken bits, wondering if she'd be able to eat it after all.

"Ann, you're too young to—"

"It's not going to happen, Mom."

"I was afraid you were going to say that."

"Then why did you bother to bring it up in the first place?"

"You gotta try, Annie. You always gotta try." She went silent for a moment while Ann held her breath, waiting for the next blow. And then Judy heaved a great sigh.

Thank God. Ann wasn't silly enough to believe her mother was giving up on the topic. But she was giving it up for *now*, and Ann was always willing to take what she could get.

"Here you go." She took a shoe-box-sized package from her bag and plopped it on the table.

It was wrapped in brown recycled paper, tied in baling twine. Judy had tucked a nosegay of dried flowers and herbs into the bow, a pretty spray of faded lavender and small white clusters that smelled like hay.

Ann took a deep breath and let the waves churning inside her settle and smooth.

"Happy birthday," Judy said, though she still sounded disgruntled.

"Thank you." Ann put her chopsticks down, carefully this time, and reached for the package.

"Oh, you don't want to open it *now*."

"I don't?"

"No." Judy shook her head as the long silver cobwebs dangled at her ears tangled in her hair. "Oh, I won't mind, but you will." She shot a meaningful glance at the next table.

Oh, help. "Mom, you didn't."

"Well, of course I did. I mean, if you're going to give up *lovers*—not that I think you should," she said sternly, "there are some scientifically proven advantages to having sex with a partner—or partners, of course—much healthier for one's body and soul. But if you insist upon giving that up, there's absolutely no reason why you should give up orgasms. They are far too important to one's physical and mental health." She tapped the box. "Hopefully you haven't been, but this is the most efficient assistance I've found. Quite effective."

The guys were openly gaping now. They were clearly never going to be the same again, and Ann figured it was pretty unlikely that she would be, either. She wondered if she could just slide right under the table and stay there, unnoticed, until the place emptied out for the night before creeping home to safety.

"And"—Judy was beaming, proud of her discovery—"it's environmentally friendly. Made completely out of recycled plastic. The batteries hold a charge for nine hours."

"Nine hours. Imagine that." She'd really rather *not*, but she couldn't seem to help it. Why would anyone need nine hours?

"But not to worry," Judy went on. "They're completely rechargeable."

SIX

Go time.

His fists jammed into the pockets of his charcoal Levi's, Tom shifted uneasily from foot to foot, his gaze glued to the escalator behind the wide glass doors in baggage claim at the Minneapolis–St. Paul airport.

He was used to a few nerves jittering around in his stomach like a kid with ADHD. He'd gotten butterflies the first time he pitched in the bigs. They'd morphed into big ol' crows, flapping around maniacally the day of the ALCS rubber game. He'd thrown up before he'd taken the mound in the World Series, and he'd struck out the side in the first inning.

So he figured nerves were good. They brought adrenaline and focus. But right now he was barely getting any air.

People were glancing his way. He felt their stares, heard them whisper to each other. *"You think that's him?" "Gotta be him." "No, he's not tall enough."*

He never bothered with a ball cap in public—most people in the state were more familiar with what he looked like with it on than off. And his hair was graying up, and with a pair of aviators, inside or out, it threw a few people off. But he still stood out in a crowd. Normally he didn't mind. People were pretty nice about it, all told, and it wasn't as if all those tickets they bought weren't the reason he had more money in the bank than a farm kid from Martinsville, South Dakota, population 382, had ever dreamed of.

But he didn't want any attention now. Today he thought if somebody talked to him he might bite his head off.

So he crossed his arms, planted his feet, and put on the scowl he'd always used to hide those nerves when he took the mound. Intimidation was half the battle. It helped to be six foot seven. Helped even more to have a fastball that could cause serious damage if it hit flesh, and a sinker that dove a good two feet before it crossed the plate.

As the arriving passengers came down the escalator, their feet came into view first. On a Saturday night there weren't many business travelers. Lots of guys coming back from golf trips, in khaki shorts and sunburns, caps that proclaimed THE OCEAN COURSE and PINEHURST and SEA ISLAND, wearing glum expressions that broadcast how thrilled they were to be heading back to work on Monday. A school choir returning from a trip, in matching T-shirts and tired faces. A grandma—had to be Grandma— with white curls tighter than springs and a beaming smile, nearly knocked over the instant she pushed through the doors by a shrieking, towheaded demon that came to her knees.

A pair of beat-up sandals and scruffy jeans had him rising to his toes, only to drop back down, deflated, when a young boy with a soul patch, a Modest Mouse T-shirt, and a backpack shuffled off the escalator.

Legs—the legs distracted him for a pleasurable couple of seconds, mile-long limbs in staggeringly high heels. A brunette in a denim mini breezed by, slanting a flirty glance his way as if to make sure he'd noticed, before planting a long and healthy kiss on a pale, balding fellow in shabby black that looked like he spent all his time in front of a computer.

Huh, Tom thought. Looked like the geeks were taking over the world after all. He'd have to tell that story to the boys, get them to pay more attention to their schoolwork. It was an uphill battle, helping them play as well as they could, having faith in them, and still reminding them that it'd be wild good luck if one of them, much less all of them, made it to the NBA. But when you're fifteen and better than nearly everyone you know, you still believe you're gonna have Wade's moves and Kobe's shot.

In some ways it didn't help that he'd made a living, a ridiculously healthy one, as a pro athlete. It got their attention, made them listen, but it also encouraged them to think it was easier than it was. And even showing them the scars on his shoulder, how quickly it could all be taken away, didn't help.

When you were that age, you were indestructible. God knows he'd thought he was.

A full ten seconds passed without someone gliding down. *Why* didn't they let you into the concourse anymore? He'd called up the airline before he left home, and her flight was supposed to be on time, a full—he checked his watch—thirteen minutes ago.

A lot could happen to a young girl in thirteen minutes. Oh, he knew all about the stupid security concerns and why unticketed people couldn't go wandering around the concourse. But it didn't help much now, did it?

He eyed the security guard who stood behind his counter, half-asleep. Another five minutes, he was gonna go talk to the guy, see if a wink and a promise of an autographed ball and a couple of tickets would get him in. A sob story about his missing daughter wouldn't hurt. How was he to know some pervert hadn't grabbed her as she was walking down the hall and yanked her into a closet?

Oh, Lord. Her plane had barely landed, and his imagination was already going nuts. How was he going to survive the summer? He was going to have a heart attack from worrying about her.

He ignored the prod from his conscience that it served him right. If he'd been worrying about her since day one, like he should have been, it wouldn't all be concentrated into such a short time right now.

Maybe she'd slipped out with the choir kids. Was it possible he wouldn't recognize her? He hadn't seen her since the last time he was in Chicago, in October, to watch the ALCS championship. He'd taken her to dinner, a mostly silent affair punctuated by his sudden, random questions, which she answered exclusively with monosyllables.

She'd been in a black phase then: hair, clothes, lipstick. But girls could change those things easily enough.

A pair of heavy black boots came into view, followed by baggy black pants hung with chains that looked like they should be confining pit bulls, and he let out a sigh of relief. Had to be her.

It was, looking small and young, swallowed up by a long black trench and a choppy swath of dark hair, streaked with neon purple. Her eyes were rimmed with dark liner, and there was a smear of Smurf blue across her lips. She was bleached-cotton pale—he wasn't sure if that was natural or makeup—and she was clutching an army-green duffel slung over her shoulder, her nails short and midnight black.

She shuffled through the doors with her head down, watching her toes. He tried to think of the last time she'd looked at him full-on, face bright, smile open.

When she was ten, maybe. They'd been uncomfortable with each other then, when he'd flown her in for the game when they'd retired his number. But she'd still been excited to see him, thrilled to be down on the field looking up at all the people cheering for him.

But over the next year their conversations had gotten shorter, even more strained, as if she'd stopped trying. And the next time he'd seen her, she'd been dressed as if for Halloween and was quietly but perceptibly hostile.

This summer was a chance for him. Maybe their last chance to salvage something of a real relationship before she ran headlong into adulthood and a life that wouldn't include him at all.

"Hey." He wondered if he should hug her, but she subtly turned away, cutting off the possibility, and he felt a pang in his chest. Well, what did he expect? He was practically a stranger. He knew that was far more his fault than hers.

He'd tried. But they lived in separate cities, and he had zero relationship with her mother beyond support checks. When he was playing he swung through regularly, and he'd get her and Cassie tickets to the game. Take her out for an afternoon, if he had a free hour. But that ended long ago, and phone calls just didn't do it. In lieu of actual contact his gifts had gotten more frequent and more elaborate. He knew it was guilt talking, and he knew even as he did it that it wasn't enough, but he couldn't seem to stop.

"Well." He cleared his throat. "I suppose we should get your luggage."

"This is it."

"That's it?" He didn't know a woman who would go someplace for the whole summer with a single duffel.

It could be her way of getting him to buy her a new wardrobe. It was partly his fault—he took her shopping nearly every time he saw her, because he didn't know what else to do with her—and probably, mostly her mother's fault, too. Cassie was as manipulative a woman about getting what she wanted financially as there was on the face of the earth.

He'd had to pay her ten grand to get to have Mer for the summer, even though Cassie'd clearly been desperate to get rid of her.

"Here." He stuck out an arm to take her bag. "Let me—"

She stepped away, tugging the strap higher over her shoulder. "I got it."

In silence they rode down the next set of escalators and trudged through the hallways that led to the parking garage.

He kept sneaking glances her way. Trying to see some hint of familiarity, some reminder that *this was his child*. She'd always looked more like her mother than anybody on his side of the family. In fact, he'd had a paternity test done right after she was born, just to check.

She was his. There was no doubt about that. But they had so little history together that the connection seemed thin, a technicality more than the solid net of family ties there should have been.

He wondered if it was too late to do anything about that.

She kept her eyes down. The black dye on her hair soaked up the harsh industrial light, leaving it flat and dull, fluorescing the brilliant purple. It was hard even to tell how big she was; her clothing flapped and sagged around her, hiding whatever was beneath.

She sure didn't look like her mother anymore. Her mother had the kind of curves usually found draped over a sports car on a calendar hanging on a garage wall, and she made good and sure everybody noticed. Her hair color was no more real than Mer's, but it was on the opposite end of the spectrum, an eye-commanding spun gold that swirled around her shoulders.

Exhaust blasted them as they headed into the dim oppression of the parking lot. A plane roared into the sky, shaking the concrete around them.

"Here we go." He keyed open the door to his truck and grabbed her pack to throw in the back of the four-door cab.

Mer stood beside the door, her mouth curving into a frown. Was that blue lipstick supposed to make her look like she was dead? he wondered. Weird choice, any way you looked at it. He didn't know fashion, but he knew weird. "This is it?" she asked.

"Yup. Climb in."

He settled into his seat, watched while she hauled herself up and plopped down.

"Buckle up."

She sighed, that exasperated sigh that was common to all teenagers when confronted with the stupidity of their elders. But she gave in, obviously deciding it was easier than fighting a battle she wasn't going to win.

"Thought you were a big shot."

"I am a big shot." He started the engine and looked over his shoulder to back out of the space. Big pickups weren't made for city parking ramps.

"Then why you driving this?"

"Because I like it." Which was partly true.

He did like the old truck. It was the first thing he'd bought when he'd been drafted, back when he thought a new pickup was the height of luxury, and it still fit his legs better than a sports car. Of which he had three: a brand-new black 911 Turbo, a classic Ferrari, which had Boom teasing him about thinking he was Magnum every time he wheeled it out, and a SL55 AMG for everyday.

They were all garaged downtown in cushy, heated comfort beneath his condo. And that's where they were going to stay.

In part because he didn't want Mer spending the summer bugging him to let her drive them. Yeah, he was going to let his kid go out on roads she barely knew with 480 horsepower beneath her.

And in part because he didn't want her to look at him and see nothing but a bank account. He couldn't blame her if she did. He'd done his share to give her that impression, and for damn sure that's all Cassie ever saw in him.

He'd been twenty-two when he and Cassie had met in a club after they'd finished a series with the White Sox. Hot women had been common for him in those days. A kid in the candy shop, all those beauties on display, and all he'd had to do was make his choice, pick between Twizzlers and jelly beans.

But she'd been more than hot. She'd been sex on legs, and she'd looked at him with lust glowing in her gorgeous eyes, and he'd bought it hook, line, and sinker.

He hadn't realized that the lust was there all right, but it was for the dollar signs she saw when she looked at him.

"You drive?" he asked Mer as he rolled down the window and tossed a twenty at the gate attendant. He shook his head at the proffered change and eased forward.

"You don't know?"

"Ummm . . ."

Through the screen of her hair, he thought he saw a hint of smile. A rueful, *Lord but the guy's stupid* one, but a smile.

"Okay," he said to her. "No use fu—" Shit. He swallowed. *Watch your language in front of the lady, punk.* "Might as well get this right out in the open, 'kay? You don't know me. I don't know you. I'm sorry about that. But I'd like to change it."

"I drive," she said flatly, without even looking his way.

Maybe he'd get her a car. Later in the summer, he amended quickly, when she'd earned it. It'd be silly for him to have to spend all his time shuttling a teenager around.

He heard the rattle of his old engine, the honk of a car that was cut off when a silver SUV merged. The distant rumble of a jet engine.

But no conversation. He was a guy. He didn't have conversation; he had beers. He relied on females to handle the talking part. They were good at it.

Mer, however, didn't seem inclined to help him out.

"That's the Mall of America, over there," he said as it loomed to their left, a hulking concrete structure with a big red, white, and blue star sign with matching ribbons waving behind it in the front, flanked with parking structures that were bigger than the airport's.

"Whoop-de-do."

"You want to go tomorrow?"

She shrugged, a small, indifferent one, as if even that was too much trouble.

"And that place, there, that's the new indoor water park."

"What, you're a tour guide now?"

Two more miles of silence. And then she reached for the dashboard and turned on the radio. "You know where any good stations are?"

"Um. What do you call good stations?"

"Don't tell me you listen to country."

"No. No, of course I don't listen to country." Oh, great. He hadn't lied to impress a female since he was seventeen. He hadn't had to.

But then, he hadn't cared all that much what any of them had thought of him, either. There was always another one waiting in the wings.

She fiddled with the dial until she found something with a heavy beat and a guy shouting about some woman's ass.

They'd played stuff like that in the locker room, alternating between rap and hard-core metal, so it wasn't a shock to him. At least on the radio they beeped out the worst words.

But it wasn't exactly a message he wanted his daughter getting. By his calculations, a good half of rap songs had something to do with some woman's butt.

The rest had to do with her tits.

"Did you start smoking?" he asked suddenly, when he took a deep breath and caught a good whiff.

She shrugged. At this rate her shoulders were going to be stiff by the time they got home. It seemed her most common response to anything.

"Answer me," he said, flat and firm. Hell, he herded teenagers around five times a week, bigger and older ones, with mouths on them, from far worse neighborhoods and backgrounds than Mer. She couldn't be that tough.

Of course, none of them were girls.

"So what?"

"Your mother lets you smoke?"

"She smokes. Didn't you know?"

"Yeah, I knew." Every time he picked up Mer, Cassie would answer the door in an outfit he knew damn well she must have spent half the day picking out, in full makeup, looking like she was heading for a Playboy photo shoot, blowing streams of white from her nose. "That doesn't mean she thinks it's okay for you to smoke."

"She says it keeps you skinny. Got forbid that she'd have a fat daughter."

"It also makes you *dead*."

"Hey, in Cassie's world, better dead than fat."

His fingers were starting to cramp around the steering wheel. Damn it. "Cassie? You call your mom Cassie now?"

That shrug again. "Says it makes her sound too old, if someone as old as me calls her Mom."

"I'm not Tom, you hear me?"

"Anything you say, Pops."

"There's no smoking in my house."

"Okay."

He took his eyes off the road long enough to glower at her. He wasn't going to have her rotting her lungs on his watch. "I mean it, Mer."

"I said okay!"

"Mmm-hmm." Now why didn't he believe her?

They turned north on Highway 100, cruised all the way to Excelsior Boulevard before he spoke again.

Just try to get a conversation going, he told himself. The house rules could wait.

"So. How's school?" His fallback first question when confronted with anyone between the ages of five and eighteen.

"How do you think it is? I'm here, aren't I? School's not out for another three weeks."

"What?" He barely noticed the red light, had to brake hard to keep from hitting the Prius in front of him, sending them both jerking forward.

"Jesus!" she said. "Some reflexes there, man. Thought it was your shoulder that didn't work."

"It is."

"Then you're just old?"

"Yup," he admitted cheerfully. The league kids teased him on a regular basis about his decrepit body and advanced age. Maybe it would bother him when he could no longer beat their asses, but that was still a decade or two away.

She gave him a quick, surprised glance, a hint of a smile on that mottled mouth. The lipstick was wearing off, splotches of lip peeking through, making it look disconcertingly like she'd been hit by a fastball two days ago and was healing slow.

God only knew what the neighbors were going to think when they got a good look at his daughter.

"So your mom let you leave school early?"

"No." Her jaw hardened. "Got suspended for the rest of the year."

"What'd you do?"

She slunk down in her seat until the shoulder strap came up under her chin. "What makes you think *I* did something? It was the stupid-ass principal. He's always riding me for something."

"Sure he is," he said amicably. Yelling wouldn't get him answers, he figured. He could yell later, if it was called for. "But what'd you do?"

Their street was coming up. He turned left beneath a huge silver maple shimmering with spring. There was a church on the corner, small and Catholic with an attached elementary school. Houses lined up beyond it, with neatly clipped lawns and warm lights glowing behind multipaned windows. Pots of petunias flanked doorsteps. A mailbox shaped like a loon squatted in front of a blue-painted rambler. Someone was walking a dog, an old man in a Gophers sweatshirt, with a froufrou little bundle of white and black fur trotting behind him. He raised his hand as they passed.

"Who's that?" she asked.

"No clue."

"But he waved at you."

"That's what they do around here."

She mulled that over for a moment. "Cute dog."

So she liked dogs. He'd just learned one thing about her, the first real thing. A normal thing, a good thing. She liked dogs. He felt better already.

"So why were you kicked out of school?"

"Didn't forget about that, did you?"

"Nope."

She sighed while he turned right, heading around the block.

Once he parked, he figured, he'd have lost her to the moving in, and he wanted to know now.

"I had some pot in my locker."

"You what?" He hit the brakes again, right there in the middle of the street, and lowered his forehead to the steering wheel.

Breathe, he told himself. Just breathe.

SEVEN

"Umm . . . He felt her shift his way, the tentative brush of her fingers along his shoulder, snatched back as if he were coated in acid. "You okay? You want me to call someone?"

"I'm okay," he said. *Breathe.* "Just give me a second."

"But—"

"I said just a second!"

Okay. My daughter smokes, and she does drugs, and she's been kicked out of tenth grade, and somehow I've got to fix it all in one summer.

"Umm—"

He lifted his head, glaring at her.

"No, I—" She waved at the back window. "There's a car behind us, and I thought . . ."

"Okay. Thanks." He shoved the shift into drive—too hard for the poor old truck, for which he uttered a mental apology—and eased forward. He was tempted to turn it around, floor it right back to the airport, shove her on the next plane to Chicago, and be done with it. He wasn't equipped for this. Didn't know what to do with her. If her mother couldn't handle her, what made him think he could? She was sixteen.

He hadn't been there for her, all along, the way his father had been there for him and his brothers. Hollering at 'em, grounding them, dumping more chores on them if they didn't do what he expected of them.

But he couldn't go back to change the past. He could only try to fix it now, and what kind of man would he be if he didn't at least try?

No kind of man at all.

He wheeled into his driveway, feeling a little soothed by the sight of his house. Vines climbed over the old stucco, and the light he'd left on in the kitchen winked through the leaded glass. There were flowers all along the edge of the driveway, planted by the old lady who lived there before, and they were blooming like crazy. Weeds were coming up, too; he'd noticed that today. Time to get a gardener.

Maybe he'd make it Mer's job. Good for kids to have jobs, right?

He parked in front of the detached garage and turned the key. The truck shuddered, gave a sigh, before rumbling off. The truck always got in the last word.

"Here we are."

"*Here?*" Her eyes were wide and shiny, staring at the back of the house as if she'd just run smack into a dead body.

"Yup," he said, swinging out of his seat and reaching behind for her bag. He supposed it was a shock to her. Cassie had an apartment on the south side of Chicago. A decent enough place, he supposed. But it was a squat old brick building, crowded in by others like it, and the only green thing on the street was the mold on the garbage. It smelled urban, too, of asphalt and trash and the odors that came from the Thai restaurant on the corner.

This smelled like the suburbs. Not the country—he knew the country. Here there were hamburgers grilling, and damp grass from somebody's sprinkler system, and potted flowers blooming. A dog barked next door, and a couple of kids shrieked. Laughter in the backyard behind his; there were people on a deck, wineglasses in their hands.

"What? You moved to fucking Norman Rockwellville?"

"First off—" He rounded the truck and yanked her door open. "I don't want to hear that word from you ever again."

"Why not?"

"It's not . . . appropriate."

She made a sound in her throat, an isn't-he-ridiculous rumble.

All right, he swore. He swore a lot. He'd spent half his life in a locker room, a ball diamond, a gym. Of course he swore. And it was one of those tricky dilemmas of parenthood, explaining why things that were okay for adults weren't all right for teenagers.

He had a feeling that "appropriate" just didn't mean much to Mer.

She'd been here a whole forty-five minutes, and he was already halfway to "because I said so."

"Just don't, okay? I don't want to hear it."

She eyed him, speculation clear in her eyes. "What you gonna do if I do?"

He wasn't such a fool that he couldn't recognize that she was testing him out.

"I suppose I could wash your mouth out with soap. Didn't get to do it when you were a kid, so we could make up for lost time."

"You wouldn't do that."

He crossed his arms, put on his fiercest "man in black" face. He'd stared down Barry Bonds in his prime; sure as hell—heck— he could stare down a sixteen-year-old girl.

Even if she scared him a lot more than Barry Bonds.

She ducked her head and slid out of the truck, and he held back a sigh of relief. One down. There'd be more, but at least he'd made it through the first.

"How'd you know about Norman Rockwell?"

"Grandma liked him. She had pictures in her house. That family at Thanksgiving, with that big, fat turkey. You know that one?"

"I do."

"Yeah, that one. And a few others," she said softly.

Cassie's mom. Tom had met her once; she'd been babysitting when he went to pick up Mer. Her husband, long dead, had been a bus driver; she was small and soft, had the kindest eyes he'd ever seen, and a voice that went with her looks. At the time he'd wondered how she could possibly have given birth to such a barracuda of a daughter.

"I'm sorry about your grandma, Mer. She was a nice lady."

"Yeah." Her head was down, her voice barely audible. "She was."

Okay, this was where he was supposed to comfort her, right? He might not know a whole lot about fatherhood, but even he knew that much.

He hesitated, his hand wavering in the air over her shoulder. It looked so big next to her, clumsy and callused. He hadn't realized how small she was. The tough-girl clothes, the ever-present stay-away scowl made her seem older, harsher. Now she seemed fragile, as if the pressure of his ungainly palm against her shoulder might break it in two.

He tried anyway, lowering it gingerly. Her shoulder was warm, but she jerked away, turning toward the back door.

Well, what had he expected? He hadn't earned that right yet.

It was heading toward evening. He could hear crickets—damned noisy things—and the peep of baby birds settling in for the night. And still the silence gaped at him, waiting for him to fill it.

"My mother died when I was twelve." It came out rusty. He never spoke about his mother. Never. His father had never been able to talk about it, not from the day they'd found out the cancer had metastasized, and his sons had taken their cue from him. "There were five of us. All boys. She would have adored having a granddaughter."

She turned to him and, for the first time since she'd arrived, looked at him fully. Heavens, but she had pretty eyes. They'd gone darker as the light faded, and now were nearly the same purple blue as the dusk. "Do you still miss her?"

No, he wanted to say. *It gets easier, it gets better, you get over it.*

"Every day," he said.

"Shit."

He chuckled. "Yeah. Shit."

"Not going to wash my mouth out for that one?"

"No. Sometimes swearing's the only thing that'll do." He pointed at the door. "Come on. Let's go in."

"You really live here?"

"Yup." Because there was no way he was living downtown with her. There were too many places to get in trouble right outside the door. Bars that were less than diligent about checking IDs. The cruising young men who hung at Block E and City Center, just looking for unsuspecting girls to snag. Perverts headed to Augie's or SexWorld.

The only recreational facility she could run to from here was the golf course, and the guys there were far more interested in whacking little white balls than getting their own off. And if she did start looking for trouble, sure as heck somebody would notice and tell him. His was undoubtedly the most-watched house in the neighborhood. People strolled by day and night, sneaking peeks at his front door. *"You know who lives there?" "Yeah, him. Imagine that."*

"In you go."

"Is this a retro thing?" she asked as soon as they entered the kitchen.

"Nope. Just old."

"What's all that?" The counters were covered with plates wrapped in foil and plastic wrap, at least two of which were tied in big floppy bows. Covered metal sheet cake pans were stacked next to the toaster, and a bundt on a strawberry-painted cake stand towered over them all.

"Desserts, mostly. Toffee chip cookies, seven-layer bars,

Nanaimo bars. Scotcheroos. Well, I guess there aren't a whole lot of those left. I like scotcheroos."

"You been working on your inner Martha Stewart?"

"Wait'll you see the fridge." He grabbed the old chrome lever handle and tugged. Cold air poured out, and there were so many bowls and casseroles and lasagna pans jammed inside he thought that maybe if they started eating right that second they might finish it off by Labor Day. "I moved in last week," he admitted. "These are all the welcome presents."

Even if he hadn't been Tom Nash, he'd still have gotten a few. This was that kind of neighborhood.

But he was pretty sure the steady stream of offerings was mostly an excuse for people to get a gander at their famous new neighbor.

Especially when their husbands and kids were in tow. Somehow he didn't think it took a whole family to deliver a Tater Tots hot dish.

"Guess we're not gonna starve for a while."

"So." He tossed his keys from hand to hand, listening to the jangle that matched his nerves.

Okay, he hadn't spent a whole lot of time in his life trying to *talk* to females. But he'd never been so damn nervous around one, either, not that he could remember.

He also couldn't remember the last time he cared so much whether one liked him.

"You want to see your room?"

That shrug again. It would be amazing if she didn't blow out her shoulder as bad as his.

"This way."

She followed him down the hall, past the dining room with its built-in buffet and a table that was meant to hold one of those Norman Rockwell–inspired Thanksgiving dinners. This one probably would never be used except as a mail drop. He turned at that floral old-lady nightmare of a room and tramped up the stairs.

"Here we are." Her room was the first at the top.

He'd told the designer the room was for a sixteen-year-old girl and left it at that. He figured she—being female—would know a whole lot better than he what Mer might like. It was kind of pretty, he'd thought when it was finished, but what the hell did he know?

Now, as she stepped past him, careful not to get too close, and took in the room through the screen of bangs that came to her chin, he realized it was all wrong.

The walls were a pale and delicate purple, the furniture creamy and thin-legged. Lace pillows buried the white iron bed like a snowdrift, and more lace swooped across the two windows.

It was the room of a princess, and his daughter was probably closer to the frog.

"I should have waited for you to get here. Let you decorate yourself." Stupid, he thought. He should have known to let her do it herself.

But he'd gotten excited. Wanted to make it special for her. To prove she was welcome. Something nicer than at Cassie's.

"No. No, it's nice."

"You can change it around. However you want."

She walked over to the windows, as out of place in her dark clothes as a crow in snow, and fingered the lace as if she were afraid it would shred at her touch.

"I like these—what kind of windows are these?"

"Dormers."

"Dormers," she repeated. "I like these. And the window seat."

"We can call the decorator on Monday. You can redo it."

She turned, shoving her hands deep in the pockets of her coat. "What difference does it make?" *Because I'm only going to be here a little while.*

He wanted to tell her that it made a lot of difference. That he wanted her to be happy, to feel comfortable here. That he wanted to make up for . . . well, for what he couldn't make up for. It just wasn't possible.

But he could start from right now and do his best.

"There's a bathroom right across the hall. That one can be yours. There should be plenty of towels, and—"

"Where do you sleep?" she put in abruptly.

"Me?"

Her face was turned his way, but her eyes were skittering around, back and forth, like a deer scenting a wolf pack.

They'd never, not once, spent the night under the same roof. A couple of times in the same hotel, but that didn't count; they hadn't even been on the same floor, and Cassie had stayed with her.

They'd never been alone before the ride home. Before, they'd been in a car or a cab, with a driver in front. In restaurants full of other people, in stores stuffed with clerks and shoppers. Never *alone*.

"Well, this is awkward."

His honesty drew a . . . Well, it wouldn't quite qualify as a smile. They'd have to work their way up to that one. But there was a little light in her eyes, a softness to her mouth.

"Kinda."

"My room's at the end of the hall. Got a bathroom down there, too. It's not far, if you need me. But . . . there's a lock. On this door." He frowned. "No smoking in here, though. I'll smell it, and I'm not too old to break that thing down if I have to."

"That's okay, then." She nodded. "Okay."

"You hungry?"

She pursed up her mouth, as though she had to think about it. The lipstick was almost gone, and her hair had slipped back out of her face, and he suddenly realized that she really did look like Cassie after all. She had those sculpted cheekbones, that perfect nose, the kind of plump lips that kept doctors in collagen.

"Yeah," she said.

"Lasagna, tuna noodle, or Tater Tots?"

She smiled then, mischief lighting up those pure blue eyes, and he thought, *Thank God she dresses like a depressed undertaker, or I'd have to shoot some boy or another before the summer's over, no doubt about it.*

"I was thinking I would finish off the scotcheroos."

EIGHT

Sundays were the busiest days at Cedar Ridge, a day of guilt and penance here every bit as much as at the local churches.

On Sunday all the people who were too busy to come during the week finally surrendered to their duty and came to visit. Children, grandchildren, nieces, and nephews all showed up in droves, clutching modest bouquets of daisies and carnations bought at the supermarket. The children had artwork in hand, bright-colored scrawls on plain white paper to be proudly displayed on walls and doors.

Ann left the door to John's room open on Sundays, despite the noise, because several of the younger visitors found Cleo a welcome distraction.

Ann understood. She felt the same way.

It was cold and gray outside, and she was deep into the newest Child/Preston thriller when Cleo, comfortably settled at her feet, lifted her head.

"Hello, Ann."

"Oh, hi!"

Martin McCrary was still a handsome man, despite pushing seventy, with a thick head of silver hair, the posture of the soldier he'd been a very long time ago, and a waistline that was only slightly softer than it had been in his thirties.

He wore a golf shirt, embroidered with Mill Valley CC, tucked into pressed beige slacks. Ann had always thought that as he aged, John would look even more like his father.

Another dream that would never come true.

Mary walked in behind her husband.

The routine never varied; the instant Martin stepped into the room, his eyes swerved away from the bed and stayed there. When Mary first entered, her eyes never went anywhere else.

"I didn't know you were coming today, Dad." He'd never been as faithful as a visitor as his wife. Had never seen the point of standing beside the bed of someone who didn't even know he was there. Oh, at first he'd been there a lot. When there'd still been hope. But now he came once a month, as much a part of the duty brigade as Mr. Schultz's great-nephew. She thought that he hated Cedar Ridge more than anything; he'd accepted John's condition, grieved, and moved on years ago. But the place itself held too many reminders of what awaited him someday; he was healthy now, but a man of his age could only postpone the inevitable so long.

"Rain in the forecast, so I canceled my tee time." He crossed the room and bent to give Ann a warm kiss.

Unlike his wife, he'd been satisfied with Ann as a daughter-in-law from the first. She was tall, athletic, and smart; she'd give him good grandchildren, and that was all he cared about.

What he'd hadn't been nearly so pleased with was the fact that his son wasn't following in his footsteps in McCrary Construction.

Martin was a builder, a big one. Big as could be had in Mallard County, anyway. Ann doubted there was a commercial building or large farm structure built in a three-county area in the last forty years that he didn't have a hand in, and he'd always assumed someday he'd pass the company off to his only son.

But John had wanted to design, and not giant pig barns or turkey processing plants.

He squatted, knees creaking, to rub Cleo. "How you doing, Cleo? How's my beautiful girl?"

Cleo's tail beat a thrilled thump against the linoleum floor tiles. If there was one person in the world Cleo loved more than Ann, it was Martin.

"Hussy," she scolded her, which only made her tail beat all the faster.

Martin chuckled. He started to rise to his feet but had to grab the windowsill when he wavered. He sucked in a breath, and Ann bit her tongue to keep from offering to help, knowing he'd hate that.

He straightened, staring out the window as if that were the only reason he were pausing there.

"You bring anything today?" he asked.

"I don't know how you stay so fit with that sweet tooth."

"Moderation in all things," he said. "Some things feed your body, some things feed your soul. I make sure I do more of the first, but you have to do a bit of the second, too."

"Tell that to my hips."

"Your hips are fine. And that's not an answer."

"Espresso brownies," she said. "They're at the nurse's station. If they haven't eaten 'em all up yet."

"Better not have." He gave her another kiss, then turned—rotating away from the bed, facing the windows, wall, television, bathroom instead—for the door. He left the room without ever having glanced at his son.

"How are you today, Mary?"

Martin had asked her to call him "Dad" on the day she and John had announced their engagement. Mrs. McCrary had only turned from Mrs. McCrary to Mary, and that's what she had remained.

Mary was still at the side of the bed, stroking her son's head. She was younger than her husband, and although she'd once been a beauty, today she looked even older than Martin. Lines cratered from her nose to the corners of her mouth, making her look sad even when she was smiling.

"I'm fine," she said.

John's hair was shaved short, easier for the aides to manage, a pale fuzz. "He used to have hair like this when he was little," Mary murmured. "We buzzed it off every summer. Cooler under his baseball cap, easier for swimming." She smiled, deepening the lines. "And so I didn't have to fight with him so much about washing his hair."

"I remember."

Mary glanced up.

"You do?"

"Of course I do. I've had a crush on him since I was six. I remember everything."

"You always said that."

"First day of first grade. He had on a Twins jersey, tan shorts that went past his knees, a big scab on his shin, and he cried when Mrs. Mortimer made him leave his glove in his locker."

"That's right. I have a picture of him in that outfit. We took one every year, on the front steps, before he went off to school." Her smile deepened.

Maybe Mary was just grateful that someone else had memories of John that were as vivid as hers, and who was willing to bring them out and share them. Or maybe she and Ann would have found a way to grow together someday, groped their way to a more comfortable relationship, if things had turned out differently.

"What time did you come this morning?" Mary asked.

"Oh." Ann shrugged. "Early. Woke up at five or so, couldn't go back to sleep. So Cleo and I went for a run. A quick one, because it looked like it was going to pour any minute. Figured I'd get the brownies here while they were still warm."

"You should take the afternoon off."

"Huh?" Was her mother-in-law still trying to chase her off from her son? Even now, after all this? "But—"

"You shouldn't have to spend your whole Sunday here." She nodded her head, and suddenly Ann recognized her offer for what it was, just an offer, Mary's way of acknowledging their mutual memories, of recognizing that this was hard on Ann, too. Not as hard as it was for her, but hard. "Call a friend. Go out for dinner. Maybe a movie."

"A friend." That was a problem. Oh, she had people she called friends at the office. A monthly lunch date with her college roommate.

But it was awkward socializing with couples, because she wasn't part of a couple, and maybe she reminded them a bit too much that someday they might not be, either. Yet she couldn't go out with the single women she knew, either: they were all looking to meet a man, laughing about their dates, complaining about the slim pickings. She wasn't single.

She wasn't anything, really. And she didn't fit in anywhere. Except here, with her husband, who'd left her twelve years ago and hadn't left her at all.

"I don't know," she said. "I'd planned to spend the afternoon."

"That's okay." Mary dragged a chair nearer the bed and plopped her bag beside her. Her knitting was blue today, a cap that was barely bigger than a fist. "I'll be here."

NINE

Not this year, Ann promised herself.

This year, she wasn't going to kill anything.

She lined up the flats of annuals along her stone patio, admiring the bold, hot pink petunias, the pristine white impatiens that would go in the shade of the maple.

The woman at the nursery had assured her that they were very easy to grow.

But she hadn't inherited her mother's green thumb. Plants thrived with wild exuberance in Judy's care, even things that weren't supposed to grow in Minnesota. Her apple trees were ridiculously fertile, her tomatoes produced enough fruit to can an entire winter's worth of sauce, and she grew more beans than any person would dare to eat.

Ann, on the other hand, killed everything. The fern in her living room, the orchid in her bathroom, the potted rosemary on her kitchen windowsill, and whatever poor plants were this year's sacrificial lambs in her garden.

She tried. She just couldn't get the hang of it. She either watered too little, drying them to a crisp, or overcompensated when they started to droop and drowned them.

She'd gotten less ambitious as the years went on, or maybe just resigned, and she didn't plant as much. But the house deserved a few flowers; it was the kind of house that called for tulips bursting out along the foundation as soon as the snow melted, for window boxes that spilled over with geraniums.

So she tried. Because Ann McCrary wasn't a quitter, never had been, never would be.

"And you," she said sternly to Cleo, who happily ignored her and continued leaping in the air, snapping at the tiny white butterflies that swooped by, "are not digging anything up this year. You hear me?"

It was still gray outside, the sky clotted with low clouds, but the threatened storms that had kept Martin off the golf course hadn't materialized. There'd been a sputter or two but nothing heavy. The forecast was for heat later in the week, so she needed the plants in before they started to bake. Wouldn't do to have them die before she even got them in the ground.

She spent a pleasant twenty minutes laying things out, moving the pots around, trying a neat line of flowers along the sidewalk, a mixed cluster beside the stairs. Imagining what they'd look like in full bloom, when the petunias started spreading and threatening to take over in a riot of color like they did every year in Mrs. Kozlowski's yard across the street. It always seemed like she started with only a few plants clumped around the mailbox and in no time she had a whole river of them, streaming along the driveway, with little more effort than tugging off the dead flowers now and then.

If Mrs. Kozlowski could do it, so could Ann. She was determined. How hard could it be? She could figure out, to the dollar, what a full remodeling of a turn-of-the-century Victorian would cost, exactly how long it would take to do it right, and what the owners really wanted when they said they wanted "contemporary historicalism." Surely she could figure this out.

She'd fetched her trowel and gloves and started digging beneath the tree—damn, why'd the sun have to pick *now* to make an appearance, it was going to get hot out here after all—when she realized Cleo hadn't bugged her for a while.

Usually Ann had only to bend down before Cleo was there, nudging hopefully at her elbow, pushing her nose under Ann's head. *Pet me, pet me, you must be down here because you want to pet me.*

She sat back on her heels, glancing around the yard.

Cleo was at the fence that separated her yard from Mrs. Hillerman's—no, Tom Nash's. It was a wood fence, five feet tall, with broad slats set an inch or two apart. Cleo had her nose wedged firmly in one of the gaps.

"What have you got now?"

There were endless possibilities. A squirrel, a cat. Garbage, smelly socks.

When Ann reached her side Cleo pulled her nose out long enough to acknowledge her presence, then jammed it back in.

Sometimes height was an advantage. Ann rose to her toes.

Ah, it was attention that had drawn hers. No wonder. There was a girl there—at least, she thought it was a girl—squatting down, her hand scratching the bit of Cleo's snout that poked through the fence.

"Hello."

"Oh?" The girl looked up. Yes, a girl after all, though it was hard to judge her age. Always was, when they started dressing like that, overwhelmed by those huge black clothes and unflattering makeup.

Ann didn't really understand it. She'd wanted to fit in so badly when she was a teenager that she couldn't understand why somebody would try so hard to be different. Though the rebellious ones ended up all looking the same, too. Couldn't just once they choose a coat in a color other than black, decorate themselves with something other than chains and spikes?

The girl jumped back. The thick band of black encircling her eyes made them look all the more blue.

"I'm sorry, I—"

"It's fine. You like dogs?"

It appeared she had to think about it. "I don't know."

"You don't know?"

"We live in the city, in an apartment. No dogs allowed. So I don't know."

"You want to meet her?"

"Meet her?"

"Sure. There's a gate, just down the fence a little. Behind the ivy. Come on over."

She shoved a few lank, neon purple strands of hair back into the bulk of flat black. She seemed surprised, surprised enough to make Ann smile.

She supposed the girl wasn't used to people who didn't know her inviting her in. A gleaming silver hoop pierced her left eyebrow, a stud the right side of her nose. Cords tangled around her neck, holding miniature skulls, vampire teeth, a tiny charm of a buck knife. Her black T-shirt was at least three sizes too big for her, sagging past her hips, and there were skulls on the shirt, too, gleaming white printed randomly over the black. Square in the middle, right below her collarbone, one of them cried blood, the vibrant red drop the only bit of color in her entire costume.

She supposed that more than a few people in the neighborhood would take one look at her and keep looking, one hand on their cell phones, their thumbs hovering at the ready over the nine.

But Cleo liked her.

It was only a mild recommendation. Cleo liked almost everybody. But Ann operated under the delusion that most of them were decent enough underneath, so why wouldn't Cleo like them?

The world was sometimes a brutal and unlucky place. She had to believe that most of the people in it were okay.

"I'm safe," Ann said. "And so's Cleo. I promise." Ann tilted her head. "You can ask permission first, if you need to."

The girl snapped up abruptly. She was a lot taller than Ann had originally thought, almost as tall as she was. That perpetual slump shaved a good three to four inches off of her. "I don't need to ask anybody anything."

"Then come on in."

The girl came through the fence with her head low, swinging side to side, wary as a young doe. She shuffled toward Ann, the ragged edge of her wide-legged pants, which should have been at least three inches shorter, dragging on the damp ground.

"Why's there a gate?"

"There wasn't a fence when we bought the house. Mrs. Hillerman, who used to live there, liked it that way. Her kids, the kids who lived here back then, ran back and forth between the two houses when they were growing up. But when I got Cleo, I needed a fence. Mrs. Hillerman didn't like it, though, so I put in the gate. Made her feel like she was welcome here anytime. Which she was."

"You put in a gate, just to make an old lady happy?"

"Yup." Hard to tell if the girl was pretty. Her face was narrow and long, her cheekbones sharp, her eyes swallowed up in all that black.

Cleo, who had been patiently waiting her turn, gave a quick, high-pitched bark to remind them she was there.

The girl squatted down. "Her eyes are blue!"

"Yup. She's a husky." They were nose to nose, grinning at each other. Didn't take much to get Cleo that way, but Ann suspected that it was a rare expression for the girl. "They're almost the same shade as yours."

"You think?" She ducked, her lids lowering, covering up before Ann had a chance to look any deeper, and gave Cleo an awkward pat on the head. Which was enough to send Cleo into exuberant wiggles of joy.

Ann bent and gave Cleo a hearty scratch behind the ears, a thump on the side. The girl took the hint immediately, running her hands over Cleo's side.

"I'm Ann, by the way. Ann McCrary."

"Mer."

Her wariness was easing. She looked like any other kid with a dog, relaxed and warm. Yes, definitely pretty, though she either had no clue or was trying really hard to hide it.

"There are tennis balls in that basket by the garage. If you want to play with her awhile."

"She'd play with me?"

"Sure. She's a ball slut."

Mer shrugged. Careful not to look too eager, to not seem like she was taking a suggestion from an adult. "Whatever."

"I'd appreciate it. If I can get the flowers in without her helping to dig, maybe I won't end up with half the yard tracked into the house."

"Okay." She straightened and jogged over to the basket. Cleo, who knew what was coming, promptly plopped on her butt, her eyes fixed on Mer, now transformed into the most important person on the face of the earth.

"You need to tell anyone where you are? So they don't worry?"

Mer gave a snort, as if the idea of anyone worrying about her was too ridiculous even to contemplate.

"He was watching the White Sox game and swearing. He'll never notice I'm gone."

"You are Nash's daughter, then."

She tossed a ball from hand to hand, Cleo's nose bobbing along with the arc, while she eyed Ann skeptically.

"Know all about him, do you?"

She ignored the niggle of embarrassment. "I brought something over to welcome him, and—"

Mer's mouth curled. "Hot dish or dessert?" She gave the ball a good hurl, flinging it across the yard, where it wedged in between the slats of the fence. Cleo took off, pawing at it when she reached it, trying to get a good grip with her mouth, unable to tug it free.

"Hmm? Oh, brownies. Anyway, it took me a good ten minutes to figure out who he was. I should have pegged it right off, but I guess when someone is someplace you don't expect him to be . . . Well, this isn't where you expect to find an all-star, is it?"

"You're telling me." Her expression cleared as quickly as it had darkened. Cleo hadn't given up, but she'd started whining. *Here, human dummies, look what you did. Come get it out for me.* "Oh, you big baby." She jogged over and tugged the ball free. "Yeah, he's my father. Technically speaking, anyway."

It seemed to call for a comment, something comforting and reassuring. But her expertise with adolescent children was limited to her memories of her own teenage years, and she didn't think that her experiences were at all universal. At least they weren't likely to apply to this glum and prickly creature.

She searched for hints of the father in the daughter. In the long and rangy build, maybe—Mer looked like she'd be lean beneath the oversized clothes. And the blue eyes, of course. She should have pegged that right off, though the eyeliner changed the look of them just enough to throw her off. But nothing in her guarded, self-protective posture echoed his sure and confident way of moving. "I'm sure it's more than technical."

"Glad one of us is." Mer quickly turned to Cleo, as if she realized she'd said too much, and winged the ball again, sending Cleo hurtling after it. It bounced off the garage with a hearty thud, rebounding over Cleo's head, so she leaped into the air, twisting her furry body around.

Ann got the message. Topic closed.

"You've got a good arm. Not into baseball?"

"God, no!" Mer said fervently.

She got half the petunias in, two irregular, hopeful patches at the bottom of the stairs and a row along the brick walkway, where they'd get plenty of sun. She'd heated up as she worked, her fleece itching her back, the hair at her temples going damp.

Mer, who'd been jogging across the yard, trying to beat Cleo to the ball, stopped beside her. "That looks nice," she said. "Really nice."

"Yeah." Ann drew the back of her hand across her forehead. "Too bad their life expectancy's about two weeks."

"You kill things?"

Her hand stilled in midmotion. *It's nothing*, she reminded herself. *Your dog is fine, your friends are fine, and John wasn't your fault. It wasn't because you didn't take good enough care of him. It wasn't, and you know it.*

"Just plants. I just can't seem to get the hang of it."

"That's okay. I can't get the hang of algebra."

"Yeah." It was nice of her to say that.

She didn't look like a nice girl. She looked like the kind of kid who'd play horrid music and stay out all night and bring home boys her parents hated. Who'd skip class, and prompt regular visits from the police, and say *"I hate you"* more often than *"I love you."*

But Cleo, panting, dropped at her feet and rested her head on her toes. And Mer smiled.

Ann wondered what Tom Nash thought of his daughter. Couldn't be what he'd expected. An all-American country boy from South Dakota—okay, so she'd Googled him, it was just natural curiosity—who had a reputation as a good guy in the locker room and who'd dedicated himself after his career was over to keeping kids off the street. And yet he had a daughter who looked like she spent her fair share of time on those very streets.

"Thanks for playing with her," Ann said. "She doesn't get that tired that often, believe me. Wish there was some way I could thank you."

"The brownies . . . Were yours the ones with the shiny chocolate stuff on the top?"

"Ganache. Yeah, those were mine."

"Then consider me thanked." She shrugged. "Had nothing else to do. Better than the baseball game." She bent down again, her hands running automatically through Cleo's fur as if petting her were the most natural thing in the world.

"She'll be coming into heat soon, and I'll be breeding her." If anybody needed a dog, it was this one. Ann thought nearly every kid needed a dog, but some *really* needed one. George, the boxer mix she'd had from five to twenty, had been the only thing that had kept her sane a lot of those years. "Maybe you'd like a puppy."

"When?"

"They'll be ready to go in, oh, late October, early November. If everything goes according to plan."

"I'll be long gone by then."

"Gone? But—"

"Mer. Mer!" The bellow came from over the fence.

Mer winced. "Oops."

"Never notice you're gone, huh?" Ann was ready to call back, but Tom was still hollering.

"Mercedes Williams!"

Mer's brows snapped together. "Here!" she screamed back.

"Where the hell is here?"

"Through the gate, Mr. Nash," Ann supplied.

There was a thud, a flurry of curses. The fence shook.

Ann hurried to the gate before the man crashed on through. "Over here."

He stormed into her yard and it was as if the temperature suddenly dropped ten degrees.

"Where the hell have you been?" He was still in black, a thin T-shirt and jeans that fit him well, anger streaming from him, filling up her pleasant little yard.

But at least he worried about his daughter. That was a point in his favor. He was overreacting and bad-tempered—she wasn't a child, after all, and this was the suburbs—but she supposed it was better than *not* worrying. Though she wondered if this was what Mer was rebelling against, because the girl was obviously rebelling against *something*.

She glanced at Mer. She was as angry as he was, huddling into her coat, her chin lowered so her hair fell forward, the stripes bright and violent against the matte black. "Game over already?"

"Rain delay."

"So *that's* why you noticed." She nodded, as if she'd expected nothing less. "Look, I was playing with a dog, for Christ's sake.

What'd you think was going to happen? Isn't that why you've got me buried out here in fucking Pleasantville?"

"That's not the point, I—"

"Unless you think *she's* a pervert. And even so, I'm pretty sure I could fight her off, if I had to. *If* I wanted to." She stuck out a hip and tossed a flirtatious glance in Ann's direction.

Ann's mouth fell open. Well.

She'd been mad at her mother in her life. Sometimes it seemed like she'd seldom been anything else. And Judy wasn't one to expect you to swallow your grievances. She encouraged—*expected*—you to lay it all out there, in great detail.

But she'd never have said something like that to her mother. It would never have even occurred to her.

He took a step in his daughter's direction, and Ann tensed, ready to throw herself in between them.

But Mer only took a step forward, too, as if preparing for battle.

"Mercedes—"

"Don't call me that!" she screamed. "Don't you ever call me that!" She sprinted through the gate. A moment later a door slammed, loud as a gunshot.

Well, what do I do now? Ann wondered. Ignore the man and go back to planting? Slink into the house and hope he goes nicely away? Or try to intervene, to discover if he was treating his daughter right?

Stalling, she bent down to stroke Cleo, who was huddled against her leg with a wary eye on her new neighbor. Even Cleo, predisposed to love everybody, didn't know what to make of him.

He was still staring at the space where his daughter had disappeared. But the anger had vanished, his shoulders bowed.

"I'm sorry," he said to her, "that you had to listen to that."

"Forget it." She waved a hand. "My afternoon was boring, anyway."

"Guess we livened it up, all right." He shook his head. "Probably livened up the whole neighborhood, didn't we?"

She couldn't disagree. The lots here were smaller than was

typical in the suburbs, and on a spring day there were open windows up and down the block. There were probably at least a half dozen people wondering what all the commotion was. "Maybe," she ventured, "you might want to back off a bit. You embarrass a kid that age, try and rein them in too much, and it's almost a guarantee that they'll rebel."

"And just how many kids have you raised?" he flung at her, and strode through the gate as quickly as his daughter had.

Ann looked down at her dog. "Okay, Cleo, guess we got told, didn't we?"

TEN

The blare of the phone shot Ann out of sleep, snapping her upright.

She scrubbed her hands over her face and squinted at the clock: four thirty.

The phone rang again. She debated not picking it up; had to be a wrong number, a crank call.

But she'd only dial in to get the message the instant it stopped ringing; she could never resist. It was faster to just pick it up.

If it was a heavy breather, he was going to be really, really sorry.

"Hello?"

"Mrs. McCrary?"

The dregs of sleep dissolved, leaving her wide awake. Nothing good could come of a phone call that started that formally this early in the morning.

"This is Erin Burkwalter at Cedar Ridge. Your husband's spiked a fever. We're assuming there's an infection, though we haven't located the source as of yet."

"How high?"

"101.5."

"Okay," she said. And waited.

"I'm calling to get your permission to treat. I'm sorry about the time, Mrs. McCrary, but if we wait until morning, it may well be too late."

"Of course. It's fine," she murmured automatically.

There was silence on the other end of the line, as if the nurse expected questions, concerns, maybe even tears. But a fever had happened dozens of times since John's accident; it was part and parcel of his condition.

There was a moon tonight, she noted vaguely, big and gleaming white. It was framed in her dormer window, streamed a ribbon of silver across the foot of her bed. Cleo lay against her feet, watching Ann expectantly.

"Do you want to treat?" the nurse asked.

For one brief, monstrous second she thought about saying no. That's all it would take, one small and brutal *no*, and the stasis she lived in would finally be over. It might get better; it might get worse, horribly worse; but at least it would be something, one direction or another. Instead she stayed frozen in place, as trapped in John's condition as he was.

"Yes," she said. "Treat him. Of course, treat him."

"All right." The nurse paused, and Ann waited. She must be a new nurse, one who hadn't had been there long enough to know that she'd been asked this question many times before, given the same answer every time.

"You can sign an order, you know," the nurse said. "To treat." There was kindness in her tone, underlaid with a faint hint of impatience. "Or not. Then we won't have to call every time."

"I know." Ann took a breath, willing the rush of anger to ease down. It wasn't the nurse's fault. She wanted things simple. It made sense to her to make a decision one way or the other. To recognize when it was a lost cause and stop wasting everybody's time. "I'll think about it."

Which was a lie. She'd thought about it the first dozen times it was suggested to her. But also she didn't want to make the orders permanent, to have him treated automatically every time, no matter what. Maybe, sometime, she'd be brave enough, strong enough, or just plain tired enough to let him go. She wanted that instant of choice.

But not yet. She wasn't there yet.

Carefully she placed the receiver back into its cradle. There was a wind outside, a brisk one, that had sprung up since midnight. She heard the whip of it through the branches, the rattle of a loose trellis against Mrs. Hillerman's—no, Nash's—house.

She stroked Cleo's head. Faithful Cleo, who filled more places in Ann's life than was probably healthy for either of them.

Suddenly restless, she got out of bed and moved to the window. Her room faced her new neighbor. The light by the back door was on, illuminating part of the backyard, exposing a pile of tools, a ladder, a pile of stacked lawn chairs. Nash hadn't gotten that far in unpacking yet.

There was a light on upstairs, too, faint and yellow, shining through a thin swatch of patterned fabric. Ann didn't know what room it was. A bathroom, maybe, to guide them in an unfamiliar house. Maybe Mer's bedroom. Perhaps she couldn't sleep in a new bed, or maybe she never went to sleep until dawn; she looked like the kind of kid who was late to bed, late to rise, more comfortable with a life lived in the darkness.

Or maybe she'd simply fallen asleep with her light on, unable to face the blackness and its nightmares. Ann knew all about being unable to face the dark.

It could even be Nash's room. Unexpectedly a vision of him filled her mind, vivid, startling. Was he restless? Worried about his daughter? He *should* be worried about his daughter, if Ann was any judge.

He was probably naked. Maybe a pair of boxers, in deference to the fact that he wasn't alone in his house anymore. She doubted he was the kind to sleep in pajamas.

He'd look good like that, with those long, lean muscles, his pitcher's shoulders.

She spun away from the window, wondering if she deserved the guilt that nagged at her.

She couldn't expect herself to be perfect. John wouldn't expect her to be perfect. He'd loved her as she was, with no boobs and a weird family, black thumb and a snore like a teamster. She'd never doubted it.

So it wasn't a betrayal to have a stray thought about another man, not really.

But it wasn't useful, either.

It surprised her sometimes, how little she missed sex. Especially given that she'd liked it a whole lot. But the first months after John's accident—there'd been too much grief, not enough sleep, no emotion left over for anything like that. And after that, when she'd finally started to accept, had begun to feel like she was, maybe, awake and alive after all . . . she'd simply gotten out of the habit of thinking about it. As if parts of her had just shut down, knowing anything else was pointless.

It was convenient, if kind of sad.

Or maybe that part of her responded only to John. Without him, that part of her stayed asleep.

"What do you think, girl?" Cleo thumped her tail against the blue and white double wedding ring quilt. Ready for anything: back to sleep, out for a run, hours of *Buffy* reruns on the sci-fi channel. They were equally appealing to her.

"Yeah," Ann said. "Crumb cake it is."

———

Wow, she sure was having fun now.

Mer kicked her boots up on the bleachers in front of her and thumbed up the volume on her iPod, letting Avenged Sevenfold blast her ears, blocking out the sounds of whistles and shouts, the squeak of new basketball shoes on old hardwood. Let "Seize the Day" blow out the junk that kept jamming up her brain.

Monday night. She'd been in Minnesota a whopping two days, and she was already bored out of her mind.

Guys ran up and down the court, whipping basketballs at each other, sweating. Oh, a couple of them looked okay, and when they started stripping off their shirts, that was an interesting bonus. Once in a while one tossed a glance her way. Curious, mostly: *"Is that really Nash's kid?"* Now and then one would whisper to the guy next to him while they were waiting in line to shoot, give him an elbow and point her way, and they'd turn away, laughing, when she caught them looking.

She knew they were making fun of her. Stupid jocks. She wasn't their kind of girl, sure as hell didn't want to be, but she didn't like them looking down on her, either.

Her mother would have been their kind of girl. Cassie'd probably practiced on guys just like this before she raised her sights and started hanging out at the back doors of stadiums and arenas, ready to pounce on whichever steroided-up idiot got hypnotized by her basketball-sized boobs and skirts that were short enough to promise easy access.

But they weren't Mer's type. Hell, her *father* wasn't her type.

When she was a kid it was cool: *"You're Tom Nash's kid? The Tom Nash? Hey, can you get me an autograph? Tickets?"*

She never told them that they knew Nash about as well as she did. He'd made the obligatory phone calls, tossed a gift her way now and then to ease his guilt. Trotted her out at a game a couple of times when he was still playing and she was still little enough to be cute—her mom had a picture of them on her dresser, all three of them, at the last game he played. He was bending down, smiling and handsome in his uniform, his arm around Mer like they were really father and daughter in some way other than just the checks he signed every month. Her mother was edging into the photo, hands on her hips, long hair blowing in the wind, her feet placed carefully to show off her legs—Mer had seen her practice that stance in the mirror, making sure she knew how she looked her best—leaning Tom's way to make it look like they were close.

Fake. It was all one giant fake.

Just like this summer. She wondered what Cassie had threatened to force Tom to take her for the entire summer. She had a new boyfriend; she'd moved away from jocks, finally. Realized she was too old for that at last, Mer figured. The new guy was no spring chicken, had to be closing in on sixty, and he owned a shitload of parking garages.

He was nice enough, actually. It was Cassie who didn't want Mer cramping her style, and who'd warned her that, if she got into trouble one more time, she was shipping her out, one way or the other. Mer figured it had been a relief for her mother when the school called. *I told you, I told you. Your fault, all your fault.*

Tom was herding all the guys together now, damn near three dozen of them, sweaty and stinking in a gym that was heating up to close to sauna temperature. He divided them into lines, started running them up and down the court while they hurled balls at each other, until the last one in each line bumped it off the glass and into the net. They hardly ever missed.

She hadn't wanted to come. Why'd she want to sit on her ass in a smelly gym and watch a bunch of jocks run up and down the floor?

But he'd wanted her here. Said he wanted her to see what he did now, now that his baseball days were over.

She figured he just didn't trust her alone in the house yet. She wasn't sure she did, either. A place that old and creaky probably had ghosts.

He jogged by and glanced her way, giving her a wink. She wondered if he was having fun playing dad and how long that would last.

On the basketball court, he didn't look so freakin' tall. Here, there were four or five other guys as tall as he was. Two of them were half a head taller; one white, one black, both popsicle-stick skinny, with that awkward, jerky lope that said they hadn't quite got used to their height yet.

There were only three guys she'd call short—shorter than she was—every one of them so quick and shifty that before your eye registered they were in one place, they were already in another, as comfortable with the basketball as if they'd been born with one in their hand. They were all high school kids, Tom had explained on the way there. Some looked it; some looked ten years older, with beards and dark scowls and the muscles of grown men who'd spent a whole lot of time in the weight room.

He'd started the league after he'd retired. A nighttime league, in the city, to keep kids off the street during the danger hours. Couldn't get in trouble in the gym, and the rules were that, if they wanted to keep playing, they had to stay out of trouble out of it, too.

But it wasn't just playing ball with her father that kept them coming. It was what happened in the summer, when the league opened up and other players started trickling in, guys who were already playing in college, some in the NBA developmental league. Even a handful of true pros, backups, mostly, but guys they'd seen on TV, players whose jerseys they owned. Sometimes superstars after their careers were over, playing for the fun of it, helping the new guys find their game, proving that they weren't over the hill yet.

There was a select team formed in June, a mix of all of the above except the real pros, the best of all the rest. The prestige, and the level of play, were huge. They'd play in tournaments all over the country by the end of the summer, and any high school kid who got to play with the big boys was guaranteed a scholarship, and not at some podunk Division II school, either. Duke, UCLA, Florida, Ohio State—they'd all recruited players from the league just in the last two years.

So they kept coming back, Tom had said. And if he used that hook to keep them off the streets, so be it.

He'd huddled them all around now, was using some kid to demonstrate, dribbling as he backed into him with his butt stuck out, shielding the ball with his body.

Mer glanced at the clock and sighed. Ten thirty. They'd be here another hour and a half at least. And the bleachers were starting to make her butt go numb already.

Next to where she sat, one set of bleachers was pushed back, stacked up flat against the wall, with a pad hanging down below it to keep anyone who ran into it from knocking himself out. A hoop was cranked down in front of it; there were eight around the gym, six of them down.

Extra balls were lined up on a cart at one end of the gym. She glanced at the team again; none of the players was looking her way. She climbed down off the bleachers, snagged a ball from the cart, and shuffled back to the corner.

They'd played a little in phys ed in junior high. But she'd long since figured out that she'd inherited none of her father's athletic prowess. Or much else from him, as far as she could tell. And so when it was basketball day she avoided the whole thing as much as possible, staying as far away from the scrum as she could, praying the entire time no one would throw a ball her way.

But desperate times . . . She cocked her arm, threw the ball at the rim. And missed completely.

She glanced back, just to make sure no one had seen. Okay, she didn't figure she'd be good. But they made it look so easy. Every now and then one would let fly from halfway across the gym, and even that would go in sometimes.

She couldn't be more than ten feet away. She tried harder this time. Maybe too hard; the ball whacked the backboard, nowhere near the basket, and flew back, over her head, bouncing onto the playing floor.

Damn it!

She turned around and found a guy standing there, the ball in his hand, a cocky grin on his face.

She'd noticed him before. Hard not to; even she could tell he was the best one, making one quick shift and flying by whatever poor idiot was assigned to guard him. Slicing down the court, out to one side, getting there way ahead of everyone else, one arm up, calling for the ball.

He was almost as tall as her dad but a lot thinner. Built like a steel rope, not an ounce of spare flesh on him, but wiry strong, like he could move his body in ways nobody else could, any way he wanted at any time, fast as a greyhound down the court.

His skin was medium-dark; mixed, she figured, with a narrow face and cornrowed hair and big, sleepy, dark eyes. His workout clothes were baggy on him, his shorts threatening to slide off his hips the next time he went up for a shot, the loose fabric flapping around his knees.

"Lose somethin'?"

She scowled. "Don't you have things to do?"

He jerked his head to the other end of the court. "Got to make twenty shots from beyond the arc." He grinned. "Already made mine."

"Yeah. Well." She crossed her arms, refusing to ask for the ball. He gave it to her, or he didn't. She wasn't playing games with him. But he just kept looking at her. He put the ball on his hip, draping his arm over it to hold it there.

"What?" she said at last, grumpy because she hated people looking at her.

"Now, no need to be snappin'." His skin was shiny with sweat, gleaming under the gym lights. "You Nash's kid, huh? Didn't know he had one."

Now there's a surprise. "Don't you have balls to play with?"

His grin flashed. "Don't like to play with myself."

"Yeah, I'll bet." She shot a glance at the other end of the court, hoping that they were almost done and her dad would call him back. No such luck. They were all still taking aim, sending balls toward the hoop, half of them knocking each other's balls off line before they got there. It was going to take all night for some of them to get to twenty at that rate. Especially the tallest one, so blond you could hardly tell he had hair, who was damn near as awkward shooting from that distance as she was.

She started shuffling off to plop back down on the benches. Tomorrow night she was going to beg to be left home. If he insisted on bringing her along, she was going to have to do something drastic. Like read a book.

"Hey!"

He thought she was going to answer to *hey*? That might work on stupid little girls who hovered around, hoping for a scrap of attention from the star-in-the-making. It would have worked on her mother.

It wasn't ever gonna work on her.

"You're not supposed to wear street shoes on the court!"

She glanced down at her heavy black boots, then turned on him. "What? You gonna tell on me?"

He flipped the ball from hand to hand. She wondered what he did with them if he didn't have a ball. "Aw, come on, don't be like that." He smiled again, a smile that said he was used to getting what he wanted. "I'm harmless. Really, I am."

She snorted in disbelief. "Sure you are."

"Okay, maybe not harmless. Girls wouldn't like me if I was *completely* harmless." He set the ball to spinning on one finger, showing off, so damn good-natured about the whole thing it was hard to hold on to a good mad at him. "I'm Tyrone."

"Okay." She plopped down on the bottom bleacher and stuck her earbuds back in her ears.

He pulled the ball down, came over, and tugged one of the buds free. "This is where you say, 'Nice to meet you, Tyrone. I'm . . .'"

He lifted his brows, waiting for an answer that never came. "Heather?"

Did she look like a *Heather*? She scowled at him.

"Ooookay." He backed up, hands up to show his innocence. "Guess it's not Heather. Lindsay?"

She deepened her frown.

"Emily, Katie, Megan?"

She shook her head.

"Umm . . . LaKisha?"

A little laugh almost escaped.

"Betty?"

Okay, it did come out that time.

"Olga, Hildegard. Oh, I know!" he said triumphantly. "Svetlana!"

She laughed and gave in. "It's Mer."

"Knew I could get you to tell me."

"Had to stop you before you got to Candi."

"Was goin' for the stripper names after I worked my way through Eastern Europe."

Yeah, she knew his type. Knew that nobody ever stayed mad at him, at least nobody who wasn't on the opposite team. Knew he got whatever he wanted eventually, that his charm came from knowing that he had the world by the tail. It was kind of troubling to discover she wasn't immune.

Of course, he was catching her at a susceptible moment, stuck here in Minnesota with nothing to do. Any distraction was looking good.

"You always so cheerful?" she asked.

"Why wouldn't I be cheerful?" He gave the ball a couple of quick dribbles, low and blinding fast, then went up, miming a jump shot, his feet well above the level of the lowest bleacher. "I'm seventeen, and they're talking McDonald's All American next season." Then he ran his hand over his rows. "And I'm pretty."

"Such a shame you got no self-esteem."

"Yeah, ain't it?" He bent over and started shifting back and forth, guarding his imaginary man. She wondered if he ever stopped moving. There was energy in him, cracking like a live wire, as if he just might short-circuit if he sat still for one second. "You always so grumpy?"

"Yup."

"I'd be grumpy, too, if I shot a ball like that."

He'd seen. Damn it, he'd seen. "I did that on purpose."

"Trying to look like Larson, huh?"

"Larson?"

He nodded to the other players. "The one who looks like an overgrown ostrich." He was the only one still shooting, all the rest were sitting, drinking water, and hooting at him as he heaved balls toward the backboard.

Tyrone shook his head sadly. "They're gonna be there all night."

"Why's he even bother, then?"

"Oh, we all gotta do it. Nash says that you never know when there's a second left and somebody's got to sink a three and you're the only one open." He bounced the ball a couple of times, spun, and went up, all pure, graceful motion, sending the ball arcing high toward the rim, a clean swish through the net. He grabbed the ball on one bounce and turned toward her, his *did ya see that?* grin firmly in place.

She refused to be impressed. "Why's he here, then? If he can't shoot?"

"Because he's freakin' tall. Seven one and still growing. You don't have to shoot when all you have to do is get in the paint and drop it over the rim." He was bouncing the ball through his legs now, forward, back, lifting alternate feet. "Plus he can swat a shot away like nobody's business. If he doesn't trip over his feet runnin' down the court, that is."

"Mmm-hmm." It was making her jittery, just watching him. But it was hard not to watch him. And what were her other choices, really? Staring at her boots? Her dad? "What do you want?"

"Huh?" He bent down, dribbling low, so the ball only lifted a few inches off the floor with each bounce, a staccato rhythm as fast and hot as a crazy drumbeat.

She stood up and grabbed the ball away. She couldn't think, couldn't talk, not when he kept pounding away; the thump was starting to make her head throb. "Why are you over here, talking to me?"

That smile again, and she found out she couldn't think anyway. Damn it. It wasn't supposed to go like this.

"You tell me what you'd pick to do, if you was me: sit with a bunch of smelly guys, watching Larson whiffing on half his shots, or talk to a pretty girl?" He leaned over, took a sniff. "You smell better."

"Humph." A pretty girl. Now she knew he wanted something. "You think, if you suck up to me, my father's gonna put you on the select team? Because I don't have that much pull with him, I promise you."

Now he looked insulted. "I don't need no help getting on that team, girl. I'm a lock."

He grabbed the ball again and started a dizzying series of moves, shifting, spinning, and he leaped, looking like he could hang right there, like the laws of gravity didn't apply to him, holding the ball in one hand. He drew that arm in a big circle before tossing the ball up low, under the basket. It skated up along the glass and dropped in. He let the ball bounce and roll to a stop at her feet.

"Okay, fine. You're good." She picked up the ball and held it out. "So teach me."

"Yeah?"

"You gonna make me say please?"

"Yup."

"Okay, *please*."

He stepped back and waved his hand at the basket. "So shoot."

"What?"

"Gotta know what you're doing wrong before I know how to fix it."

So stupid, she thought again. Stupid to let him talk her into making a fool out of herself. Stupid to do it so he'd stay around and talk with her. He was bored, or trying to impress her father, or having some kind of bet with his buddies.

But she was starting not to care. He was hot—silly to pretend he wasn't—strong, and cocky, with those sleepy dark eyes that made you want to look at him and keep looking. And he was amusing, and he had a sense of humor, and he wasn't deterred by her shit. And really, what else was she going to do?

She didn't bother to even try to make the shot. Nothing she did was going to impress him. She slung the ball toward the hoop, surprised when it clanged off the rim.

"Huh. I'm getting closer."

"Ookay," he said. "Everything. You're doing everything wrong." He grabbed the ball. "Put your hands like this. One on the bottom, one almost on the top. And bend your knees. You shoot with your legs."

"Funny. Thought you shot with your hands."

"Yeah, but it's all about your legs. Stronger muscles, you know? Your legs get tired at the end of the game, your shot starts goin'." He bounced up and down. "That's why we run so much. Gotta keep your legs strong, your wind up."

She carefully placed her hands around the ball. It felt too big for her, awkward as hell, and she gave her knees an experimental flex. "Wait a sec." She put down the ball and stripped off the baggy twill shirt she'd bought at a surplus store and dyed black. It was a men's large, way too big for her, which was exactly how she liked it. But it was getting in the way, she wore a T-shirt underneath, and the gym was warm.

She turned to find Tyrone staring. "Hey." She snapped her fingers an inch in front of her nose. "Up here, sport."

"Sorry." He dragged his eyes up. "Just didn't know you were hiding *that*."

"Yeah, well, I catch you slobbering again, and you'll be lucky if you can walk for a week, much less go up for a rebound."

She had boobs. Better ones than her mother, even after Cassie had shelled out for a boob job six years ago. *"You've got a gift, Mercedes,"* her mother had said when Mer turned thirteen and went from an A to a D in six months. *"Why don't you use it?"*

"Sorry." He dragged his gaze up, fixing it a bit too obviously on her face. "It's a reflex."

"Yeah, well, my knee's got a few reflexes, too."

"Gotcha." He handed her the ball. "Assume the position."

She tried, she really did. But somehow she shot while she was still on the way up out of her crouch, instead of at the peak, and her hands must have been off center, because it went way right.

"Whoa! Little strong with the left hand, there."

"Oh, screw this." Temper flared, and she grabbed the ball, hurling it against the wall.

"Easy, there." He caught it as effortlessly as if it had been tossed his way. "Come on."

He set himself up at the painted-on free throw line and waited. "Well. Come on."

"What?"

"Come here." Impatient, he reached out and tugged her over. "No knee reflexes, now." Too late, she realized she should have protested. He couldn't haul her around like that. Except he just had.

He turned her around and planted her right in front of him. He was hot; the heat rolled off him. And he smelled like sweat. But clean, too, some sort of deodorant soap. "Here." He placed her hand on the ball, where he wanted it, and moved the other one on top. They looked so different, his hands and hers, hers looking white as a sheet on top of the dull, pebbled orange, his darker, twice as big. His fingers were long and kind of elegant looking. There was a scab on one knuckle and a pale scar across the back. Her stomach turned over.

"Yeah, like that. Don't move 'em."

His hands moved to her sides, settling on her hip bones, and pressed down. "Okay, now bend your knees, easy, back up . . . shoot!"

Pretty as a picture, the ball arced toward the net and swished through.

"Hey! I did it!" She turned to find him smiling at her, his face only a few inches from hers. Way too close, but man, he had nice eyes, and there was a fun little shiver going on inside, and it felt really good, and jeez, why not?

"Those real?" she asked.

"What?"

"Those." She touched the big sparkly stud in his left ear, cool and clear and the size of a jelly bean.

"Not yet," he said. "Ask me again in three years. Maybe four."

"Hmm."

"You sure don't look much like your dad, do you?" And then he laughed. "Now, don't frown like that. Wasn't a question. Just an observation."

"Uh-huh." She should be moving away. But what was she going to do? Go back to sitting on the damn bleacher until her butt turned to cement?

"Not like I look anything like my mom, either," he said. "She's as blond as you are under all that black dye."

"What makes you think I'm blond?" *Blond* implied all sorts of things she wasn't. Perky, cheerful, pretty, looking for male attention.

Not that she didn't like guys. They were useful enough now and then. But she wanted to be the one who got to choose.

But she'd overlooked the fact that it was nice to be flirted with. Especially by someone like Tyrone, who could clearly have had his pick. It was like being asked to the prom, in front of everybody, by the hottest guy in school.

Not that she'd ever want to go to a prom.

"Light blue eyes," he said. "Light eyebrows under the gunk you got drawn on them." He drew his thumb down her jaw. "Pale skin."

"Think you know a lot about women, do you?"

"No use denying the facts."

She wondered if he was going to kiss her. He looked like he was getting ready to. And he wasn't the least bit nervous about it, like it never occurred to him that she might pull away.

Damn him, he was right.

"Hey!"

They flew apart immediately. *Dad* shout, *coach* shout; it worked the same on both of them.

Her dad was glowering at them. His famous icy stare—she had a *Sports Illustrated* tucked away where he was on the cover, on the mound, but in an all-black uniform instead of his usual white and blue, bent over as if ready to pitch, one arm behind him, with that exact same look on his face. Cold as a snake, twice as mean, ready to strike.

He had a ball hooked under his arm, his black shirt soaked with sweat. "You playin' ball tonight, Becker?"

"Sure thing, coach," he said easily. He held out his hands, and Tom zipped the ball to him, hard enough to knock over a Chevy. Except Tyrone caught it, no problem at all, and started dribbling back down the court, smooth as you please, throwing in a spin move now and then for the benefit of his audience.

Mer's turn. As if he thought that look was gonna work on her. He could stare all he wanted, but really, what was he gonna do to her?

"I didn't bring you here to distract my guys."

His guys? She wondered if he ever spoke of her that way, *his* daughter, without any thought behind it, just claiming her.

"What *did* you bring me here for, then?" she asked, putting a sneer in her voice, a tone that always sent her mother into a crazed rant about ungrateful daughters and dumb, pissy teenagers.

It stopped him for a moment, his expression dark and bewildered.

He might as well have said it out loud: *I have no idea why I brought you here, and I'm really sorry I did.*

No surprise there. Her mother didn't much want her around, either.

"I thought you might like to see what I do," he said at last. "This place . . . It's important to me."

"Good for you."

He frowned at her tone. "Be careful around that one."

"Tyrone?" She was as careful around guys as she wanted to be. But her father didn't have to know that. It was none of his business. "I've been handling my own love life for years, thank you very much. It's a little late for you to start worrying about it now."

His scowl grew fierce. She got the feeling he was tempted to drag her home and lock her up until she was forty.

Good luck to him on that one. He was new to being a father, but she wasn't new to being a daughter. She knew her way around all sorts of parental commands.

"Better late than never," he said. "Look, Tyrone's a good ball player. And an okay kid, underneath all that swagger. Be a better kid when some of it gets knocked out of him."

"Good for him."

"He's got a baby, Mer."

She kept her face still, masking her surprise. He had a kid?

"Little girl. Cute as can be, almost a year old. He was sixteen; the baby's mother was barely fifteen."

She lifted her chin. "So?"

"You don't care?"

"Nope."

"You should care, Mer."

"Why? Is he mean to the kid? The mother?"

"No," Tom said, his voice flat. "But I don't think that he pays a whole lot of attention to them, either."

"There's a lot of that going around."

He jerked back as if her words carried a physical force behind them. "Mer . . ."

"Don't worry, *Dad*." She used the term deliberately, and reached up to pat him on the cheek, curbing the anger enough that it wasn't quite a slap. "I'm on the pill."

ELEVEN

Her new neighbors had lived next door for two weeks, and she'd only seen Tom Nash twice.

Oh, she'd been busy. She'd gotten two new clients: one, a nice couple who'd just learned that the baby they were expecting via surrogate was triplets and whose classic bungalow just wasn't going to fit them all; and a newly retired pair of empty nesters who'd discovered that the shabby family cabin, which had functioned well enough for weekends, lost a lot of its charm when you were living there for weeks at a time. The 1940s structure wasn't worth saving, so they were crashing it all and building a snug new place that looked even older, but with a fully functional heating system and a dishwasher.

It had taken John a full week and heavy doses of intravenous antibiotics to kick whatever infection he'd picked up. It was a common problem for one in his condition; one little bedsore could allow entry to a nasty bug, and the infection could rage through before anyone could stop it.

She heard Nash a couple of times, roaring out of the driveway on that motorcycle, the rumble loud enough that she felt it in her chest.

She'd looked him up again online. Okay, she couldn't help it. He was her *neighbor*. She scanned a dozen articles before she worried that she was crossing the line from curiosity to stalker and closed it out. But not before there'd been that photo from *Men's Fitness*, the one on ex-athletes keeping up their physiques after the game, that showed him in running shorts and nothing else.

He wasn't as skinny as he'd looked in a baseball uniform. At least, not anymore. And he had damned impressive abs for a guy who'd been out of the game eight years and was heading for forty.

Yeah, she'd noticed. If she hadn't, she'd have to turn in her girl card.

Tonight she was already getting home late. Potential clients had been late for her last meeting, and then there'd been an endless phone call when Mrs. Schmitz, who was turning her attic into a master suite, felt the need to discuss every detail of travertine versus limestone versus ceramic.

Poor Cleo, she thought as she zoomed down her street as fast as she could without worrying Mrs. Kozlowski would call the cops on her. The dog had to be about ready to burst.

Except as she rolled into the drive, she saw that Cleo was already outside, wriggling in ecstasy on the ground as Mer rubbed her belly.

She drove into the garage but left her briefcase in the car. No reason to hurry, she told herself. They both looked fine. But a low hum of anxiety started anyway.

"Mer?" The girl looked up at her, big sad eyes which she'd rimmed with black, spikes of fake eyelashes drawn a good half inch long underneath. Her lipstick was black today, too, and she'd put something in her hair that looked like wax, pulling it into stiff chunks.

"Hope you don't mind," she said. "I heard her whining, and . . ." She shrugged, which Ann already recognized as her all-purpose answer.

"I guess it's okay." Her dog was certainly happy. But she wasn't supposed to be out here.

"Did I leave the door unlocked?"

Mer looked up again, as if considering something. She stood. "No."

"She wasn't just out here?"

"No." Mer walked over to the fake boulder by the back door and turned it over, revealing the space where Ann kept her spare key. "How often you get ripped off?"

Ann winced. She'd thought the rock was a good fake, and she'd been locked out twice, when she forgot her keys at the office. John had told her, over and over, that it was a bad idea. But really, what could happen here?

"Never."

"Not yet, at any rate." The girl shook her head sadly. "You want to be stupid about yourself, no skin off mine. But you got Cleo to think about."

Ann debated about just how angry she should be. The girl had broken into her house. But she had given her an easy out. All Mer would have to do was agree: "Yeah, you left the door open." Instead she'd chosen to tell her the truth. That had to count for something. "Mrs. Kozlowski'd notice if there was anything weird going on over here. She lives for weird things happening to other people."

"She's too busy spying on Dad's house to bother with yours anymore. Apparently we need more watching than you do. Might run a brothel or a drug ring out of there or something."

Dad's house, she'd said. Not mine, or ours. "More than me?" Ann asked in mock outrage.

"Yeah, I know. It's you quiet, boring types that you really gotta worry about."

"Boring? You think I'm boring?" She tried to make it sound like a joke. Mostly meant it that way. But there was a little hurt prickling beneath it.

Okay, she probably *was* boring. No surprise there.

"Sorry. I didn't mean it like that. I meant . . . good. A regular, good person."

"I know you didn't mean it like that. I . . . Well, I had a lot of not-boring when I was growing up. Maybe I am overcompensating a little." She knelt down to give Cleo a scratch. "Hey, you hussy. You gonna give me any attention at all?"

"She's a good dog. Barked like crazy when I opened the door, stopped the instant she saw it was me. Remembered me, I think."

"Of course she remembered you." It was already after six. She should have given Cleo a quick run, thrown a sandwich together, and bolted for Cedar Ridge. They'd be waiting for her.

But Mer was in no hurry to go anywhere. Shouldn't she be? Didn't someone her age have much better things to do than hang out in a backyard with a dog and a boring woman hurtling toward middle age?

She glanced at the fence that separated her yard from Nash's.

"Where's your dad?"

Mer's face closed up, going dark and wary. "Why?"

"He know where you are this time?"

"Why would he care?"

"I'm sure he does," Ann replied automatically, wondering if she was right.

Mer straightened. She was almost as tall as Ann, who skated just below six feet herself.

Cleo nudged Mer's hand—*Why'd you quit?*—and Mer laughed, a brief burst of sunshine through the clouds, and obediently began stroking her head again. "You never get enough, do you?"

"No, she doesn't. You can just tell her to go lie down if she's bugging you."

"She doesn't bother me," Mer said. "And Dad's at practice."

"I thought he didn't play anymore."

"No, not him. A bunch of kids that he coaches in a basketball league. Some program he started. He's all hot about it. I'm not allowed to go anymore; there are *boys* there." Her mouth flattened. "Guess he thought I was going hump one of 'em in the middle of the gym floor."

"I—" Ann shut her mouth. Yes, Ann'd been having sex when she was Mer's age, technically speaking. But she sure as heck wasn't thinking about, much less talking about, humping random strangers in public. "Okay, I feel like I should have a comment here, some wise and guiding platitude, but darned if I can come up with an appropriate one."

It felt good to earn a smile. She had a feeling Mer didn't give those out easily.

"Well. I should get going," Ann said.

"Yeah." But Mer just kept her hand on Cleo's head. The wind blew her loose shirt against her, a thin, charcoal gray cotton that came nearly to her knees. She was reed thin, her hips narrow.

Ann had never been a mother, but even she had enough of Judy in her that her automatic reaction to a skinny teenager was to want to feed her.

"Have you had dinner?"

"Not yet." She shrugged. "Dad left me money. Said I could order a pizza. Or I could walk to Arby's if I felt *motivated*."

"How many times this week have you had pizza?"

"Three."

"God forbid." Sympathy battled with duty. "You know how to cook?"

"I know how to pour cereal."

"Come on," Ann said, and headed for the gate. "I'll teach you how to make something."

The guilt started right off. Just a little now, but it would get worse.

She shouldn't be going into Nash's house without his invitation, but she was curious. Too curious, if it came right down to it. His daughter, his house, and he were none of her business.

And of course she was going to be late, way late, to Cedar Ridge. Her visit there would have to be brief tonight. And the relief she felt about that made her feel guiltier than anything.

But the kid needed food, didn't she?

Mer followed without protest, as Cleo trotted along beside her.

"Okay if we go in the back?" Ann asked.

"Yeah. But you're not going to find anything to make in that kitchen."

"There's always something to make." She prided herself on her ability to throw together a good meal with the bare essentials. She and John had married at twenty-one, and they'd had a lean few years until they'd graduated. Good practice for desperation cooking.

"Oh, heavens." She'd been in Mrs. Hillerman's kitchen before. It had been ugly and inefficient then, but at least it had been spotless and loved. Now, there were dishes piled in the sink, a bunch of rotting bananas on the counter. Pizza boxes were stacked haphazardly on the table, one good breeze from toppling, and her shoes stuck to something the instant she stepped onto the worn floor. Her nose wrinkled; someone really needed to take out the garbage.

"The cleaning lady comes tomorrow," Mer said.

"Good to know."

Ann went straight to the fridge, ignoring the urge to pull out a garbage bag and start pitching. She might feed his daughter, but she was not shoveling out Tom Nash's trash.

The fridge wasn't much better. There were a lot of Tupperware containers and bowls wrapped in foil. A least four Chinese take-out boxes, and two of the Styrofoam containers used by the nearest steakhouse for doggie bags.

"Let's see." She gingerly lifted a corner of the foil that covered a blue Corning Ware casserole dish. "You have any idea what this used to be?" Mold crept over a pale surface, and a burned crust edged the upper rim.

"Dunno. Tuna noodle, I think."

"I pity whoever's getting that dish back." She slid open the vegetable drawers, which were as clean as an operating room. Because she was pretty sure there hadn't been any actual vegetables in there since Nash had moved in. "Okay. Maybe this is going to be harder than I thought."

No eggs. No milk. Orange juice, yes, and a two-liter bottle of Mountain Dew. And lots of putrefying leftovers.

She tried the cabinets. There was a bag of day-old bagels on the counter, but no other bread. A hefty stack of brand-new cobalt blue Fiestaware, which looked completely unused; a couple of good pots, but not so much as a can of chicken broth.

"Okay, change of plans. We're going over to my house."

Her kitchen was almost exactly the same size as Nash's; their houses, the same vintage. But she and John had concentrated the majority of their remodeling dollars here and stolen a closet from the first-floor bedroom to make a tuck-in for the refrigerator, now hidden behind cabinet panels.

They'd done a good job, the perfect blend of his contemporary edge and her old-fashioned coziness. White subway tiles made a backsplash, edging up against the creamy marble that topped the countertops. They'd saved one wall of the original cabinets, stripping them down to their original mellow oak, and mixed in cream-glazed maple for the new. The walls were red, warm and rich as spices.

"Wow. This is really pretty."

"Thank you," Ann said, with a warm glow of pride. They used to get a lot of compliments, back when she and John had people over nearly every week. But that had ended with his accident; she'd been too busy, too lost, to think of it for most of the first year. And after that . . . Well, it had seemed too late. Too much like trying to go on as if he'd never been there. "We designed it ourselves."

"*You* did?" Mer spun slowly, taking it in. "How'd you know how to do this?"

"I studied for a long, long time." She opened her bread box, pulled out a day-old loaf of Italian bread. "That's what I do."

"Never met a designer before."

"An architect, actually. Houses, mostly, new and rehabs. Though I did a church once. That was fun."

"Who's we?"

"My husband, John. And me."

Mer looked around the room, searching for a sign of male residence. "Your husband?"

Okay, Ann thought. Might as well get it out of the way right up front. She knew from experience it only got more awkward, harder to say, the longer you waited.

"He was in a car accident," she said, as she grabbed a big pot from a cabinet and filled it with water, careful to keep her face on the task, her voice level. "Almost twelve years ago. He's been in a nursing home ever since."

"What? You mean like in a coma?"

"Sort of." She placed the pot on her baby, her Viking stove, and cranked the heat up to high. "It's called a permanent vegetative state, if you want to get technical about it." She'd rather not; *coma* sounded better. Kind of romantic, the things that people on soap operas woke up from, as their beloved's tortured voice called them back. But vegetative—she couldn't think of John that way, as something inanimate, mute and still and unthinking.

But she forced herself to use the precise terms to stamp out the flicker of hope that had proved very hard to kill.

"Come here," she said, motioning Mer over and popping the top off of her food processor. "We're making pasta with bread crumbs. You like pasta, right?"

"Who doesn't like pasta?" She peered skeptically at the chunk of bread Ann handed her. "With bread crumbs?"

"It's a lot better than it sounds. I promise. A classic Italian dish. And the longest time it takes is heating the water, and it's about as easy and cheap as possible, and who doesn't have bread and pasta in their kitchen?"

"Well . . ."

"Okay," Ann admitted. "You didn't. But your dad is clearly food challenged."

"Not just food," Mer said.

Apparently Mer wasn't too impressed with her father's take on a lot of things. But the girl's face was grim, with those narrow black stripes standing out against her powdered skin, and Ann figured prying was definitely the wrong approach.

"Here. Just tear off chunks and throw them in the processor. We're making crumbs."

"Can you use any kind of bread?"

"Sure. But it's better if you've got something hearty, a good ciabatta, or some baguettes. But anything'll work. Good way to use up bread before it molds."

"Got any way to use up a hot dish before it molds?"

"Eat it."

But Mer barely smiled and was silent until the bread was all whirled up into crumbs.

"My mom got pregnant with me on purpose," she said suddenly, an awkward burst of words in the quiet kitchen.

Ann passed her a box of pasta and pointed at the boiling water. She figured that keeping her mouth shut was the best way to encourage Mer to keep talking.

Mer dumped the penne into the boiling water, keeping her gaze on the task. "Her eighteen-year plan. Get knocked up by some rich jock so he has to pay child support." She shrugged. "She probably would have picked someone else, if she'd known that he was going to blow out his shoulder in a few years."

"I see," Ann said, as neutral as she could manage.

She figured this was the girl's attempt at comfort. Ann had told her something hard, something from her past, and now Mer was doing the same thing.

But she didn't know what to say about a woman who'd tricked a man into fatherhood for the money. And who'd let the child who resulted know that she'd done just that.

"That's why my name's Mercedes. Because I was her ticket to one." She flattened the box between her hands, pushing hard, as if she could squeeze it down to nothing. "I *hate* that name."

Ann pulled out a cutting board and broke off three cloves of garlic from the bulb that sat in a small basket near the stove. "Ann's not my real name."

"It's not?"

"Nope." She showed Mer how to pop a clove with the side of a knife, then handed it over for her to try. "I changed it when I was twelve."

"Your mom let you change your name?"

"Sure. My mom's real big on following your own path. I just told her that I'd had a vision of what my real name was, and she had to go with it."

"Did you?" She whacked the knife with her palm and the clove went flying, bouncing off the backsplash. "Oops."

"No problem. Good for getting out your aggression." Ann rescued the clove and let Mer have another shot at it. "Did I have a vision? No."

"You lied?"

"Yup," she admitted cheerfully. "I'm sure my mother knew it, too, but she was so thrilled with the idea of me having a vision that she didn't dare question it."

"There. Got it that time." Mer plucked out the papery skins, leaving a smashed clove of garlic.

"Great. Here's how we mince them now." She gathered the smashed cloves, pressed down on the tip of the big chef's knife with her left hand while she moved the handle up and down with her right. She handed over the knife. "Anyway, my real name's worse than yours."

"No way."

"It's Wildflower Meadow."

Mer stopped in midmince. "You're not serious."

"Yup."

"Your folks are hippies?"

"Yeah. Well, my mom is. My dad considers himself that, but the truth is he's really just kind of a slacker. Can't be bothered with changing the world."

"Well. Still. I'd rather be Wildflower Meadow than Mercedes. At least your name doesn't remind everyone that you're basically a giant ATM machine."

"You did a good job on the garlic." Ann scraped the minced cloves into the olive oil and butter she'd started heating in a large pan. "And that's not the worst part."

"Don't tell me."

"Oh, yes. They named me that because that's where I was conceived."

"Oh, God." Mer winced. "You should never have to know, or think, about your own conception."

"Exactly. So when I picked out a name, I chose the plainest one I could think of." She'd handled that okay, she judged. Shared a little bit of herself, distracting Mer, however briefly, from of her own problems. Taught her how to cook something so she'd never starve, let her pet a dog. Next she'd get her fed, then send her on her way better off than she'd found her.

That was about as much as you could hope for when dealing with a teenager who wasn't yours. Maybe with one who was.

Then Ann would scurry off to Cedar Ridge and try not to think too much about the fact that she'd enjoyed this evening about as much as she had any in a very long time. Because that was just bordering on the pathetic.

"Okay," she said when the crumbs were in the pan, too, crisping up nicely. "Salad now."

"Salad?"

"You didn't think you were getting out of here without ingesting vegetables, did you? That's the downside of eating with an actual grown-up."

"Which my father isn't?"

"Hey, that's not for me to judge." She pointed at the big, dark green bottle with the gold foil label that she kept handy on the counter. "Grab that olive oil, will you? We're making our own dressing tonight."

"Why would you make something when all you have to do is open a bottle?"

"Because sometimes things are worth the trouble." She watched the girl bend over a bowl, whisking carefully as instructed, dribbling oil into the balsamic and mustard, and thought: *I bet you're worth the trouble, aren't you? I wonder if either of your parents knows it.*

TWELVE

Ann careened into the Cedar Ridge parking lot at eight o'clock, breathless from the rush. She'd skipped her evening run, something she almost never did, but Mer promised that she'd give Cleo a good shot of exercise after she left.

It meant essentially giving Mer permission to come and go in her house as she wanted. Ann wasn't sure how she felt about that. It didn't seem wise; she barely knew the girl. But Mer'd gotten in that afternoon, and nothing unusual had happened. And Ann knew what it was like to be home alone, night after night. She'd gotten Cleo for a reason. It was pretty clear that the girl needed her, too.

Dinner had been . . . nice. She cooked for people all the time, but she rarely ate with them. Not a relaxed meal in her kitchen, anyway. A quick salad at the office with her office manager and her intern didn't count.

She hurried through the parking lot—emptying out already, people heading home—and into the lobby, nearly careening into Ashia. "Oh! I'm sorry I'm so late. I should have called, I—"

"Easy there, girl." Her headdress tonight was Colorado sky blue, her smock yellow, the Crocs on her feet bright purple. "You're not late. You're not punching a clock."

"Well, yes, but—" She stopped, took in a breath. "I always call, though."

"Doesn't mean you have to," Ashia said gently. "We're not your parents, you know. And you should know by now we take good care of him."

"I know." She still felt like a kid who'd gotten caught sneaking into class after the bell. "I had a guest for dinner, and—"

"A handsome one, I hope."

"A handsome what?"

"Oh, honey, if you have to ask, you're in worse shape than I thought. Guest, of course."

"Guest?"

"A date," Ashia said patiently, as if translating for someone who had a weak grasp of the language.

Date. It was not a word that had any relevance to her, not even a word she'd thought for years and years.

"I don't date."

"I know that, Annie," she said. "And it's a shame." She hooked her hands on the stethoscope that hung around her neck. "Got rounds now. Have a good visit."

Ann stood rooted in place, her mind buzzing too fast for the rest of her to move. A shame that she didn't date? It had never occurred to her that people—regular people, not her "what does marriage have to do with it?" mother—thought she *should* date.

Last she checked, her marriage vows had said nothing about allowing dating. The "for better or worse, forsaking all others" part seemed pretty clear to her. Though now, looking back at the naive, love-struck young bride she'd been then, she realized she'd had no clue what they meant. Had never conceived of just how bad the *worse* could be.

But she'd meant them then. Still meant them, for the blessing of having gotten to love John.

"Ann?"

Ann spun to face her mother-in-law, as guilty as any teenager caught sneaking in after dark. "Mary! I'm so sorry, I should have called. There was no need for you to stay."

"I was just leaving."

"Oh, good!" Shoot. She was still a tongue-tied girl, saying the wrong things. They'd been family for close to two decades; she shouldn't be intimidated by Mary anymore. "Not good that you're leaving, of course. But that you weren't waiting for me."

"Of course," she said, her voice crisp as her white cotton blouse, which only reminded Ann what a mess she was, stumbling over awkward words.

"I had someone for dinner—you know I have new neighbors, I told you, remember? And—"

"You mean that baseball player?" Her mouth flattened, a razor line of disapproval.

"No. Well, yes, he's the new neighbor. But it was his daughter I had over for dinner. He was gone, and she was alone, and, well, she just looked like she needed a good meal. And some company."

Stop justifying, Ann told herself. There was nothing to justify. She'd been here virtually every day of the last decade. This place was the focus of her life, the touchstone around which the rest was formed.

It was the same for Mary. Ann knew Mary's life revolved around John, that she was the one person on earth who was as trapped by this situation as she was. And Ann was grateful to her, her and Martin; they'd paid for John's care over the years, the hundreds of thousands of dollars it cost to keep him here and safe. If they hadn't, Ann would have lost her house, her firm, during that first horrible year.

Don't even think about it, they'd told her, when she'd first tried to thank them, once she'd come out of the fog long enough to realize she hadn't gotten a bill in months. He's our son; of course we'll take care of him. And we don't want you to sell John's house, John's business.

"Oh." Mary had an apple-green sweater draped over her shoulders, pearls at her ears, and peach on her mouth. Fresh as spring, twice as elegant. "How old is she? The girl?"

"It's kind of hard to tell." Ann waved her hand over her face. "There's a lot of stuff covering her up. Over twelve, I'd think, and younger than twenty. Anywhere in there, you got me."

"It's hard to tell these days, isn't it? Some of those girls, I see them out walking with their boyfriends, and the boys have pimples and no shoulders and, except for the way they're draped over each other, it looks like the girls should be babysitting them."

Mary knew her duty. Ann had expected to be reminded of hers as well, with a subtle but effective laying on of the blame for putting someone else—someone she barely knew, who certainly wasn't her responsibility—before her husband.

But she'd forgotten that Mary was first and foremost a mother. The great tragedy of her life was that she'd only been able to have one child and no grandchildren. She'd mother any young one who came into her sphere.

"I didn't look like that when I was that age, that's for sure."

Mary laughed, surprising a smile out of Ann. It had been a very long time since anything she'd said had made Mary laugh. "No, you certainly didn't. Wait, don't screw up your mouth like that. I didn't mean it that way. Of course you were lovely. Would John have chosen you, if you weren't? But when you were fourteen, you looked fourteen. Coltish and fresh, not like Ann-Margaret's tarted-up baby sister. And that, my dear, was a good thing."

Ann had to lock her jaw to keep it from dropping. "Thank you. I think."

A man wheeled by, careening his chair around the corner at a speed just a shade too fast for safety.

"Good evening, Mary!" he called. "I enjoyed meeting you."

"As did I, Henry."

The man zoomed down the hall and out of sight. He was broad-shouldered enough to keep that chair moving at racespeed without the assistance of a battery, his hair thick and steel gray. He'd worn a warm-up suit in basic black, and, except for the chair, he looked the picture of health.

"Can you get traffic tickets for wheelchairs?" Ann wondered.

"Of course, when somebody that age can move one like that, I suppose you should give him a medal, rather than a ticket."

"Yes," Mary said, a hint of wistfulness in her voice, gazing after the careening chair.

"Who is he?"

"Him? Oh, that's Henry."

"And?"

"And nothing. Just Henry."

"Seems to know you, Mary."

There was pink on her cheeks, barely perceptible under the foundation, a sparkle of fluster in her eyes.

"So you have an admirer, do you?" Ann teased.

"Don't be ridiculous." In all the time Ann had known her, Mary had only once evinced a hint of interest in another man besides her husband. Come to think of it, she'd never betrayed much interest in her husband, either; she was too circumspect for that, too reserved.

Judy, on the other hand—Ann was forever catching her kissing in the kitchen or making eyes at a nice-looking man. If Judy had shown such obvious interest in Ann's father, she might have found it cute, endearing, a comforting sign of her parents' strong relationship, rather than something that made her want to slap her hands over her eyes and run off shrieking.

But Mary—once, a good fifteen years ago, after Mary'd had two glasses of wine on her birthday, and they'd all gone to see *The Unforgiven*, she'd sighed and murmured, "Now, that's a man!" when Clint Eastwood had sauntered on-screen. When she realized that Ann had heard her, she'd looked exactly like she looked right now: mortified but a bit excited, too.

"And why wouldn't he admire you?" Ann asked.

"Oh." She swallowed, and the mask dropped into place. "I just—I was walking down the hall, on my way out, and he merely asked me a question about the nearest ice machine, and we struck up a conversation. I think he's lonely."

"It was kind of you to give him some time, then. I'm sure he appreciated it."

"I think he did," she said with some surprise. "He had a hip replacement, and there's no one to watch him, so he has to stay here until he's on his feet again. It's very sad. His son's in the Middle East, and his daughter lives in Seattle, and she has two little ones, and his son-in-law's an intern, so there's no one to help." Her voice dropped, as if saying it louder would be tempting fate. "His wife died five years ago. Breast cancer." The last two words were barely audible.

Mary had had a mastectomy herself, six years ago, followed by four months of chemo. She never talked about it, had allowed neither her husband nor her daughter-in-law to go to treatments with her, preferring to take her sister, Helen. Ann had never seen her without her wig, her makeup, and she'd never even missed an evening at Cedar Ridge except when she herself was hospitalized. Mary probably wouldn't even have told her if Martin hadn't called to ask Ann to keep an eye on her, because she'd refused to let him cancel his annual golf trip to Scottsdale with his regular foursome.

"It's hard to be alone," Ann said, the words out before she thought better of them.

Mary flinched. "Yes," she said quietly. "It is."

THIRTEEN

The house was dark when Tom rolled into his driveway. The clock on the dashboard of his truck had flicked over to twelve forty-five.

The house. He was still working his way up to calling it "my house." Wondered if he'd ever get all the way to "ours." Or if she would.

He'd never given a whole lot of thought to what he wanted in a house. Once he started making some money he'd pretty much just gone for the same kind of place the other single guys on the team bought, something slick and fancy with a lot of toys. A place where you could invite your buds over and they'd whistle, low and admiring.

If you'd asked him what a home looked like, he'd have immediately conjured up the farm where his dad still lived. One of his brothers had taken over the bulk of the work, though he knew damn well his dad was still out there every single day, bad knees and a double bypass be damned.

He thought of the way it looked years ago, a plain, boxy white farmhouse with the porch sprawling all along the front, two poplars sticking up on either side of the front door. Back then, there was clematis climbing up a trellis on the side, and lace curtains at the windows, and a birdbath, its base bordered by marigolds, smack in the middle of the yard that one of the boys had to mow every Saturday.

His house, when his mother was alive.

He had bright, clear memories of her. Not Hallmark memories. Mostly memories of her hollering at the boys, breaking up wrestling matches in the kitchen, nagging them to pick up their socks, ordering showers before she'd give them dinner.

She was a tiny little slip of a woman—he'd been taller than her when he was ten—with a voice like a bullhorn and no tolerance for fools. She cooked with more volume than taste, tried valiantly but with little success to install a few manners into her boys, and knew exactly where to cuff you on the ear to make it sting for an hour.

Lord, but he missed her. It was the last time he'd lived with a woman, which was probably why he was making such a muck of it now.

He kicked off his shoes the instant he came in the back door, started stripping off his sweat-soaked shirt and shorts before he remembered he couldn't do that anymore. Walking around in his underwear was a casualty of having a daughter in the house, along with swearing and drinking and watching any movie that had naked people doing stuff he didn't want his daughter to know about.

She'd laughed at him at that one. After three days of awkward silences, with her mostly locked up in her room doing God only knew what, he'd gone to Target and bought every DVD that looked even vaguely like a chick flick. She'd been disgusted by *The Notebook*, complaining about the cheese factor until she'd finally popped it out after an hour, to his everlasting gratitude. So there was hope for the girl after all.

She'd liked *Love, Actually* a whole lot better. So had he, until the story line about the sweet, shy porn stand-ins had gotten just a bit too graphic about their work. His face grew as hot as it had been when Melissa Dillard had caught him peeping down her shirt at Homecoming in ninth grade, before his growth spurt had given him a competitive advantage in blouse-peeping. *He'd* been the one scrambling to eject the DVD that time, while Mer just looked amused.

The door to her room was closed when he got to the top of the stairs.

He stood outside it, debating with himself.

This parenting thing was tricky. Especially when you were trying to deal with a teenager you barely knew, and you hadn't had all the experiences along the way to get you in shape for the job. Like trying to jump from A-ball to pitching to A-Rod.

Philosophically, he figured there was something to the advice about respecting their privacy, showing them you trust them. And he knew damn well that riding herd on a kid only made her all the more creative in getting around you. He didn't know if he'd have put so much effort into smuggling booze into the prom if his dad hadn't warned him he'd tan his hide if he came home drunk.

So he hadn't come home. Problem solved, except for the fact that he'd had to shovel manure every morning at five for a solid three weeks afterward.

But Mer had already proven she couldn't be trusted, hadn't she? That's how she'd gotten here in the first place.

Though he wasn't sure he agreed with the school's take on that. Getting kicked out of school didn't seem like proper punishment for getting caught with pot in your locker. Heck, when he was her age, getting suspended from class would have seemed like a reward—if it hadn't meant getting kicked off the baseball team, too. Three weeks without Mrs. Zimmer, old dragon breath herself, breathing down his neck in English? Hell, yeah!

If they really wanted to give her a consequence she'd remember, they should have made her go to school round the clock for a month.

So he knocked. A couple of wimpy little taps at first. Harder when he got no answer.

He took a deep breath, praying with more fervency than he knew he had in him that she slept in some big, thick nightgown, and opened the door.

The bed was empty. Easy to tell when the blankets were on the floor, the top sheet twisted at the foot of the bed, the fitted bottom one half-off.

Panicked, he ran to the open window, where the pretty curtains fluttered in a soft night breeze, before a thread of sanity wiggled in.

Of course she hadn't climbed out the window. He hadn't been here; she could have just walked out the door. And while his daughter certainly had a flair for the dramatic, she didn't strike him as the type who'd put forth that kind of effort when it wasn't necessary.

He tried the spare bedroom, pin-neat, with a white and rose quilt on the sleigh bed and a cluster of silk flowers in an old pitcher on the dresser. Neither of them had set foot in the place since they moved in.

The living room was empty, too—she hadn't fallen asleep on the couch, but who would? With its swooped back and a whole lot of buttons tucking divots into the sheared velvet back it was as uncomfortable as a bull-pen bench.

There was no reason for her to run away, he told himself as he ran for the basement. He pretty much left her alone, didn't he? Didn't have too many rules, hadn't raised his voice except when she'd been flirting with Tyrone, and that was for her own good. Okay, he shouldn't have done it in front of Tyrone—tactical error there—but he'd taken one look at the way Tyrone had been smiling down at her, bumping his hips against her rear as he pretended to show her how to shoot, and he'd had a sudden flash of Mer with her belly swelling out of her T-shirt. Just the way Tyrone's baby's mama, Clarice, had looked when she'd stopped by practice once a month before she was due. Tyrone had told her never to interrupt him again when he was playing.

No father should be held accountable for his actions when his head was filled with a vision like that.

Basement. Basement, and then the police.

But she was there. Of course she was there, curled up in one of the theater chairs fast asleep, a quilt she'd dragged from her bed over her shoulders. The only light down there came from the big screen, the bright blue eerie and cheerful.

He picked up the empty case on the side table: *Love, Actually*.

He decided not to be upset that she'd immediately watched it when he was gone. Better that than some druggie/slasher movie, at least, full of blood and pain.

The fridge was full of root beer and Dr Pepper; the beer had been one of the first things to go the first time he'd left her alone in the house.

So he grabbed an IBC root beer—not the same, but it would have to do—and settled down in the recliner to contemplate his daughter.

Asleep, she looked younger. She'd still had on that horrible makeup, but it was smudged, like she was a kid who'd played at being a grown-up, drawing fat black lines around her eyes with a thick marker, smearing color across her lips.

So. What was he going to do with her? He could keep her safe for a summer—he thought—but beyond that? Could he teach her how to keep herself safe, make the right choices . . . make better choices than he had?

Her eyes fluttered open, unfocused and confused.

"Hey," he said. "You fell asleep watching the movie."

"I did?" She yawned, looked around as if trying to orient herself. "Oh, yeah. Guess so."

"If you were so tired, why didn't you just go to bed?"

"Couldn't sleep." She was awake now, her eyes narrowing in his direction in a way he wasn't sure he liked. "I heard a noise. Like there was somebody at the door."

He snapped up. "Did you call the police?"

"No, I didn't call the police. It was probably nothing." She shivered. "Probably."

"Next time, you don't take any chances, okay?"

"Sure. I'm going to call the police every single time a branch blows off a tree. Which happens about every ten seconds out here." But she was gnawing the last of the lipstick off her bottom lip.

She was probably right. Probably.

"Maybe—" He stopped before "you should come to practice with me after all" got all the way out. He knew where the real danger lay. "I'll call and get a security system installed tomorrow. Been meaning to do that anyway."

"Okay." But Mer's eyes were wide, her body still huddled beneath the quilt as if it could protect her. She was so thin. Fragile. "It's okay, really. I should get over it."

"Over what?"

"Being afraid." If she shrank any deeper into the covers she was going to disappear "Mom—well, she goes out a lot. I should be used to being alone by now, shouldn't I?"

Damn it, Cassie!

He should have hired his own damn nanny. Insisted that she move in with Cassie from the first, make sure Mer was looked after. He should have known that Cassie wouldn't pay enough attention to her, wouldn't come running home to her kid if there were open bars and a man willing to buy for her. And there was always a man willing to buy for her.

Maybe that's why Mer always tried to look so tough, with her crypt-keeper clothes and her foul mouth and her just-try-and-mess-with-me attitude. Because this was the real Mer, all scared inside, vulnerable and unsure.

"And at least," she was going on, "well, in Chicago, I had friends. And there was always *someone* in the building. But here . . . Not that I'm asking you to stay home with me," she added hastily. "I know your work is important. But it's . . . It's just kind of lonely, you know?" Her voice quavered.

"How about . . ." He thought a bit, sorted through options. He was of the firm belief that there weren't many things—oh, a few, mostly medical, but not many others—that money and a little ingenuity couldn't solve. "I'll find someone. Someone to stay with you."

"You're not going to get me a *babysitter*." He thought she might cry at the suggestion.

"No, no!" he hastened to reassure her. "Just a . . . companion. Until you have a chance to find your own friends."

"Oh, yeah, I'm really gonna have friends when they find out I'm a sixteen-year-old who can't stay home alone."

Home. She said *home*. His heart slopped into mush.

"Maybe." She chewed on a thumbnail. "No, you wouldn't want to do that. It's too much trouble."

"What?" He was ready to do anything short of inviting Cassie to move in herself to help things along. "Try me."

"It's really not . . . I mean, I'd like it. I'd *love* it. But it's a lot to ask. Mom would never let me."

"She wouldn't, huh?" That could be a great recommendation right there. "Never know until you try, do you?"

"That's true," she said slowly. She raised hopeful eyes to him, the exact eyes his own mother had, the only thing Tom had inherited from her, the only thing Mer had inherited from him. "I would really—" she said, and took a deep breath. "I would really love a dog."

FOURTEEN

Tom figured his neighbor was getting murdered. Had to be the only thing that could make her shriek like that.

He took off running, blasted his way through the stupid gate—why *did* they have that, anyway?—and skidded to a stop in a slick of mud and crushed petunias.

She was alive after all, soaking wet in a thin purple tank and a baggy pair of khaki shorts, a smear of mud on her cheek, a dripping hose in her right hand, and a world-class scowl on her face.

"What?"

She pointed with the hose head. *"That."*

He took a look, then another one, and started laughing. "Coop's having fun, huh?"

He'd found Cooper chained to a fence, FREE scrawled in black marker on a hunk of corrugated cardboard propped up beside him. Tom had stopped for gas in north Minneapolis on his way to practice, and the dog had barked once to get his attention, then laid down, his big head on his paws, his eyes sad and hopeful, his tail thumping once every thirty seconds or so.

Tom had known he was being played. He wasn't stupid. By the dog, and by his daughter, who'd sniffed and drooped and sighed around the house for a good ten days. She'd taken to sleeping with a baseball bat under her bed, even after he'd had ADT installed, and when he'd seen that poor dog, all by himself, it had seemed like a sign. So he'd caved.

They'd had a dog on the farm, a collie with Lassie's looks but none of her brains, who'd lived mostly in the barn and who loved nothing so much as following a baseball, back and forth, back and forth, snapping at the air as Tom and his brothers played catch, a cheerful idiot who didn't seem the least bit deterred by the fact that he never actually caught the damn thing.

Dogs weren't meant to be in the city, surrounded by acres of concrete, chained to a fence. So he'd loaded the thing into his truck—damn dog smelled like a sewer—and carted him along. It was a nice cool night, so he left him in the truck's cab with the window cracked, checked on him every fifteen minutes, and climbed in at the end of the night to find a tear in the front seat, a chewed-up baseball glove, and the half-empty Starbucks cup he'd picked up at the drive-through long gone.

That should have been his first hint. The dog ate like Boom but with even less discrimination. He confiscated Tom's favorite leather chair in front of the big screen, claimed a spot at the foot of Mer's bed and growled if anyone but her came close, and left drifts of pale brown fuzz all over the house.

But Mer had fallen in love. She'd named him Cooper—after Gary, she'd said, and Tom was happy that she even knew who Gary Cooper was. She had stopped complaining about him leaving her every night for practice, and had even—once—condescended to join him and Coop on a walk.

Of course, Coop had everybody crossing the street when they saw him coming, but that was okay. He hadn't been asked for a single autograph since Cooper came to live with them.

Coop was pushing 125 pounds and was, at best guess, a mix of Saint Bernard, Rottweiler, and, as far as he could tell, any other breed that drooled. Once they'd gotten in the habit of not leaving anything resembling food on the counter, things seemed to be going okay.

But his neighbor wasn't okay. She was damn near purple, her

eyes bugging out of her head. "You didn't get him *fixed*?" she screeched at him.

He joggled a finger in his ear and waited until the ringing subsided. "What? I dunno."

"You don't *know*?" She looked at him as if he'd just admitted to boiling bunnies.

He shrugged, aware he'd picked up the gesture from Mer. It was useful, he'd discovered. And he kind of liked the idea that they had something in common, the way his brother Mike had Dad's walk and Eric Mom's smile.

"Wait. Just where did you *get* that dog?"

"From a gas station."

"A gas station." She pressed fingers to her eyeballs, shook her head. "Mer said he was a rescue."

"He was chained to a fence. Figure that counts as a rescue."

She winced, her automatic pity—*oh, poor doggie*—warring with her anger. "I thought . . . I figured you got him from the humane society, or some rescue organization. Where he'd have to be fixed."

"Well, I guess he wasn't." He glanced at the dogs. They'd quieted now, and were standing rear to rear. "So you want me to drag him off?"

"Too late now. They're tied."

"Tied?"

"Stuck together. Until it's over." She sighed. "She was supposed to go to the stud tomorrow."

He grew up on a farm. Okay, he knew a fair amount about birth. But their pigs, their cows, hadn't had any fun along the way. They were all artificially inseminated; easier to control, and a frozen vial of sperm was a lot easier to ship than a whole steer.

"Aren't you supposed to keep her inside when she's in heat?"

The look she gave him should have sliced him in half, clean through the heart. He was glad the rake was out of reach, glad that she didn't look like the type who kept a gun handy.

"Everybody else around here gets their animals neutered like responsible grown-ups!"

"Shouldn't have left the gate open."

"The gate wasn't open!" She stomped over to the lilac bushes and pointed at a huge hole that angled under the fence. "He *dug* his way through."

"Determined fellow."

Her hands shook, as if she couldn't wait to wrap them around his neck. "You—"

"Look, your dog's fine. See?" They'd moved apart and were both curled up on their rumps, licking away. The canine equivalent of a cigarette, he figured. "Ann . . . It is Ann, right?" He put on a smile, the one that disarmed mothers and reporters. It always helped to remember their names, too: *He knows my name, Tom Nash remembered my name!*

It was a crock, of course. But that didn't mean he was reluctant to use it. If you had to put up with the crap that being famous brought, you might as well enjoy the upside as well, whether it was suddenly available restaurant tables or a slick way out of a difficult situation.

He would never abuse it. He'd decided that his second year in the league, when he'd watched a teammate use his name to skate by on a weapons charge.

But if it kept his neighbor from hating him, well, that was a fair deal all around, he figured.

"No reason to make a bigger deal out of this than it is," he said. "Whatever the puppies were worth, I'll pay, okay? Just let me know." He'd add a little extra, just to keep the peace, and—

The water hit him square on, smack in the middle of the face, with enough force behind the spray to sting. He sputtered, shut his mouth so he wouldn't drown. He jumped aside, out of the way, but she just followed him, her aim unerring, her expression as fierce as Joan of Arc's.

There was nothing to do but rush her. Surrender to the fact that he was good and wet, and another few gallons wouldn't hurt.

He was still pretty quick for an old guy—God bless the boys for keeping him in shape—and he caught her by surprise, wrapping one arm around her waist to hold her still while he wrestled the hose from her death grip.

She didn't give up easy—being that angry helped, he figured—and she was stronger than she looked. He gave the hose one last wrench and yanked it free.

He gave a heave, whipping it across the yard. "What the hell was that!"

"It's not about the money!" she shouted at him. And then she wedged her arms in between them and shoved, breaking his hold.

Until she pushed him away, he hadn't given one passing thought to the fact that he had a woman all pulled up against him, nice and snug, and that she smelled like sunshine and vanilla, and she was tall enough that it wouldn't have given his back a crick to have to bend down and kiss her.

Now that she'd shoved him away, he couldn't think about anything else. Her shirt was damp, clinging to a waist that looked smaller than his forearm, and her legs would have made a supermodel jealous.

Okay, she wasn't exactly pretty. So what? He hadn't had a date since April, since Cassie had started hinting around about Mer coming for the summer and he'd gone into serious father-training. And he wasn't going to have a real one, not until she went home; their relationship was complicated and prickly enough without bringing his sex life into it.

But September was starting to look a long, long way away.

"It is not about the money," she repeated, slow and even. She stepped forward, ready to face him down, her eyes stormy, and he realized she had to be pushing six feet. "You're finding a home for those puppies. Every last one of them. A *good* home, one that I approve."

"Sure," he said. How hard could it be, finding homes for a bunch of puppies? Puppies were cute.

She narrowed her eyes at him, as if trying to figure out if he was telling her the truth or simply agreeing for expediency.

"You will," she said again. "Or I'm telling your daughter on you."

"Yes, ma'am."

She scowled. Oops, he thought. He'd meant it to be funny, agreeing with the woman in charge. But he'd forgotten that a lot of women were touchy about the *ma'am*. His dad had drilled him good when he was young about being respectful, but that was with church ladies, teachers, women who were closer to his grandmother's age than his own.

Younger women didn't like it so much. He'd learned that lesson when he was in the minors, when he'd made the mistake of being a bit too polite to a sexy thirtysomething he'd met in a bar in Rochester.

Just to punish him, she'd slept with their shortstop instead, who'd crowed about it the whole bus ride to Toledo, making sure he knew exactly what he'd missed.

"Come on, girl." She tapped her leg to call her dog along, who trotted obediently after her. At the top of her steps, she spun to spear one last, dark look his way.

It was probably a really bad idea to tell her that she was more sexy than scary that way. He'd always liked women with a little fire. Up until now he had no idea she had any.

"You—" she said, stabbing her finger at him like it was a spear, "take that . . . *stud*"—she spat out the word with the same tone he used when he said *White Sox*—"*home*. And fill up that damn hole!"

He waited until she'd disappeared inside. Her house had a small back porch, and her door was painted chocolate with dark green trim, and there was a fancy little rusty-colored light fixture hung beside it, and somehow it looked a hundred times better than his grungy back door.

Coop was by his side, curling up in the dirt, settling in for a good rest. The splotches that used to be white were streaked with mud, and his paws were black.

"Oh, yeah, you got what you wanted, didn't you? Pretty happy with yourself."

The dog gave one thump of his tail, which was apparently all he had energy left for.

"But you're getting me in trouble with the ladies, and I hate that."

The dog laid his head down on his paws. "Come on, then."

He started for the gate, expecting the dog to follow as promptly as Ann's had. He got halfway there before he looked back and realized the dog wasn't coming.

"Coop! Come on, Coop!"

The dog didn't move.

He sighed and trudged back. He wrapped his fist around Coop's collar and gave a tug. The dog still didn't budge. He pulled harder, dragging Coop a good six inches in the wet grass.

"Come on, Cooper!" This was why he hadn't had a dog before. He remembered now. They were damn near as obstinate as women.

He couldn't tow the fool beast all the way across the yard. That wouldn't be good for him. And he'd already been yelled at enough for one day; he didn't want to know what would happen if Mer caught him mauling her dog.

He sighed and bent down.

A hundred and twenty-five pounds should be nothing. He'd lugged women who weighed that to bed more than once, no trouble at all.

But the dog was dead weight, and he was heading for forty, and he felt his back twinge as soon as he straightened.

"Hope she was worth it," he said as he carried the dog home. "Because tomorrow, bud, I'm calling the vet."

FIFTEEN

Keeping Mer occupied was proving a problem.

Oh, the dog helped, even if having Cooper meant his sexy neighbor was going to hate him forever. Which was probably a good thing anyway. She still wore a wedding ring, although he'd never seen a man over there. And she wasn't exactly easygoing, and she was his *neighbor*, which meant there was no getting away from her when it was over, not until he moved.

But Mer didn't know anybody in town and it just wasn't normal for a sixteen-year-old to spend so much time alone. He had vague memories of the girls he went to high school with. They were *never* alone, giggling in frilly clumps in the school hallway, chattering at each other on the phone as soon as they got home. Hell, they even went to the bathroom together; it had taken some effort to get one alone long enough to do anything interesting with her.

Mer had asked for a computer, but he was still stalling on that one. Seriously, chat rooms? He was going to let her go wandering unsupervised in chat rooms while he was at practice? Never gonna happen.

So she watched movies, one after the other. She played with Cooper. She spent endless hours in her room doing God only knew what. He preferred not to think about it.

It just didn't seem healthy. Hell, if he'd tried to live like that, he'd certainly have done something guaranteed to give his father a heart attack.

Twice he took her to practice with him again. Gave her a job. That was a good thing, right? Had her keep stats when they were scrimmaging. And played Tyrone every second of the game so he had no time to flirt with her.

But he'd apparently underestimated Tyrone, who was brilliantly inventive when it came to flirting. He'd give her a look every time he loped by after making a shot. Tom finally had to scream at him about getting his ass back down the court before everybody started racing the other way again.

At least Tyrone made her smile. In a way it seemed he couldn't. But when Tyrone missed practice tonight, it worried Tom enough that he turned it over to his assistant, Leo Lowenstein, an Energizer Bunny of a player who was the shortest guard who'd ever seen the floor for the Minnesota Gophers. He was twenty-five, a grad assistant for the team during the year who now spent his summers working for Tom.

The kids were terrified of Leo, which Tom considered one of his best assets. That, along with the fact that he had enough energy for six kids. He could run them into the ground and still have enough legs left to dunk.

So he left the kids in Leo's competent hands. Because he just had to make sure that Tyrone wasn't with his daughter.

He wasn't sure what he'd do if he found them together. He just knew he wouldn't be able to be any good to anybody until he knew, one way or the other.

And then he sat in his truck in the parking lot beside the old gym and wondered where to start.

Home, he figured. If they weren't there, then he could call Mrs. Becker, who was probably the one person on the face of the earth who scared Tyrone.

He angled southwest, winding his way through the darkened streets. Half the houses were boarded up, and a good share of the rest should have been because they sure weren't in good enough shape for anybody but rats to live in. A café squatted on the corner, Millie's Kitchen, closed down for the night. Next door was a convenience store, with bars covering the grimy windows plastered with cigarette and milk ads. A clump of kids huddled in the weak light. Tom saw the orange glow from their cigarettes, heard the heavy bass thump from the boom box they'd put on the steps.

He hit the brakes, rolled down the window. "Hey!"

"You don' wanna be stoppin' here," one of them said, a gray knit cap pulled down to his eyebrows, his Oakland Raiders jacket sized for someone who played for them.

"That you, Mack Johnson?"

A skinny boy leaning against the window stood, then shuffled slowly over to the truck, too cool to hurry, with that odd, uneven hitch in his step they all seemed to adopt, like one knee kept giving out. "Mr. Nash?"

"Yup." Mack was one kid he'd lost. He'd come to league for a good five months, and he'd been a decent player. Not enough heft to play forward, not a good enough shot to play guard, but he would have gotten better. Then he'd missed one practice, then three, and here he was, back hanging out on street corners where nothing good could be going down.

"Hey, y'all, this here's Tom Nash." He waved his buddies over, and they stuck their hands through the window to shake, grinning.

"How's school going, Mack?"

He ducked his head—aw shucks, all innocence—then stepped back into the streetlight. He had on a graying wife-beater that showed his ribs, a pair of kicks that couldn't be more than a day old. "Quit."

"No good, Johnson."

"All good, Mr. Nash." He did a little bob with his head. "Gotta make the benjamins, y'know?"

"Yeah, I know." Except the way he was making those dollars was more than likely some way that was going to end with him in a cell. "Anytime you want to come back, Mack, we'll be waiting."

There was a glimmer in the boy's eyes. Sadness, temptation, a recognition of what he was giving up?

Probably just a stray beam from the streetlights. He'd learned the hard way, over the years, not to romanticize the whole thing too much. It didn't help anybody.

He popped the truck back into gear and drove home. In Chicago, was that what Mer spent her time doing? Hanging out on street corners, waiting for trouble to find her?

It always did, when you waited for it. Sooner or later. If you were lucky, or smart, you got out before it was too late.

It couldn't be too late for her. He refused to allow it.

He was heading for the back door when he heard the dog bark next door, quick and delirious, loud as a bullhorn, and he knew immediately it was Cooper. *Her* dog was far too well behaved to sound like that.

Damn fool dog, he'd gotten in Ann's backyard again. He wondered what it was going to cost him this time. He'd asked around about the puppies she would have been able to breed; turned out that they ran close to 2K apiece. But if she caught him again, he figured this time the price would involve a lot more than money.

He looked over the fence. The dog was loping back and forth, with his tongue hanging out, dripping saliva, chasing after Ann's dog.

"Coop." He kept his voice down low, trying to sound firm, but not wanting to shout in case Ann was home. He was sure she'd just love the fact that his pervert dog was chasing her princess around the yard again.

Though he supposed the damage was done. He didn't figure she'd see it that way, though. *"Coop,"* he repeated, harsher, louder. But the dog didn't even bother to glance his way.

The kids—tough ones, some of them, who rarely listened to anyone—got up and started running when he used that tone, no questions asked. So how come he couldn't get a damn dog to obey?

Of course he wasn't having much better luck with his daughter. Apparently he could only intimidate kids over whom he had no actual legal authority. His own family, canine or human, ignored him completely.

"Coop! You get your sorry ass over here or it's gonna be really sorry."

Ann's dog took a sharp right, a graceful cut that rivaled Tyrone on a good day.

Coop tried. His front legs planted but his rear kept going, sliding right into the thick of one of those pretty flower beds, uprooting a good dozen plants on the way, stopping in the middle of the garden surrounded by purple and pink blossoms, a spot he apparently decided was the perfect place to lick his butt. Though it seemed like most places were the perfect place to do that.

"Come *on.*"

The back door opened. He ducked, the same reflex that had stood him well when a pitch came right back at his head. *Incoming!*

But it was his daughter, coming through with a platter in her hands and a smile on her face. Same clothes as always, a pair of pants with legs so wide they looked like a skirt, a T-shirt held together with a long line of tarnished safety pins.

But it didn't look like her. Her hair was out of her face, tucked behind her ears, and her mouth was bare of paint.

Ann followed right behind her, a big wooden bowl in one hand, a clear pitcher of water in the other. She was laughing about something as she closed the door with her hip and he thought, *So that's what they look like, the two of them, when they're not pissed off at me.*

There was a table on the stone patio, painted brilliant white, with striped cushions on the chairs and a copper pot of bright geraniums on the tabletop. They put down their things, Mer deftly blocking Coop—who'd decided that food was far more interesting than his own parts—with her leg. "Not now, Coop!"

"I'll get him," Tom said, jogging over to help, and could have bitten his tongue.

The relaxed and happy girl morphed back into his daughter immediately, her shoulders hunched, her chin tucked, her jaw obstinate.

Ann just went still, the pitcher she was holding hovering mid-pour, as her eyes went flat and wary.

"Sorry," he said quickly. "I didn't mean to interrupt, I—"

"What are you doing here?" Mer flung it out, an accusation more than a question.

"Looking for you," he snapped back, and immediately saw it was the wrong thing to say.

Somehow, whatever he said to her was the wrong thing. If he *hadn't* looked for her, she'd have believed he didn't care what happened to her. Since he had, she thought he didn't trust her.

"I let Leo take practice tonight," he said, deliberately mild.

"You let Leo take over?" she said in disbelief.

Apparently she knew him far better than he knew her. He had no idea what went on in that head; she'd already figured out that he hated ceding control, even to Leo.

The league was his baby. The only reason he'd gone quietly into retirement was because he'd already had the program in mind. No money in it, of course, but he didn't need money. No glory, either, but he could live without that, and he'd had more than most already.

But a higher purpose . . . That was a good thing. Or so he'd told himself, over and over, enough that he finally stopped spending March in a foul mood, wishing he was in Florida at spring training. Enough that he could finally watch the series two years after he retired without getting pissed every single second that he wasn't the one on the mound.

It was better than a lot of guys did when they retired. There were some who were ready, who'd had long and healthy careers, who'd seen years ahead when their skills were starting to erode and had plenty of time to plan for the right time to walk away.

Who were sick of the travel and were more than ready to play daddy for a while.

But that wasn't most of them. How did you replace something that had been in your bones since you were four or five? Most people didn't achieve their biggest dreams when they were in their twenties. Most people didn't have to deal with "What now?" when they had fifty years ahead of them to fill, knowing that nothing else would ever give them quite the same rush, because where else could you walk out to the shouts of sixty thousand people and *win*?

Because, when it came right down to it, it really was about the winning. The task was clear, the results even clearer. Real life was a whole lot tougher to figure out when you were getting it right.

"Leo was sniveling about whether I trust him or not," he said. "Besides, a guy's gotta have a night off now and then. Thought maybe we could go out for dinner."

"Oh." Mer glanced at Ann, who'd filled the glasses and was now bent over the bowl, tossing a salad. "We already . . ."

Ann straightened. She had on pale shorts, long ones that came to her knees, and a T-shirt, and her hair was clipped severely back. It was probably the most dressed up he'd seen her. He suddenly realized that in the right clothes, she was probably an all-out stunner.

"Why don't you join us?" she asked, polite but without a trace of warmth. "There's plenty."

"I don't know. A lot you can hide in my food if you're the one dishing it out." He nodded at the dogs, who'd taken up residence beneath the table, their heads on their paws, tails thumping hopefully, eyes glued to the platters of chicken. "You decided Cooper can be allowed back in the yard, obviously. Am I forgiven, too?"

"*He's* hard to stay mad at." But there was a quirk at the corner of her mouth, like she was trying not to smile, and he wondered what it would take to get it to come out, real and full. "Will you stay? I'll even take a bite of everything on your plate first, if you're that anxious."

He'd hoped to get his daughter to himself. But maybe this would be easier, with a female to play buffer between them. She'd know what to talk to Mer about. Maybe he'd learn a few things, make it easier the next time. "Yes. Thank you."

"I'll get another plate."

Mer slumped down in her chair, her arms jammed across her chest.

"And aren't you happy to see me?" he said. There was no point in circling around it anymore.

"Oh, I'm just thrilled."

SIXTEEN

Might as well get all the fun stuff out at once, Tom decided. "You're going to get even happier," he said. "Stopped by the Quick Mart. You know the one on the corner? Had a nice chat with the guy who runs the place. Turns out he's kind of a fan."

"How nice for you."

"Yeah. Showed him a picture of my darling daughter, too."

"Oh, joy, I . . . wait. You have a picture of me in your wallet?"

"Yup."

"You do not."

"Want to see?" He pulled out his battered, black leather wallet, a present from the niece who'd drawn his name at Christmas four years ago. He flipped it open, showing her the photo in its torn, plastic flap. Her teeth were bared, a strained approximation of a smile that was a whole lot closer to a snarl, her neck rimmed with at least a dozen thick chains, an army jacket swallowing up her narrow shoulders. "Look at you, all dressed up and grinning for the camera. Such a sweet smile."

"Hey, you're the one who likes to have his picture taken."

"I do not."

"Sure. That's why you were never in those magazines."

"Part of the job, Mer. Part of the job."

"Uh-huh." She flicked the edge of the wallet with her finger, flopping it shut. "Where'd you get that?"

"Your mom sent it to me."

"Oh, sure she did." She twisted the knotted strings on her left wrist, a tangle of cords that had to be cut off to be removed. Her fingernail polish was chipped, flecks of black speckling short, broken nails. She must bite them; it seemed like the kind of thing he should already know about his daughter. "*She* doesn't even have a picture of me in her wallet."

Damn it, Cassie, he thought. *Can't you at least make a stab at mothering?*

"Well, you know Cassie. She doesn't like the competition."

"Riiight."

"But yeah, she sent it. Why wouldn't she?" He'd had to remind her a half dozen times, but Mer didn't have to know that. "Anyway, the guy who owns the store, he could hardly believe you were sixteen. Called all his employees over to show 'em and everything."

Her head came up, her eyes glittering. "Imagine that."

"Yeah. Imagine that."

Okay, she was mad at him again. Maybe he should have left it alone. But this was his job, wasn't it? His duty as a father.

He wondered if she really thought he was that stupid. Or if she thought he simply wouldn't bother. He could always smell the smoke on her, though it seemed like she kept it out of the house. But her clothes, her hair, nearly every time he came home . . . Yeah, she was still smoking. Maybe just 'cause she liked it. Or maybe she was making it so obvious on purpose, testing to see if he'd do anything.

He figured the nearest convenience store was a likely source. It was three blocks away; the next closest was another two beyond that.

So he paid them a visit. Made sure they knew she was underage, and that he'd have no problem reporting them for selling cigarettes without carding to check for minors. Had no problem giving out a handful of autographs, either, in exchange for a promise to give him a call if she came in looking for smokes anyway.

Because if she couldn't buy them outright, she might try to steal them, trade for them, or charm one of the clueless young men who worked the counter into giving them to her.

"Mer," he said seriously, "I'm not going to let you smoke." There wasn't a whole lot he could change about her in a summer; that was getting more obvious all the time. He wasn't even sure what he *should* be changing. But smoking was easy.

"*Let* me?" she said angrily. "What are you going to do? Follow me around for the next three months?"

"If I have to," he snapped, his own anger kicking in. Did she have to make everything so hard between them? Why couldn't she, just once, say okay and go along with him? It wasn't as if he was trying to make her do something that wasn't good for her.

"Gee, aren't we all having a lovely time." Ann slipped a plate in front of him, simple thick white china with chunky silverware tucked into a blue-striped napkin on top. She took her own seat, glancing from father to daughter. "So? Are we ignoring all the tension floating around out here, or are you going to tell me what's got you both all ticked off?"

"He thinks I'm not old enough to smoke."

"How old are you?" She handed Tom a platter of chicken, then started piling salad on her own plate.

"Sixteen."

"Then you're not old enough to smoke."

Tom felt himself grinning. He'd known he was right. And he was going to get fed, too. If her brownies were anything to go by, dinner was going to be damned good.

Mer's glare flipped between the two of them. The grown-ups were ganging up on her on this one. She'd never expected Ann to take her father's side against her on anything.

"But what difference does it make? Sixteen, eighteen . . . Those two years don't mean anything. It's all about maturity, anyway, not actual chronological *age*, and—"

"Eighteen's not old enough, either," Ann said placidly. She

handed Tom the salad bowl and reached for the napkin-lined basket that held a sliced baguette.

"What is old enough?"

"Hmm." She broke off a piece of bread, chewed while she considered. "Ninety? Somewhere around there."

"*Ninety?*"

"Yeah, that's about right. Old enough that the odds are high you're gonna die of something else before the lung cancer or emphysema catches up with you." She gave a theatrical shudder. "It's not pretty, by the way. I personally wouldn't want to chance it even at that age, to tell you the truth, but I suppose I couldn't yell at you too much if you were ninety." She pointed at the blue crockery bowl that rested in front of Mer. "Pass the potatoes, please?"

Mer did, grudgingly.

Tom appreciated Ann's attempt. But emphysema and cancer weren't gonna hold much sway with his daughter. Because those things were years away—*never*, in teenage time—and here, right now, she could piss off her father much too effectively to give up smoking without a fight.

But he didn't have much choice, either. Was he supposed to ignore it, just to take the challenge out of it and see if she'd give it up on her own?

Too big a chance to take. Too easy an out to abdicate his responsibility like that. And if he had to pass around her picture at every place that sold smokes within five miles, he'd do it.

"My mother forbade me to do something once," Ann said. "She wasn't much on forbidding things, mind you. She believes in experiential learning."

"Experiential learning?"

"Letting you screw up, so you learn things but good. But she outright forbade me to dye my hair blond when I was thirteen. Said going blond was buying into society's impossible standards of beauty." She poked at her salad. "I just wanted to be pretty."

Her smile was rueful. "My hair turned green. Not a nice, vibrant green, either, like I'd planned it that way. It was the color of neon puke, and the dry straw in our barn was softer than it was. Had to cut it all off. Took a good year and a half to get back to normal."

It was a good try, Tom thought. Point out the folly of doing something that only harmed yourself when you were really trying to bug someone else.

He just wasn't sure his daughter cared all that much if she hurt herself in the process, as long as she hurt him and Cassie.

The meal went on in silence, except for the angry chatter of the crows on top of the garage and the familiar whines of the dogs, reminding the humans that they were under the table and hey, a scrap here and there would be appreciated.

But the three of them didn't have much to talk about it. He shouldn't have been surprised that it was so awkward, having dinner with two women he barely knew.

Guys, he knew how to have a conversation with. They talked about sports and cars and women. Straightforward. Easy.

Women . . . Who knew what the hell women liked to talk about?

Yeah, he dated. Sometimes a lot. But really, talking wasn't high on the agenda. He skipped that part if he could get away with it. And if he couldn't, well, an actual conversation never seemed necessary. Either the women just went on their merry way, babbling about stuff that he could barely translate and had no interest in, but they—bless them—were perfectly happy if he simply nodded now and then and paid the check, or they did the work, asking him questions about his career, nodding raptly at his stories of the big leagues as if every sentence he cranked out was the most fascinating thing they'd ever heard.

Some were really interested. Some were just trying to get *him* interested. Either way, it didn't require him to take the lead in anything until they headed for bed.

Neither his daughter nor his neighbor, however, seemed inclined to help him out this time.

So he ate. He was really good at eating.

There were raspberries and glazed almonds in the spinach salad, lemon and rosemary in the chicken. The little brown potatoes were so crispy they almost popped when he bit into them.

"This is really good," he said. "*Really* good."

"Don't tell me," Ann said, and pointed at Mer with her fork. "She did it."

"*Mer?*"

Mer shrugged. One of these times, he thought, he was going to get some duct tape and strap her shoulders down, just so she couldn't do that anymore. Maybe there'd be more words coming out of her mouth if she couldn't express herself with her shoulders.

"I didn't know you could cook."

"I couldn't," she mumbled. "Ann's been teaching me."

"Really?" He sat back, settled his gaze on his neighbor. "Just how often have you two been having dinner together?"

"Hmm." Ann cocked her head, as if considering it. "Two, three nights a week, I guess." She flashed a fond grin at his daughter, the kind of easy and open affection that he didn't know how to give her, because things were just too damned complicated between them. "I don't like cooking for one, so I usually just have a sandwich. Mer's been indulging me, letting me think I get to pass on a useful skill, keeping me company."

"Well, you must be a damned good teacher."

She waved it off. "Natural ability."

Mer slunk down into her chair the more they talked about her. Embarrassed, probably, to be complimented on such an old-fashioned and domestic skill as cooking.

He leaned back, comfortable in the chair, and admired Ann's yard, the welcoming and pretty space she'd made with flowers and pots. "Your garden looks great."

"It does, doesn't it? Not quite sure how that happened." Ann stood and started stacking plates. Apparently she wasn't one to sit around after a meal, enjoying the evening and an after-dinner chat.

Which was too bad. Not that he cared about the conversation, but his daughter wasn't hiding herself in her room, the dog wasn't destroying anything, and he got to look at a nice-looking woman. Which was about as good as evenings got for him these days.

Lord, how the mighty had fallen.

"Mer," he said, crossing his fingers that she wouldn't pitch a plate at him for daring to suggest it, "why don't you help Ms. McCrary—"

"She doesn't have to clean," Ann interrupted. "House rules. Whoever cooks doesn't have to clean." She shoved a plate at him. "Which means you're helping."

"I'll feed the dogs," Mer said. She whistled and ran off through the gate, the dogs loping after her like they knew the routine.

He piled up plates, grabbed the three glasses in one hand, and followed her into the kitchen.

"Okay," he said. "Who is that and what have you done with my daughter?"

She laughed as she flipped open a dishwasher hidden in the cabinetry and slid plates into their slots. "Don't you remember? You're never the same with other people as you are with your parents."

"You, too?"

"Oh, *especially* me." She pulled a plastic tub down from a cabinet and started packing away the remnants of chicken while he stood there like an idiot with a couple of dirty plates in his hands. She was all smooth efficiency, and he was clueless in his own kitchen, much less in someone else's.

"I find that hard to believe." He knew her type. They got straight As, never got kicked out of class, and made their parents proud. He might have managed the last, finally, but he'd never come close to the first two.

"Yeah, well, you've never met my mother." She spun toward the fridge, caught sight of him standing helpless, afraid to move for fear he'd screw something up. "They go in the dishwasher."

"I knew that." He winced when he banged a plate against

the metal edge of the door, and sighed in relief when he realized it hadn't chipped.

"You want some wine?"

He looked up to find her standing with a bottle in one hand, a glass in the other.

"God, yes."

"Long day?"

"It's not that. I had to empty the house out. Came home one night and there were four empty beer cans in the trash."

"Here you go."

The wine was light and white—not his kind of drink at all—but he gulped it gratefully. She sipped hers, watching him over the rim while he took in her kitchen.

"This is nice," he said. Old, new, he couldn't tell. It looked old, except the stove, but it didn't feel it. There was no flaking paint for one thing. The floor gleamed, the cabinet doors all hung straight, and the grout between the tiles behind the stove was pure and clean. "Really nice."

"Thank you," she said. "I could do this to yours."

"I, uh—" It wasn't the first time it had happened. Women he dated often came into his life and started taking it over, fixing his wardrobe, his house. Nesting, as if showing him what good wives they would be, how much easier his life would be with them in it. But usually they waited until he slept with them first. "I couldn't ask you to do that."

She laughed, her smile easy and relaxed. The way she should look, he realized suddenly, though he'd never seen her that way before. Tense, sad, angry; happy didn't seem to be her usual state. "Well, I *am* pretty expensive. But I'm *really* good."

His brain blanked out, a quick flash of lust burning through rational thought.

Not what she meant, he reminded himself. It just sounded that way because he wanted it to.

"How long you been feeding my daughter?"

"Ah . . ." She screwed up her face in thought. "A couple of weeks?"

"We're imposing on you, and I didn't even know it." He wandered around the room, taking in the bottles by the stove—olive oil, balsamic vinegar, dry vermouth—and a ceramic box painted in swirls with *sel* scrawled on the wooden lid.

He wasn't the least bit interested in her kitchen. But he was a little too interested in her, and he'd finally figured out that he couldn't just sleep with whoever he wanted. Some people brought complications, and he had more complications than he could handle already.

He liked things simple. Do your work well, don't spend more money than you have, take care of your friends, love your family. He could never figure out why people insisted on fucking that up with all sorts of complications.

"It's no imposition," she said. "I wouldn't do it if it were."

"You must have better things to do than feed a surly teenager who isn't even yours."

"She is surly, isn't she?" She closed the lock on the dishwasher and pushed the button. He heard the rush of water as it filled, the thump of the arm starting to turn.

"Oh. You noticed."

"Yup." She dribbled more wine into her glass and leaned back against the counter while she sipped. He wondered how old she was . . . Older than him? Not much, if at all. A tiny diamond glinted on her finger, a blink of an engagement ring butted against a plain platinum band. No kids, though; there were no signs that a child was living there, even part-time, and in his experience kids always made their presence known, littering the house and yard with as much equipment as an army battalion. But there was no way she was old enough to have them grown and out of the house.

Hadn't wanted them, couldn't have them, just hadn't found the time for them? She seemed like the kind of woman who'd want kids. Otherwise, why would she spend so much time with his?

"Seems like she's earned a little surly, though," she went on.

"What did she tell you?"

"Mmm." She was appraising him over the rim of her glass. Trying to get a grasp on what kind of father he was, he guessed. Mer could have told her anything, said he had orgies in the kitchen or a drug den in the basement. Gaining sympathy, looking for a way out . . . No wonder Ann fed the poor, neglected waif. "Not that much. Only that her mother didn't seem too sorry to see her gone."

"Yeah." He gulped the wine, held out the glass for her to fill it up again. "I screwed that one up, didn't I? Should have paid more attention. Should have spent more time with her." Those nasty, persistent *should*s. "Should have picked someone better to be her mother."

"Why didn't you?"

"Well, *picking* didn't have a whole lot to do with it. Just picking up."

"You picked up her mother in a bar?"

"I'd say she was the one who did the picking up, though I wasn't smart enough to recognize it at the time."

"You smart enough now?"

"Yup. Been smart enough for years."

"Smart's good."

"Yeah, but I was a little late to that party."

"Long as you got there."

"Not soon enough for Mer."

There were bookshelves by the little breakfast nook, stuffed with actual cookbooks. A chubby ceramic pot with a lid, a nosegay of dried flowers in a slender vase, a clutter of pictures in small silver frames. She was young in the photos, laughing, her hair free down her back. A prom picture—imagine that—with Ann in a sweep of dark satin, her hair piled on top of her head, and a blond guy, stiff and tall in a classic black tux. The same guy in a football uniform, bending on one knee with his helmet tucked under his arm, his bangs falling over his eyes. Him again, in what looked like the same tux, next to Ann in a frilly white wedding dress, both of them grinning and frighteningly young, as if they had no clue what they were getting into. And her, beautiful on a beach in a simple black one-piece, laughing at the camera.

Must be the ex, he thought. Surprising that she kept their wedding pictures around, the wedding ring on. Maybe it was recent, and she hadn't given up hope. Though in his experience once somebody moved out, it was over. Everything else was just to roust out the guilt, be able to tell yourself you tried your best and did everything you could. Better just to say "done" and get it over with.

"It could be soon enough," she said. "You don't know that."

He glanced back at her. She looked like a different person than the woman in the pictures. Oh, she was older, but it wasn't just that. It was that those years had taken something from her. Her eyes were somber now, her smile contained.

"I hope it's not too late," he said. He wondered what it would take to make this woman laugh like she was laughing in that picture. Wondered if he could do it, if he put his mind to it.

She set her wineglass aside and walked over to him—jeez, but the woman had legs—and he held his breath, wondering, too, if she was going to come on to him, and if he was smart enough to say no. He'd been smart for a long time. Sometimes it was hard, though. He had a feeling it was going to be really hard this time.

Especially since he *really* liked her legs. He'd never realized he was such a leg man.

Maybe he could sleep with her after Mer went back to Chicago. The thought cheered him considerably.

But she just took his glass and placed it on the creamy marble counter beside the sink—clink, clink—and damn it, she wasn't coming on to him.

"Okay," she said, "you have to go now."

SEVENTEEN

He wasn't even in his house before he heard her car roar out of the driveway.

She was in a hurry. Must have a hot date.

He jogged up the back steps and couldn't help but notice that his backyard didn't look nearly as good as hers. A few flowers struggled up here and there, ones that must have been planted by the lady who had the house before him. The lawn was pocked with holes—Cooper'd been busy—and the flower urns on either side of the steps were empty except for dirt.

Maybe he should get a gardener.

"Mer?" He pushed open the back door. She was in the narrow back entry, pouring dry dog food into a bowl the size of a watermelon, while blocking the beast with her foot.

"Wait!" she said. "You have to sit. Look how good Cleo is sitting? Ann says you have to sit before you get your food."

The dog whined but plopped down.

"Okay, go ahead." The dog plunged forward and started crunching.

"Hey, look at that. You got him to listen."

"Sometimes." She tucked the bag back in the closet and carefully shut the door—they'd learned that one the first day. And that Cooper didn't understand the concept of "enough food."

"He's a good dog, though," she went on.

Tom prudently reserved comment. Cooper was not a good dog, not even close. But he was good for Mer; the fact that she remembered to feed him without any prompting, and took him for a walk every day, was more than Tom had expected. Plus it had won him fifty bucks from Boom, who'd bet that the novelty would start to wear off in three days and Tom would be out in the yard scooping poop all by himself before a week was out.

"You're doing a good job with him," he said.

She blinked, and he thought, *Just say "Thank you." Say "Thank you," and let it go. Let it, just this once, be a nice normal parent-kid interaction, so we can both see, for once, what it could be between us.*

"I *like* the dog," she said.

"Ouch." He bit back the retort that he wanted to let fly.

It wasn't in his nature to simply sit back and take her needling. He was a battler, the fourth of five boys, defending himself from the day he was born.

But they'd only end up arguing. And arguing wasn't getting them any closer to where he wanted to be.

"You eat over there a lot, huh?"

Her brows drew together, as if that wasn't what she expected to hear.

Good, he thought. She'd been ten steps ahead of him from the instant she stepped off the plane, and he was still running to catch up.

"Sometimes." She pushed past him into the kitchen.

"Maybe we should invite her over here for dinner."

"I suppose we could." She looked around, at the fridge that froze milk on the top shelf and let oranges rot in the fruit drawer, and at the white sink that had stained to brown. "Her place is a lot nicer, though."

It was, that was for sure. Although, beneath the clutter of empty dishes and half-eaten bags of chips, the bones of his kitchen were the same as hers. Except hers invited you to settle in, and his made you want to skip dinner. "She seemed in a hurry to get out of there tonight."

"Not used to being kicked out, huh?" She opened the fridge and pulled out a bottle of orange juice.

"Oh, I've been kicked out before."

The bottle of juice stopped halfway to her mouth as she eyed him curiously. "By who?"

"Maureen Sorenson. Freshman year of college. Finally talked my way into her room, and then she got a phone call. Apparently a senior quarterback trumps a freshman pitcher."

"Poor fellow." Mer set the bottle down and leaned up against the counter, resting her hands on the edge.

A chat in the kitchen, Tom thought. Kind of homey, kind of how he'd imagined it. Except his daughter still looked like something that crawled out of a zombie movie.

"Anyway," Mer said, "I suppose she was in a hurry to go see her husband."

"She's still married? I've never seen him over there."

Never seen anyone over there but Ann, come to think of it. Not that he was turning into a nosy suburban neighbor who kept an eye on the woman next door or anything.

"That's 'cause he's in the hospital."

"The hospital?" Jesus. Here he was sitting at her table, letting her feed his daughter, eating her food, when all this time she was having a crisis. No wonder she looked so sad.

Mer waved a hand. "Well, it's not really a hospital, I guess. A nursing home."

"Her husband's in a nursing home," he said flatly, trying to put the pieces together. Either the guy in the pictures wasn't her husband after all, or they were really old pictures and she was the best-preserved seventy-year-old he'd ever seen.

"Yeah, he had a car accident. Been there for like ten years," she said. "It's really sad."

Part of him noticed that it was the first hint of genuine compassion he'd ever seen from Mer. He was relieved to know that she had it in her, that she could feel something besides anger for another human.

But half of him was thinking, *Boy, bud, you pegged that one*.

Complicated. Really complicated.

"What do you want?"

"Gee, Cassie, it's good to hear from you, too."

"Oh, it's you." The impatient snap in her voice softened to a husky purr. "How ya doin', Tommy?"

Why did women who wanted something from him always call him Tommy? Girls in bars, women hanging out behind the stadium or who'd somehow found out which hotel room was his. Even Tamara, when she'd tried to sweet-talk him into encouraging Boom to give their marriage another chance.

It must be some female code he'd never deciphered, though he'd finally wised up enough to realize that when a woman called him Tommy, he should start running the other way.

"I'm doing okay." He paced across the floor of his bedroom, barefoot on the scratchy rug, his cell to his ear, wondering how to broach the subject without giving Cassie too much ammunition. "Okay."

"That's good. How's our girl?"

Our girl. He wasn't sure Mer was anybody's girl. Not even her own. "Well, that's what I wanted to talk to you about." Damn. He should have thought this through a little more. He couldn't just say, "*How do I get to know my daughter? How do I get her to talk to me the way she talks to my neighbor? How do I be a father?*"

"She in trouble? 'Cause I told her if she gets arrested again—"

"*Again?*"

"Oh, didn't I tell you about that?" How had he ever found her laughter seductive? He knew he must have; he had a vague memory of sitting in that bar and thinking that her laugh sounded like sex, that *everything* about her made him think of sex. Now it grated, enough so that he had to hold the phone away from his ear until she stopped. "Nothing for you to worry about. Little misunderstanding. Forgot she put a CD in her pocket when she left the store. Won't be on her record if she stays out of trouble for a year."

He sat down on the edge of the bed and pressed his free hand to his temple. *Christ.* "Why didn't you tell me?"

"Sure, Tommy, you always wanted to know all the little problems I had with that girl while I was raising her." Sarcasm was as much a natural talent to Cassie as baseball was to him.

"Maybe I did."

"Then you would have asked, wouldn't you?" she said, more amused than anything. "What's this about?"

"I just think we should be clear on the house rules. I keep telling her she can't do things, and she says that it's okay with you, and—"

"And you figured the girl might be fudging to get her way?"

"Yeah."

"Well, have at it. What'd she say?"

"Did you know she smokes?"

"Of course I knew. You think I don't notice what my own daughter does?"

Crap. Clearly, he was getting no help from this quarter. The only surprise was that he thought he might; desperation was making him stupid.

"Look, Tommy, she's *sixteen*. How're you gonna stop her if she really wants to do something? You gonna tell me you didn't do a little hell-raising when you were that age? I know you better than that, and so do you."

"Well, yeah, but—" But he was a *guy*. A few beers on a hot summer night by the river were normal. Maybe even more than a few now and then. What else were they going to do out there? And yeah, okay, he'd slept with his girlfriend in high school. Girlfriend*s*. They were more . . . mature than she was.

They weren't Mer. They weren't his daughter.

"Put her on the phone," Cassie ordered.

"But—"

"I want to talk to Mercedes."

He padded down the hallway with its fussy flower-patterned wallpaper—jeez, if he was going to stay here past September, that was going to *have* to go—and rapped on her door.

No answer.

"Mer?"

When she still didn't respond he pushed open the door.

"Dad!"

"I'm sorry."

She sat up the second he opened the door, tugging her earbuds free. She was curled up on her bed with Cooper at her feet. There was a tattered black T-shirt, no better than a rag, tossed over the frilled rocking chair, and her boots were on the floor by the bed. Otherwise, nothing had changed from the day she'd arrived; she wasn't settling in at all.

He held out the receiver. "I did knock, but you didn't answer. Your mom wants to talk to you."

"My mom?" He wondered if there'd ever be a day he spoke to her without getting that wary suspicion in response. As if she thought he wanted something but she couldn't quite figure out what it was.

"Yeah." He handed her the phone. He backed out of the room as quickly he could, wondering if her room would ever seem like anything but forbidden territory and him as unwelcome as Elvis in a convent, and closed the door behind him.

Huh, he thought as he stood for a moment with his hand on the doorknob.

She'd yelled at him when he'd burst into the room.

But she'd yelled *Dad*.

———

"What's going on there?"

"Miss you, too, Mom."

"Oh, come on, you haven't even been gone three weeks."

Good ol' Mom, Mer thought. *At least she didn't try to fake sentimentality.*

"Why'd your father call me?"

He'd called Cassie? Was he trying to get rid of her already? She scooted down on the bed, curling up around Coop. He sighed and relaxed against her, big and warm. "How the hell should I know?"

"You do something?"

"I didn't do anything."

"Sure you didn't." Cassie's sighs were a whole language on their own. That one was one of her favorites, the big, gusty, "why is my daughter so difficult?" sigh. "You guys getting along all right?"

"We're getting along fine." As long as they stayed out of each other's way, which they were managing to do most of the time.

"Good. That's good." She could almost hear it over the phone, the impatient click of Cassie's fingernails on the table, *tap-tap-tap.* Wasting time talking to her daughter, when she could be getting on with the business of being Cassie. "You got a shot here, baby. Don't blow it."

"A shot at what?"

"You're gonna be eighteen before we know it. But you have all summer with him. He's not that hard, Mer. He likes to think of himself as a good guy, as a responsible guy. You play up being daddy's little girl, you could walk away with a nice trust fund."

"I don't want his money."

"Oh, honey." Cassie laughed so long Mer nearly hung up on her. "You go ahead and try that one on him. It'd probably work, come to think of it."

It'd serve her mother right, Mer thought. If she *did* get some money out of her dad, a great big pile of it, she'd wave it in Cassie's face and wouldn't give her one stinking penny.

"Why do you think I sent you there?" Cassie asked, stern now. "So don't screw it up. You gotta look after yourself in this world. Sure as hell nobody else is gonna do it for you."

Yeah, Mer'd figured that one out a long time ago.

She buried her nose in the fur at Cooper's neck, breathing in that sweet-awful dog smell. He needed a bath. Maybe she'd give him one tomorrow. But she kind of liked being able to come in the house and know that he was there, even before he came running.

"You hear me, Mer?"

"I hear you."

EIGHTEEN

He blamed it on the pizza.

He wasn't a kid anymore. He couldn't leave a pepperoni special out on the counter and eat it for breakfast, the way he used to nearly every day the one year he'd spent in college.

He'd had one drink at Escape—*one*—before he had to make a trip to the can.

The club was full. Friday night, summer, the place dark and throbbing, the girls wearing scraps of clothing that wouldn't look out of place on a beach. Behind the glass doors of the VIP room Boom was surrounded by females, all sizes, all colors, all smiling up at him. There was a bottle of Shakers vodka on the bar next to him, and his arm was draped around the narrow, bare belly of a girl who could really use a cheeseburger.

But they were all young. Too young. He looked at them and saw Mer. Saw Cassie, when they'd met. Somebody should have shot him, he thought, for touching her. She'd been *nineteen*. Yeah, he'd only been three years older, but . . . Crap, they'd been idiotically young, both of them.

He pushed through the doors, keeping his gaze straight ahead so he didn't encourage any of the women there to shimmy his way. The music—he supposed that was music—was starting to pulse behind his temples.

"Hey!" Boom pulled over an empty glass and sloshed vodka into it. "You're falling behind."

"I'm going home."

"Already?" He craned his head, as shiny under the low lights as if it had been waxed, to see who was behind Tom. "With who?"

"With me."

Boom shook his head sadly. "You're getting old, man. Took me half a day to convince you to come out, and you lasted, what, fifteen minutes?"

"I'm ten months younger than you."

"Well, technically." The girl was walking her fingers up Boom's bare arm; he'd torn the sleeves off of his black silk shirt, the better to show off the guns.

"And how old are you?" Tom shot at her.

Her mouth pursed into a pout so pretty she had to have practiced it. "Twenty-five."

"Yeah, right." Silver hoops the size of Frisbees brushed her shoulders. He'd have been scared to touch her, worried they'd snag on something and tear a hole in her ear. Wasn't slowing Boom down a bit. "Something I ate's not agreeing with me. I'm going home."

"It's a sad thing, when a man forgets how to enjoy himself. Ain't that right, sweetheart?"

"Don't worry," the girl purred. "You'll enjoy yourself."

It was all Tom could do not to roll his eyes.

"Boom, you're not driving home."

"I never drive myself home," Boom said.

"And don't—hey, hey, hey!" He snapped his fingers in front of Boom's face to snag his attention, which had gotten firmly fixed on the way the girl's halter top was slipping to the side. She looked down and shrugged, as if her imminent nipslip was too insignificant to be bothered with.

Two more shots of vodka, Tom figured, and the halter was going to be decorating the top of Boom's head.

"You." He pointed at Boom. "You make sure and check her ID, all right?"

"You going all parental on me, Nash?"

"I got sixteen years of it all saved up. Gotta use it on someone."

"I always check, Nash."

"Yeah, I know." Boom may have liked to flirt with pretty girls in bars, but he was damned careful about which ones he brought home, and he always suited up when he did.

Boom sighed and surrendered to the inevitable. "If it's a heart attack or somethin', and not just that you got a stomach like a grandma, you call me, all right? And I'll be over tomorrow to check on you."

"Bring beer."

It was a beautiful night, cool and breezy, with a thin gauze of clouds over a half-moon. Tom drove west, easing the truck down the highway with the radio turned low. He wished he'd stopped and swapped the pickup for one of his convertibles. A night like this sang for an open top.

His stomach wasn't hurting as bad as it had at the club, he noticed. Must have been something in the air. Maybe he was allergic to amped-up pheromones and hair spray.

He felt almost okay by the time he turned at the golf course. His neighborhood looked peaceful, resting quiet and ordinary in the moonlight. A bunch of cars sat in the driveway of a well-kept Tudor, and lights streamed through the diamond-paned windows. Card club, he figured. Hot night in the suburbs.

The old guy was out hoofing it with his dog again, wearing a light-reflective vest that blazed orange in Tom's headlights. He caught the blink of flashlights in a backyard; kids, out late playing flashlight tag.

The only light on in his house was high in Mer's room. He glanced left; there was a light at Ann's house, too, upstairs as well, a soft, low glow. She was home, probably alone.

Another Saturday night, and I ain't got nobody . . .

Darn it, now he was going to have Cat Stevens—or whatever his name was now—in his head all night long. He hoped he could slide it over to "The First Cut Is the Deepest"; he liked that song better.

The back door was unlocked. "Damn!" He grabbed for the nearest wall, caught himself before he hit the ground. "Damn dog."

Coop was sprawled an inch inside the door. He lifted his head and whined.

Weird. Cooper was never more than two feet from Mer when she was around. Maybe she was next door again, and had just forgotten to shut off the light in her room.

He took the stairs two at a time. Cooper shot past him, nearly knocking him over. "Damn dog!" he muttered again. The beast was going to be the death of him yet. Coop just wagged his tail—Tom suspected he was starting to think that "damn dog" was his name—and took up station outside Mer's door.

"She in there, boy?"

Maybe it was the pizza after all, and Mer was sick, too. He heard a whimper. "Mer?" Rustling. A thump.

"Mer?"

"Dad, stay out. Stay out!" There was an edge of panic in her voice.

Which was the last thing that would keep him out. "If you're naked, Mer, cover up. I'm comin' in!"

The door wasn't locked, thank God; he didn't think his shoulder could take breaking a door down. He took in the room at a glance: Mer, tugging the covers up to her neck, her hair mussed, eyes wild with anger. And a bare male ass, halfway out the window.

"Stop." He grabbed on, hauled back, and had him slammed up against the nearest wall before he realized he'd moved. Adrenaline surged: *Protect the girl, protect the girl.*

He hauled back his arm, ready to let fly, before the face in front of him finally registered.

"Tyrone?"

"Hey, sorry, man, I—"

Tom hit him. He knew he must have, from the way the kid

doubled over, coughing and gagging, but for the life of him he couldn't remember deciding to do it.

"Dad. Dad! *Stop!*"

He looked down at Mer, who had both hands wrapped around his forearm, hanging on. Her elbows were jammed against her sides, barely trapping the sheet she'd wrapped around herself, and her shoulders and arms were thin and bare. Her makeup was smeared, her mouth swollen, and his vision started to haze.

"Get dressed," he snarled, and returned his attention to Tyrone, because if he looked at his daughter for one more second, he wouldn't be responsible for what happened next. "And make that dog stop barking! She's *sixteen*," he snarled at Tyrone. *"Sixteen."*

"Yeah. I know." Tyrone sniffed and brought up his chin, a good show of the bravado that he lived on, but beneath the forearm that held him against the wall Tom could feel the kid's heart flutter, quick as a trapped rabbit's. "I'm seventeen. So what?"

"So what?"

"Hey, man, she called *me*."

"I did, Dad. I did."

"You're not helping, Mer."

"So what then? What are you going to do now? Beat him up?"

"Sounds good to me." Sweat streaked down Tyrone's temple, and his jaw, with its pitiful fuzz of beard, trembled.

A kid. He was just a kid, too.

Tom stepped back and let go. He shut his eyes so he didn't have to look at either one of them, because he wasn't sure how long his control would hold. "Get dressed," he said. "Get dressed, and get out, Tyrone. If I open my eyes and you're still here, you're gonna be here a lot longer than you wanna be."

"Dad."

He ignored her. He had to. He flexed his fingers rhythmically. A fist, stretch them out, form a fist again. Breathing through it, like he used to do on the mound when the adrenaline got raging and he knew if he didn't get it under control he'd be overthrowing and he'd never get the ball to go where he wanted.

He heard the rustle of clothes, a quick flutter of steps. The murmur of urgent voices. "Shut up, Tyrone," he said. "If I don't want to see you, I don't want to hear you, either."

Don't think about it, he told himself. *Don't think about it.*

But the more he warned himself not to think about it, the more it was *all* he could think about. That boy, and his daughter, in this bed—

Don't think about it.

Oh, God, how did fathers do it? How did they ever let their daughters out of their sight? How did they ever let them get *married*, knowing that it meant some guy was going to *touch* them?

He waited until he heard the front door slam before he opened his eyes. "Okay," he said. But he didn't turn around. Not yet.

He wasn't sure if she was there. Wasn't sure if he wanted her to be. Maybe if he had to spend the night looking for her, he'd have time to burn off some of the anger. Let the worry tamp it down a little, remind him that things could be worse.

But then she'd be with *Tyrone*, and he'd really have to hurt someone.

"Okay." He thought he could be reasonable now. And so he turned. And saw her there, in a thin black tank over a baggy pair of plaid men's boxers, her arms crossed over her chest, her chin up and eyes shooting sparks.

"What the hell was that for?" she hollered.

"*What the hell was that for?*" The fury came roaring back, and he had nothing useful to do with it, nobody to spend it on, nobody to beat to a pulp.

She was mad? She, this *child*, who was screwing a boy in the bed he'd bought for her, and *she* was mad?

"Yeah!" she shouted. "I told you to stop coming into my—"

"Stop!" He held up a finger, vaguely surprised when she shut up. "Not now. Can't talk about it now. Later. We'll talk about it later."

He had to get out of there. He felt the press of it, the words that he knew he'd be sorry for, the need to lock her up and be done with it until she learned what the world was really like. What boys like Tyrone were really like.

"I'm going out," he said. "You're not." He narrowed his eyes at her, willing her to take him seriously, to *listen* to him just one damn time. "If you know what's good for you, you're not."

"But—"

"But nothing. We'll talk later. Don't think we won't." They'd talk when he thought there was a chance in hell of it doing any good. But not now.

NINETEEN

He recognized it was none of her business. Knew he would be imposing, that it was getting late, that he was asking more of her than he had a right to do.

He knocked on Ann's back door anyway. Pounded, when nobody came fast.

Cleo barked inside. Again, closer, coming to see who dared bang on the door in the middle of the night.

Good dog, guarding her mistress. Unlike that useless Cooper, who didn't have enough sense to bite Tyrone on the ass when he'd come calling.

A light flicked on inside. The curtain pulled back briefly, then the bolt snicked open.

"Tom?" Her hair was down—great curly clouds of it, so pretty, tucked behind her ears—and she pulled the belt of her robe tight, fuzzy dark chenille as plain as dishwater. "What is it?"

"You got booze in the house?"

"Well, sure, I . . ." She ran a hand through her hair, then stepped back. "More wine, I guess."

He moved by her into that picture-pretty kitchen, and the knot between his shoulders unkinked a notch. The room smelled of cinnamon and coffee. "Anything stronger?"

"Nope. I'm afraid not."

He stood like an idiot in the center of her kitchen while she went to the small wine refrigerator installed under the counter. "Red okay?"

"Anything."

He should have offered to open it, he realized belatedly. He hadn't come here to have her wait on him. But she was reaching up, high on a shelf behind a cabinet with glass doors, and pulling down two wineglasses before he thought of it.

"You're still standing?" She handed him one glass, pointed at the table with the other. "Sit."

"I'm imposing."

"Yup," she said cheerfully.

She put the bottle on the table in front of them, next to a cut glass vase with a cluster of pale lilacs in it. She settled back, waiting.

He looked at her, and something inside him relaxed a bit. She was pretty in her old-lady robe with a bit of plain T-shirt peeking out above the neckline. Dark shadows scooped beneath her eyes, and in the dim kitchen a few lines were starting to show at the corners of her mouth, her eyes.

Well, she'd earned them, hadn't she? When he'd met her, he'd thought: *Another perfect suburban woman. Good looks, good marriage, good kids, good house. Nice and simple.*

But life had knocked her around some, too. He felt sad about that; she hadn't earned it, hadn't opened the door and let the darkness in. But it made her more interesting, too. Not so simple after all.

"So," she finally said. "What'd she do?"

"How'd you know she did something?"

She tilted her head and rubbed her thumb against the thin stem of the wineglass. "You show up at my door in the middle of the night looking for alcohol. What else could it be?"

"Thanks for that." He lifted his glass to her, which was already down to a red stain in the bottom—funny, he couldn't remember actually drinking it—and she lifted the bottle, filling it an inch shy of the rim. "Don't have any at my house anymore."

"I heard about that." She leaned forward, elbows on the table. "So?"

He drained the glass—he was gonna need it if he was going to have to talk about this—and poured until it was about half-full. He held the bottle over her glass, which held only a restrained splash.

"No, I'm fine."

"Okay." He nodded. "So. Okay." All at once, he told himself. Like tearing tape off a leg when you'd been wrapped for a game. The hair was coming with it, one way or another, and it was going to hurt like a bitch, but at least you got it done with fast. "Came home early. Went out to a club with Boom—he's been after me for weeks, and I thought . . . Doesn't matter." Doesn't matter that it just didn't interest him anymore. Wasn't sure it ever had, or if he'd just thought it was supposed to, part of his place in the world, the things a guy like him did, hitting up the hot spots, living the life. "She was there. With a boy."

"Okay," she said.

"In bed."

"Okay."

She kept looking at him with those big smoky eyes, her mouth calm. Obviously she just wasn't getting it.

"In bed, with a boy, *naked.*"

"Okay."

"One of my boys." That one took the rest of the wine in his glass; damn, but the bottle was three-quarters empty already. "You got more of this?"

"As much as you need. It's not like you have to drive home." She moved her glass aside—she hadn't drunk any of her wine yet, as far as he could recall—and leaned forward, folding her hands on the table. Nice hands. Nothing flashy, short, bare nails and that modest wedding ring. The hands of a woman who had other things to worry about or who just didn't care about things that really didn't matter. "Is it worse, that it's one of your boys?"

"Hell yes, it's worse!"

"Why?"

"Because they should know that my daughter's off-limits."

"Why's she off-limits?"

"Because she's sixteen!" He'd considered Ann a smart woman. Obviously he'd misjudged her completely.

"I slept with my boyfriend when I was sixteen," she said. "In fact, I was barely fifteen. Of course, I was in *loooove*." She had a fond, amused smile on her face, remembering the silly girl she'd been. "I don't suppose she's in love with him, is she? That'd complicate things."

"How could she be? She hardly knows him."

"I'm not sure one has much do with the other when you're that age."

"Oh God." He stared glumly into his glass. Except he kept seeing them, the way they'd looked when he'd burst into the room, and he had to gouge that image out of his mind. The wine wasn't working nearly fast enough.

So he concentrated on Ann instead and tried to figure out why he enjoyed that so much.

He knew prettier women. A lot of them, actually. But he'd gotten to the point where pretty wore off damned quickly. Not sure when that had happened, when pretty stopped being enough. When he realized it couldn't hold his interest for more than a week or two.

Ann was a lot better looking than he'd thought at first. He liked the way her head tilted when she listened, that grave and thoughtful expression that said how seriously she took what you said.

He'd admired her legs from the first. He wondered why he hadn't noticed the rest of her, the smile that didn't come often but was worth the wait.

"So what do you want to do?"

"Do they still make chastity belts?"

There it was, that smile. It started slow and then flashed into brilliance. "I think so, actually. But I think they use them for an entirely different reason now."

He blinked at her; the wine must be kicking in after all, because it took him a while to realize what she meant.

But then he couldn't think of anything else, about how this innocent and ordinary-looking woman knew about such things and how she kept smiling at him while she said it with such a perfectly pedestrian voice.

It distracted him, though, and for that he was grateful.

"You okay now?"

"Not okay," he said. "But I'm getting there."

"All right, then." She refilled his glass, finishing off the bottle, and went to fetch another one. Her robe was perhaps the baggiest one he'd ever seen, covering her from her neck to just above her ankles, the hem unraveling. It was the sort of robe women wore when they curled up with soup and old movies, when, if they had men in their lives, they were telegraphing "not tonight."

But he watched her butt swaying in it, smooth and easy. A good butt. He'd seen her out running, a lot, and she had the long, strong strides of someone who'd spent a fair amount of her life moving.

And he really had to stop thinking about sex. His daughter with Tyrone; his neighbor, period. Because either one wasn't something his brain needed to be dwelling on.

"Okay." She put the fresh bottle of wine on the table, well within reach, before sliding back into her seat. "It's gonna get harder. You ready?"

He groaned and slid back into his chair, sticking his legs out into the room. "No. Yes. Do I have to keep talking about this?"

"Nope," she said. "But, unless you plan to ignore it completely, it might be a good idea to desensitize with me before you bring it up with Mer."

"Can I ignore it completely?"

"I don't know. Can you?" she said, all amused sympathy.

"No," he admitted, petulant as a teenager turning down something he knew was bad for him but that he really, really wanted.

She leaned forward and touched the lilacs in the sparkly vase. "Last ones of the season," she said, giving him a moment. "So. Do you think it was her first time?"

"I don't know." He took a couple of breaths, too, big and deep, to calm himself. And he smelled the lilacs, sweet and delicate. And her, maybe, something light and just as sweet. "I suppose not, right? Shit." *Others? There were others?* For the first time he was grateful that he hadn't been around for so much of her adolescence; he hadn't had to think about this every time she set foot out of the house. "Which is better? Or worse?"

"Well, if it was her first time, it might mean it was . . . important. She could be feeling a little fragile. Especially if it wasn't . . ." She fingered the lilacs, her smile going wistful. "Well, you might not want to start off yelling, for instance."

"I'm not sure I can promise that." Or much else. "How about you?" he asked. "Did you feel fragile?" He told himself that he asked for informational purposes only. She was his only insight into the female mind. He wasn't the least bit curious about what moved her, what made her feel.

"Honestly?" The smile bloomed into a grin. "I was thrilled. I was in love, remember?"

"I bet your mother wasn't thrilled."

"I never told her."

"Good move. Parents should not have to know this. Parents should go to their grave thinking their children are virgins, and that any grandchildren were conceived immaculately."

"That's not why I never told her." A curl of hair had fallen forward over the corner of her eye, and she tucked it back. "I never told her because she'd ask too many questions. She'd want to know every detail. How it was. Make suggestions as to how we could have done it better." She shook her head. "I didn't want her in the middle of it. I wanted it to be just him and me."

Lucky guy. Whoever he was, wherever he was, he'd been a lucky guy. "Your mother is weird."

"You don't know the half of it."

"Okay. No details. I can do that."

"Well, you'd better ask one detail. You need to make sure

she was safe." Her voice became urgent. "Right away. There are things they can do, a morning-after pill . . ."

"Goddamn motherfucking hell," he said distinctly, and dropped his head to his hands.

She laughed at him. Lord help him, she laughed at him. "It'll be okay."

"I can't do this."

"Yes, you can." She touched his hand, a wisp of contact. "You don't have a whole lot of choice."

He looked up hopefully. "You could do it."

"Oh, no."

"Sure." He didn't know why he didn't think of this sooner. It was genius. "You're a girl. She's a girl."

"No."

He played his trump card. "But she *likes* you."

"She likes you, too."

"Sure she does."

"Oh, don't look so skeptical. Of course she likes you." She swirled the wine in her glass. "Did you think about why she did it there? At your house?"

"Because there was a bed there."

"Hey, I don't know about you, but a bed was optional when I was sixteen." She took a sip, slow and easy, as he struggled not to think about her in a bed. "They could have gone anywhere. She chose your house."

"You think she wanted me to catch her?" He shook his head. "She had no way of knowing I was coming home early."

"Maybe not this time." She shrugged. "But she wasn't exactly playing it safe."

"But—" Females were strange. There was just no way around that undeniable fact.

"Look, I don't know what she was thinking. It could be nothing. But it's also possible that, maybe without even realizing it, she wanted to see what you'd do. If you'd ignore it, ignore *her*. Send her home."

"So you're saying I have to get this right?"

"Pretty much." She patted his hand, comforting. And she should probably stop doing that, if he was expected to concentrate on the matter at hand. "Don't worry, I'll help."

"She said she was on the pill," he said, perking up at the memory. At least he didn't have to worry about *that*.

"She could have said that just to annoy you," Ann said, not without sympathy. "And the pill's not enough, not these days. You're still gonna have to ask."

Maybe he could stay here instead. Move into her kitchen. There'd be good stuff to eat, and he'd get to see her now and then, and *her* dog was good company. Wouldn't be so bad.

Damn.

"That's how I got Mer, you know."

"How? By not asking?"

"Oh, I asked. Even back then I wasn't a complete idiot, though I suppose a few people would disagree. But Cassie—that's Mer's mom—swore she'd taken care of it." He shook his head. *Jeez, what an idiot.* "They'd warned us about that. The guys who'd been on the team for a while, my agent, the financial planners we were required to meet with. But she promised, and I wanted to believe her."

"Mer said that her mother had her on purpose."

"She told you that?"

Ann nodded.

"See, I *told* you she trusts you. You should talk to her."

"You're not getting out of this one, Tom."

He knew that. He just didn't like it. "Yeah, you're right. Probably how I ended up here now." And oh, he was sorry about that. If he'd moved her in at four, at six, it had to have been easier. And he would have worked his way up to bigger problems. "I wasn't there for her, all the time she was growing up."

He'd never been a man for regrets. They didn't do any good, got in the way of moving on. But these, it seemed, were here to stay.

He waited for her to say something encouraging, like most

of the other women he knew: *Oh, it wasn't your fault, you supported her, what were you supposed to do?*

But she just waited, her face calm, eyes level on his.

"Oh, I supported them. Tried to remember to call, visited when I was in town. Sent her stuff from wherever I was. But I wasn't *there*."

"It happens."

"Not to me." He'd had enough wine, he realized abruptly. She was starting to look a little blurry, and he was feeling relaxed. Like if he drank any more, he'd much rather just crawl into bed than do anything he was supposed to do. "My brothers, they're right there with their kids. Eric coaches his son's Little League, for Christ's sake. Kevin's in charge all the time when his wife's at the hospital. My dad, hell, he didn't talk to me for a month when I told him I wasn't marrying the mother of my child. Said a man steps up when he's going to be a father, and I wasn't stepping up."

"Was he right?"

"About the marrying? God, no. I hardly knew her." He'd actually considered it, for all of about two hours. His oldest brother, Mark, had knocked up his college girlfriend and married her the weekend they found out. They'd been together ever since, had three more kids before they were done, and were still gooey in love.

The horror of being married to Cassie made him shudder. He had barely known her back then, but he knew her well enough now. "We'd have been divorced inside of two years, and those two years would have scarred Mer for life. Not to mention me. But about stepping up?" He didn't like to think about it. He tried to do the right thing. "Maybe. Maybe more than I'd like to admit." *Okay,* he thought. *Time to put that one away.* He could learn from it, but he couldn't change it, and it was getting in the way of moving on. "I do know one thing. After Mer, I swore I'd never again believe a woman who told me it was safe. That I'd never have another baby without being married to her mother first."

"Did you keep that one?" she asked, seeming far more curious than judgmental.

"Absolutely."

"How can you be so sure?"

"Well . . ."

"Hey, accidents happen."

"Yeah, but I was really careful. And believe me, in my world, if you got a shortie running around, somebody's going to come after you for child support."

"I suppose that's true."

"Yeah, I kept that promise. But I'm not sure I did right by Mer. I made sure she was taken care of financially, but the rest . . . I didn't do enough." That was clear to him now, though he hadn't paid much attention to it before. He'd had good intentions. Always meant to become a bigger part of her life, be all parental before it was too late. But it always seemed like there was plenty of time. She was just a kid, and the days they did spend together seemed artificial and ultimately pointless; he knew damn well he wasn't influencing her in any major way during his brief and structured time with her.

"So what has changed now?" She seemed interested in his tale of woe, asking all the right questions, with that cute tilt to her head that encouraged him to keep on spilling. Even though he'd obviously pulled her out of bed, was keeping her from sleep now.

But he didn't want to go home.

"I mean," she went on, "you moved her in with you. You bought this place to make a home for her. What changed?"

"I lost a kid." He hadn't put it all together, not until right then. Christ. Score one for self-awareness. "His name was Gil. Gil Brockmann, and man, he could play. Best passer in a high school kid I'd ever seen. Always made the right decision. Had a scholarship waiting for him—no big-shot place, just community college, until he got his grades up and proved that he played bigger than he looked. It was a start." The highlight reel flashed through his head, Gil screaming down the court, sending a perfect behind-the-back no-look to anybody who managed to keep up with him. "But he couldn't get a high enough SAT score, not to be eligible to play Division I ball. Took it three times, and still no go."

"What happened to him?"

"Got pissed, I suppose. Got scared. Robbed a liquor store and got caught. He's in Stillwater."

"I'm sorry to hear that."

"Yeah. I was sorry, too." It didn't matter how much he preached individual responsibility to his boys, how often he drilled into their heads that their actions were their choice and anything else was an excuse. Or how many people told him that it wasn't his fault, that he couldn't be held responsible for what the kids did twenty-four hours a day. It still felt like a failure. "But then Mer started getting in trouble."

"So you figured you could save her."

"No. Yes." He debated about more wine but figured he'd reached his limit. And even though he might have preferred oblivion, he didn't dare go there. It wouldn't be fair to Mer, wouldn't be fair to Ann. "I don't know. I just knew that I had to try, if I wanted to live with myself."

"Hmm." She nodded thoughtfully. "She's sixteen, Tom."

"Are you telling me it's too late?"

"I don't know." She smiled to soften her words. "Neither do you, though. And it's better to try than not, isn't it?" She slid her glass aside; he didn't think she'd sipped more than an ounce, had obviously taken that much only to be companionable.

"You don't like the wine?"

"Oh, yes. But I've got to get up in the morning, and any more than that would make it hard." She seemed amused with herself. "I have no tolerance at all. I'd be tipsy in no time."

"I bet you're cute tipsy."

She looked surprised, as if it were something she'd never considered before. "I don't know."

"You could try it out," he said. "I'd make sure you got to bed safely. And I'll tell you the truth in the morning."

Damn it, he thought when her smile faded. She shifted back, her posture going from relaxed to wary in an instant.

"Sorry," he said. "Old habits."

"It's all right."

Okay, he thought. *No flirting, even of a harmless sort.* Wasn't allowed; that was obvious, a big blaring off-limits sign. It was a shame, that. He'd like to flirt with her, even if it was impossible for it to be any more than that.

"So what do I say to her?" he asked.

"I'm not sure I know her well enough to help you there." She was still sitting back in her chair, tugging the collar of her robe together at the V over her breast, even though she had a shirt on underneath and he couldn't see a thing.

"Hell. You probably know her as well as I do. And at least you're female."

"Maybe you should talk to her mother."

"Oh, no." He'd spoken to Cassie once this month already. That was his max. "Tyrone's a good player. I mean, really good. Cassie would probably be thrilled that Mer was finally listening to her and continuing the family business."

"I'm sure that's not true."

"You don't know Cassie." They were different species of women entirely, Cassie and Ann. Thank the blessed Lord.

"But—"

"You're going to have to trust me on this one, Ann."

"All right," she said but didn't seem convinced. "I think . . . Well, I really think you should just say what you feel."

"You've got to be kidding me." What he felt? How the hell was he supposed to know something like that? He was more accustomed to burying what he felt than identifying it, much less sharing it. "What? That I want to beat him senseless and lock her up until she's forty? You think telling her that'll help?"

"I'm betting she already knows."

"Gee. Thought I was subtle."

"Yeah. Subtle. That's the first thing I noticed about you."

Time to go. She'd said as much without saying as much.

But his butt stayed rooted to the checkered cushion, which was a lot more comfortable than it looked. He couldn't figure out why he wanted so badly to stay. Did he really like her that much? Or was that just a convenient excuse, convincing himself that he wanted to stay here and admire her rather than go home and deal with his daughter?

"Okay. I can do this." He wondered if it sounded as hollow to her as it did to him. This was parenthood, he supposed. He'd imagined things like sending her off to preschool, taking her to the zoo, tipping his hat to her as he walked off the mound after a no-hitter, watching her come down the stairs for the prom or sprint across the stage to pick up her diploma.

It was all the middle stuff he hadn't thought about, all the stuff he'd missed. All the days when you didn't know the right thing to do, or the right thing to say. You just knew it might matter, and you were terrified you'd get it wrong, and it would be the one thing that screwed up your kid forever and you'd never know until it was too late.

He creaked to his feet. Jesus, it was his shoulder that was bum; he was too young for the knees to be going, too. "Ann?"

"Hmm?"

"Thanks."

"Sure. No problem." But there was a slight curve to her mouth, a softness that he hadn't seen there very often.

Weird how he'd come to her first. Without even thinking about it, so late, when he had no right to impose. When, to come right down to it, they weren't even close to being friends.

He could tell himself that it was because she had a connection with his daughter, and no one else did. Because he'd needed a woman's opinion, and his brothers would kill him if he bothered his sisters-in-law at this time of the night.

"You said I should figure out if it's important," he said. "That, when you were fifteen, it was important for you." He tried to imagine her at fifteen, couldn't manage it. Not even with that image of the young girl in the prom picture or the wedding picture. Because he couldn't connect that laughing girl with Ann, with her grave eyes and solemn mouth. Because that girl had believed that life was mostly good, and this woman didn't. "When it was over, how bad was it for you? Am I going to . . . Am I going to have to worry about her?" That she'd hurt herself, that she'd be permanently wounded, that it would knock something important out of her, and she'd never get it back. "What was it like when it was over for you?"

"You're going to worry, anyway, aren't you? No matter what I say?" she asked, and he had to acknowledge that it was probably true. He'd always considered himself a straightforward kind of guy. No good worrying about something, because that wouldn't change it. Do something if you can. If you can't, let it go.

But that was before Mer was there, every day, and the worry had slithered its way in and taken over, all the more potent because it hadn't found its way in before.

"Besides," she said. "It never ended. I married him."

TWENTY

Mer had been grounded for two weeks, and Tom was absolutely certain it was far worse on him than her.

It had been a reflex. He'd gone home from Ann's, battling the urge every damn step of the way to keep from turning around, sprinting back to her, throwing himself on her mercy and asking—or begging or bribing—her to handle it for him.

He had money. Everyone had a price, right? And there was no doubt in his mind that she would do this better than he could.

But he also knew that sometimes you just had to pay the cost yourself. Hurt yourself and you had to do the rehab. Drink yourself stupid and you had to have the hangover. Spend the money and you had to pay the bill.

Where Mer was concerned, he was just beginning to understand that he had a really big bill coming due. Oh, maybe some of it was Cassie's responsibility, too, but he'd handed her the credit card.

He'd gone into his house. Let the dog out, went to the can, splashed some cold water on his face. Drunk a glass of juice, practiced what he was going to say. And when he couldn't delay another second without feeling like a bald-faced coward, he'd schlepped up the stairs and peeked into her room.

She was fast asleep. Or faking it; he wasn't so stupid he didn't acknowledge the very likely possibility that she was pretending in order to escape The Talk. That's how it always was in his head: The Talk, big, harsh, flashing neon letters. When his father said you had to have The Talk, it was time to start worrying, 'cause you'd fucked up big.

They'd had The Talk the morning after the prom, after he'd skipped out on English class three times his freshman year. When he'd decided to leave the U after one year to try the minors, and when he'd told him he'd gotten Cassie pregnant. Maybe a few more; he'd blocked the rest from his mind. You didn't have The Talk unless it was something that mattered.

Nevertheless, whether Mer was faking sleep or not, he was grateful to delay it a bit.

The morning would be better, he convinced himself. Calmer. They'd both have some time to settle down, so they could discuss things unemotionally and logically. Morning's always better.

So he'd told himself. But he'd been dead wrong.

His unemotional and logical attitude had lasted all of about three minutes. She'd finally stumbled out of bed at nearly noon. He'd been waiting for her in the kitchen.

He'd come away from The Talk with a strong notion that his daughter was (A) not in love with Tyrone, (B) it was definitely not her first time, and (C) she had every intention of doing it again.

It was the last one that blasted logic into insanity. "Sixteen," he shouted. "You're *sixteen*!"

"How old were you?" she'd shot back.

He tried to cover. "Not sixteen."

"Because you were younger, right?"

Dilemma. Option one: lie to your child. He preferred this one, strongly, but had a deflating notion it was the wrong one. Option two: admit the truth, with a heartfelt parable about the horrible regrets, and say how much you're hoping to save them from making the same mistakes you made.

Except that would be lying, too. He didn't regret it. His luscious night with Marlene Olberman, the head football cheerleader, ranked as one of the fondest memories of his life, and his only regret was that he suspected it wasn't quite as transformative an experience for her. However, at nineteen, two weeks after he'd been drafted, when he'd gone home to South Dakota in triumph, he'd made it up to her. Repeatedly.

So he was stuck with dancing around it. "This isn't about me," he said. "We're talking about you."

"No, *you're* talking about me. And at me."

"But you're a—" Mercifully, for once his mouth didn't run away from his brain, and it shut up before "you're a *girl*" made it all the way out.

Okay, maybe he was a sexist. Particularly when it came to his daughter and sex.

But even he—though many would argue—wasn't dumb enough to say it.

"No more," he said. "While you're here. My house, my rules. No more . . . dating."

She laughed at him. Out-and-out laughed, her face opening up in a way that would have thrilled him if she'd been laughing for any other reason. "We weren't dating, Dad."

"Okay," he'd said. "You're grounded."

She hadn't believed him. Not at first. And then she'd said, "Well, how is this different than any other day for me, stuck in Nowhereville with nothing to do?"

It wasn't until later—Monday, in fact—that he realized he'd forgotten two very important things.

He hadn't asked her about the whole safety factor. Truthfully, he couldn't even think about it without getting the icks. And he wasn't at all sure she'd tell him the truth, anyway.

So he begged Ann—visiting Ann, he'd decided immediately, didn't fall under the grounding rules; she had to be a good influence—and she'd taken pity on him. She'd also assured him—*Thank you, God*—that things were okay in that department, both on the baby and the communicable disease front.

Okay, his daughter was sexually active, and indiscriminate at that. But at least she wasn't stupid.

He'd also forgotten to figure out exactly how he was supposed to enforce the grounding, short of chaining her to his wrist.

After a very long Sunday, with Mer locked up in her room except for the semihourly door slamming to remind him she was there and she was ticked, and an equally long half of Monday, he'd realized he didn't dare go to work.

Except he had to go to work. He hadn't set a foot out of the door for fear she'd go running straight to Tyrone, and if he had to stay in that house for the whole evening, he was going to go stark, screaming nuts.

Funny how, all those years he spent on airplanes and in hotel rooms, he couldn't wait to get home. Now he had to get out.

So he cheated. He called in the big guns.

He went to Mrs. Kozlowski.

She'd been surprised when he'd knocked on her door late Monday afternoon, her eyebrows climbing almost to her corkscrewed white hair, which was tucked under a plain blue bandana. Flattered, and terribly understanding, when he'd tried to explain his delicate dilemma.

She'd understood immediately. Her second girl, Lauren, had been a bit of a wild child, she'd confessed. Not that she'd gotten away with much; her mother was too vigilant for that. And of course he, hopeless male father that he was, could never be expected to be as efficient as Mrs. Kozlowski in that regard.

But she'd taken pity on him. Fed him a cup of coffee and a stale powdered donut—the domesticity she lavished on her garden apparently didn't extend to her kitchen—and patted his shoulder consolingly, assuring him that his daughter would come out the other side all right, as her own Lauren had. She was a cardiac nurse in Denver now, and a fine mother herself.

But it was the simple expediency of his offering her tickets in the second row, right behind the Twins dugout, that had her eyes shining. Her grandson, despite being dragged off to the godforsaken territories of Billings, was a Twins fan, a fact that earned what he assumed would be her most assiduous efforts on Mer's behalf.

He shook his head as he crossed the street, heading home. He wasn't the star of the team that mattered anymore. He was just the conduit to the team that mattered.

That was okay, he decided. Whatever worked.

And Mer would be safe. He had no doubt of it. And he made absolutely certain, before he left the house, that Mrs. Kozlowski was on the case.

And so the two weeks had crawled by. She hardly spoke to him. Hardly *saw* him, spending most of her time in her room, and when she did slink out and join him downstairs, she'd confiscate the remote—obviously she knew exactly where to hurt him—and flip back and forth between Animal Planet and MTV.

Animal Planet wasn't bad. Those meerkats were cute, and he found himself on the edge of his seat during *Animal Cops*; those people who left their animals in that condition were *sick*, and deserved far worse than they got.

But MTV gave him nightmares. Though he now knew where his daughter got her ideas about appropriate male-female relationships. And all this time he'd blamed Cassie.

Instead, she'd gotten them from people named 50 Cent and Nate Dogg.

He'd tried to talk to her a couple of times. Got no response, and gave up. He'd already grounded her. What else could he take away?

But tonight was Saturday, and he was getting out. He was pathetically grateful about that, though he usually hated gigs like these, where he had to dress up in a monkey suit and pretend that he was thrilled to meet every person in the place, listen to them all tell him where they'd been when he'd won the game that clinched the series, and moan about the state of his shoulder and his lost career.

He did it anyway. It was a particularly good cause tonight, the Children's Cancer Research Fund. Though a hard one, as they always insisted on playing one of those videos of sick kids which ensured that there wasn't a dry eye in the place but plenty of pens scratching over checkbooks.

If his chatting up every baseball fan in attendance old enough to remember who he was helped crack open a few more of those checkbooks or add an extra zero to the number on the *Dollars* line, it was worth it.

Maybe not the damned bow tie, but everything else.

Mer was coming up the stairs as he was going down. Her eyes widened, then skittered away, as if he was something repulsive.

"Hey," he said, "I didn't think I looked *that* bad."

She stepped aside to give him room to pass on the stairs. For a moment he thought that would be it, that she'd ignore him as obviously as she had the past two weeks.

The constant tension, the having to tiptoe around for fear of setting off an explosion, was wearing on him. For damn sure the girl had more stamina than he did.

He just wanted things back to normal. More than normal. Easy, comfortable, a regular father-daughter relationship.

He ignored the tiny nudge at the back of his brain that said this *was* a regular father-daughter relationship.

"I'm leaving now," he said.

"Really? Thought you just looked like that for the fun of it."

"Yeah, well." He cleared his throat.

There should be something he could say that would ease this. Make it okay between them, so that they could at least get back to where they started.

She looked him over again, up and down. "You got a date?"

He did. Sort of. Heather McVay was a local news reporter who made absolutely no secret of the fact that she had her sights on an anchor chair and a bigger market. That worked out well for both of them; there were no expectations on either side.

They'd been lovers, at least technically, though that was an overromantic term for something that was mostly a convenience to both of them. They'd spent a couple of long vacation weekends together, when both of them could get away. Enjoyable, but little more. They looked good on each others' arms, however, and he couldn't go to a function like tonight's alone. She had hosting duties, and she could be counted on to entertain herself. She'd be as busy working the room as he would, with far more enthusiasm and charm, and she'd never complain that he'd abandoned her to stand in a corner with a bunch of guys, reminiscing about the glory days.

"Well, don't worry about it," Mer said. "I won't wait up. Take your time. Don't give me a passing thought. Stay out all night if you want."

"Not a chance," he said, with only a little pang.

He missed sex. Damn, but he missed sex, but he knew his priorities. He could hold out until the end of summer. Didn't mean he was going to *like* it, but he could. He was a grown-up.

"I'll be fine," she said, though he didn't believe her for a second. "Besides, I'm sure the old bat across the street'll keep an eye on me."

"Don't call her that," he said automatically.

Maybe she was an old bat, but he was grateful for her every day when he went off to practice. Tonight, though, Tyrone was on the loose, and his daughter was clever, and he needed more assurance than Lorraine Kozlowski, as talented and dedicated as she was.

"Come on now. You go ahead and get laid."

"Mer!" he said warningly. He could not get used to it, didn't know how to get her to shut up. He suspected she talked like that mostly because it shocked him so much, and so he tried his best not to react like . . . well, like an outraged father. But he failed routinely.

He wasn't, generally speaking, particularly uncomfortable about sexual matters. He'd spent too much time in a locker room, too much time on the road.

When it came to his family, as far as his father knew, Tom had had sex exactly once in his life, which resulted in Mer. Wayne Nash studiously ignored any evidence to the contrary, and they both preferred it that way.

"But it's making you grouchy," she said. "You'd be happier with the edge off."

"I'm not grouchy."

She snorted, that sound of utter disbelief and disgust perfected by adolescents.

"Okay, maybe I am," Tom said. "But the only reason I'm grouchy is *you*."

"How'm I making you grouchy? I'm hardly any trouble at all."

"When you're the least trouble is when I start worrying the most." He tried to scowl at her, a proper parental warning. But this was the most she'd spoken to him in weeks, and it was—almost—normal. Making fun of her father, seeing how far she could push.

"Well, don't worry tonight." She reached up and gave his tie a tug to straighten it, a gesture that had his throat tightening as if she'd pulled it a whole lot tighter. "You're not bad, you know. Not for an old guy."

Maybe, he thought. Maybe they'd find their way after all.

"Thanks," he said. "And I'm not worried."

The doorbell gave its bright peal. "See?" He started for the door.

"What?" The—it wasn't a connection between them, more the possibility of one—was gone as quickly as it had come, her frown snapping back into place. "You got me a *babysitter*?"

"Yup," he said, and pulled open the door.

"Hey!" Boom filled the doorway, black Oakleys wrapped around his shiny round head, wearing a pair of jeans—he had them custom-made to fit over his thighs—and a purple silk Hawaiian shirt with pale flowers that looked like vomit stains. A gold chain as thick as Cooper's collar wrapped around his neck, with the three-inch-long diamond-encrusted bat he'd had custom-made when he'd won the American League batting title dangling against his chest.

Tom heard Mer bang up the stairs. He didn't have to turn around to know that she was stomping off in a huff. She whistled to the dog and headed up to her bedroom. Amazing that she could make that much noise, even though there was a carpet runner on the treads. An ugly, patterned carpet runner, but thick enough that it should have dampened the sound more than that.

"Wait for it." Tom held up one finger, counting it out in his head. "And . . ." He brought his hand down. "Now!"

His timing was impeccable; the door slammed within a split second of his arm reaching the bottom of its motion.

"All the ladies are just always *so* glad to see me," Boom said, as he stepped in. He had a black leather duffel bag over one shoulder and a six-pack in each hand.

"Thanks for doing this, Boom." It was a horrible imposition, and Tom knew it. Sooner or later he'd have to pay and pay big. But there was no one else he could trust with this. No one else who owed him as much as Boom did.

Boom might have shrugged. There was too much muscle lying thick over those shoulders to tell if they moved. "Hey, no problem. I like kids."

He did. He had a fleet of nieces and nephews, and it had been a rare game that there weren't several of them cheering him on. His cell phone had a special ring for them, the theme song for *Good Times*, and he answered when he heard it, no matter what. Now that he was retired, he flew off to see one batch or another nearly every month.

"Yeah, well, I don't know about this one." She wasn't happy about this. And when Mer wasn't happy, one way or another it spilled over onto the nearest human.

He figured he should feel guilty that, for once, it wouldn't be him. But he was too relieved for guilt.

"Hey, man, don't worry about it."

"I'm not." Not really. He wouldn't have asked Boom to come if he was going to worry. "I owe you, though."

"So what else is new?" Boom said cheerfully. He looked Tom up and down. "Gee, don't you look pretty?"

"Shut up." He tugged at his collar, which was digging into his neck like it was made of cardboard.

"Almost go for you myself, when you look like that." He leaned forward and made a show of taking a good whiff. "Smell good, too. Who you goin' with?"

"Heather."

"She fine, that one." Boom nodded, his face grave. The relative merits of the females of the species was a serious matter. "Thought you might be taking that neighbor of yours."

"Why'd you think that?" he asked, ignoring the tiny flush of guilt working its way up. It meant nothing.

"Oh, just the way you been talking 'bout her."

"I have not. I mentioned her, *maybe*, once, and that's only because of Mer."

"Yeah, once. That's a lot for you."

"Some of us aren't the kind to kiss and tell."

"Hey, somebody's gotta share with the less fortunate. Let you all live vicariously." Boom's grin flashed. "That implies that there's some kissin' to tell, by the way."

"Nope. No kissin'." And he was a whole lot sorrier about that than he should be.

Boom shook his head sadly, which he was doing with more and more frequency around Tom these days. "You should do somethin' about that tonight, then."

"I don't think so." He grabbed his keys from the side table, thought better of it. "Hey, can I use your car?"

"Excuse me?"

"Look, all I've got here is the truck and the bike. No way Heather's gonna be seen in, or on, either one. I don't have time to go downtown and pick up something else."

Boom gave him a hard glare, then dug in his pocket and tossed him the glittering silver key chain with its huge, diamond-studded charm in the shape of a dollar sign. "You take care of my baby, now."

"And you take care of mine."

"Yeah, but I'm more trustworthy than you."

"I don't have time to argue." And it really was a case-by-case basis. On some things, Tom was more responsible, on others, Boom. It was just that Boom's version of trustworthy and the rest of the civilized world's didn't always match up. "She's tricky."

Boom waved his hand as if shooing away a fly. "You gotta be kiddin' me."

"Okay, okay." He turned for the door.

"You know, Nash," he said. "It's not gonna somehow keep her from having sex if you give it up."

In his head, he knew that was probably true. But logic hadn't kept him from eating the exact same meal—three pieces of Popeyes fried chicken, two biscuits—before the start of every game, or from wearing the same shorts every day when he was on a winning streak. Logic only went so far, and why take the chance?

"You never know," Tom said and jogged out so he didn't have to hear Boom's answer.

That wouldn't keep him from answering, Tom knew. But he didn't have to listen to it.

TWENTY-ONE

Mer lay flat on her back and stared at the ceiling. That perfect, clean white ceiling, with a frosty glass fixture that was probably fifty years old square in the middle.

She wanted to throw something at it, see it shatter and rain down shards.

She couldn't believe her father had called in a babysitter. As if she were too young, too stupid to be left alone. As if she were eight.

Okay, he'd blabber about how it wasn't because she was young but because she couldn't be trusted. But trusted to do what? Do what he wanted, and nothing else? What she wanted obviously didn't enter into it at all.

Maybe, if he'd actually been around to hire her babysitters when she was eight he'd have more right to be snooping around now. But he hadn't been, and somehow he thought he had to make up for lost time by being twice as strict as any sane parent.

She rolled onto her side and pulled a pillow up against her chest. It had a flounce of lace around it, scratchy against the inside skin of her forearm. Outside, it wasn't even dark yet; she could see the tops of the trees, swaying in the breeze, revealing a glimpse of the dark shingles on Ann's house through the leaves.

Ann didn't treat her like she was eight. Oh, now and then she tried to slide in some adult advice, all sneaky and casual. But then she let it go. Let Mer decide if what she'd said was worth listening to or not.

Her dad could learn a lot from Ann. Because her dad was a complete and utter control freak.

She wouldn't have figured it. He'd always seemed so easygoing, ready to try anything she suggested, give her anything she wanted as long as it wasn't ridiculous and she pretended to ask nicely.

There'd been lots of times, back when she was young enough to be stupid, that she'd wished he'd invited her to live with him. Had to be better than living with her mom.

But at least Cassie let her be most of the time. Oh, she nagged her about how she looked, but otherwise she didn't much care where she was and who she was with, as long as it didn't bother Cassie. Which was how it should be.

She sighed and sat up, jiggling her legs up and down.

She couldn't stay in this room all night. She was getting twitchy, as if she were going to bust right out of her own skin like something out of a horror movie, the alien spawn fed on boredom exploding straight out of her chest. And she was getting dead sick of spending so much time in her room, though what else was she supposed to do? Hang out with her dad?

She'd only been with Tyrone twice since her dad pulled this whole grounding bullshit, when Tyrone had climbed into her window sometime after two a.m. Thank God her dad slept soundly, and the nosy biddy across the street checked out about midnight.

Tyrone was fun. Decent in bed, though he liked her to do a little too much of the work. Girls had been just too easy for him to get, ones who'd do anything to snag his attention, and so he was used to pretty much lying back.

She'd made it clear it wasn't working that way with her. She thought he kind of liked that; people didn't bother to challenge him too often. So it was okay. More exciting, for both of them, to be putting one over on her father. And neither one of them was dumb enough to bother to pretend that it was anything more than a good time. When wasn't it, really? She was pretty sure that all the love stuff people wrapped sex up in was just an excuse to let them do what they wanted, anyway. Everything'd be a lot simpler if they were just straight about it.

She reached down, gave Cooper a good scratch behind his ear, which made one of his rear legs start to quiver like he had the DTs. It was like he had some wires crossed somewhere in that brain of his: scratch that spot, the leg starts shaking.

That was okay with her. She didn't want him to be like every other dog, just like she didn't want to be like the girls she saw walking down her street once in a while. They all looked the same; smooth shiny hair, smooth shiny teeth. Little robot daughters, exactly what their parents had ordered up.

Suddenly she felt like she couldn't breathe, like all the flowers and lace were starting to choke her.

It was quiet downstairs. The big bald mountain that masqueraded as her dad's best friend couldn't be that interested in watching her. He just couldn't. She wondered what her father was holding over his head to get him to stay with her on a Saturday night. Had to be something good.

He was probably staring goggle-eyed at the television screen. The thing mesmerized men; she'd seen it happen with her father a dozen times. And she was pretty sure it was game six of the NBA championships; Dad had whined about it all afternoon, plotting ways to smuggle a TV into the party.

For sure he'd brought plenty of beer. With any luck, he'd never know she was gone. And honestly, once she made it out, she didn't much care if he found out. What was her dad gonna do? Ground her? Been there, done that.

And if he sent her home a couple of weeks early, well, that wasn't that big a deal, either. It wasn't like she expected him to ask her to move in for good or anything.

She found a pair of Converse sneakers, quieter than the boots, and eased open the door, wincing when it squeaked. Stupid old house; the stairs weren't any better. She took her time, placing her feet on the edges. Cooper shot down the stairs before her, skidding around the corner and heading for the kitchen. If there was the slightest chance there was food involved, he wasn't missing the opportunity.

She kept the lights off, pausing in the hallway to listen. The entire first floor was dark, except for a lighter rectangle where the open doorway marked the top of the stairs to the basement. She could hear the television, a murmur of fake-excited announcer voices, the roar of cheers. Yup, the game. He wouldn't move for hours.

She tiptoed down the hall, keeping one hand on the wall as she eased into the kitchen. The light over the back step was on, so all she had to do was shuffle her way over—

"Hey."

Busted. "Why are you sitting in the dark?"

"Didn't need a light." She heard a click, the hum of the fluorescent bulbs struggling to come to life, and then a flare of light, bright enough to make her blink.

He was sitting comfortably at the table, a sandwich in one hand, a beer on the table next to him. "You hungry, too?"

"Well, no, I—" She should just say, "I'm going out" and do it. How was he going to stop her?

But she eyed his arms, one of which was thicker than both her legs put together, and figured that, if he wanted to make a fuss about it, she wouldn't put it past him. She'd bet twenty bucks Dad had given him permission to use all means necessary.

"I was just . . . taking the dog out. Yeah, Coop was whining. He has to go out."

"Really?" He looked down to where Coop had curled up happily at his feet, his nose following every move the sandwich made. "Doesn't look like he's bustin' his bladder to me."

Traitor. "Yeah, well, he gets distracted easily by food."

"I know the feeling." Boom moved the sandwich to the left, up, down, grinning as the dog's nose followed.

Boom looked scarier grinning.

"Well," he said. "Go ahead. Take him out."

"Uh. Sure." She slapped her thigh. "C'mon, boy."

She ended up having to wrap her hand in his collar and practically drag him out the door. Once they got there, however, Cooper decided he liked it in the yard, taking his time to sniff under every single bush, to investigate each tuft of grass in case there was something new there. And all the while she was getting dive-bombed by mosquitoes the size of bats.

She'd bet there were bats out here, too, she thought, and backed up against the door, under the pitiful shelter of the overhang.

The moose came out and leaned against the doorjamb, stuffing another sandwich into his mouth. "You okay?" Boom asked.

"Oh, yeah, we're fine." So fucking fine. Saturday night, and she was hanging outside her father's house, getting her blood siphoned out by buzzing vampires, waiting for her dog to find a toilet spot that suited his delicate requirements.

In Chicago, she'd be out. Someplace where there was music, loud and hard, the beat so mean it filled you up until you couldn't think of anything else. God, she missed it.

And her mother wouldn't be grounding her, either. Because her mother'd be out, too.

"Coop," Boom said, sudden enough to make her jump, "dump!"

The dog hunched his back immediately, did his business, and came trotting back to them.

"How'd you do that?"

"What? He doesn't do that for you?" He smiled, teeth white as pearls in the dark light. "I'm good with dogs. They like me. And it's all about knowing you're in charge, so they know it, too."

"Dad can't get him to sit without holding a treat over his nose."

"Yeah, well, Nash's got a problem with that being in charge thing. Too nice."

"Could have fooled me."

He stared at her. There was no expression on his face, no disapproval or anger, just staring, without so much as a flicker, until she started shifting under his regard. "What'd you expect him to do?" he finally asked her. "You're his daughter."

No, she was his mistake. And now, apparently, his problem. "I don't know." She dropped her gaze to the dog, who was a lot easier to look at than Boom. "Nothing."

"You're smarter than that." The last half of the sandwich disappeared into his mouth in one chunk, and he spoke around it. "I'll be down watching the game. You're welcome to join me whenever you want. Gotta be getting sick of your room."

She couldn't bolt now. He'd be listening. He didn't think she was stupid enough to take that bait, did he?

So she tromped back through the house, making sure her footsteps were heavy on the wood floors, and up the stairs. Then she watched the clock, a good fifteen minutes, waiting for him to get involved in the game, to suck down a couple of those beers he'd brought.

She eased up the window. Evening had come barreling in, turning the sky a deep lavender, making lights flick on all over the neighborhood. She could hear the shouts of kids, smell charcoal and steaks.

She looked down, plotting her route. If Tyrone could get up to that window, for sure she could get down from it. He had to weigh more than she did. Then three blocks to the bus stop, and she'd be free. She didn't know any of the routes, but she figured anything headed east would get her into the city eventually, and that was good enough for her.

Okay.

There was ivy against the side of the house, thick with leaves the size of her palms. She swung over the sill, scrambling around until her feet found a place to rest, then eased her weight onto it.

Good. She wasn't going crashing down.

It must have taken her another fifteen minutes to get to the bottom. A lot longer than it looked, though it looked plenty long when she'd been dumb enough to glance down. She'd never been afraid of heights. Still wasn't, she figured. She was just afraid of entrusting her weight to a bunch of plants.

In the daytime, in a breeze, the ivy rippled against the side of the house, soft and pretty and delicate. But the plant was pricklier than it looked; she had scratches all over her forearm, another one on her cheek. And all the while those damned bugs were feasting on the back of her neck; she could feel welts popping out, itching like a fiend, but she didn't dare let go long enough to slap the little bastards.

But it was worth it, she thought as she hit ground. She hadn't been out and had fun, real fun, since she'd gotten here. It was unnatural.

She dusted off her hands on her pants, turned, and ran smack into Boom.

"Jesus!"

He was the size of a house, a big solid stone one. He had his arms crossed across his chest and was grinning down at her like she amused him.

"You scared me."

"Really?" he asked. "You don't look like you scare all that easy."

"Yeah, well." She wasn't going to be flattered by that. "I was just, well . . . kind of an experiment. Read about it in a book, wanted to see if climbing down the ivy really worked."

"Now, which of those lies do you figure I'm gonna buy? The one about it being an experiment, or the one about you reading a book?"

Damn, but he was a pain in the ass. She would go ahead and hit him, if she didn't figure that she'd probably break her hand on that chest.

"Hon, I got six sisters. *Six*. My whole life has been about two things: baseball and keepin' them outta trouble. There ain't *nothin'* you can try that I ain't already seen."

He left her there, standing beside the house. Like it never occurred to him that she wouldn't follow, that she'd obey as brainlessly as Cooper.

She should run. Except, even though he was big, she was pretty sure he was faster than she was, and she had a feeling he knew exactly where she was, and if she turned the wrong way, he'd be on her like Cassie on an All-star.

Fine. He wanted her home, she'd stay home.

But she wasn't staying in her room all night, a meek little charge. She was going to make sure he wouldn't enjoy the evening any more than she would.

She followed him down the stairs. He was already settled in front of the TV, his chair kicked into full recline, a beer snugged into the cup holder. Coop was all curled up on the chair next to his, besotted eyes fixed firmly on Boom.

Casual-like, she wandered over to the fridge, opened it, and stared inside as if pondering her options. There were the usuals, Orange Crush and Sprecher's Root Beer and Coke in bottles—Dad liked bottles. And the beer that Boom had brought.

She bent over, reaching slow so as not to attract his attention.

"Don't even think about it."

Her hand was an inch from the bottle of Summit Pale Ale. She glanced over at the seating area. He wasn't even looking at her.

"Okay, this is enough." She stomped over to him, planted herself between him and the screen. "Why do you *care?*"

"I don't," he said easily. "But your dad does, and that's good enough for me."

Great. The guy was the responsible sort.

But he could be scared into leaving her alone. Had to be possible, because she could do things his sisters couldn't to frighten him off.

She reached for the hem of her T-shirt, lifted it up slow and easy, giving him a good glimpse of the ring through her navel.

"You go one more inch," he said, low and calm and lethal, "and I'll lock you in a closet until your father gets home."

She paused, her strip of belly still bare. "Why?" she asked, trying to inject a note of seduction into her voice, wishing for once that she had a little more of Cassie in her after all.

Not that she wanted to sleep with him, though. He was *old*, old as her dad.

But she wanted him to leave her alone. "Come on," she said. "You like the young ones. You know you do." Wasn't much of a guess; they all did. It had been a problem, the last year or two, when one of the guys Cassie brought home was just a bit too interested in her daughter.

Except for her new boyfriend, Howard. He treated her with vague and affectionate befuddlement, like she was a great-niece he'd never met before but was predisposed to like, even though he had no idea what to do with her.

She made herself meet Boom's eyes, hoping he'd see that she was willing to go the distance, that his life—at least, his evening—would be a lot more pleasant if he just let her do whatever she wanted.

But she couldn't hold it. His eyes were fierce without being the least bit angry. Angry, she could have handled; she could have worked on that anger, prodded him into doing something stupid. But it was clear he was willing to wait all night if he had to, and it wouldn't bother him a bit.

"*Fine.*" She stomped over to the fridge, dug out the last bottle of Dr Pepper, chose the theater seat the farthest from him, and plopped down before she realized she'd forgotten to pop the top off the soda. "Damn."

He reached over, took the bottle from her, flicked the top off with his bare hands, and handed it back without taking his eyes off the game.

She wasn't going to say thanks.

"You're welcome," he said placidly.

Mer endured three minutes of the game, which included a time out and two Budweiser commercials, before taking custody of the remote and flicking through the channels.

What would annoy him the most? Not MTV; it drove her

father nuts, but Boom looked like his taste in music was a little more contemporary. Some sappy movie on Lifetime?

No, then she'd have to sit through it, too, and it wasn't worth it.

She rolled over an episode of *LaVerne & Shirley*. Okay, that'd have to do it.

"Oh, man," he said as she settled in. "I love me some Lenny!"

Mer knew when she was beat.

"I remember you, you know," she said. "When I used to go down on the field."

"I remember you, too. You were the prettiest little thing. Hair like dandelion fuzz, eyes like blueberries."

"And I'm not now?"

He glanced over at her. "Who can tell under all that crap you wear?"

"Hey!"

But he was grinning, and that took the sting out.

"I used to buy you snow cones."

"I remember that, too. Rainbows, and you'd tell them to make sure they gave me extra syrup."

"All it took was a little sugar, and you were the happiest kid around."

"Yeah," she agreed. She still loved sugar; it just didn't fix things the way it used to.

But it helped. "Do you like fudge? I could use some fudge."

"Fudge?" His eyes lit up. "You got some?"

"Nope," she said. "But I can make it."

"You can cook?"

"I'm getting there." She was getting damn good, if she did say so herself. Of course, Ann was a decent teacher. But she liked cooking; you could take certain steps, and know that a short time later you'd have something good. And you could fiddle around a bit, try out stuff, and make something new. Creative and straightforward at the same time. Do stuff right, and it turned out right.

It wasn't like school, back when she'd used to actually try, when she'd do everything she was supposed to and sometimes it didn't turn out anyway. It wasn't like life. And if you really screwed up, you could just dump it in the garbage and start all over again. No harm done.

"Hot damn," Boom said. "If you decide to move out on Nash, you can come live with me."

TWENTY-TWO

Ann was late to Cedar Ridge again.

Though she supposed it hardly counted as late any-more, when she hadn't had any intention of getting here until at least eight.

The one night a week she ate with Mer had turned into two, and finally three. And at least one of them included her father.

She enjoyed her time with the girl. Fancied that she was good for her, that Mer needed some time with a grown woman who appreciated her company and encouraged her to make good choices. And she loved hauling out her cookbooks, planning what they would make, trying them out. It was so much more fun than slapping together a sandwich to eat at her mute husband's bedside.

She left cookies—oatmeal, bittersweet chocolate, and a good dose of the Korintje cinnamon she'd bought at Penzeys—off at the front desk. There was a new nurse on duty tonight, one who looked scarcely older than Mer, crisp in her light blue scrubs with clouds of pale brown hair curling around her face, and she introduced herself.

"Oh, yes." The girl's tag read Jennifer, and her face immediately drooped into sad concern. "I've seen your husband's chart."

"Enjoy the cookies." What else could she say? Ann wondered. Tell the girl not to worry, it was okay, she was fine, when that was anything but true?

The only person in John's room was Mary, her knitting needles flashing in and out of a sky blue half-finished sweater that was the size of a Cabbage Patch doll.

"Is everything okay?"

Mary kept knitting as she looked up. Her hands were always moving; Ann sometimes wondered if she stopped, if she'd fall apart. So far, she never had. Unlike Ann, who'd wailed and cried and wept regularly for a good two years.

"Oh yes," Mary said. "He's in the pool. They got backed up today, but that nice therapist didn't want to leave without John getting his exercise."

It was one of the best things about this facility. No matter how long John was in his condition, how dim his prognosis, they treated him like they expected him to wake up tomorrow. He got regular therapy: being rolled on mats on the floor; moving his limbs in a steel, X-shaped tub of water; being cranked up to vertical and transferred to a wheelchair; having his joints flexed and massaged routinely. It was a lot of work to care for him, feeding him through his gastric tube, changing his external urine collector, smearing antibiotic salves on any red spots so they wouldn't grow into bedsores. She admired the work they did here, was grateful for it. And they'd never once betrayed the slightest hint that it was pointless.

Of course, the facility was also paid very well to do just that.

"He should be back soon," Mary went on. She flipped the minisweater around, ran her fingers swiftly over the loops of yarn, counting them out, before starting back in the other way.

Ann sat down, watching in silence while Mary knitted, the steel click and slide of the needles loud in the room.

"You don't need to stay until I get here," Ann said. She'd told Mary that more than once, to no effect. She'd managed to mostly wrestle into place the guilt of spending less time with her husband; the bald truth was he didn't know the difference. And even if he did . . . Well, John would want her to enjoy herself, to have a life. It was her own conscience that got in the way, not him.

But the guilt of imposing on Mary was a constant nag. She spent all her time here as it was, and now those hours were expanding even further as Ann took a little time with Mer.

John would want her to take care of his mother, too.

Okay, Ann thought. *I have to try.* She owed him that much.

"Mary," she said, and then more sharply. *"Mary?"*

She looked up in surprise, because Ann never used that tone with her, and the poke and slide of her needles slowed. She had on her pearls, a pretty blouse striped in blue and white. She was still handsome enough that Ann could only hope she looked half as good at that age. "Is something wrong?"

"Yes," Ann said. "You have to go home, Mary."

"I will," she said. "Once he's settled in for the night."

"No, that's not what I meant." Ann shook her head. "You're a wonderful mother, Mary."

"Oh." She looked so surprised, so pleased, that Ann made a vow to compliment her more often. "Thank you."

"Nobody could do more for a son than you do. No mother could be more faithful. But you have to stop spending every single moment here. You have to have a life."

"Don't be silly." She sniffed, as the tempo of her knitting picked up. "This is where I want to be."

"Mary." Ann put her hand over her mother-in-law's, forcing her to stop and look at her fully. Her age was starting to show in her eyes, the blue that was once brilliant as cornflowers fading into clouds. "John wouldn't want this. He wouldn't want you to sit in this place every hour of every day. He'd want you to get out of here."

Mary's sniff turned into a sniffle. She gazed at the empty bed, a gleam of moisture in her eyes. "But where else would I go?"

Ann sat back and let her hand drop to her lap. The room was not unpleasant. Plants bloomed on the windowsill, replaced as soon as the petals dropped. An album's worth of photos were affixed on the wood veneer closet door: John from babyhood to twenty-eight, snapshots from family trips to Disneyland and the mountains, John with all of his sports teams, with his best friend in their caps and gowns, giddy and proud in front of the first house that he'd designed and had built. The two of them, growing up together, arm in arm.

She'd framed some of his favorite plans, his senior project and the north side community center he was working on before the accident, and hung them on the plain buff cement walls. A knitted afghan, royal blue and gold—Mill Valley school colors—blazed bright at the foot of the bed.

But it was what it was. Sterile and plain and dreary, a purgatory for humans who were scarcely that anymore.

How many hours had she spent here? Ann wondered. She'd never actually counted. Sometimes it felt as if she'd spent her whole life here, as if those wonderful times she'd spent with John were merely the dreams and this was the reality, the whole of her world contained in one twelve-by-fourteen nursing home room.

Her chest hurt, the pressure swelling from inside.

Was this what the rest of her life was going to be, too? John could be here another twenty years, another forty. It was unlikely, but he'd lasted this long, and nobody'd predicted that, either. She'd merely kept going, one day after the other, and it had all added up to this. One day she'd look up and realize that she was as old as Mary, and this place had consumed her life, too.

She could get sick tomorrow. It happened all the time. And then this *would* be her whole life, and she would have wasted so much of it. Because she was afraid of doing anything else, because she'd let the guilt and the *shoulds* keep her here, frozen.

"I'm going to have a party," Ann said. "And I want you and Martin to come."

———

Ann had just let Cleo out for the last time when she heard the thump-thump of a basketball next door.

They never bothered to shut the gate between the two houses anymore. If they did Cooper just paced on his side and howled. Two nights of that and she and Mer had made a pact to just leave the damn thing open, as long as Mer filled any holes and picked up any Cooper-sized droppings on Ann's side of the fence.

She leaned against the rough wood in the opening. The back light was on and bugs flailed in a cloud around it. The air was thick and heavy, waiting for a storm. There'd be thunder by midnight, she'd bet.

Tom had put a hoop up over his garage two weeks ago; she'd heard him doing it, a lot of pounding, even more swearing. A steady stream of comments from the huge black guy who sat in a lawn chair, a cooler at his feet, and laughed at him.

Now he was shooting. Aim, flex, let it fly, corral the ball, do it over again. And again, the rhythm as regular as a meditation. His black T-shirt was sleeveless, his equally dark shorts long and baggy. When she was a kid, basketball players used to wear gym shorts tight and small enough to get a good view of their rear, except then she'd been too young to appreciate it.

She wasn't too young anymore.

The ball rebounded off the rim, bouncing into the grass, and Tom swore.

"If you cleaned the lightbulb so you could actually *see* the basket, it might help," she said.

He turned in her direction and looked glad to see her. Glad to see *her*. It had been so long since someone had looked at her like that, that it made her heart stutter a bit.

"I don't need no stinkin' light." He tossed the ball over his shoulder, the way they did in the commercials. It hit the peak of the garage, a foot above the backboard, and landed in the tangle of bushes that edged the drive. "That worked better in my head."

"It was worth a shot. I would have been thoroughly impressed if it had gone in."

"You're not impressed anyway?"

"I'm impressed that your legs are so white they damn near give off enough light to shoot baskets by all by themselves."

He whistled. "You decide to start jawing about a man's game *and* his legs, you better be ready to take what comes."

"I can take it."

"Really?" He bent over the scrubby bushes, fished out the ball. There was a bone in there, a couple of tennis balls, and something that stank so bad he didn't dare investigate further. Cooper had a stash. "Prove it." He fired the ball at her, surprised when she caught it and tucked it beneath her arm, against her hip.

"Where's Mer?"

He jerked his thumb over his shoulder, at the high window where light flared through the curtains. "In her room."

"How's the grounding going?"

"Grounding's going just frickin' dandy." He held out his hand. "You ain't shooting, give it over."

She bounced a pass to him, watched him while he fired it up and it swished through. "Nice shot."

The evening was quieter than usual. The frogs who held regular orgies in the wetlands of the golf course had apparently worn themselves out. All over the neighborhood windows were closed, sealing in the sounds of televisions and conversations, everybody waiting for the storm.

"Can I ask you a question?"

He stopped dribbling immediately and turned toward her, listening like it mattered, like she had his full attention. "Of course you can ask me a question."

"I promise it won't be too personal."

His eyes darkened, a flicker that was there and gone before she could identify it. "I don't care if it's personal."

Oh, man, he shouldn't tempt her. She knew her boundaries; they'd been laid down the day she said "I do," and nothing that had happened since then changed them. Truthfully, she rarely gave much thought to the limits she lived with. What was the point? They were what they were, and she'd grown comfortable with them.

At least until he'd moved in next door. Him, and his daughter, and she'd rather spend time with the two of them than almost anybody else. She was getting itchy, unsettled, uncertain in her own skin. Like a storm was brewing inside her, too, ready to blow in and scour the moldy old stuff away.

Sometimes when they were having dinner she wondered what they'd look like to a stranger. A family, comfortable together, sharing a meal, sharing their day, sharing their lives . . . She was getting a glimpse, however pale and artificial, of the life that John's accident had stolen from her. And for the first time in a long time she was mourning it again.

"Your league," she said. "Why basketball? Why not baseball?"

He let the ball roll around in his hands. "Lots of reasons. The kids, in the city, they're more into basketball than baseball. And we can run it year-round, and one guy can go out and practice by himself, and . . ." He leaned forward, as if he were confessing a secret. "The truth? I like basketball better."

"Then why didn't you play it? You're actually kind of tall. In case you never noticed."

"Not tall enough." He backed up and took aim, holding the ball poised in shooting position. "Not tall enough to be the big, slow, white guy, anyway. I got two out of three, but not the one you need for that."

"So don't play center."

He shook his head and took another shot. This one hit the back of the rim, bounced forward to the front, and rolled all the way around before dropping through. "Not quick enough, not a good enough shot." He looked as glum as if he'd lost his last friend. "Got no ups, babe. Got no ups."

"Let's see."

He gave her a curious glance, then took a run toward the garage and leaped. He touched the bottom of the backboard, but only just. "I could dunk," he said, "but I gotta take a good run at it. With somebody hanging on me? Not a chance."

"Yeah, you're right. No ups." She chased down the ball herself, tossing it from hand to hand. "So how long are you going to keep her grounded?"

"It's been working so far."

"You're going to keep her grounded all summer. Because it's just so much fun, and because it's so great for your relationship."

"Hey, at least I get to sleep. If she was out at night, no way I'd get a wink until she came home. So that's something."

She weighed the ball in her right hand as she weighed what to say.

She was butting in, no doubt about it. None—absolutely none—of her business.

But she liked Mer. No getting around that. She wasn't exactly sure why; there wasn't a teenager on earth less like herself at that age than Mer.

Except in that feeling of being apart from everyone else, of not quite fitting in. Though she figured more adolescents felt like that than not. She just hadn't realized it at the time.

Oh, Mer was no doubt hanging around her out of desperation. There was nobody else, and no teenager could spend *that* much time alone. And she liked Cleo, and certainly the food was far better than at her house. That was enough reason.

But it felt like more. It felt like, maybe, Ann was making a tiny bit of difference there.

Except it wasn't enough. She wasn't a parent, wouldn't get to see her after she went home to Chicago, didn't figure Mer was going to be calling her weekly to report on things. This was the only chance she'd have.

And Mer was right on the edge. Ann didn't have to be a child psychologist to realize that. She was either going to start growing up, or she was going to spiral down, getting lost in the anger and the rebelliousness, and who knew when she would find her way out, if ever?

Somewhere along the line she was going to have to start talking to her father. If her mother wouldn't parent, he would have to do it. And he'd be decent at it, if he'd stop beating his chest, remember what century they were in, and get on with it.

"She talking to you at any time except when you all are having dinner with me?"

"She doesn't talk to me then, either. She talks to you and you translate."

"Fair enough."

"So maybe we should have dinner with you every night."

He was smiling at her with an easy grin that didn't tell her a thing. He could be kidding. Probably. It was only her imagination that made it feel like more.

She was just lonely, she decided. Funny how she hadn't realized it before. How having two more people around made her suddenly recognize how she hadn't had anybody for a long time.

"I know it's none of my business," she said. "But I think you should let her off."

"It's kind of your business. But no." He shuddered. "I can't. Every time she set foot out of the door, I'd think of her and that . . . I just couldn't."

"It's going to happen sooner or later."

"Yeah, but I don't have to see it." Funny how that famous scowl, all fierce and laser-sharp, no longer seemed the least bit mean to her. It was just Tom. "There should be a rule. No children should be allowed to have sex until they go off to college, so their parents can go on in the blissful and innocent delusion that nothing's happening and nothing ever will."

Ann let the ball bounce on the asphalt, heard that sharp and hollow ring when it hit, and caught it again when it came back up to her, debating.

None of your business.

But it felt like her business, Tom and Mer. She claimed them, even though she had no right to. And when they left at the end of the summer—oh, hell, she was going to miss them—at least she'd know that she tried to put things right between them.

"I'll play you for it."

"Play me?" His head came up, and he glanced back at the hoop. "In basketball?" There was as much shock in his voice as if she'd just suggested he go sashaying down Nicollet in a miniskirt, stilettos, and full makeup.

"Sure. Why not?"

His grin widened, a shit-eating, humor-the-silly-chick grin. He looked younger then, and full of himself, and she thought, *Hell, if I were nineteen and saw him in a bar in Chicago, he could have been in hock up to his eyeballs and I still would have jumped him. Cassie'd have to be crazy if the only thing she'd wanted from him was the money.*

"Well, I *have* seen you shoot . . ." she teased. "Okay, so you are a fair bit taller than me, and I'd be at a terrible disadvantage one-on-one. I suppose it'll have to be . . . What's that called? Horse?"

His grin widened, and her breath gave a little stutter step. Oh, shoot, she was really going to have to start watching herself with this one. Except for that one night he'd came knocking on her door—and she was still far too flattered by the fact that he'd come to her, right away and automatically, as if she was the first person who'd come to his mind—they never spent any time together that didn't include Mer. That'd been dangerous enough, reminding her what she was missing.

But she was missing this, too, attention from an attractive man. The thread of anticipation and uncertainty, the breathless wondering if he was feeling it, too.

There was a scary and dangerous part of her that wondered if it was so bad. It wasn't as if she was going to have *sex* with him, for heaven's sake. Not even go out with him. It wasn't a betrayal of her vows just to flirt a bit. What was the harm? Hadn't she earned some mild fun?

Except there was nothing at all mild about Tom Nash. And there *was* harm, because she didn't know how long just that would be enough.

"Knock yourself out." He stepped back, waving at the backboard. "Ladies first."

"Whoever said I was a lady?" She took off toward the basket, dribbling low and easy, the rhythm as steady and familiar as a heartbeat. She went to her left, laying it in as simply as snapping her fingers.

She turned, caught the ball in midbounce, and whipped it at him in one motion.

He had one brow raised, his head tilted. "Not bad."

"I used to play. A little."

"Hmm." He took off, kissed the ball off the backboard even though he barely left the ground.

"Nice," she said. Not the shot. The shot was elementary, one she could do when she was nine with her eyes closed. But there was no denying he looked damn fine doing it.

She didn't want to make it too obvious. What would be the fun in that? She didn't want it over too soon. Though she had to struggle not to laugh at the way his confidence deflated as his surprise grew. When he'd already had H-O-R she missed one shot, an easy one from about ten feet away, at what would have been the baseline if they had one.

He chased down the ball, then whirled to face her. "You missed that on purpose," he snarled at her.

She laughed at him. She couldn't help it. "Competitive much?"

He gave her another glare, as if that would force her to admit it, then paced off the distance. He made the shot—not easily, it almost rimmed out, but it went down.

He had the honors now, and she had to match his shots.

He banged the ball on the driveway, *bounce*, *bounce*, *bounce*, enough force behind it that she was afraid the ball was going to split open. He stared at the basket as if trying to read the fate of the world in it, then looked at her and nodded.

He took off, great big strides that ate up the space, and went up, just jamming the ball over the rim.

"That," she said, "was the damned *ugliest* dunk I've ever seen."

"Probably," he said smugly. "But I made it." He rolled the ball to her gently, as if he were rolling a toy to a baby. "Your turn." He tried to take a step and winced, grabbing at the back of his leg.

"That's not fair."

He shrugged. "First rule of horse. No rules on the shots." He continued to hobble toward her.

"You should probably ice that."

"Oh, no," he said, and tapped the ball she still held. "Your shot."

"I concede that one."

"Chicken?"

"*I* am not stupid enough to pull a hamstring just to show off."

"That implies you could do it," he said.

"No, I—" She scowled and shoved the ball so hard in his stomach he sucked in a breath. "Shoot."

He did, two more simple ones before he missed a long, arching shot that would have been about two feet beyond the three-point line.

She made it and left her hand up in the air after the shot, a pretty arch to her wrist, showboating like Reggie Miller on a roll.

"From the rosebushes," she said. "Nothing but net."

It was at the far end of her range, one she hit no more than one out of four times. She took her time setting it up, closing her eyes for a moment to visualize the ball swishing through, sweet as life.

It was a great shot, a beautiful arching rainbow she knew was good from the instant it left her hand, sending a surge of adrenaline and triumph up her spine. Didn't matter, she thought, if you were playing in front of a thousand people or in a backyard. It still felt damned fine.

She sneaked a glance at him. His jaw was hanging low until he caught her looking. He snapped it shut, game face snapping back into place. "Gimme the damn ball."

"Sure thing," she said cheerfully.

He missed it, of course. He'd never had much of a long-range shot. He didn't bother to watch it bounce off.

"Okay," he ordered her. "Spill."

"I was on a basketball scholarship my first two years," she said. "Division II, not Division I. But we were good, and I was all conference my sophomore year. Second highest scorer in the league."

"You hustled me."

"Yup," she agreed. "And don't turn that glower on me, Nash. It might have scared opposing batters, but you aren't throwing a ball at me, and I'm over it."

He tried to hold it, finally laughed instead. "I'm famous for that glare, you know."

"I know," she said, not without sympathy.

"Why is it," he asked, "that grown men cower in front of it—I used to send reporters skittering from the locker room routinely, without saying a word—and you and my daughter are completely unaffected?"

"We're better judges of character?" she suggested.

"Flattery will get you nowhere." The rising wind carried the smell of fresh-cut grass and ruffled his hair. He still had all of it, too. "Well, that's a complete lie, but still." He tilted his head, studying her as if he could read the past in her face. "Why'd you quit?"

"Wanted to be an architect. They didn't have a program at Mankato, so I transferred to the U." She picked up the ball because she needed something to do with her hands. "I know it's probably inconceivable for you that someone would give up their sport for school, but there you are."

"Not just for school," he said.

"No," she agreed. "Not just for school." Because she and John wanted to be together. Later, she'd been so glad of that, that they'd had those two extra years.

"Miss it?"

"Sure, I miss it sometimes. How could you not?" She still felt more at ease with the ball in her hands than not. She'd lived on her shot, because out there on the farm she'd had no one to play with, too far from the other houses to even bike over until she was a teenager. But there'd been a rusty hoop on the side of the garage, and as long as she was practicing, no one bothered her. "But it was the right decision. I love my job, I wanted to be with John, and I was ready to get on with my life."

"You were ready to get on with your life at what, nineteen, twenty?" He grimaced. "I don't know if I'm ready yet."

"So you're a late bloomer. Nothing wrong with that."

"You a forward?"

"Nope. Shooting guard."

"You're awfully tall for a guard."

"Which is exactly why everyone had such a hard time stopping me."

He watched her slide the ball from hand to hand, then sighed and glanced up at Mer's window. The light was still on, the night still. "So I have to let her go out, huh?"

"Yup," she said, "and if you think those pitiful eyes are gonna work on me, remember I have a dog, she's cuter than you, and I'm immune."

"Cuter than I am?" He sighed. "Do I have to let her go out with Tyrone?"

"No, but she'll do it anyway." He had to know his daughter at least that well. She wasn't the kind to meekly accept. Ann wished she'd had a little more of that in her at that age. "Honestly, it won't be nearly as much fun if they don't have to sneak around. I'm bettin' it'll wear off pretty quickly."

He brightened. "You promise?"

"Nope. I never promise where young love is concerned. It's too tricky."

He slapped at a mosquito on his arm, harder than he needed to, and scowled. "Okay, fine. I'll let her go out with Tyrone. On one condition."

"What's that?"

"You have to come hold my hand when I do it."

TWENTY-THREE

He was kidding. Of course he was kidding. So she'd believed.

It turned out she didn't have to hold his hand. But she had to give him booze, and chocolate chip cookies, and finally—her secret weapon—a giant platter of superspicy nachos.

"Okay," Ann said, as he stared out the front window of his house a good ten minutes after Mer had left. "You did it."

"Yeah." He had his arms crossed across his chest—the better to keep them from grabbing Tyrone—and his gaze fixed where Tyrone's beat-up old jeep had disappeared around the corner.

Forget worrying about her and Tyrone and what they might do. He'd moved on to sheer terror when he'd gotten a gander at Tyrone's car, which was a death trap if he'd ever seen one. It looked like it was going to shed pieces all the way down the highway as soon as Tyrone cranked it over forty miles an hour.

"You gonna stand there all night?" Ann asked him.

"Pretty much the plan."

"Is that gonna help?"

"Nope."

"You want . . . dessert? A drink?"

He didn't answer, just glowered as if, if he stared hard enough, he could watch them the whole time, no matter how far away they got. Parental superspy abilities.

That'd be cool. Or horrible, depending upon which side you were on.

"I should have bugged the car," he said. "Or put on one of those electronic trackers."

"I knew you would be bad, but I didn't think you'd be *this* bad," she said. "I swear, I could strip naked and dance a jig, and you wouldn't even notice."

His head swung around, and his gaze settled on her with the same intensity with which he'd watched his daughter leave. "That, I'd notice."

Oops. She knew better than to head down that road.

She'd never been the kind of woman drawn to the dark side. John had been the sunniest person she had ever known. His mother claimed he'd been born smiling.

She'd never been one to risk, either, someone who danced along the edge of convention, daring life to suck her over. She left that for her mother.

But somehow she couldn't help it where Tom was concerned. Things she knew better than to say popped out of her mouth before she thought about them. Mostly because it had been so damn long since anyone had looked at her like that, and she was afraid that pretty soon it would be too late.

"I should go," she said. Running back to safety, running back home.

"You made me do this," he said. "You can't leave me alone."

"You'll be fine."

"I will not. I'll be miserable."

"Be good for you. For your character. Teach you . . . something."

"How did your father ever do this? How'd he ever let you go out on a date?"

"He wasn't there."

He just waited, one brow raised. She sighed. "Bruce . . . travels. Showed up for my high school graduation but missed my wedding."

"Idiot."

"Yeah, well, my parents aren't exactly conventional." She laughed at his surprise. "Yeah, I know, how'd they have me? My mother asks herself regularly how she managed to raise such a boring daughter."

"You're not boring," he said, sounding like he meant it.

It would be so easy to fall into it. Into believing that there could be something between them. Even indulging in it, in fantasy. Enjoying the possibilities, even though there could never be anything more, because even a possibility was far more than she'd had in a very, very long time.

"I should go," she repeated.

"You can't. I'll just sit here all night, imagining. It would be cruel."

"So it's my job to distract you?"

"Hey, I wouldn't have to go through this if it weren't for you."

"Nice to see that you take full responsibility for your own actions."

"You know what they say about us pro athletes. Permanent adolescents."

"Oh, *that's* what they say. I heard something else."

"Lies. All lies."

Funny, how you get a picture of someone famous. From an article here and there, a press conference, the way they conduct themselves during a game. She'd pegged him as intense, competitive, moody, but basically decent. Sexy, in that mysterious way that somehow always seemed to work, even though every woman over the age of sixteen knew better.

She hadn't expected the charm, though. And she'd never, ever suspected she'd be so susceptible to it.

"Cleo needs to be let out."

"Bring her over. God knows she has better manners than

Coop. Maybe, if I'm really lucky, you'll get confused and take the wrong one home."

Shoulds. Shoulds were annoying things, nagging at the back of your brain, bumping away the *wants.*

"I can't."

"We can watch a movie. Pull out the tequila I've got hidden away in my jock drawer. And when I've drunk myself into a stupor so I can forget that my daughter's off with Mr. I'm-a-Stud-and-Know-It, you can tuck me into bed."

The image flashed, hot and compelling. She shook her head. "I'm sorry. It's late, and I—"

"Okay, let's just stop dancing around this." He stepped in her direction, closing the space between them, and she wasn't smart enough to move back. "I'm attracted to you. So what? I know nothing can happen between us. *Understand* that nothing can happen."

She tried to listen to what he said, she really did. But her brain just kept circling back to that one sentence and ignoring the rest. *I'm attracted to you. I'm attracted to you.* She vacillated between shock and pleasure, a stunned *oh-my-God* excitement like the school wallflower who'd just gotten asked to the prom by the biggest man on campus, the one who made her giggle just by passing her in the hall.

She was almost forty, and it was disconcerting to suddenly discover she hadn't grown out of such foolishness at all.

"I might not like it," he went on. "In fact, I pretty much hate it. But I understand it."

"Wait." She threw up a hand. "Stop. Go back. Start over."

"Which part didn't you get?"

"Pretty much everything after the 'I'm attracted to you' part."

"That can't have been a surprise to you."

"Oh, yeah." Breathe, she reminded herself. Breathing was always good. "It was a surprise."

"And here I was all impressed by how perceptive you are," he said. "Look, I know that it's inconvenient. And pointless. Can't seem to help it. But is that any reason we can't—" He seemed stuck on the right term. "Hang out?"

"Hang out?"

"That wasn't a euphemism."

Too bad. "Euphemism. Big word there, Nash."

"Yeah, aren't you proud of me? I know a few. Antidisestablishmentarianism, even." Maybe they'd had this conversation in her dreams. But not in real life, never in real life; she was completely unprepared. And completely flattered. "I just don't see why the fact that I think you're the hottest thing this side of Heidi Klum should get in the way of us being friends. It'd be unfair for you to hold my urges against me. They're not my fault."

It seemed like it had to be a bad idea, them "hanging out." She just couldn't figure out why. "Heidi Klum? You like Heidi Klum?"

"Who doesn't?"

"Seems awfully cliché," she said. "Blondes and boobs. Couldn't at least one of you guys show a little more creativity?"

"Hey, we're simple creatures."

"Yeah. Sometimes I forget."

"But well-meaning," he added.

Okay, she thought. Two options. Go home, curl up with her dog. Cook, read, cycle through the channels looking for something decent to watch. A night like every other damn night since she was twenty-seven, a night like all the ones that stretched ahead of her, one dull and tarnished bead after another on a plain string.

Or she could stay here. With him. Her friend.

"Okay," she said. "We can try it."

"I promise I'll be good."

Too bad, the wicked, dangerous part of her piped up. The part her mother had somehow managed to plant, a part that she'd never managed to stamp out completely despite her best efforts.

"I've got some cupcakes at home," she said. "Mexican chocolate, a little bit of cinnamon. I'll go get them and the dog. Then I'll be right back."

"Bless you."

TWENTY-FOUR

"So," her mother said. "You sleep with him yet?"

"Nope." Ann was in her kitchen, refilling a platter, while Judy gazed out the window at the party in the backyard.

The day was cool for late June, but clear, with enough of a breeze to keep the bugs away. The yard was in full bloom, the dogs were behaving, and nearly everybody who was invited not only came but brought food.

"You didn't even ask who?"

"First off, it doesn't matter." She stepped back and considered her work. Lemon bars, snickerdoodles, three kinds of brownies, gooey caramel-cashew bars that were the one recipe passed on from her mother that she'd actually kept. They violated most of the rules of health and ethics, Judy said, but they were just too good to give up. "Since I haven't slept with anybody, the answer applies no matter who you meant."

A few berries tucked here and there, a fresh green sprig of mint to set off the near-black brownies. That'd look good. "And second," she went on, "I know who you're talking about."

"Aha! You did notice how yummy he is."

"You want to take this out for me?" She slid the tray aside and turned to the bowls of sauces. She'd grilled meat in advance, pork tenderloin, chicken breast, beef, and put out a sandwich bar. Simple, made better by the not-so-simple fixes: six kinds of cheese, caramelized onions, and a whole array of sauces: spicy peanut, creamy gorgonzola, chipotle-spiked ketchup, a boozy barbecue sauce, and a smooth red pepper/goat cheese puree.

"Nope." Her mother snagged a bite of brownie, chewed while she watched her daughter.

"You're no help," she complained.

"I'm trying," Judy said. "But my idea of help and yours isn't the same."

"Isn't that the truth?" Ann mumbled beneath her breath.

The sauces were ready, in little crockery bowls in a mix of crayon-bright colors.

"Okay." She turned to her mother, debating. Fight or flee? Either way, her mother wasn't going to leave it alone. "I'll say it once, and it's done. I know he's gorgeous and sexy. I'm not blind. I know he's—"

"Hey!" Tom poked his head in the door, a Twins cap backward on his head, a pair of aviators shielding his eyes, his dark polo shirt open at the collar. "Can I help?"

"See what a nice boy he is?" Judy asked.

"He's not nice. He's hungry."

Tom grinned. "See how well she knows me? Out of that salsa. Damn good stuff."

She whirled to the fridge, grabbed the jar that held the salsa she'd made that morning. "Here you go."

"You put enough jalapeño in there?"

"I put enough jalapeño in there. Now, shoo."

"You're an angel."

"You're getting fed whether you suck up or not, Nash."

"Some things you should never take chances with."

He backed out, the screen door closing behind him with an emphatic bang.

She turned to find her mother grinning at her, looking far too pleased with herself, and realized she herself was smiling. Too much, though; too broad. She let it fade.

"Okay, then." She mentally ran through her lists and turned for the fridge. "We should—"

"He likes you."

"Did you see if there are enough rolls out there?"

"Annie."

She knew that tone. There was no way she was getting out of the kitchen without either giving in to her mother or yelling at her.

"Fine." She blew out a breath. "Fine, he likes me. I'm likable."

"Not that kind of like, Annie." Her voice gentled, with a wisp of sadness underneath that caught Ann by surprise and settled her anger. "He's attracted to you."

"Yeah, well." She shrugged, felt a flush start to head up from her neck to her cheeks. "He's a healthy adult male. He's probably attracted to three-quarters of the females in the world."

"Not that kind of like, either." She smoothed her hand over Ann's head, tucking away a curl that was going wild. "Something a little more than that, sweetheart."

Oh, damn it. She didn't want to know that, even if, way down deep, she hoped it was true. Because it was pointless, and it only made it harder.

"You've been through a lot," Judy went on softly. "You deserve to have something nice for yourself."

"I'm not sure what deserve has got to do with anything," she said. "I didn't deserve what happened, Mary and Martin didn't deserve what happened, and John sure as hell didn't deserve what happened." The heat behind it surprised her, the way her voice cracked on the last word. She'd gotten control of it so long ago, and she didn't understand why it was suddenly getting harder, instead of getting easier.

She handed her mother a big bowl of fruit salad, balanced the tray of sauces herself. "Let's get this stuff out there before the hordes start drooling."

"Annie—"

"Mom. Please." And for once, thankfully, her mother let it go.

⁓

"I'd like you to meet someone, Ann."

"Sure. In a minute." She put down a bowl of pita chips next to her homemade hummus and appraised the table. It'd hold the ravaging swarm for another fifteen minutes, she judged. Who would have thought that every single person she'd invited would have showed? And that they were all bleepin' starving?

"Okay." She turned and linked her arm through Mike's. "You know you're my favorite client, don't you, Dr. Mike?"

"I bet you say that to all the boys."

"Nope. Only you." Mike Roberts did transplants, bone and stem cells and cord blood, on kids at the U. It was, Ann thought, the hardest job she could think of. And yet he was the kindest man she'd ever met, his smile always there, gentle and open and hopeful for all that he saw terrible things every day. "And Eric, of course."

"You just like him because he's pretty."

"And you don't?" she asked as they crossed the yard.

His partner, Eric Ruiz, was without a doubt the best-looking man she'd ever seen in real life. He owned a bookstore, a funky little place where he made, he'd told her, no money whatsoever, and had turned the gardens around their classic South Minneapolis bungalow into a miniature paradise.

Eric hovered over a very, very pregnant woman in a lawn chair, who looked ready to pop at any moment, even though she wasn't due for another three months.

"Yeah, I know," he said. "Sometimes I wake up in the morning and look at him and think, okay, there's gotta be a catch. Somebody who looks like that has just got to be a horrible person. Except it's Eric."

"Oh, he's horrible, for sure. You know it. All that good nature and humor and kindness . . . It must be a terrible burden to live with."

"That's what I love about you, Ann. You're so understanding." Now that they were closer, she could see the resemblance between Eric and the woman sitting near him, the same regal cheekbones and dramatic coloring and warm eyes. "I'm going to have to buy another house when we're done with this one," Mike went on, "just so I can keep you around."

"You let me babysit, Mike, and I'll be around."

"Oh, Lord. Don't say that unless you mean it." He bent down, gave the woman a quick kiss on her cheek. "And this is Marie. Eric's sister."

"I've heard so much about you," Marie said. She put her hands on the armchair, as if ready to push herself up from it but Ann rushed to forestall her.

"Oh, no, don't get up."

She sighed and sat back. "Despite what my brother thinks, I am *not* going to go into labor if I so much as walk around the yard."

"We're not taking any chances," Eric said fondly.

She waved his words away. "You're doing a beautiful job on their house," she said to Ann.

"It's a lovely house, and they're great to work with. Good vision, good taste."

"Please," she said. "This one's got enough ego as it is. No need to blow it up any further."

"And they don't skimp on the budget when the materials are worth it."

"And there's the truth of it. You just like us for our copper downspouts and our Italian tile."

"You've found me out."

"It's worth it," Mike said softly. "That house is going to hold precious cargo."

"Would you listen to him? You'd think he'd be beyond romantic notions of children, considering they throw up on him regularly." Her smile was as lovely as her brother's. "You make those cookies?"

"Which ones?"

"The ones with the white chocolate and the dried cherries."

"Yes, I made those."

"You give me the recipe," she said, "and I'll have *your* baby, too."

Ann laughed. "I'll go get it."

"No, I'm coming." Marie struggled up from the chair, her belly looking the size of a Volkswagon beneath her sunny yellow dress. "If I sit here any longer, my ass's gonna leave a permanent imprint in the chair, and I don't want to see that. Besides, I have to pee. Again."

She waddled beside Ann, people parting in front of them like the Red Sea before Moses, their anxious eyes drawn to her belly like people are drawn to an accident, unable to look away.

"You sure cut a wide swath, don't you?"

"They're all afraid I'm going to pop right in front of 'em. Spew babies out in all directions and they're going to have to catch one." She put her hand to her back, wincing. "I think I'm going to keep the maternity clothes afterward and walk around with a half dozen pillows stuffed underneath. So I can get the special treatment, but without somebody kicking my bladder this time."

Ann held Marie's elbow as they made their way up the stairs, gripping tighter as Marie swayed.

She wasn't used to pregnant women. Or babies, for that matter. She and John had both been only children, and nobody'd asked her to babysit, not her, that strange Judy Baranski's daughter. Marie unsettled her, made her both terrified and fascinated.

"It's a good thing," Ann said, once she'd gotten her safely settled on a chair in the kitchen. "What you're doing for your brother."

"Oh, well, he begged. And I wanted a niece or nephew." She rested her hand on her belly, splaying her legs to give it enough room. "Wasn't planning on getting both in one swoop, but hey, as long as we're doing it." She shrugged.

Ann pulled out a cookbook and a piece of paper, bent over to the counter to scribble out the recipe. "You all know what they are?"

"Didn't they tell you? Found out this week. Eric wanted to know, but Mike didn't. Well, you know who always wins things like that. Two girls, one boy."

"That's wonderful." So why did it hurt, a quick little razor squeeze around her heart?

"Do you . . . ?" Ann shook her head. It was none of her business.

"Worry about giving them up?" Marie shook her head. "Not really. I've got two of my own already, you know. I know that's why they insisted on using Nita's—that's our other sister—eggs, instead of mine. So I wouldn't feel as much like the babies were mine." She smoothed her hand over the mountain of her belly. "But I never have. I thought about it a lot, before I offered. They're Eric's babies, his and Mike's. And it's not like I'm not going to be able to see them. I must get extraspecial auntie points for this, don't you think? I have to be the favorite." She grinned. "And Eric is going to owe me for frickin' *ever*."

Could she have done it? Ann didn't know. She supposed you didn't know until you were faced with the situation.

But that was true of a lot of things. You could think all you wanted, but you were never sure how you were going to react until you were right in the middle of it. "Here you go. All done." She handed Marie the slip of paper. "Gotta get good white chocolate, though. None of those chips. Chop it up yourself. And real butter. That's the key."

"Got it." She tucked the recipe in her purse, a sleek billfold of embossed brown leather, and pushed herself to her feet. "Oh, shit. I really do have to go. Where's your bathroom?"

"Down the hall, to the left."

Marie had just waddled down the hall, out of sight, when Mike burst through the door.

"Where is she? She okay?"

"She's fine. In the bathroom."

"Yeah, she does that a lot." He ran his hand through his hair, ginger with a thick frost of gray.

"Not that I know about such things, Mike, but you're kinda panicky. For an all-grown-up, important doctor and all."

"I know." His smile was rueful. "I can't help it. I just . . . never thought we'd get here, you know?"

"I know." Ann had ended up a lot of places she never thought she'd be. "Do you mind if I ask you a question?"

"Sure, I'll marry you. Eric won't mind." His face registered mock shock. "What, that wasn't the question?"

"No. But now that I know it's an option . . ." He was almost homely, pale skin and a nose that veered to the right, plain brown eyes. But you didn't talk to him for more than thirty seconds before that disappeared completely. "No. It's just . . . what you do all day. The things you see. How can you . . ." She didn't know how to put it into words. All the ones that covered it sounded too awful to say out loud. *How do you watch children die, and have one of your own, and not go crazy with it?*

"What I do every day, that's *why* I'm doing it," he said gently. "I'm not going to say it's not going to make me crazy. Of course it will. But that comes with the kids, doesn't it, no matter what a parent does? The insane worry? But I need to see the other side of it. I need to remember that some kids, *most* kids, make it through just fine."

"Yeah." She wasn't sure she could. She hadn't thought twice about it, back in the days when she and John had planned children. But now that she knew how easily it could change, how quickly "okay" could disappear, she wasn't sure. "I suppose."

"You could, too, you know." He poked beneath the foil on one of the pans on the counter, dug out a corner of a caramel bar. "Have a kid. You'd be good at it."

"You think?" It warmed her that he thought so. He saw parents all the time, at the worst and best times of their life. If anyone knew what made a parent, he did. "Yeah, 'cause you all make it look so easy."

"Well, you have one advantage we didn't: a uterus."

"There is that. Though I don't know if it's in working order."

"Easy enough to find out." He grinned as he gave up his bit-by-bit strategy with the bars and pulled out a chunk the size of a fist. "You ever think of adopting? We thought of it before we decided to do this."

She shook her head. "No. I'm married. We're required to adopt as a couple. And that's . . . That's just not going to happen. I checked into it. There's no way I'd get approval, not given the situation."

"You checked?" His eyebrows climbed high. "You didn't tell me that you'd checked."

She nodded, her eyes blurring. "Three years ago. I thought . . . It doesn't matter what I thought." Oh, *shit*. She'd locked it away, in a shiny little hope chest, never to be opened. Couldn't be opened, because it hurt too much.

His eyes were warm, sympathetic. She knew he was a brilliant doctor. But this would be the part that his patients, and their parents, clung on to the most. That look in his eyes that said he understood, and he *felt*.

"It doesn't have to be that complicated," he told her. "All you need are a few healthy swimmers."

"Somehow I think it's just a titch more complicated than that."

"Only if you make it so." They heard the slap-slap of Marie's sandals as she came back down the hall. Mike turned to her immediately, his face lighting up as if everything good in the world was contained in that one woman. And maybe it was.

"There," she said. "That should hold me. For twenty minutes, at least."

"You want me to put a sign on one of the bathrooms? Reserve it for your private use? Pregnant women only. Wouldn't want you to have to wait."

"You're gonna be sorry you teased me when I take you up on it."

Mike tucked her arm through his, reached out a hand for Ann. "You coming?"

"In a minute," she said. "I think we could use some more ice."

"See you then."

She made her way down to the basement. It was dark, and cool, and musty smelling no matter what she did. The rest of the house betrayed little evidence that it was nearing ninety, but down here the old girl showed her age.

Ann went to the big chest freezer and tugged the top open. Cold air curled out, and her vision blurred.

Doesn't have to be that complicated.

Not true. Oh, not true.

But she couldn't help wishing it was.

TWENTY-FIVE

Yeah, Mer was having fun now. So much fun she might just shoot herself before it was over, just to make the day complete.

She'd helped Ann with the food all week long. That had been okay. Ann had asked and thanked her like a billion times when all she'd done was cook, and hell, she liked that.

The food was good, if she did say so herself. Oh, mostly she just followed directions. But she'd tried one thing herself, a surprise for Ann, a cake that she'd seen on the cover of a magazine the last time she'd gone to Target. It had taken her one whole evening to make, layers and layers of cake she'd made with real vanilla beans, all spread with a lemon cream she'd made herself and decorated with little purple violets made of sugar.

The kitchen had looked like the baking aisle of Cub had exploded by the time she was done. But it sure was pretty, and it was the first thing Ann had eaten when she'd stopped feeding everyone else and sat down for two seconds herself.

She'd even asked for the recipe. At first Mer figured she was just being nice, but she'd taken a sliver herself, just to make sure, and it *was* really good. Not quite as good as Ann's brownies, but close.

But the party—honestly, calling it a party was stretching

it. When did you forget how to party? By twenty, twenty-five? When you got married? When you moved to the suburbs? For sure as hell, these people had forgotten.

Anyway, that was the high point, and from there it had gone downhill fast.

Oh, there were girls her age, three of them. She knew damn well Ann had invited them for her sake. But crap, didn't she know her better than that? She was no more likely to be friends with them than with George Bush.

The girls had probably known each other forever, moving in a tight little knot as if they'd keel over if they didn't occupy the same airspace. They even looked the same. Same cute minis and wedge sandals, same loose baby-doll tops that showed off their shoulders. Different hair colors—two blond, one brown with red highlights that must have cost a hundred and fifty bucks—but interchangeable haircuts, sleek below their shoulders, thick side-swept bangs that swung by their cheekbones.

They kept sneaking glances at her, then turning away with those superior smiles before anybody caught them looking.

Yeah, she knew what girls like that thought about girls like her.

She didn't care. Would have walked right over to them and given them something to talk about, if it weren't for her dad, who kept glancing her way, then theirs, with that stupid hopeful look on his face. Wanted her to make *friends*, nice, normal friends. Shallow twits who didn't know any better, had no idea what life was like outside their shiny little world. Oh, yeah, they'd have *tons* in common.

So she escaped. Dragged a lawn chair around the back of the garage and dug out her last pack of smokes. Dad was making it harder and harder to get more, hard enough that it wouldn't be worth the trouble, except that it ticked him off so much.

She tapped out a cigarette, lit it up, and took a good drag. The plastic straps of the lawn chair were going to leave a criss-cross on the back of her thighs like grill marks on a chicken breast. They were getting sticky in the heat, and the metal frame dug into the back of her knees. Still, she tipped back, staring at the sky through the screen of the leaves above.

Only a couple more months. Then she could go back to Chicago. Maybe sooner, if Tom got tired of playing daddy. If he figured he'd done his duty and could send her on his way with a clean conscience, then she could go home.

She waited to feel something about it. Relief, excitement.

Nothing. Everything was all scooped out inside her.

Yeah, okay, going home meant moving back in with Cassie. But at least she left her pretty much alone, let her go out with her friends without interrogating her when she came home.

She let the smoke spiral up, through the leaves.

But so what if she could go out? She'd been getting tired of it, anyway. Same people, same parties, same music.

She leaned back, kicking her feet out in front of her. The hubbub of the party burbled around the edge of the garage. Jeez, those people could talk, happy light conversations about kids and jobs and summer vacations. Pretending they knew each other, when none of it meant a damn thing.

She wondered what they were all like underneath. If any of them were half as happy as they pretended to be. Were they all as mixed up inside as she was, and she was the only one with the guts to let the darkness show? Or maybe they weren't dark. Maybe there was just nothing there, bright shiny shells that were empty inside.

She was almost sorry she hadn't invited Tyrone. Ann had given her permission to invite him or anyone else she wanted. Like she knew anybody else in Minneapolis.

But she and Tyrone were just about done. They both knew it, just hadn't made the effort to finish it off yet. He was playing night and day, getting ready for the upcoming tournaments, and he didn't have much time to hang out with her. Truth was the novelty of screwing the coach's daughter had worn off, and if she had anything else to do she wouldn't be bothering with him, either.

"Oh, hello." It was Ann's mom. Ann had introduced her to Mer a couple of hours ago, when she'd shown up bearing a basket of cheese and lettuce and eggs.

Hard to believe this was Ann's mom. Mer knew hardly anybody ever pegged her as Cassie's daughter, but this was even further off. The woman had some sort of sari fabric wrapped around her waist, a faded old T-shirt above it, and ancient Birkenstocks on her feet—talk about a cliché—and she waved her hands around when she talked, which seemed like pretty much all the time. And she always had this half smile on her face. Mer figured maybe she was on something.

Well, Ann had said her mom was a hippie. Mer thought it went a few steps beyond that, heading into downright weird.

"Another outcast, I see." She glanced around her, selected a nice patch of grass, and started to sit down.

"Ms. Baranski—"

"Oh, Judy, please."

"Judy, then." She stood up and gestured toward the lawn chair. She wasn't naturally polite. She just didn't want to have to be the one to help Ann's mom get back up off the ground. "You can take my chair."

"Oh, darling, that's so sweet." She tugged one foot up to her other knee, and crossed the other leg in front of it, yoga style. "But that rickety plastic thing? I don't think so. Besides, the human body was designed to sit on the ground. And, like all things, if you don't use it enough, you start to lose the ability."

Mer shrugged. If the old lady wanted to sit on the ground like a swami, it was no skin off her nose. She'd tried.

Her smoke was almost done. She watched the ash burn low, weighed how much she wanted another one versus how much work she'd have to go through to get another pack when this one was gone. She caught Judy staring at her, still with that weird half smile, and waited for the lecture, the it's-so-bad-for-your-health spiel. Like she'd didn't know that already, and they were going to tell her some new information that would cure her of her awful habit. Sheesh.

She'd quit if she wanted to. But worry about what was going to happen in forty years? Forget it. Odds were she wasn't going to make forty years anyway. Wasn't even sure she wanted to.

But Judy just dug in her potato sack of a purse and came up with a pack of Camels. She kept matches in a little wooden box, and she scratched one on the bottom of her shoe to light it up.

"Ahh." She put both hands on her knees, the cigarette tucked between the fingers of the right one. Any minute, Mer thought, the woman was gonna start oohhmming. Or set her skirt on fire. "So, my dear, why are you hiding out here?"

Mer lifted one brow. She'd figured that was pretty obvious. But she didn't want to admit she was hiding out to smoke. If she was going to do it, she should be brave enough to do it right out there, daring her father to say something. Anything else seemed kinda juvenile.

But sometimes it just wasn't worth the trouble.

"You smoke?" she asked instead. "I thought you were, I don't know, sort of a health food freak or something."

"I try to be," she said. "I could give you a long and quite well-argued spiel about how tobacco is a natural product, and smoking it is an activity of spiritual significance in many Native American communities." She took a drag, held in the smoke, and blew it out in a slow, wavering stream. "But the truth is, I started when I was kid, and I've never been able to break the habit. It's very weak of me, of course. But self-discipline has really never been my strong point."

"Uh-huh." What the hell was she supposed to say to that? She dropped her butt into the dirt, moved to step on it with her boots.

"Oh, heavens, don't do that!" Judy plunged into her bag again, came out with what looked like an old baby food jar with a metal lid. She screwed the top off, then plucked the still-glowing butt off the ground with two fingers and dropped it in the jar.

"I might not be able to break the habit," she said. "Wish to high heavens I'd done it when I was young and strong. But I can make certain I don't leave remnants of my weakness behind in my wake."

"Uh, yeah. Sure." Whatever. Mer didn't want to argue with this one.

She went back into her bag, coming out this time with a tin of rock-shaped chunks the color of tea. "I make these myself. Honey and mint. Freshen your breath."

That bag looked like something that belonged to Mary Poppins. Mer half expected her to pull out a hall tree next time. "What else you got in there?"

Judy's smile broadened. "Oh, no. My daughter would never forgive me if I told you."

That perked her interest. "Yeah?" She tried to imagine it. What could an old lady like that be carting around?

She popped the lozenge into her mouth, gagged when the taste hit her tongue. Jesus. Honey? It tasted like something that had come out of the rear end of a rat. She wondered just how long it had been rolling around in the bottom of Judy's bag, picking up lint and crumbs and who knew what else.

Judy's lids started drifting down, her smile turning woozy. The exact same expression that Mer's friend, Katie, whose boyfriend Mack was a drummer in a band, got when she was tripping on some good stuff.

Mer decided to let the old lady do her thing. She leaned back in the chair, trying to get into the spirit of the thing. Except she was never good at relaxing, at doing nothing. It made things go all tight within her, cranking up and up, screeching like a swing chain did when you twisted it around and around, tight as you could, before letting it go to spin so fast it nearly made you sick.

Shit, she thought. Her dad wasn't going to have to ship her back to Chicago. He was going to have to find an asylum for her, 'cause she was about two steps shy of snapping.

"Judy?" she asked, just because she had to do something to shake things up. "You know where I can get some weed?"

She figured that the lady was either going to freak or give her some. She gave it even odds.

Judy opened one eye, aiming it on her like a laser sight, green and fiery. "Yes," she said.

"Well?"

She waited, but the lady didn't say anything else.

"Well?" Mer said at last. "Are you going to tell me?"

"No."

"Well, why not? You're not going to tell me it's evil, or bad for me, or makes me go blind or something?"

"No, that's masturbation," she said placidly. "And we didn't believe those warnings in my day, either—obviously—so I wouldn't be silly enough to try them on you. No, that's not it." She crushed out her cigarette on the inside of the baby food lid, then dropped it in the jar and screwed the lid on tight. "But here's the thing. I love my daughter. And my daughter likes you."

"So?"

"So it would make her unhappy. And I'm far more interested in *not* making her unhappy than I am in making you happy."

Yeah, she knew Ann liked her. She'd been really nice to her. But she knew, too, that it probably was because Ann had nobody else. If she had a bunch of rug rats of her own, if her husband was still—alive, awake, whatever you called it—she would for damn sure not be spending all her time with Mer, and Mer knew it.

"I'm going to tell you a secret," Judy went on. "It's not nearly as much fun as you think it is."

"Yeah, right." Just her luck. Ann's mom was going all belatedly suburban just when Mer needed her not to be.

"It isn't. The brain is a powerful thing, dear. Mostly it's fun because you're determined it will be."

Sure, Mer was buying that line when she knew damn well Judy had had plenty of "fun" along the way. "Well, isn't that for me to find out? Never thought that you'd be the hypocritical type."

"Nothing hypocritical about it," she said. "I'm not pretending. I'm not lying. I'm simply acknowledging that Ann wouldn't like if I assisted you. And that's good enough for me." She rose to her feet, as quick as a cat. Must be something to that whole sitting on the floor to keep things working after all. "It was nice to meet you, my dear," she said, and she sounded as if she meant it.

TWENTY-SIX

Ashia had brought her daughters, three and seven, who'd spent the last hour rolling around in the dirt with the dogs.

"The puppies'll be born in three weeks or so," Ann told her.

Ashia sent her a dark, ferocious look. "You're killing me, Ann."

"Just a suggestion," Ann said, smiling. She realized it was the first time that she'd ever seen Ashia outside of Cedar Ridge. Kind of silly, when you thought about it, given how long they'd known each other, how much she liked her. She'd just never really thought of it before.

"Okay, now stop that, Liberty!" Ashia shouted at the three-year-old, who had a good grip on Cooper's collar and was trying valiantly to swing her leg over the dog's back.

The girl giggled, tipped over, and got up, ready to try again, studiously ignoring her mother.

"You," Ashia told Ann, "are not to mention to either one of them that there *are* going to be puppies, or I will pay Mr. Mac-Evoy to flash you. I swear I will."

"Oh, now that's just cruel."

Liberty'd found her balance, but Cooper just plopped his butt down, and she slid right off into the dirt. That was the good thing about Coop; he wasn't half as smart as Cleo, but nobody could say he wasn't good-natured. Ann thought Liberty's shirt had started out pale yellow, but it was hard to tell now; it was so smeared with brown and gray that it blended into Coop's coat. "Besides, I already told them."

"I hate you."

"I'll bring raspberry muffins tomorrow," she said.

"Okay, I love you again." And then, "Liberty, *no*," she yelled, and went to grab her daughter, who was now inspecting the dog's molars, one chubby hand yanking Cooper's black upper lip skyward while her other fingers poked in the back of his mouth.

Laughing, Ann took in her yard. At last it looked as she'd imagined it when they'd bought the house. Filled with friends, laughing kids, animals. Bright flowers wrapping around the base of the house, the table she'd set up on the patio jammed with good food.

Martin had appointed himself bartender, and he moved easily through the crowd, handing out bottled beer, glasses of sangria with orange slices hanging on their rims. There was a root beer keg at the end of the table, next to a carton of ice cream in a bucket of ice.

John would have loved it. He'd be everywhere, introducing her neighbors to his work friends, his mother to their clients. He was far more outgoing than she was. They'd been a good team that way.

But she was doing okay, anyway. Nobody was sitting alone, everybody was smiling. John would have been proud of her.

"Can I get you all anything?" She'd circled a group of chairs on the lawn, underneath the big old maple. Mary was there with her knitting bag at her side, next to Marie, who Eric had finally planted in a chair. He'd threatened to reveal what she used to stuff her bra at her quinceañera if she didn't stay put in the shade.

Mao was there, too, steadily working her way through a plate of food and chatting with Mrs. Kozlowski, who'd pulled out her best capris for the occasion, neon green and embroidered with pink and purple butterflies.

"Don't be silly," Mao said, patting the empty chair next to her. "We're all quite capable of fetching for ourselves. Except Marie, of course, but Eric and Mike ask her, oh, about every thirty seconds, so I think we've got that covered."

Ann took a quick, assessing glance around the yard and decided it wouldn't hurt to sit.

Mao Xiong was two years out of the university, the first person on either side of her huge family to graduate from college. She had one more year, and one more set of boards to pass, before she was a full-fledged architect. Ann intended to offer her a partnership.

It would change things, she thought. Wouldn't be her and John's firm anymore, and it gave her a little pang to think of it. They'd started planning it when they were sixteen, and it was hard to let go of it. But Mao was simply too talented to lose, and she couldn't pay her what a bigger place could. A partnership was the only way Ann could think of to keep her.

"Thank you for bringing the papaya salad," she said. "It's delicious."

"I'll bring you the recipe on Monday," Mao said. She claimed to be five feet tall, but she was lying by at least an inch and a half. But she made up for it in personality. "I was just telling Lorraine what a beautiful job she's done with your gardens."

"What?"

Lorraine was suddenly fascinated by her plate, her doughy cheeks flushing.

"I'm sorry." Mao winced. "Was I not supposed to . . . Didn't you know?"

"Know what?"

"Oh. Well." She shot an apologetic look at Mrs. Kozlowski. "I stopped by Tuesday afternoon. You remember, I dropped the

Winston plans off on my way from the job site, because I was headed to the dentist rather than back to the office?"

"Yes. I remember." They'd been in the front door when she'd gotten home. Brilliant work, too; it was a warm and modest cottage, and the clients had decided at the last minute they'd wanted to work in a more contemporary edge than the original plans had called for. Mao's tweaks, opening up the living room in such a way to give it an airy feeling without overwhelming the rest of the house, had been perfect.

"I met Lorraine then," she said. "She was working on the bed right beside the front stairs. I thought for sure you knew."

The flowers. She'd been so pleased with them this year. The petunias had spread like crazy, blooming so thick and brilliant purple they almost looked fake. The hollyhocks were tall, a delicate blue against the base of the house, and even the impatiens were thriving.

"Lorraine? Have you been taking care of my garden?"

Mrs. Kozlowski pursed her lips tight, as if someone had popped a segment of lemon inside.

"I'm sorry," Mao said again. "I thought you knew. I mean, I figured that *you* hadn't done it."

Of course she hadn't done it. She'd gone through a bonsai, a ficus, a fern, a jade plant, and a cactus in the first year that Mao had worked for her before she'd finally given up, and she had to replace the rosemary in her kitchen window at least every two months.

"Lorraine?" Ann asked.

"Well," she clipped out. "I just couldn't watch those poor things shrivel up one more year."

"Oh." Of course.

Her yard was beautiful. Every day when she came home from work and saw it, it made her smile.

So she decided to put away the disappointment that she hadn't pulled it off herself and just be grateful.

"Thank you so very much," she said. "It's absolutely gorgeous. I love it."

"You do? Oh, well." She waved a hand, flustered as if some young man had just come up and planted a good one on her. "Well, that's fine then. I mean, I enjoy it. No problem."

"Are you going to quit?" Ann asked. "I mean, I can't ask you to continue. It's a terrible imposition. But—" She imagined all those flowers withering away, dying off one by one.

Lorraine's jaw firmed. "Those key lime tarts? The little ones, with the whipped cream? You made those, right?"

"Of course."

"My George, he loves them. And the pecan bars, too." George Kozlowski was in a clutch of other middle-aged men, wearing a shirt printed with swordfish. His Bermuda shorts exposed his knobby knees, and socks as white as his legs were stuck into black leather sandals. "I bake as well as you garden. Just never had the taste for slaving in a hot kitchen when I could be out growing things."

"You'd like me to bake something for you?"

It was hard for Lorraine to ask. You could see it in the tremble of her mouth, the way her shoulders hunched. But her gaze swept the yard, taking in the wild splotches of color that made the whole house look better than it ever had, gave it the lush life it had been missing, and she smiled. "You bring something over. Once a week. Something sweet—my Georgie's got a terrible sweet tooth, and those desserts are so expensive at Lunds—and you've got a deal."

"Oh, thank you!" Ann said fervently. Her plants weren't going to die. Life was good.

"You've done a beautiful job with the place," Mary commented. "I hadn't realized. It's lovely."

They hadn't been to her house in almost five years, Ann realized suddenly. She saw them frequently, of course, but always at Cedar Ridge. Brunch, now and then on the way over there, when one of them had a birthday. But she hadn't invited them over in a long time. They hadn't seen the new paint job, the new landscaping along the front walk, the fence.

"What are you making today?" Ann asked her mother-in-law. The yarn she was using was pale and fuzzy, light as cotton balls.

"Another sweater," she said. "For the church bazaar. But I'll have to put it aside for a little while. I'll have to get moving, if I'm to make three crib blankets before the triplets are born."

Today was just full of surprises. "You're making blankets for the babies?"

"Of course. Triplets! How exciting. That nice young man, Eric, promised I could come see them after they're born. I've never met triplets before."

Ann had worried a bit about introducing Martin and Mary to Eric and Mike. It was just not the sort of thing that came up often in Mill Valley. No worries about her own mother, of course—for once, having alternative parents was a blessing. Eric and Mike were positively conventional compared to Judy; they'd been together for seven years, wore shining platinum circles on their left ring fingers.

But Mary and Martin, it had to be a new thing for them. And Martin had been a bit too hearty in his "Nice to meet you fellas!" Mary, perfectly polite, had her eyes wide, the rest of her face so carefully blank that it was obvious just how shocked she was.

But you had to give the woman credit for a rapid adjustment.

"Wait until you see them," Ann said to Marie. "Mary has a real gift."

"Oh." Mary's smile was pleased. "It's nothing."

"That's not true. She tried to teach me once. How old was I, Mary?"

"Heavens. Seventeen, eighteen?" Her needles flashed as always, but her smile was fond. "You were just trying to suck up to me."

"Was I that obvious?"

"Of course you were," she said. "But that was okay. If you're not going to suck up to your boyfriend's mother, who, then? But you were *hopeless*. I've never figured it out. How someone as intelligent as you, and as coordinated, simply couldn't make it through a single row without tangling things up as badly as if a kitten'd got in the knitting basket."

"So you kill the plants, and you can't knit," Mao said. "It's a darn good thing you cook like a dream, or you'd have no domestic talents whatsoever."

"Hey, what I'm good at, I'm *really* good at." They'd stayed away from the memories, Ann realized suddenly, she and Martin and Mary. The memories were *there*, all the time, wrapped around them the instant they stepped into John's room, like air so thick with moisture that you couldn't take it in. But they never talked about them, pulled out the good times and laughed over them. And there had been good ones, so many of them. Maybe she'd been afraid of them, that if she started thinking about them she'd never be able to stop.

But it was nice to think about them now. To remember Mary, how careful she'd been not to hurt Ann's feelings, how encouraging she'd tried to be, patiently showing her stitches over and over again. Mary had finally snapped, snatching the little, uneven rectangle Ann had managed to produce. She'd grabbed onto the end of the yarn and pulled, unraveling it in an instant. And then she'd apologized, over and over again, for her quick display of temper. Except Ann had been just relieved to have it done with, and pleased to find out her boyfriend's perfect mother actually did have a cranky side.

She took another quick peek at the food table, just to see; yup, still okay. Tom was next to the root beer keg, a glass in one hand. Her mother stood beside him, her head tilted back to look up at him, thick gray hair waving almost to her hips.

Tom looked Ann's way, and she saw in his glance a quick flash of desperation. He took a long pull on his straw, as if wishing it were something far stronger.

Judy put a hand on his arm, leaning in, and he gulped. In the guise of needing more root beer, he took a step away, bent down, and pumped more pop into his glass. The look he shot Ann was now openly desperate. *Help me,* he mouthed, then plastered on an instant smile when Judy turned to him.

"Are you just going to leave him there with her?" Mao asked.

"He's a big boy," Ann said.

"He's not that big." Mao cast a sympathetic look in his direction. "Nobody's that big. Besides, what did he ever do to you?"

"He got my dog pregnant."

"Oh. Forgot about that," she said, deflated. "But still—"

"Come on. Don't you want to see how long it takes? I'll lay odds on him suddenly remembering a phone call. Five minutes, tops. What do you think?"

"He'll never make it that long."

His cheekbones were turning scarlet as if he'd been standing in the sun all day. He took off his baseball cap, wiped his forehead with the back of his hand, and put the cap back on, tugging it low over his eyes, already shielded by his sunglasses.

"Rescue the poor man!"

"Oh, fine. You're a softy, you know that?" She got up, took her time strolling across the yard, and noticed with pleasure that his face started to light up hopefully.

"Mom?" Ann touched her arm in midmotion; Judy was wearing at least a dozen bangles, silver and gold and intricately worked. "You remember Mao, who works for me, right? If you wouldn't mind . . . She had a few more questions about the goats."

Judy's gaze bounced between Ann and Tom, while a smile she was trying to hide tugged at the corner of her mouth. "Sure," she said, "the goats." She bounded off, hips swishing in her long skirt.

"Thank you," Tom said. He sounded as grateful as John had the first time she'd let him go all the way.

"So was she trying to get you to sleep with me, or did she want you for herself?"

"You. Maybe. God, I don't know. Maybe both."

It was impossible not to laugh at him. Big scary Tom Nash,

with the brutal fastball and the even more lethal stare, had been thrown into a state by a sixtysomething hippie.

"Come on, now. I'm sure you've chased off dozens of determined groupies in your day." She tucked her tongue in her cheek to stop the giggles. "And you can't handle a little old lady?"

"She's not little. And she's not that old." He pulled off his glasses. Shoot, why did the impact of that blue not diminish? He tucked them into the neckline of his polo shirt and put his hands in his pockets, loose black linen that made him look casual and rich at the same time. "I think all those years just made her trickier."

"Or maybe you never chased them off before," she said. "Only like them young, do you?"

"Okay, now just stop. I'm too traumatized to fence with you. Have a heart."

She took pity on him. She grabbed the glass he held forgotten in his hand, scooped a hefty dollop of ice cream in it, and filled it with root beer, the foam rich and creamy. "Here," she said as she handed it to him.

"You got anything harder?"

"I have beer. Sangria. But trust me, this'll work better."

He gulped half of it down as if it were a whiskey shot, and when he finally lowered the glass, he had a mustache of foam.

"You were in a milk ad, weren't you?"

"How'd you know?"

Smiling, she reached up with a napkin, skimmed it over his upper lip, and just like that, his eyes went dark.

Okay, she thought. Can't touch him, not like that. Not safe for either one of us.

She looked down at the napkin, made a show of scrubbing her fingers clean, and tossed it in the garbage can she'd set up at the end of the table for plates and cups. When she finally figured she could look at him and not have her expression give her away, she lifted her head.

He'd made it to normal, too, friendly but little more. If you didn't look at his eyes too closely, where his pupils were still black and something hot flared deep inside them.

"You warned me about her,", he said. "But I had no idea. None."

"Nobody does. Not even me, most of the time. I have no idea how she does it, and then all of a sudden I'm in the middle of some conversation I did not want to have, and she's got me so turned around I don't even know what I think anymore. And I've had a lot of practice."

"The government should have hired her. Sent her to Russia, would have ended the Cold War a decade earlier."

"Yeah, but she hates the government. Likes communists, though I don't know if she's ever met any real ones. Lots of pretend ones, though, and for all the U.S. knew, she might have saved the Soviet Union."

He nodded. Took a sip of his root beer, nice and relaxed, and Ann just let herself look. An indulgence, for sure, but a minor one that she assumed every woman there had let themselves enjoy, at least for a moment or two. She'd never seen him out of jeans or shorts, she realized, certainly not in a loose shirt with a collar and black loafers. She kind of figured he'd look silly like that, because he looked so damn fine in the jeans. That long, lean body—anything he put on probably looked good on him, elegant and male.

"Can I ask you a question?"

"You always say that," he said. "Have I ever said no?"

And didn't that just open up a world of questions. She reined them in, but not without a little—okay, more than a little—regret. "Why only black?"

"Hmm." He leaned in, his voice pitching low. "It's a secret."

"I won't tell," she promised.

"If you do, there'd be repercussions."

She flicked a finger across her heart, a quick promise.

"All right," he said slowly, then came closer still, his mouth hovering inches from her ear. "I'm color-blind."

"Really?"

He nodded.

"Everything?"

"Just red and green. Enough that my mom, before she died, used to lay out my clothes every night. Afterward, I asked my brothers a couple of times. Couldn't figure out why everybody kept looking at me weird at school."

"Brothers," she said, all amused sympathy.

"Hey, I was stupid enough to trust them." He put down the drink, slid his hands back into his pockets. "So I just bought black from then on, so as not to have to worry about it. By the time I made enough money that I could have hired somebody to help me, the press had latched on to it. They liked that whole 'man in black' thing. Made me mysterious, I guess."

"Oh, yes, you're just so mysterious." It seemed impossible that she used to think so.

"Hey, I am," he insisted. "Anyway, who cares enough about clothes to worry about it? Okay, Boom, but that's Boom. This is easier."

She sighed in mock regret. "But you're missing my best feature."

Now why did she keep doing that? She knew she was treading close to the edge, and that just wasn't like her.

But the tingle that chased all the way down to her fingers, the joyful, terrified little skip her heart gave; she was getting addicted to the feeling. Couldn't come up with a good enough reason why she should give that up, too. She hadn't had a choice about giving up so much. This she did, and she wanted to keep it.

She *wanted*, which was stupid and dangerous and useless, but she hadn't wanted for such a long time.

He looked her up and down, nice and slow in a way that would have had her mother cheering, if she was watching. "I don't think so," he said. "But what feature were you referring to?"

"That would be my eyes," she said, trying to keep it light, while inside her nerves jittered and danced. She batted her lashes at him. "What color are my eyes?"

He took his time, looking deep. "Brown?"

"Nope."

"Hazel?"

"They're green," she said sadly. "Smoky, they've been called. The only thing I'm glad I got from my mother."

"They're still pretty." And he was still holding her gaze, a prekiss kind of eyelock, are-we-aren't-we, and she could have slid right into it and forgotten everything else.

Forgetting would be nice, she thought. Just for a little while, let it all slip away and just be. Except sooner or later you have to remember. And maybe there'd be something else to remember, then, another regret in a long line of them.

"I should get more food." But the table was still three-quarters full; people were easing down, a nibble here, a bite there, but mostly full. More drinking, less eating.

"It's a nice party."

She was more than a little surprised to discover that it was true. A half dozen men, neighbors all of them, were clustered at the other end of the table, holding beer bottles and laughing, snagging chips and salsa from the bowl beside them every now and then. Her mother had moved on to Eric and Mike and Marie, gesturing animatedly beneath the red oak. Natural childbirth advice, no doubt.

Ashia had joined the circle of women beneath the tree—why did parties so often sort by sex, anyway?—chatting with Mao, beside Lorraine and Mary, who was staring across the yard, her hands still and white against the pale yarn.

Ann followed her gaze. Martin was beside the cluster of white and purple petunias, dapper and youthful in his casual clothes, grinning down at Sherryl Mularkey. She lived three houses over, and had been widowed very suddenly; her husband, barely fifty, had simply pulled over on the side of 169 one evening on his way home from work and had a fatal heart attack. She dealt with the loss by trying to live it up. Within six months her hair had gotten blonder, her skirts shorter, her chest bigger. And she was waggling it all in Martin's face.

There was an edge of desperation behind all the bright laughter that anybody with half a brain could pick up on instantly. Surely Martin could, and was merely being kind. Had Mary such a jealous streak then? She'd never noticed it before. And Martin was simply an outgoing man. Part of his business, part of his charm, something he'd passed down to his son.

"You okay?" Tom asked, but she shook it off. They'd been married forever, been through a lot. Had to be her imagination. Mary was probably just missing John, here in his house, his yard, with his wife.

"I think so," she said slowly. "All these years. I've been . . . distant from people, I guess. Thought it was them. That they were uncomfortable around me. Reminders of how quickly good could go bad, how random and brutal fate could be. Couldn't blame them."

"Sure you could," he said. There was heat behind his words.

She shook her head. "No. People can't help it. They don't know what to say, so they stay away. But now I'm thinking." She gestured, taking in all the neighbors, the coworkers. The friends, if she'd been brave enough to let them be. "I think maybe it was me, too. I didn't want to see them happy, watch them fall in love and have babies, and be slapped with what I'd lost. I was too scared. Maybe I didn't want to care too much about somebody again, knowing how easily he could be taken away from me."

"That's perfectly natural."

There was something soothing about having him beside her. Solid. She had a friend after all, and he'd slid right into the role when she wasn't watching. And she fully intended to let him settle in right there.

"It's no good, though," she said. "I'm . . . okay. Just okay.

And though that's a whole lot better than I was for a long time, it's not great. And it's not where I want to be for the rest of my life."

"Looks pretty damn good to me," he said, and she smiled.

"Yeah," she agreed. "Today, it's pretty damned good."

TWENTY-SEVEN

It was her last cigarette. Mer slid it out of the pack, smooth and white, while she pondered whether she really wanted to smoke it now, and leaned back in the lawn chair, sticking her feet up on another one she'd dragged around back.

She could still hear the murmur of the party on the other side of the garage, punctuated by bursts of bright laughter, a child's happy shout. Why the hell wasn't anyone going home?

Of course that didn't mean she couldn't. She'd stayed around at first because Ann had asked her to help keep the bowls full, the platters stocked. And because she wanted to hear what people said about the food.

They liked it, of course. Loved it, from the way they scarfed it down like none of 'em had eaten for a week. And Ann had made sure that everybody knew that Mer had cooked a lot of it. It was a little weird, and damned obvious, how hard she was trying to encourage her. But still nice to hear how much they liked what she'd done.

She'd planned on staying till the end, to help clean up. But it was going on and on, and if one more adult tried to have a conversation with her, with those fake-hearty interested questions and forced smiles, she was gonna puke. It was obvious they were trying—for Ann's sake, maybe, or because her father was Tom

Nash, or just because that's what people like them did—but it was awkward as hell. One of these times, when someone asked her what she liked to do, she wasn't going to be able to stop herself from saying "fucking, and meth," just to see them keel over.

Even from the back side, the neighborhood looked like something out of an old sitcom. Small, pretty yards, with fences more for decoration than anything, and short trees that had been one big mass of pink flowers in May. Swing sets, expensive ones made out of wood and bright-colored plastic, sat in a good half of the yards, with tube slides and pretend tree-houses, with all the danger and fun stripped out.

Nobody left junk out. The bikes were all stowed away in the garages, along with the minivans and SUVs. There were hedges, clipped to such sharp, level tops they looked as if they'd been mowed. Lots of lawn furniture, Adirondack chairs on some patios, tables with striped umbrellas on the others. A grill in every single yard she could see, hulking shiny things that looked like they could be driven down the street.

No weeds, no broken-down old Chevys or rolls of wire, no rusty barrels or overgrown gardens.

Nothing where she could possibly fit in. The kids in houses like this went to class, and to college, and their parents hung their graduation pictures along the hallways.

She hadn't exactly been happy in Chicago. What the hell was there to be happy about? But at least she fit.

"Hello."

Crap. It was one of those kids, with his navy blue striped polo shirt and his clean cargo shorts and his black hair clipped short as a junior banker.

She'd seen him sometimes as she walked Coop. Out in his yard, pushing a shiny black mower with a blue cap on his head. Tossing a duffel into the back of a clean white Subaru, then climbing into the driver's seat and backing carefully out of the drive. He'd always waved at her, smiling that happy smile. Once, he'd even started to jog her way, but she'd put her head down and kept on walking, like she hadn't seen him.

But now he had her cornered.

He stuck out his hand, his smile friendly and open. "I'm Josh Rabinowitz."

She ignored the hand, gave him a skeptical eye. "You don't look like a Rabinowitz."

She didn't deter him in the least. He picked up her feet and moved them aside before plopping down, his smile never wavering. "Adopted. From Korea, when I was ten months old."

"Good for you."

"Yup," he agreed cheerfully. "It was."

Then he just waited, as if it were her turn to share some tidbit about herself.

Finally he must have gotten tired of the silence. "So," he thumbed up his glasses, small metal-edged rectangles, "you want to play chess?"

Chess. Not only a geek, but no problem admitting it right off the bat.

"Do I look like I play chess?"

"I try not to judge by the cover," he said, unperturbed by her tone. "You should try it." She wondered what it would take to piss him off. If she stood up, clubbed him over the head, and called him an asshole, he'd probably just keep smiling at her like she was the nicest girl he'd ever met.

"Christ. Is there something wrong with you?"

"Depends what you mean by wrong. I guess we've all got something wrong, don't we, depending upon your perspective?"

"You know." She drew circles in the air around her head. "Wrong. Like you don't understand what I'm telling you."

"Oh, heck no." Heck. He'd actually said *heck*. "I'm first in my class. I'd tell you what I got on my SATs, but that would just be showing off."

"What do you want?"

"Honestly?" He leaned forward confidingly. "Mrs. Kozlowski was heading my way. She's nice enough, you know, and Mom always said I should remember it's hard for her, now that her kids are gone, but . . . Well, a guy can only take so much."

"Yeah." That one she understood.

"So? How about that chess?"

"I don't know how to play."

"That's no problem. I'm a great teacher."

"Okay, you're just not getting it. Why in the hell would I *want* to play chess?"

"You got something better to do?"

It was incredibly depressing to discover she didn't. She could stay here and be pissed because she was out of cigarettes. She could go back to the party and listen to old people babble about their gardens and their jobs and the Twins. She could go home and sit in that damned house alone again. Without Cooper, because for damn sure he wasn't leaving a place where there was food and kids who might drop it.

She gave him a good once-over. He was about two inches shorter than she was—call it five foot eight, five foot nine. And too thin; if he lost a couple more pounds, his belly was gonna go concave. But there was a hint of muscle in his shoulders, his arms, like it might turn into something in a year or two.

"Chess," she said. *Damn it.* "Okay. But you're gonna be sorry."

The puppies arrived in late July, the first one squirting out at three in the morning. Ann had fetched Mer and Tom an hour earlier.

Mer was happy about that. Tom was not. But Ann insisted. It was his fault, so he was losing sleep, just like she was.

Ann had put a child's play pool smack in the middle of her kitchen, lining it with old towels and quilts. Ann and Mer sat on the floor, close enough to comfort, not close enough to disturb.

Tom had pulled over a kitchen chair, stretched his legs out, and promptly nodded off.

Ann would have none of it. Every time his head dropped, she poked him. Hard. A merciless woman, that one.

Mer was so excited she could hardly contain herself. City girl. He was a farm boy; an animal's birth wasn't a big thrill for him.

There were five puppies: two boys, three girls, little yelping fuzz balls in a range of patchy colors, white and brown and caramel. He'd forgotten how tiny the buggers were.

Then Mer had smiled. A great big pure smile without any shadows, any ulterior motive wheeling behind it. He hadn't seen a look on her face like that since she was nine and he'd taken her to Six Flags.

She'd stayed right there on the floor, cooing and oohing—put a female next to a puppy or a kitten and she immediately turned all girlie—until she started nodding off about six thirty.

She hadn't wanted to leave. Ann told her to take the couch, close enough to hear if anything happened, and promised to wake her up so she didn't miss anything.

Then, finally, she relented, shooing Tom home for some sleep. He was tired. His butt hurt from the kitchen chair. They were just puppies, for God's sake, though he had to admit they were cute.

Weirdly, he didn't want to leave.

So he looked at Ann, at the purple that smudged beneath her eyes, at the paleness that drew color from her cheeks, and wanted to tuck her in, safe and sound. Make sure she got some rest, too, now that Mer had lain down on the couch and started snoring before she'd gotten all the way down.

Her eyes were tired, too, but warm and triumphant. And it didn't matter what color they were, he could still look at them day and night and want to just keep on looking.

And so he left. Because he had to.

———

The puppies were a week old, getting cuter with every moment, opening their eyes—most had brown eyes, that warm and friendly brown that said "love me" like nothing else on earth, one had blue eyes, another one of each—tumbling around in the pool, pretending to bark. And poor Cooper was starting to think he was Tom's dog, because Mer spent every waking moment over at Ann's.

Poor Cooper? Hell, poor Tom. Last night, he'd woken up to find the dog sprawled in bed with him, crowding him into a stingy corner, and the lovely and unmistakable aroma of dog farts clouding the air.

He'd stayed late at the gym tonight, though. Summer'd finally decided to hit back but good, punching in with heat and steam that had the streets sparking with violence. Tempers were short in that weather; people stayed out late because it was too hot in their bedrooms to sleep, and they were damned cranky about it.

It was the time he needed his boys off the street most of all. So he'd run an extra shooting clinic after practice, bringing in a former Gopher who'd held the record for three-point percentage for years.

If he could keep them late enough, he could keep them safe. Hopefully tire them out enough so that they'd go straight home to bed, bypassing the danger hours.

His neighborhood was dark, no witching hours here. One light was on, at the Michelson's; they'd just had a baby, six weeks ago now, and he figured it was nighttime feeding. Another light in the kitchen at the Richardsons'; Mrs. Richardson—Dr. Richardson—was an ob-gyn, and her husband always left the light on when she was out on call so she wouldn't come home to a dark house.

God, he was learning way too much about his neighbors. The suburbs were sneaky that way, entangling you in the lives of others before you knew whether you wanted to be or not.

His house was dark, too. Quiet, peaceful, the way he'd imagined it when he'd bought it. He stood in the yard, the air heavy with the scent of mowed grass, still thick with the day's heat.

He thought—maybe, though he was afraid to get his hopes up—that Mer was getting better. Settling in. He didn't think she'd seen Tyrone in weeks, though he was afraid to ask. Asking might send her running that way, just to piss him off.

And she was spending a lot of time with that Rabinowitz kid. He shook his head. Couldn't picture it: his delinquent daughter and the geek. A very nice geek, perhaps the most self-possessed young man he'd ever met, but strange after all the swagger and testosterone of the athletes Tom was used to. But if there was ever a young man it was safe to leave your daughter with—though he doubted that there ever was; he was far too familiar with the male of the species to believe that—Josh was it. And even if they were having sex—damn it, now he was shuddering again, he had to stop thinking about things like that—he was pretty sure they weren't drinking or high or some other thing that just thinking about made his head hurt.

He headed for the door but stopped when he heard a muffled sound from next door. Letting the dog out, probably. Or maybe he was hearing the puppies from the kitchen? No, it was too hot to have a window open. It was why the neighborhood was so quiet; the sounds of conversation, of the Macallisters arguing, the television that old lonely Mrs. Wilson left running all night, were all sealed up by energy-efficient windows that kept the air-conditioning inside, where it belonged.

Leave it alone, he told himself. If she needed him, if there was something wrong with the puppies, she would call him. Why wouldn't she?

But his feet veered that way anyway. His brain might be reasonable, logical, but his body simply headed for Ann.

The moon was hazy and bright yellow, maybe a few days away from full, and it seemed as if it put out some heat of its own tonight instead of merely reflecting the sun's.

He could see her sitting there alone in the dark and the heat, on the back step.

Sick? he wondered. Maybe her air-conditioning was on the fritz, a fuse blown, something like that. He could hear the whirr of his unit clicking on behind him as the air heated his lungs, and he wondered how they used to manage it on the farm all those years ago before they had AC. He couldn't remember it being this bad, but it had to be. He was getting soft, he decided.

Well, he'd offer for her to come over. Her and the dogs. No reason for them to swelter when he had guest rooms. And Mer's presence to make him behave.

He walked over to her. She must have heard him coming; he wasn't even trying to be quiet. But she didn't turn, just stared off into the shadows at the back of the yard, her eyes wide and glassy.

"You okay?"

"Oh, yeah." She lifted a bottle of wine by the neck, tilted it in his direction as if making a toast. "I'm just fucking fine."

He'd never heard her talk like that. He had no real objection to women with colorful vocabularies, but it was different enough for her that it worried him.

"Mind if I sit?"

"Suit yourself."

She scooted over on the concrete step, making room. Except there wasn't much, and his hip and thigh pressed up against hers, sticky from the heat.

She had on an old pair of shorts. When he was in high school the girls used to wear shorts like that, gym shorts with slit sides and white piping. They were all the rage, and all the boys had been grateful. Except none of those girls had legs half as good as hers.

"Want some?" She held out the bottle.

"Sure." He grabbed it, swirled it around to see how much remained. Maybe two glasses' worth in the bottom. "There's not much left."

"My second one," she said. "And don't worry. I've got plenty." Instead of slurring, she spoke more slowly than normal, biting each word off carefully like someone learning English.

He took a deep swig, more to keep it from her than because he wanted it himself. It might have been good when she'd opened it—he'd never known her to have bad wine—but this was as warm as the air, thick and heavy in his mouth, with a harsh bite that lingered after he swallowed.

She grabbed the bottle back, tilted her head, and let it pour in. Her hair was tied back, but pieces had pulled free around her face, curling wildly, clinging to her damp skin. Her shoulders were shiny; she had on one of those camisoles with two thin straps holding it up and the rest clinging to her like something from a wet T-shirt contest.

Thank God she was too blitzed to know he was looking. He wasn't proud of it. But there was only so much you could ask of a man.

"I thought you said you got friendly when you were tipsy."

She studied him. His eyes, his mouth, and his breathing went slow and deep. "You shouldn't look at me like that," he said.

"Like what?" Her pupils were huge and dark, her mouth open, slick from the wine.

"You know how." He shifted, his butt going numb from the concrete, trying to find a comfortable spot. A safe spot. "Not when a guy's not allowed to do anything about it."

"Who said you're not allowed to do anything about it?" she said, and his heart stopped. Just went still from the shock and the hope. And then she laughed, tipping her head back again. Frowning, she upended the bottle over the ground, one last drip clinging to the lip, sputtering free when she shook it. "Damn it," she said. "You hogged too much." She looked at him, impish and young and mischievous. More like that girl in the photos than the woman he knew. Oh, she had been trouble once, hadn't she? Even if she claimed she'd always been careful, always stuck to the plan.

"Shh." She put her finger over her lips. "I shouldn't have said that, should I?" Then she stood up abruptly, her hand coming down on his shoulder when she wavered. "I'll get more wine. We need more wine."

"I'll get some. In a minute. You just sit down. Enjoy the moon."

She plopped down obligingly. She was a lot more tractable when she was drunk. Her face lifted to the sky, and gold drifted over it, lit those hazy eyes and damp skin.

"So," he asked. "What's the occasion?"

"It's my wedding anniversary in three days," she said. "Hot as this the day we got married. No air-conditioning in the church, either. John started swaying just before he said his vows, got 'I d—' out before he toppled over." She shook her head. "Pastor Koval told him not to lock his legs. But he was nervous. I was sweating in that big poufy dress—cheap satin, felt as hot as my band uniform in the Fourth of July parade— but I wasn't nervous. Not one little bit."

She never talked about her husband. Not at all, not the man he'd been, not what had happened to him, not what he was like now. He didn't know whether to encourage her or not, if it was good to let her get it out or better to simply keep the dark stuff locked away.

Shit, he wasn't any good at this. She should be talking to her mother, to her friends. He just happened to be there at a weak moment, he told himself.

Except he still felt . . . honored. He couldn't think of another word that fit.

"Eighteen years," she said.

"It's a long time."

"Damn right it is!" And then her face fell, her mouth curving into a sad droop. "We had twelve years together, from our first date. And now it's twelve years like this. From now on, it's more time without him than with him."

"I'm sorry," he said. Fucking inadequate thing to say, small and bare and unhelpful. He remembered how he'd felt when his mother died, the hollow ache that carved out his insides. It had never filled up all the way; he'd just learned to live with it. But he'd expected her death, had fifteen months to prepare. They'd done a lot of the mourning before she'd gone, and you expect to lose your parents someday, even if you hope you're too old and gaga yourself to care by that time. It wasn't a shock.

Ann looked shocked now, her skin drawn, eyes wide, blinking too seldom to keep them wet, then a quick flurry when she felt the grit.

"Yup," she said. "Twelve years ago today. He was going to a

job site. A new one, a community center on the north side. North Side Freedom Center, you know it?"

"Absolutely. I drive by it every night." He knew the place. White, still white, surprising enough in that area, with more glass than they usually dared to use around there. But there were murals on the wall, people from the neighborhood and all the places they'd come from. Somalia and Cambodia, Ethiopia and Tibet, Mexico. They had parenting classes there, a food shelf, job training programs. After-school tutoring, flu shots in the winter. "He did a good job."

She nodded. "I've never seen it. Not finished."

"They've kept it up. There's a chain-link fence, of course. But a garden, too. Vegetables on the east side, flowers on the west. It's blooming now."

"Good. That's good." Her words were coming slower now, but they'd lost that clipped cadence, as if grief were blurring the edges of the words. "He was going to check things on it. When a project was going up he couldn't stay away. Loved to see if it looked the same in the flesh . . . " She laughed at herself. "I suppose the steel and concrete, but it was the flesh, really, to him. Anyway, he couldn't wait to see if it turned out the way he'd imagined it."

He'd just let her keep talking, he decided. As long as she wanted. If she stopped, he wouldn't push her. But if she needed to say it, he would hear it. Hear her.

A car went by the next street over. He could see its headlights flashing against the side of each house as it passed; white, white, brick, the Andersons' creamy stucco. Must be a kid coming home late from a date, he decided. Somebody'd be getting grounded.

"I was waiting for him at home. Packing. We had reservations at a B and B in Stillwater, to celebrate our anniversary." She swallowed, rubbing her fingers over her throat as if it hurt, as if she were catching a case of strep. "The timing was right. The house was done, the firm was making money. The timing was right in me, too. We were going to try to have a baby."

He almost said it again, that ridiculous little "I'm sorry." But it just wasn't enough, didn't make any difference, and so he kept silent, thinking it. Letting it float silently through the air.

"Even a week later—" And that's where she finally broke off, her voice shattering high and hard.

A week later, and she might have been pregnant. Might have had something of him, something to hold on to, something to push her forward. Someone to love.

"There wasn't even anyone to blame," she said. "A drunk driver, a kid showing off. Just an old lady who had a stroke behind the wheel of her Olds '88. She died, too."

She settled her head on his shoulder, wiggling until it fit just so, and he went rigid. Damn it, she was so sad. She wanted comfort, needed someone to lean on for a change. And he was so inadequate to the cause.

Cautiously, he eased his arm around her back. She sighed and relaxed, heavy and loose against him. For a while he thought she'd fallen asleep.

That was okay. Good, even. He could hold her while she slept in the heated yellow moonlight. And get her through the worst of the night. He owed her at least that much, and things always seemed a bit better in the daylight. It seemed that humans were programmed for hope with the dawn.

But she wasn't asleep. She burrowed closer, her nose brushing his neck. He felt the flutter of her breath, warm and moist as the summer air.

And then—oh, damn—she kissed him.

TWENTY-EIGHT

It was exactly like he'd imagined and better than he'd hoped, a simmer of soft lips and heated skin.

"That friendly enough for you?" she murmured.

"You're drunk," he said regretfully. He'd love to take advantage of her. But he liked her too much to do it.

"Not drunk enough." She drew back enough so he could see her eyes, the wet shimmer of tears and the raw slice of grief. The same kind of grief he'd seen in his father after his mother died, the kind that ripped a chunk of you away and maybe, if you were very lucky, could be patched up but could never be repaired. And you'd never even want it to, because they'd earned that much, the people you loved. When all you had left of them were the scars, even the scars were welcome.

"It hurts, Tom," she said in a voice so soft and raw that it broke his heart. "It hurts."

"Yeah," And there wasn't a damn thing he could do about it. He would have moved a mountain, caught the moon, sawed off a limb, to take it from her.

"Make it stop," she said. "I just don't want it to hurt for a while."

So he did it. He knew he shouldn't. Knew he'd pay for it tomorrow, and for a long time to come. Knew it wasn't getting rid of the hurt, only putting it off. But sometimes, if that was all you could hope for, you took it and worried about it later.

And so he kissed her. Hard and long enough to try to push anything out of her mind but him. Not because he needed her concentrated on him to the exclusion of anything else. There was nothing possessive about it. But because he wouldn't let her hurt if he could hold it at bay, if only for a little while.

She climbed right on top of him. Put her knees on the concrete steps on either side of his thighs, settling down on him with enough pressure to make him nearly burst right there, wrapping her arms around him as she started to move.

There was desperation there. He couldn't pretend that it was nothing but passion that drove her, that she wanted him for himself and nothing else. But he didn't care. Because he'd wanted her from the first, and because he could do this for her, and it was probably the only thing he could.

"Annie—"

"Hush," she said, while her mouth kept busy at his. "I haven't had sex for twelve years. I'm not interested in talking."

"Christ. Way to take the pressure off a guy."

She rocked against him, and he could feel her mouth curve up into a smile. "You're up to it."

She sounded sober enough to know what she was doing. Enough that he didn't have to worry that he was taking advantage of her. And if tomorrow she needed to blame him, well, he could take the hit.

She lifted up, fumbling at the snap of his jeans.

"Hell. We doin' this right here?"

Her eyes flew wide in surprise, and then her lids came down, seductive and wild. "Why not?"

"Don't you want to—"

"Twelve years, Nash. Twelve. You think I'm waiting one more second?" She kept her mouth on his while she rose and backed up enough to strip off her shorts, laughing against his mouth while she tried and failed to keep them fused. And then she just moved her panties aside and sank right down, and his mind exploded.

"Okay, wait," he said. "Wait."

"No. No more waiting." And then she grabbed his hand and pushed it down between them, so he could stroke as she moved.

She went off immediately, her head falling back, her mouth open, shaking like the leaves that tossed overhead in the rising wind. And heaven help him, he went, too.

"Oh, Lord." She dropped her forehead to his shoulder, her body limp against his, as if all energy, all life, had been drained away. She shuddered again. An aftershock? Or the regrets beginning already?

No, he thought. Not that. Not yet.

He kissed her softly this time, a whisper: "It's okay, it'll be all right, I promise." He could promise no such thing, of course. He knew the lies even as he made them, as his hands and his mouth eased her back up into passion, into letting her body shut out her brain.

He wrapped one arm around her back, put one big hand on her rump, and rose to his feet, turning to enter the house with them still joined.

"Impressive," she whispered.

"Hon, you ain't seen nothin' yet."

Keep it light. That was the plan. He didn't want her sliding back down that slope into the murk of memories and loss. Sex was perhaps the greatest anesthetic of all. How many people since the beginning of time had used it to block out reality, to forget?

He walked her through the dark house—she'd no lights on, not even over the porch, the stove—and managed somehow not to run into a wall. He knew the first floor well enough but not upstairs. But the curtains were open, the moon powerful, and his eyes had adjusted.

She was busy all the way, almost frantic, with her mouth and her hands. The bump of his steps moved her away from him, then together, a hint of rhythm and motion that was nowhere near satisfying, just enough to make him insane. But he made it all the way to her room.

He registered it dimly: clean and perfectly neat, spare wood floors and modern furniture with sleek lines that somehow suited the old room with its slanted ceilings and rippled window glass.

He leaned over the bed with her. She kept her arms, her legs, wrapped around him.

"Let go, Ann."

"No." She shook her head, her lips skating over his mouth with the motion, back and forth, and her grip tightened.

"I'll make it worth it," he murmured. "I promise."

She sighed and released him. He pushed away, dislodging their connection, though it was hard. He could have stayed there, sunk into her, and powered through quick and fast, letting the world blur into oblivion.

He wasn't the kind of guy who ever thought about tomorrow. Not in the middle of things, anyway. You just enjoyed and let the rest take care of itself. Whether there'd be a relationship or not, another night or not, was immaterial to what happened in bed.

Except they already had a relationship of sorts. One he was aware he might be sacrificing by doing this, and he didn't want to lose her.

But he didn't want her to hurt right now. The pain that had been in her voice, her eyes, had nearly shattered him.

He didn't know if he could give her happiness. But he knew damn well he could give her pleasure, and that would have to do.

He looked at her first. Let his eyes touch every part of her, drink in the sight of her sprawled across the bed. Her hair'd come loose, messy clouds of it; no wonder she always kept it tied back. It had a mind of its own. Wild hair, the hair of a woman who danced on bars and gave herself over to the music. An anomaly, or did she have that in her, born to the risk and the adventure? Girls rebelled against their mothers. It was human nature. Perhaps she'd boxed that part of her away, diligently stamped it out until she was controlled and safe.

Except nothing was ever safe.

Her shirt was still on, twisted around her waist, pulling low over one breast. Her legs, those long, long legs, bent slightly, loose and relaxed over the bed. Her eyes were sleepy, unfocused as if she were close to drifting off. But lazy and sweet, without hurt.

"Oh, no you don't," he said. Later she could sleep. Not now, not during his night. He bent to her, began to slide her panties from her hips. Plain white cotton, cut high, and as sexy as any black lace thing he'd ever seen. His breath caught as they came off, slipping over those legs, and her lids lowered further, but there was nothing sleepy about her eyes now.

The little top was harder. It snagged on her arms, her shoulders, tugging tight beneath her breasts. Small breasts, he supposed, if he were being objective about it. But Ann's breasts, as pretty and sweet and feminine as existed on the face of the earth. Perfect breasts.

"Oh, for Christ's sake," she said impatiently, sitting up, dragging it over her head, and tossing it away. She flopped back down, completely exposed, completely open to him, and the room swirled. He was going to pass out, he thought. Pass out because there was no longer any blood flow above his waist.

"Now you," she murmured.

"You want naked?" he said. "You got it."

His clothes were gone in a blink. Didn't take much. Socks, shoes, a T-shirt and gym shorts and the compression shorts he wore beneath when he played ball.

"Impressive."

"I'm not always fast," he promised her.

"Wasn't talking about how quick you stripped."

"Oh." He swallowed. "Oh. Well." He felt stupid with it, flummoxed by the idea she would admire his naked body.

"Now come here."

He obliged, levering himself over her, looking down at her face in the moonlight.

She urged him on, spreading her knees, lifting her hips to bring him inside.

But he was done with her setting the pace. She wanted the speed, the drive and violence to hurtle her away from reality.

But he knew better ways. Ones that wouldn't be over so quickly.

He explored her. His mouth, in every place he'd ever admired. There were dozens, hundreds. Her neck, behind her knee, that luscious spot on her shoulder, inside her elbow. With his hands, he touched all the other places he'd never seen, the ones he now realized he'd been dreaming about for weeks.

She shivered in his arms. Sighed in all the ways he'd imagined. And when at last he slid into her again, she cried out in joy and release.

But when it was over, when he held her close and watched her eyes fog into sleep, he made a terrible mistake.

"You okay?" he asked her.

Her eyes went wide, wounded. He saw the tears that sprang to them, the pleasured blur that snapped immediately into focus.

It was his fault that awareness had come back to her. His responsibility to drive it away. So he rolled her beneath him again, drove her into the madness once more. And took himself with her.

———

She slept at last, hard and unmoving, one hand against his chest, one thigh drawn over his.

But he didn't. He watched over her instead, waiting for the light, waiting for the regret.

He knew better than to hope there wouldn't be any. She simply wasn't the kind. And if she regretted what they'd done, so would he.

That was the problem with doing things to postpone emotion, to block out feeling. It only worked for a little while.

They'd made love four times. *Four*. What was he, a teenager? She'd come nine times. Okay, yes, he counted. But she had a lot of years to make up for, a lot of empty nights. He did what he could. Would have done more, one way or the other, except while he was gathering himself, planning what else he could do, she'd slipped off, content and exhausted.

Made love. He'd termed it that way in his mind, automatically and without pondering the matter, and the fact of it whapped him aside the head like a fastball that came right back at him, too quick to even turn away.

He didn't make love. He had sex. Got laid. Fucked.

But none of those things applied to Ann.

It had to be heading for five. Light was sneaking through the clouds, rosy and soft.

He knew the instant she awakened. Her eyes stayed closed, but her body betrayed her, muscles going taut, the steady rise and fall of her breasts becoming uneven and sharp.

"I know you're awake," he told her.

Her cheeks went red as if she'd been scalded. Her eyes, when she opened them, were wary and . . . not horrified, perhaps, but considering it.

His fault. It clumped in his stomach, cold and regretful. He'd known she was hurting, known she was drinking. He'd convinced himself it was a kindness, a way to help her through a hard and long night.

But maybe it had been purely selfish. He'd wanted her all along. More than he'd been willing to admit, even to himself. He had jumped at the first opportunity, and now he was going to have to live with the aftermath.

She looked like she'd had a long night. Her hair had gone crazy with it: the tangles of that clumped around her ears and were piled high on the left side of her head. Red rimmed her eyes, her lids and mouth puffy.

And damn, he wanted nothing but to lie back, pull her on top, and lose himself in her again. Put off the aftermath a little longer.

"Do you want me to go?"

She closed her eyes, swallowed hard. "Yes," she said. "I want you to go."

TWENTY-NINE

"You're grounded."

Mer caught him sneaking in. His shoes off, easing the door open so the fool dog didn't give him away, and yet she saw him before he saw her.

Busted. He turned slowly, giving himself time to arrange his features into what he hoped was blank innocence.

She was on the couch in the front room, struggling to sit up, with a rose and blue granny afghan tucked over her legs that he was sure the decorator had spent the price of a plane ticket on. Her face was scrubbed clean, and she had on one of his old T-shirts, white washing to gray with a Vikings helmet on the front. She looked young and sleepy eyed, with her ink-black hair—the purple was fading, he noticed—sticking up in cowlicks like it had when she was a child waking from a nap. Because Mer, even at two, had never slept peacefully; she tossed and turned and mumbled, waking up as mussed up as if she was wrestling bears in her sleep.

"I'm sorry I'm late," he said quickly. "Practice ran late, and—"

She laughed at him. "Jesus, Dad, did you *ever* get away with anything when you were a kid? 'Cause you look so guilty that they wouldn't even bother with a trial if you ever got arrested, just convict you and toss away the key."

"I'm not guilty," he tried. "Just tired, and—"

"Dad." She pushed the afghan aside and swung her legs to the floor. Thick, fuzzy socks sagged around her ankles, and beneath the T-shirt she wore, her legs were long and bare. "Seriously. No need to get all weird about it. Unless you're a lot better at hiding things than I thought—and apparently you're *hopeless* at it—you haven't had sex since I moved in. Figured you were going to cave sooner or later."

"But I—" He snapped his mouth shut. Whatever he said was only digging himself in deeper.

"I mean, you don't want my sex life to be better than yours, do you? Wouldn't be cool."

"Mer—" he said warningly.

She crossed over to him, patted him on the cheek. "You earned that one. You worried me."

She was right. Though he couldn't help but be a little flattered—not fair of him, not cool, but still—that she cared enough to be worried. He'd been convinced a good portion of the summer that she didn't care about him at all.

"You're right," he said. "I should have called."

"I'm right," she said. "You say that again, okay?"

"You're right."

He'd made mistakes last night, he reflected. Hard to feel like making love with Ann was a mistake, but intellectually he knew that there was going to be an aftermath. All that remained now was to see how big the shock waves were.

Ann went running. Alone, and long, and hard, hoping the pain in her legs, the sharp slice of each breath in and out of her chest, would jolt her into sanity. Back into herself.

It didn't work. She couldn't figure out what to feel, *how* to feel.

She'd broken her vows.

She knew women who cheated. Went to school with some,

lived next door to one once, had a temp at the office who zoomed out with a guy who wasn't her husband every other day at lunch and didn't care if they all knew about it.

She wasn't like them. Had never imagined a situation where she could be like them. Not that she judged, mind you.

Okay, she judged. She wasn't proud of it, but she couldn't help it.

It was the one thing her mother, for all her lovers and sexual adventures, had done right. She'd never pretended to be anything else, never made a commitment that she didn't keep.

You made a promise, Ann always believed, you kept it. The people who didn't were those who couldn't ever think beyond the moment, who were so caught up in a frantic search for excitement that they never considered what happened after, that the newness faded fast and what you were left with was no better—and quite probably worse—than what you gave up.

That was before life got . . . complicated. Before things got messy.

That was before Tom.

She showered, running hot water over her face with her eyes open, until her vision blurred and her eyes stung. She checked on Cleo, the puppies. And then she bolted for the one place she knew she could find herself.

She headed for John.

It was six thirty when she hit Cedar Ridge. Early; they'd just changed shifts. There were nurses at the station, reading charts, double-checking carts of little paper cups of morning medication. Metallic clatter rang from the kitchen, a vacuum zoomed in the activity room where a dozen folding chairs formed a half circle around an old upright piano.

John's wing was quiet, the doors open only a few inches, the hall empty, the floor gleaming from a new wash.

She eased open the door, as though she could still wake him up somehow.

And then she heard the sound, an exhausted half sob with a hiccup on the end, like the leftovers from a good weep fest, when you'd already cried it all out but weren't quite ready to give it up yet, and she shoved the door open the rest of the way.

"Mary?"

Her mother-in-law was in a chair dragged close to the bed, her head resting, forehead down on the edge of the perfectly made bed with its bleached white sheets. When a patient couldn't move, the bed never got rumpled.

"What happened?" Her gaze arrowed to John. But he looked the same, his skin no paler than it always was, his head tipped awkwardly back, his eyes open a bare slit. His left arm curled above the covers, the wrist cocked, fingers bent; no matter how much stretching therapy you did, some of the muscles tightened, pulling the extremities in unnatural positions.

Not dead, then. Relief came out of her in a fervent gush, even as she recognized and regretted the reason: if John had died while she was with another man, she never would have recovered.

God, she was more selfish than she thought.

"Mary, he looks fine. Was the doctor in? His fever—" His forehead felt warm, but no more than usual, the skin thin and delicate; he spent no time in the sun, the wind, to toughen it up.

Mary shook her head. Her eyes were swollen nearly shut, tears making tracks down her cheeks, seeping makeup into the lines around her mouth. Her hair was dull and flat, clinging to the side of her face, and her lavender blouse was rumpled.

"It's not that."

"Is it—" Oh, God. Not that. She lifted a chair, set it carefully beside Mary, and put one hand on the two that Mary had folded on the bed. "Is it Martin?"

She sniffed, an unflattering wet sound, and nodded.

"Why didn't you call me—"

"He left me!"

"What?" Her world spun wild again, a crazy wobble like a top coming to the end of its rotation. "Martin? But—"

Mary and Martin. Martin and Mary. She never thought of them as individuals but as one entity, two parts of a whole that wouldn't function without the other. They'd honed their roles in the marriage, defined themselves in relationship to each other. She'd never seen them argue, never seen them make a decision without consulting the other.

And they were old. They'd been together more than forty years. What could possibly split them apart after all this time?

"What happened, Mary?" It couldn't be what she thought. Surely Mary was overreacting, blowing some minor disagreement completely out of proportion, taking some comment way out of context. Ann couldn't imagine it; Mary wasn't the type, had never been the dramatic sort, had never jumped to conclusions. But that was easier to swallow than the idea that Martin had left his wife.

"He said—" She drew a sleeve across her nose, leaving a trail of wet slime on the fabric that covered her slender forearm. "He said he wanted to live a little before he died."

"What?" Sounded like some weird delayed-onset midlife crisis. Even if he was a *really* late bloomer, though, shouldn't he have gotten over it by now?

"Said that, if I wasn't going to do it with him, he'd find someone who would."

Ann's tongue felt stuck in her mouth. There had to be something she could say, something that would help. But she couldn't think of a thing.

"I'm sure that it's just . . ." *What?* "It has to be a mistake, Mary. Some sort of . . . Has he been to a doctor recently? I mean—"

"Oh, he's perfectly *healthy*," she said, her tone as bitter as rotten lemons. "Too damned healthy."

Ann gaped at her. Her mother-in-law had sworn. Unimaginable. But then, so was Martin leaving his wife.

"I should go home," Mary said. She put both hands on the bed, as if preparing to push herself up, but went no further. Her shoulders slumped with exhaustion, her eyes swimming with tears.

"Have you been here all night?"

Mary nodded, her gaze going to John's face. Her mouth

curved up in a smile, sad and lonely. John had always been able to make her smile.

"I don't think you should drive," Ann said.

"I can drive," she snapped. "I can make that drive in my sleep. I could make that drive in a coma."

Which was probably true. She'd gone back and forth between Mill Valley and here what, a few thousand times? But Ann knew how long even a mile was when you were in that kind of shock. How someone, when their world had just fallen apart—again— might look at a telephone pole or a bridge abutment and think, just for a second, how easy it would be to turn the wheel and finally have it all over.

She pictured her in-laws' house. A perfect white Colonial, four bedrooms up, with a big yard that used to hold beautiful gardens back when Ann was in high school, so vivid and color-ful they'd held their wedding reception there. The gardens had shrunk every year of the last twelve; Mary hadn't had time to keep them up, not when she was spending so much time here, and she'd plowed them under rather than watch them go weedy and barren.

It was a lovely house, tasteful and classic, but relatively mod-est given Martin's success. He'd built it early in their marriage, and Mary had chosen to stay, even when he'd offered to build her something new and grander.

Ann believed that the house held too many memories for Mary to leave. And, apparently, too many for Martin to stay.

"Why don't you come stay with me for a while?" Ann asked. It was an impulse, but what else could she do? She'd only worry about Mary, driving home alone and then rattling around in that empty house.

"You don't want me to stay with you," Mary said flatly.

"Yes, I do." It was, Ann found to her surprise, true.

It could be that she didn't want to think about last night. It could be that having her mother-in-law there was a convenient buffer; Tom could hardly come bulling in and force her to face what she'd done if Mary were there.

But John had loved his mother. And, in watching over her and sheltering her for a time, she could finally do something for him, too, when she'd hadn't been able to do that for so very long. "Fair warning, though," she said. "There are the puppies. And they're . . . puppies."

Mary's smile firmed. "I like puppies."

THIRTY

"Have you seen Ann lately?" Tom asked, trying for casual. Apparently he failed miserably, because Mer's head snapped his way, her mouth freezing in midbite.

Then she chewed while she studied him, the sandwich bulging out her left cheek, and he contrived to look innocent.

"I saw her today," she said after she swallowed. "I see her almost every day. Why?"

He shrugged. "Haven't been asked over for dinner for a couple of days."

"What? My cooking's not good enough for you?"

"No! No, not that." He picked up his sandwich, made a show of yumming over it. "What's in this, anyway?"

She narrowed her eyes at him, the thick lines of eyeliner on each lid coming together in one black slash. "Turkey, Granny Smith apple, Brie. Honey mustard I made myself. Why?"

"It's good."

"Hmm." Her mouth pursed, as if she were trying to read him. "Okay. Well, she's got her mother-in-law with her now. Probably figured we didn't want to have dinner with an old lady like that."

"Don't call her that."

"What? Old lady?"

"Yeah. You'll be one someday. You don't want someone to call you that, do you?"

"When I'm that old, I won't care," she said. "And you'll be long gone by then, old man."

"Smart mouth." He was going to miss her, smart mouth and all. He was getting used to having her around. And he sure was eating better lately. "So what's her mother-in-law doing there?"

"How should I know?"

"Didn't you ask?"

"I figured she'd tell me if she wanted me to know." She stood up, picked up her plate, and headed for the dishwasher. "You want to know? Ask her yourself."

———

Okay. Okay, he could do this.

He stood in her backyard, three feet from the bottom of her steps. He'd been standing there for a good ten minutes. He'd be ready soon. He was almost sure of it.

Hell, but it was hot out. Funny that he hadn't noticed it before. That weather girl with the shiny teeth and tight sweaters on the morning show had predicted a nice day. Accuracy apparently wasn't the reason she'd been hired, because sweat trickled at the back of his neck, coated the palms he wiped on his thighs for the third time.

It's okay, he told himself. *Just ring the doorbell and talk to the woman.* He'd done it dozens of times.

The door opened, and his heart stuttered. Jesus, she was pretty, with a brown and white fluff ball of a puppy cuddled up against her faded Gophers Basketball Final Four T-shirt, the one from the season that no longer existed, her expression warm.

"Oh," he said. "Hey." Yeah, Mr. Eloquent, wasn't he? He should just go back to staring and scowling and forget all the talking stuff. There was a reason the press always considered him the silent type: because he couldn't think of anything clever to say.

"Oh." Her smile faded, her eyes going wary. And he hated that just seeing him made that happen.

"Haven't seen you for a couple of days."

She buried her nose in the puppy's neck while color climbed into her cheeks. "Been . . . busy. Figured Mer would tell you that Mary's been staying here."

"Yeah, she did." He was sure he'd practiced what to say to her. Stayed up half the night figuring it out, and here they sounded like a couple of twelve-year-olds noticing each other for the first time, who couldn't dredge up a thing to talk about. And damn, he'd always been able to talk to her. "But I thought that maybe . . . Oh, *damn it*." The hell with it. "I'm sorry."

Her head snapped up. "Are you?"

"Well, I . . . I'm sorry if you are," he said cautiously. This was virgin ground for him. He'd always gone into a . . . Relationship wasn't a good word for what he'd had, for they'd been far too temporary and unimportant for that. But he'd gone into them with both parties knowing from the beginning how it would end, simple and clean.

But there was nothing simple about this.

She put the dog on the ground—one of the females, he thought, the runt of the litter. Mer had dubbed her Zon, for Amazon, though Ann had warned her not to name them. The little thing almost disappeared into the grass. "I'm not sure if I am," she said. "I should be. I know I should be. I suppose I will be someday, won't I? But mostly when I start thinking about it, I end up *thinking* about it."

"Yeah, I've been doing a fair amount of that, too." He took a step, managed to stop himself, just barely, and shoved his hands in his pockets. Because if he didn't, he was going to touch her, and that had to be a bad idea. He'd forgotten why, but it had to be.

"If I took advantage of you . . ." She'd been tipsy, and he'd known it. Hurting, and lonely. He'd convinced himself that he'd touched her only because he wanted to chase the pain, to give her some respite, no matter how brief. But he'd gotten what he wanted, hadn't he? He'd wanted her so much it had kept him up nights, haunted him through the sleep he did manage to catch.

Her chin came up. "Maybe I took advantage of you," she said. "I needed to forget. I used you."

"Hon, anytime you want to use me, go right ahead. Just so you know."

She laughed and the weight lifted off his shoulders. Was there anything better than her laugh?

"Are we okay, then?" They had to be. Mer needed her. And he . . . Well, he *something'd* her. Wasn't quite ready to figure out quite what. "When we didn't see you for a few days, I thought that maybe we weren't."

"I think so." She paused for a moment, as if trying to figure it out. "I was just embarrassed, I guess."

"Embarrassed? What would you have to be embarrassed about?"

"Well, I did kind of . . ." She put her hands to her cheeks and blew out a breath. "I was . . . demanding."

"One might even say *insatiable*."

"That, too."

"Oh, yeah," he said. "We men *hate* that."

It would be easier, he decided, if she just weren't so damned kissable.

Before, he'd thought the curiosity was as bad as it could get. That the not knowing was what was driving him crazy, that he'd have more control after he'd had her.

He was dead wrong.

"Besides, you hadn't had an orgasm for twelve years," he said. "You had some catching up to do."

"Who said I hadn't had an orgasm for twelve years?"

"You did—"

"No, I said I hadn't had sex for twelve years." She couldn't meet his eyes, but laughter played at the corners of her mouth. "Not the same thing. I know you guys would rather not think that we can be self-sufficient in that area, but—"

"Oh, no, we like to think about it. In fact, I can guarantee I'm going to be thinking about it for days."

"I'm sorry," she said, though she didn't sound a bit sorry.

"Besides, I hope it's not quite the same."

"Okay, now you're just fishing." But she grinned at him, with that mischief that lit up her eyes, all the more fascinating because it was so rare.

"I'm glad we're okay," he said. "Mer needs you. And I'd hate it if she lost that because of something I did."

"You think I'd do that?"

"No," he said quickly, as the storm clouds gathered in her eyes. He wondered if he'd ever seen her angry. Well, yes, he realized; she'd been mad as a hornet when Cooper had mounted her dog. "I guess I haven't been doing a lot of thinking lately. Apparently I'm still not."

"Did you ever?" she asked, but there was no heat behind it. She reached down and scooped up the puppy, which had fallen asleep in the sun. It didn't open its eyes, just snuggled into her arms as if it belonged there.

"Ann, do you—" Mary poked her head out the door, took in the two of them, and her face went blank and careful. "Everything okay out here?"

Ann gave him a long look, while he held his breath and hoped. "Yeah, it's okay," she said. "I was just inviting Tom and Mer for supper."

———

Three weeks. It had been three weeks since she and Tom had . . . well, since they'd done that. One night. Just one night. And yet, when she first swam up to consciousness every morning, she opened her eyes expecting to see him there.

Just some weird psychological trick of her brain, she decided. Nothing had happened in that bed for so long that her mind had gotten fixated on the one time it had and refused to let go.

It was still awkward between them. She missed the easiness,

the warmth. Oh, they saw each other. Buffered by Mer, by Mary, all conversations filtered and translated through them. She had to be careful what she said. How she looked at him.

Often she wondered if it was worth it. Worth the niggles of guilt, worth having to readjust her view of herself. Worth losing him as a friend.

But then she'd remember. How much it had hurt before he'd touched her, and how quickly that had fled. He'd chased it thoroughly, held it at bay for one long night that she'd needed so desperately, and she knew she couldn't have done anything else.

But she was uneasy. Her stomach unsettled, her thoughts insubstantial and fuzzy. She couldn't concentrate. Didn't feel much like eating.

Even this morning, as she sat in the warm sunshine at her kitchen table. Mary was puttering around in slippers and a robe, brewing up coffee.

She wasn't much trouble to have around, careful not to overstep her boundaries. If Judy had moved in for a couple of weeks, Ann knew, the whole house would be rearranged by now. She'd have thrown out half the ingredients in the kitchen, turned down the air-conditioning, installed a half dozen pots of plants in the living room, started a compost pile in the backyard, all in the guise of helping.

Mary helped. But she always asked first, tentatively, as if she were afraid to step too hard. She let out the dog when Ann worked too late, cleaned up after the puppies, had the rosemary in the kitchen window looking lush.

But it was still weird to have someone else in the house. Ann had lived alone a long time. It was nice, sometimes, to come home to someone instead of an empty house, one that had been scrubbed so efficiently in her absence that there was still an orange-oil shine on the dining room table.

And it kept her from running to Tom on lonely and frightening nights. She wasn't sure she would have been strong enough otherwise. And while she might—maybe—be able to live with one lapse, she couldn't deliberately and continually ignore her vows.

Mary hit the button on the coffee grinder, the smell of the beans hitting the air with a deep, toasty punch. Ann looked down at her plain piece of whole wheat toast, and her stomach lurched.

There wasn't much to bring up, though she hugged the porcelain bowl in the first-floor bathroom for another couple of minutes to be sure. The black-and-white tiles on the floor blurred before her watery eyes, and acid burned her throat.

"Okay," she said. "Okay."

She splashed cold water on her face, buried it in a soft, sunshine yellow towel.

"How far along are you?"

She braced her hands on the edge of the pedestal sink and took a couple of deep breaths before turning to face Mary.

She stood in the doorway, her hands deep in the pockets of her celery green robe, her face neutral.

"I'm not—"

"Don't lie to me, Ann," she said sharply.

"I wasn't going to lie." Hadn't exactly worked her way to the truth, yet. She was still lodged firmly in shock, numb and disbelieving. "I'm just not sure, yet. Haven't taken a test."

Mary tightened the robe on her belt, yanking the ends sharply. "Who needs a test? You've thrown up every morning for three days. How late are you?"

How late was she? She'd never been that regular, never paid all that much attention to her cycle. There hadn't been a reason to, and the cramps that came a day or two before her period always gave her plenty of warning.

"Maybe a week."

Mary nodded. "What are you going to do?"

What was she going to do? She hadn't gotten to the point of thinking about that. Too busy trying to wrap her mind around the truth of it.

The room decided to take a spin, whirling like a carousel. "Can we sit down?"

"Of course. Is the kitchen okay? The smell of the coffee—"

"It's fine," Ann said. "I'm done now."

"For now. When I was pregnant with John, they kept telling me it'd be okay as soon as I finished the first three months." She stepped aside, allowing Ann to head down the hall before her. "But then I threw up *twice* a day for the next two."

"Gee, something to look forward to. Thanks."

Was it true? She slumped into a kitchen chair, slid her hand over her belly. It didn't feel any different. Shouldn't it feel different? Could be a bug. Could be that part of her that longed so much to be a mother tricking her body into thinking it was so.

Mary sat down. Slowly, with her hands pressed to the table, as if otherwise she might topple over.

Ann saw her so frequently that she never noticed the signs of aging. They were too gradual, and she'd known Mary too long. She looked at her and saw the woman she'd always known. But Mary's hands were pale against the table, the skin thin as plastic wrap, blue veins twining across the back like a river map.

She'd gotten thinner since she'd moved in. Ann was pretty sure she forgot to eat when Ann wasn't around to prod her into it. She drank too much coffee, and sometimes Ann could hear her up in the night, light footsteps down the hall and on the stairs. She'd followed her once, afraid that Mary was ill, and found her on a pillow on the floor in the kitchen, her face buried in the fur of one of the puppies. Ann left her there. The dogs would do as much good as anything, she figured.

Mary wrapped her fingers around her coffee cup, drumming them along the sides, as if she didn't know quite what to do with them without needles and yarn in them. "How far along, do you think?"

"Not long. It was . . ." She winced; this was not something she was comfortable discussing with her mother-in-law, and, unlike Judy, she was pretty sure Mary was going to be mortified, too. "It was only three weeks ago. Just before you moved in, and . . . Well, it was only once."

"Isn't it always?" She took a sip, the cup quivering in her hand. "Some young girl gets carried away one night and boom!

Baby. No matter how dearly I wanted it, I always had a hard time getting pregnant. Oh, how I used to cry every month." She took another sip, then grimaced. "Cold."

"Let me get that," Ann said when Mary made to rise.

"No. You stay here." She pushed up, wound around the plastic wading pool that still held the puppies. She'd had them out early in the yard, and now they were all sleeping, curled up around their mother. They were getting so big, grew so fast. Soon enough it would be time for them to leave.

Mary dumped her coffee in the sink, refilled the cup from the pot. Steam curled up, and she leaned against the counter, with her back to Ann. "I had an even harder time staying pregnant. Lost three babies after John was born before the doctor finally said no more."

"I didn't know."

"It was a long time ago." She turned, her smile fixed, her eyes flat. "Now then." She crossed the floor with more speed this time, her hands clutched around the cup, and took her seat again.

"Yeah. Now then." Mary was clearly ready to talk. Except Ann had no clue what to say. Her brain felt set on slow, as if the thoughts were stuck in mud. She couldn't sort through them, couldn't find her way to clarity. "You haven't asked me whose it is."

Mary gave a short bark of laughter, abrupt and sharp in the quiet morning kitchen. "What were you thinking? That I'm blind, that I'm stupid, or that I'm ridiculously naive?"

"None of the above." Ann smiled, but it felt strange, the smile of another woman. "I guess I thought I was more discreet than that."

"Well, honey, I didn't figure it was Eric or Dr. Mike. And there aren't a whole lot of other options."

Her smile broadened, settled in, and then, just as quickly, faded. "I thought maybe . . . I thought you'd be mad at me."

"Honestly? I thought so, too." Birds sang wildly outside. A car roared by; Mark Benson was late for work again. "You know why we paid for John's care, all these years?"

"I—" *What?* "My brain doesn't seem to be working that well

right now, Mary. You better give me warning if you're going to change topics that quickly."

"Oh, that's going to get worse, too," she said serenely. "But it's not really a change of subject. Did you know why?"

"I was too grateful to think about it much," Ann said. "I know how much the two of you loved him. You wanted him to have the best care, no matter what it cost. I couldn't do that for him."

She would have tried. Oh, she would have tried. And she would have lasted, maybe, if she'd been very lucky, a year or two. And then the state would have had to take over, and who knew where John would be now?

"Not just that." Mary shook her head. She'd brushed her hair back from her face, and the lines ran straight across her forehead, deep and parallel. "We didn't want you to have any reason, any reason at all, to let John go."

Ann's stomach twisted, and she tensed for another dash to the bathroom. "I wouldn't do that."

"Not purposely, no. Probably not." Mary's shoulders lifted, fell. Still her fingers were curled around that cup of coffee, but she hadn't taken another sip since she'd refilled the cup. "But if you were losing the house, ruining the business, by trying to keep up his care? I knew how brutally expensive it was going to be. At some point, maybe, you'd just wonder if it was worth it. Convince yourself he wouldn't have wanted to live like that and maybe you should shut things down."

"I'm not sure that's not what he would have wanted," Ann said. That thought had kept her up many a night. "But I just couldn't do it."

"I know. Me, either. But I think, if we're not ready to let him go, that'd be okay with him, too. He'd wait for us."

"Yeah." Crap. Her eyes were flooding now, her emotions swinging wild.

"I should move out."

"Oh, no!" Ann reached across the table and grabbed her mother-in-law's hand. The bones felt narrow and fragile, but her grip was strong. "I mean, sure. If that's what you want.

But don't do it on my account." They hadn't discussed it. Ann hadn't asked. Didn't really want to know, didn't want to pry in Mary and Martin's business. They'd handle it better without her interference, she thought. "Have you . . . talked to Martin?"

"Yes. Twice." Mary clipped the words out, short and rapid. Perhaps, Ann thought, if she said them quickly enough, she wouldn't have to feel them. "Nothing has changed. We haven't been . . . It's been difficult, ever since John." She held her eyes open, as if afraid to blink. "I couldn't . . . How could I be happy, how could I live, when my son wasn't? But Martin wants to. And I—how'm I supposed to change now?"

"I don't know." Ann didn't seem to know a whole lot this morning.

"But I don't—" Her hand turned in Ann's, the fingers convulsing. "I don't think I can go back to that house."

"Then don't." Ann understood, better than anyone, what houses represented, what they meant. Homes were her business and her passion. And that house stood for something that had ended a long time ago. "Not till you're ready. If ever. It's just a house." *Now*.

"Yes. You're right." She nodded. "Just a house." She patted Ann's hand with her free one. "So."

"So." She'd have to deal with this, wouldn't she? Sooner rather than later. There wasn't going to be time for her to think about things, the luxury of being able to adjust. "Mary?"

"Hmm?"

"I don't know if I can do this."

"Of course you can do it, my dear." She said it with such conviction that Ann nearly believed her.

"Just keep telling me that, okay?"

"Whatever you say." She tried to smile. Trying to be happy for her, to project positive encouragement. But Ann knew that this had to hurt. She'd imagined Ann's child would be her grandchild, and the one thing Mary had always wanted, more than anything except her son back, was grandchildren.

"Mary? You can say no to this, if you want. I won't be hurt. Not in the least. But . . . Well, you know, Tom's mother died when he was young." *Tom.* Shoot, she'd hardly given him a thought. She was too busy trying to wrap her brain around the idea of *me* and *pregnant* to even consider him. But he'd be in this, too, wouldn't he? Somehow. And she was going to have to think about how she felt about that. "I only had one grandmother, and she was . . ."

"I know. The woman she was, was gone before you had a chance to know her. But she was a lovely woman, Ann, she really was. Made the best caramel rolls I've ever tasted, and as soon as there was trouble, as soon as anyone got sick or lost a job or anything of the sort, she was there with those rolls and an offer to help. And she meant it." Mary nodded. "She would have *loved* you."

"Yes." Okay, she wasn't going to get all misty about that, too. There were plenty of waterworks lurking as it was, and it was going to be all she could do to keep them in control. She wasn't even sure if she wanted to blame it on the hormones or not. It was a good excuse, but did that mean she was going to wander around feeling like this for months yet? No, thank you.

"Anyway," she said. "I always wanted a grandmother. Children need them, I think. And my mother'll be . . . well . . ."

Heavens. She'd love the child, Ann had no doubt about that. But she wasn't going to be, well, a grandma, not in the way that the storybooks talked about them. Ann tried not to feel too guilty about thinking that. But she had a child to consider now, and there was no such thing as having too many people to love you.

"No need to go on. She'll be a grandmother of a rather untraditional sort."

"Yeah." Ann nodded. Mary'd known Judy since they were both in elementary school. She understood. "Anyway, if you could . . . Well, would you think about considering this one your grandchild?" When Mary's chin wobbled, Ann rushed to go on.

"If you can't, I really will understand. And maybe you won't know until it's here. I just think that . . . Well, I think that any kid would really like to have you for a grandmother."

Mary was silent and unmoving for so long that Ann was afraid she'd offended her terribly and started rehearsing her backpedaling speech.

"I'll think about it," Mary said at last. "So? What are you going to do?"

"Have a baby, I guess."

Oh, God. She was having a baby.

"When are you going to tell him?"

"I don't know." Her stomach sloshed again. "I haven't thought about it yet."

"If you don't mind a bit of advice . . ."

She latched on like it was a lifeline. "Please! Advise me. Tell me what to do!"

Mary smiled. "Don't wait too long. It'll only get harder, and the longer you wait, the more, um, upset he's likely to be."

"Oh. Yeah." Upset. Was he going to be upset?

What was she thinking? Hell, yes, he was going to be upset.

"This afternoon," she decided. Might as well get it over with. "But I think I'm going to go tell John first."

THIRTY-ONE

She felt better after she'd gone to Cedar Ridge. Calmer, the way he'd always made her feel. She'd be all worked up, fussing over a grade, pissed off over a bad game, and John would smile at her, and everything all twisted up inside her would just smooth back down, like a storm abruptly sliding into calm.

This was going to be harder.

She filled up her cheeks with air, pushed it out through pursed lips. Again. And then her head swam and she had to put her hand on the wall to steady herself.

Shoot. There was no reason to do this *today*. She should practice more. Think things through, so she had everything solidly lined up in her head before he could start mucking it up.

Excuses, Ann.

Yeah, she knew. She was still petrified.

But Mary was right. That was only gonna get worse. The more nights she lay in bed thinking about it, the more terrible reactions she could come up with. The more she'd convince herself that he was going to be really, really ticked off.

She punched the doorbell, jumping when it ding-donged. Cooper went nuts. She heard him thumping inside, the skitter of claws as he tried to put on the brakes, the whomp when he slid right into the wall beside the front door.

And she heard Tom. *Great. He was swearing already.*

He was scowling when he opened the door. But then he saw her, and his brows went up in surprise, and his mouth softened. "Hey," he said softly.

He was barefoot, in gym shorts and a T-shirt that had been washed so much it was more gray than black. His hair was mussed, and there were reading glasses on the top of his head.

"You need glasses?"

"What?" He grabbed the glasses off the top of his head, chuckling sheepishly. "Yeah, I guess. Got LASIKed a couple of years ago, and they told me it'd speed up the need for reading glasses. Guess that means I'm officially old, doesn't it?"

Better and better. He felt *old*. Crap, she was old, too, too old to be doing this for the first time.

"Is Mer here?"

"Nope. Went over to Josh's."

"And you're relaxed enough to read."

"It's Josh. He's scared of me."

"No, he's not." Josh, Ann thought, wasn't much scared of anything.

"You're right, he's not. He should be, though. Why isn't he scared of me?"

"Because he's Josh."

"Yeah. He's a weird kid. I think he's more grown-up than I am."

"Except for the reading glasses."

"Yeah."

Silence bullied its way between them, the absence of conversation far more noticeable than any actual words would have been.

It had been awkward between them ever since that night, no matter how diligently they'd tried to pretend it wasn't. A couple of times she'd caught Mer studying them with a puzzled look on her face, as if she was picking up on something but couldn't quite figure out what.

They were too careful not to bump up against each other. Too cautious in what they said, how often they looked each other's way. Too determinedly impersonal in their conversations. She'd had some hope they'd settle out of it, back into the easy relationship they'd had before.

Guess that one was out, too.

"You want me to tell her you came by?" he asked at last. "Or I can call her, if you really need her. The puppies—"

"Are fine," she said. "And no, actually, I need to talk to you."

Heat flashed into his eyes. "Talk?"

"Yeah, talk."

"Shoot. And here I thought you couldn't resist me any longer and you came to jump my bones."

"Oh." She snapped her fingers. "Is *that* what I came for? Huh. Guess I forgot."

"A guy can always hope."

"Yeah." Hope. She had it now, more than she had in a long time. Silly hope, ridiculous giddy hope, tempered with a solid slug of terror. *A baby.* "Let's go inside, hmm?"

His cheerful expression clicked immediately into concern. "You sure you're okay?"

"I'm fine." *I hope.*

He stepped aside to allow her to enter. She headed down the hall, straight for the kitchen. She felt comfortable in there, as faded and inefficient as it was. She liked kitchens, didn't like that fussy, formal living room. And there was a sink handy if she had to throw up again.

She felt the presence of him behind her, the sound of his footsteps, the heavy bulk of him. Could almost convince herself that she could feel the heat of him, too—a body that big had to put out a lot of heat; she remembered how warm she'd been that night together. Hot, really, in more ways than one, hadn't even needed a sheet.

"You want something to drink?" he asked.

"No." Her hands were sweating, her mouth dry. "Yes. Water."

"Okay." He filled up a glass from the pitcher in the fridge and handed it to her. She stared into it, ripples spreading on the surface as her hand trembled.

"All right, you're worrying me," he said. "And I suck at worrying. So tell me fast and get it over with."

Good plan. She squeezed her eyes shut, took a deep breath, spilling it all out in a rush. *"IthinkImpregnantgonnahave-yourbaby."*

Nothing. No response at all.

She dared to open one eye. He still had the pitcher in his hands. The door to the refrigerator was open and spilling cold air.

"Think?" he said. "Or know?"

"The test said—"

"Test? You took a test? Without telling me?"

She winced and nodded. And then she rescued the pitcher right before it slipped from his hands. She put it back in the fridge, gently closing the door.

"A baby? My baby?"

"Yes."

He was swaying, his skin the color of chalk.

"Maybe you should sit down, hmm?" She guided him to the table, eased him into one of the retro metal chairs with the green vinyl seats. He sat there, compliant, hands loose on his thighs, staring off into nothing.

Heavens. She figured he'd be shocked. Worried he'd be mad. Hadn't guessed, though, that he'd head right for unconscious.

Minutes passed. Five, ten? Enough that she wondered if she should call someone. Not 911—he was still breathing, she checked—but, hell, his dad? Boom?

"Well," she said. "I know it's a lot to take in at once. You've probably got a lot to think about. I'm just gonna go now. Let me know if you want to talk about—"

"No." He nodded, slapping his hands down on the table with enough force to make her jump. "No, there's only one thing to do."

He slid off the chair, right down to his knee. He wavered there a minute, wincing until he got everything arranged just right, and then held out his hand to her.

"Ann McCrary," he said, "will you marry—"

"What the fuck is going on here?"

THIRTY-TWO

Tom scowled at the interruption. "What's it look like? I'm proposing to—"

"Oh, stop it," Ann said to him, and pulled her hand free. "You're doing no such thing."

"Yes, I am." He reached for her hand, but she stepped away, toward Mer.

"Mer, it's not what it looks like. I mean, it sort of is, but—"

Mer had gone so pale that the dark swipes of lipstick and eyeliner she wore looked like zebra stripes.

"Mer." Tom pushed himself to his feet, grimacing as his knees cracked like snapping twigs. "Ann and I, we've something to talk about. If you could just leave us alone a moment, we'll explain later."

She just crossed her arms over her chest, glaring at them both, waiting.

"Okay. Fine." Tom turned back to Ann. "I guess she's part of this, too. How soon before you can get a divorce? Because before the baby gets here—"

"*Baby?*" The word burst out of Mer, and she rounded on Ann. "You're having a baby," she said flatly.

Ann folded her hands before her waist, twining the fingers together until the skin burned. "Yes. I'm having a baby."

Mer whirled and ran. But not before Ann caught a flash of her face, suffused with anger and betrayal and hurt.

Her feet beat a harsh staccato on the wood floors, and the front door slammed like an ending.

"We'd better go talk to her."

"No point," Tom said. "Not till she's ready. And we're not done here."

"Tom, we've got eight months to figure out about the baby! Mer's a little more pressing. God knows what she'll do out there."

"Walk off some steam, no doubt. It's not as if she's going to get far." He took Ann's hand, turning her to face him. "Okay, now about the wedding—"

"Tom, I'm not marrying you," she said.

"Of course you're marrying me. You have to."

"I do?" She kept trying to read his face but couldn't find a thing. Not anger, not concern, nothing. He looked as if he'd gotten beaned in the head with a quick line drive up the middle and hadn't quite come back to his senses yet. "Look, you're in shock, and you're not making sense. You know that's impossible."

"It's not impossible. I told you. I told you I was never having another baby out of wedlock."

"Wedlock." An old-fashioned word. Not a very appealing one, with its implication that marriage strapped you in to something that you couldn't leave, not even if you wanted to, like handcuffs or stocks or a jail. "I'm already married, Tom. Just in case you forgot."

Her shock was wearing off, and in its place came panic. And a spurt of anger.

Tom shrugged, as if her marriage were a mere inconvenience to be dispensed with as soon as possible. "So you get a divorce. There has to be some legal standing in a case like this. For God's sake, you haven't really been married for twelve years! Don't know why the hell you didn't take care of it years ago—"

"Take *care* of it?"

A man with all of his brains working would have noticed she was heading toward all-out fury, and backed off. He would have figured out that his case would be better made in a calmer moment. "Yeah. But now—"

"It is my marriage," she said with gritted teeth. "I took a vow. It is not something to *be taken care of* like a leaky pipe or a failing roof."

"I took a vow, too. Right after Mer was born. And I swore I would never do that again."

"Well, you shouldn't have gotten me pregnant then, should you?" She whacked at him with the flat of her hand, a solid *thwack* against his upper bicep. It didn't faze him in the slightest, but it felt good, good enough that if he said something else stupid, she was going to hit him again. She could blame it on the hormones, she figured. They had to be good for something.

"So it's all my fault?"

"Hey, I bet if I go upstairs and start scrambling through your drawers, I'll find a nice stash of condoms," she said. "I haven't had sex in twelve years, and I was drunk. You expect me to know what to do?"

"Oh, I knew that you were going to throw that back at me, sooner or later. I just knew it."

She jammed her arms across her chest and glared at him.

"We have to get married," he repeated. "I promised myself."

"Yeah, that's just how a woman always hopes to be proposed to."

"You're turning me down 'cause I didn't do it right? Cut me some slack, sweetheart. You kind of caught me by surprise."

"No, I'm turning you down because I'm married." She stepped closer, drilled her finger into that solid chest. "*Married*. And if you don't see how a legal, moral, and religious vow taken before a man of God trumps some weak-ass promise you made to yourself when you were twenty-two, I can't help you."

She turned on her heel and headed for the front door.

"Hey! We're not done," he called after her.

"Yes we are," she said. "And, since it doesn't seem as if you're going to do it, *I* am going to find your daughter."

————————

Shit, Mer thought for what was approximately the 567th time.

Yeah, she'd counted. Wasn't as if she'd had anything else to do.

She'd waited until she saw Ann head off to work, Mrs. McCrary drive out in her Lincoln for the nursing home. Nobody'd be back until at least lunchtime. Usually Mer took that shift, checking on Cleo and the pups, but she figured Ann wasn't going to be trusting her to do that today. She'd be wrong, though. Mer still liked the *dogs.*

So she had Ann's house to herself at least until twelve thirty or so. She'd gone to Josh's, but he'd already left. He was counseling at tennis camp this week; he was good, apparently, expected to be ranked second in the state in singles this year. He hadn't told her that. His mother, proud and beaming, had spilled it, when she'd told Mer how much the kids loved him.

It was a different world out here. She was pretty sure her parents had never once talked about her with their faces glowing the way Josh's mother had. It was kind of freaky, she told herself. Maybe Mrs. Rabinowitz was just making up for the fact that Josh was adopted by gushing, didn't want him to think that he wasn't wanted.

Oh, hell, being adopted had nothing to do with it.

She leaned back in the kitchen chair, let the cig roll around in her fingers. The sun came in strong and yellow, turning the tiles to cream, shining off the stainless stove like it was made of silver.

Yup, it was still a damned nice kitchen. Too bad its owner was such a bitch.

She couldn't go home. Her dad was there, hadn't set one foot outside. She'd checked. And she just didn't want to see him right now.

She thought maybe being with the dogs would calm her down. But puppies made her think of babies, and . . . Shit! Ann and her father were having a baby.

She thought Ann had liked her. Had really, truly liked her.

Well, she should have known better. It wasn't the first time someone had tried to get to her dad through her. Usually she could spot a suck-up a mile off. But Ann had been trickier, so slow and careful Mer had never seen it coming. And it pissed her off that she hadn't noticed.

Not to mention her dad. Getting all jacked up about her and Tyrone, when all the time he was grinding it with Ann. Nagging at *her* about being safe, for God's sake. What a hypocrite. Pretending to play dad, making a fuss about how she was his only daughter. Yeah, he hadn't been that great a father, hadn't paid all that much attention to her, but at least she'd always known that she was the only kid he had.

Shit, she thought again. Time to go home to Chicago, soon as she could buy a ticket. Might as well not wait until they shipped her out so they could concentrate on the *baby.*

She ran her fingers down the white tube she held. It was misshapen, bent at the tip, the paper a sickly, stained beige. But it was the last damn one she had; she'd gotten it from Tyrone the last time she'd seen him, and there weren't going to be any more where that came from.

But this was as good a time as any, wasn't it?

She flicked open her lighter. The little flame glowed bright, swimming in front of her eyes, and she blinked hard until her vision cleared.

———

"Ann?" Mary Ellen Swanson, their office manager, poked her head in Ann's office. "Your neighbor's on the phone. Says it's important."

"My neighbor?" Her heart started thumping hard enough to remind her it was there.

He'd asked her to marry him. For all the wrong reasons, and it was impossible, and she hadn't been able to stop thinking about it all morning.

She'd driven around for an hour, trying to catch a glimpse of Mer. She'd stopped at the Rabinowitz's, and Josh's mom had said he was gone and wouldn't be home until five, that Mer had stopped by and left, and promised to call if she saw her.

She'd finally given up and come in to work. She had a meeting with a potential client at one, was interviewing a new contractor at three. Mer could be anywhere. And maybe, at work, she could get her head to concentrate on something else long enough for stuff to start sorting itself out in the back while she wasn't paying attention. Sometimes it worked that way; she'd be cooking, and get the perfect solution to a difficult design problem.

"Tell him I'll talk to him later," she said.

"Him?" Mary Ellen had to be pushing sixty, a widow fond of hair dye the color of Santa's suit and earrings that could have been chandeliers in Graceland. Ann figured the firm would be able to survive without her all of about a day and a half. "It was the one from across the street. Lorraine? The one with the great pants at your party?"

"Lorraine?" *What could she want?*

"She said it was important."

Okay, now she was working on hyperventilating, her breath fluttering along with the wild heartbeat. Lorraine had never called her at work. Her house had to be burning down. Or her mother had gotten arrested again. Something.

"Okay." She took a deep breath and lifted the receiver. "Lorraine?"

"Oh, Annie, thank God I caught you," Lorraine said. Breathless, but not sobbing. So at least nobody was dead. "I went over to water the flower beds and—just accidentally, you know—while checking on the window boxes, I happened to glance in the window. And Mer was there."

"Thank God." She should have known Mer wouldn't do anything dumb. She was just hiding out until she got used to the idea. Ann felt like doing that herself. "She's in my house a lot, Lorraine. I asked her to keep an eye on the dogs."

"But she's *smoking*," she said, her voice chirpy with the scandal of it. Lorraine liked nothing better than a scandal.

"I know, Lorraine. It's a terrible habit, and I thought she was trying to quit, but you know, we all slip up sometimes. I'll talk to her when I get home."

"You don't understand," Lorraine said, around quick, staggered breaths as if someone had kissed her silly. "I'm pretty sure it's not tobacco she's smoking."

THIRTY-THREE

She called Tom.

She debated about it in the car on the way home. Her house, her relationship with Mer. Maybe she should just handle it. Bring him in when she knew more, if it became necessary. But she finally decided he had to know. In the end, Mer was his daughter.

So she called him on her cell, and gave him a brief rundown, careful to point out that she was only going on Lorraine's information, and they really knew nothing at all yet. When she finished, the line went silent so long she wondered if they'd lost the connection. And then he'd just said, "Thank you," formal and distant, and hung up.

She stared at the phone, frowning. Then she flipped it onto the seat next to her and drove faster.

Nobody was home at her house except for the dogs. The back door was locked, but she only needed to take one step inside before she knew that what Lorraine had claimed was true. One didn't forget that smell, burning rope underlaid with something sickly sweet.

She took a minute to soothe the restless dogs. Too much excitement for them, she figured. Tom must have done a lot of hollering. Then she headed next door.

She had a right to butt in this time, she figured. It had happened at her house.

Tom was tall and dark and glowering when he answered the door, his mouth set hard, his expression forbidding.

"I'm sorry," he said. "That she did that at your house. She won't be bothering you anymore."

"What?" She glanced behind him, expecting to see Mer pouting. Or mad. One could never be sure with Mer. "Where is she?"

"She's in her room. I'm calling her mother."

Ann nodded. "Probably a good thing if you're together on this one."

"Yes. And then I'll book the flight—"

"What flight?" Ann broke in.

"Her flight home."

"You're sending her home? Just like that?"

Weariness crept into the set of his shoulders, his eyes. "What else can I do?"

"You can work on it. That's what you do, in a family."

"Because you know all about how families work," he said, and she stepped back, stricken.

"I'm sorry." He reached out a hand to her. "I didn't mean it. I'm just so . . . Damn it, I didn't mean that."

"Is this the kind of parent you're going to be with our child?" she asked, her anger rising fast. "You ship her off when things get a little uncomfortable for you? If that's the way it's going to be, I need to know now. When I can count on you and when I can't."

"*Shit.*" And she saw it then, what was behind the tough expression. Not anger, like she thought. It was fear. "What the hell am I supposed to do, Ann? Obviously I'm fucking this up. She *has* to be better off with Cassie."

"Are you sure about that? Cassie had her for sixteen years. You've had her for two months. Just how much of this can you blame on yourself?"

He didn't have to say a thing for her to read his answer. He'd blamed all of it on himself, all of those years he was there only peripherally, all the days since then when he'd failed to make a difference.

"I'd like to talk to her."

He gave her a long look, then shrugged. "Suit yourself."

Okay, Ann thought to herself as she slowly made her way up the stairs, with its cabbage-printed wallpaper and fusty, patterned runner. *What are you going to say to her now? What do you think you can do that's going to change anything?*

But she only knew she couldn't walk away from Mer now. She wasn't stupid. Mer'd been hurt when she'd heard about the baby, hurt and angry.

She knew, too, that parenthood wasn't all gurgling babies and well-behaved teenagers. Far from it. You could do your best, do everything right, and still sometimes things didn't turn out how you expected. Kids had minds of their own, and fate liked to throw her own curve balls at you, too. Hadn't Ann learned that a long time ago, better than anyone?

If she was going to be a parent, she might as well start groping her way through the tough stuff now. She wasn't so naive as to think there wasn't plenty more of this ahead.

"Mer?" She tried to sound light and friendly, knocking just hard enough on the door to be heard.

"Go away."

"Well, that's not happening," Ann said. "And frankly, you owe me that much."

"I *owe* you?" She waited for the explosion. Instead, what she got was: "Come in, if that's what you want. It's open."

She came in and took her time, studying Mer's room. She'd never been in there before. It was filled with lace and pastels, frills and white furniture. Pretty enough, she supposed, though unimaginative and fussily old-fashioned.

"Doesn't look much like you in here," she commented.

"What do you mean?" Mer said in mock insult. "I'm just the princess of all things girlie and boring."

Mer was flopped on the bed, with her eyes fixed on the ceiling. She had on black pants, belted low around her hips, ballooning out in legs as wide as a sail, hacked off just below her calves. Her T-shirt had a hand with an upraised middle finger printed on the front, and her nails were a sickly green. And despite it all she looked as young as Ann had ever seen her. Or maybe, Ann thought, she was finally starting to look beneath all the camouflage and see the girl.

Ann sat on the end of the bed, earning a scowl and stubborn silence. She plucked at the yarn that tied the quilt, purple and white, delicate as floss.

"You've got me at a loss here, Mer," she said at last. "I don't know the right thing to do."

"I'm sure you'll figure it out. Don't you always know what the right thing to do is?" Mer said, her voice heavy with sarcasm.

"I should be mad at you. You used my *house*, for *that*. Hell, I am mad at you." And she was going to wreck the quilt if she kept pulling on the ties like that. She folded her hands in her lap. "But I'm also not stupid, you know."

"Really?"

"Yup," she said. "And you don't have to be a genius to figure it out. You're kind of obvious, you know. So I'm torn."

Mer turned her head toward the window.

"You see," Ann continued, "I believe that our behavior has consequences. You did something illegal, in my house. There should be some fallout from that."

Mer rolled her eyes.

"But I'm also aware that you were testing me. Seeing if I'd send you away, too, for doing something bad. If I'd cut you out of my life."

That got her to turn Ann's way. "When did you start watching Dr. Phil?"

"No Dr. Phil. Just logic."

"Don't go looking for hidden meanings." Mer had left makeup on the pillow, a smear of black against the pure white linens. "I like dope. There was nobody at your house. Just that simple."

"Just that simple," Ann repeated, but she didn't buy it for a minute.

"Besides, it's not that big of a deal. Not like you never tried the stuff."

"Nope," Ann said.

Mer snorted in disbelief. "With the mother you got? Never? Who the hell has never even tried it once?"

"Maybe because she's my mother," Ann said. "And the answer to who, is me."

"Shit, I knew you were a nerd. *Christ*, McCrary, live a little. I'll give you some, if your mom won't."

"Oh, I can get it anytime I want. My mom used to grow it in the grove." It wasn't any big secret. "And she's still there, on that damned farm. Never wanted to go anyplace else. And I hated that place. Hated that damned house that was freezing in the winter. Hated the beat-up walls and the mold that seeped in and the jumble of furniture they'd gotten from the dump. Hated that I couldn't invite anybody over without being mortified."

Mer was listening now. Trying to look like she wasn't, pretending to be bored, but she was absolutely still, her eyes fixed.

"Mom swears she's happy there. Maybe she is, I don't know. But if that stuff had anything to do with putting a nice rosy haze over the place for her, I knew I wanted nothing to do with it."

"Jeez. Is there anything you liked about it?"

Ann considered. "The goat. I liked the goat." And her mother. Sometimes. "I always knew that my brain and my body were the way out of there. I wasn't doing anything that might mess that up."

Mer looked her up and down, her eyebrow lifting in skepticism, and Ann couldn't help but chuckle. "Not that kind of using my body. No, I got a basketball scholarship."

Mer sat up on her bed pulling her knees up to her chest and tucking her arms around her legs. "I know you used me to get to Dad. Just like Mom."

Ann shook her head. "Nope. I was just stupid and careless and well, lonely. No long-term plans there." She still was having a hard time believing it. "Hard to imagine, isn't it? I was careful my whole damned life. The most responsible teenager you ever saw. And so I had my careless moment twenty-five years later and got caught."

Mer seemed to be thinking about it. She turned her head, resting her cheek against her knees, and plucked at the threads that trailed from her hem. "I am *so* grounded, aren't I?"

"Oh, yeah," Ann said. "That consequences thing."

"Great." She sighed heavily. "And I'm not getting rid of you, either?"

"Nope. Not that easily."

"Crap," she said, but there was no heat behind it.

Ann glanced around the room again. An old milk-glass lamp sat on the sawn oak chest, a delicate piece of tatted lace drooping over the edge. There was a silhouette on the wall, framed with a twining of pale lavender ribbon. The only sign of Mer's occupancy was the pile of shoes beside it on the floor, black Chuck Taylor sneakers and scuffed boots and a pair of rubber flip-flops with soles three inches thick.

She had to decorate, she thought suddenly. Something for her child, something much better than this.

"Mer?"

"Whaddya want now?"

But when Ann swung her gaze back, she caught her smiling. She had two silver loops through her eyebrow today, one like a bull's ring through her nose, and her hair had been greased into stiffened chunks.

She's trying so hard, Ann thought. She wondered how many people bought it for more than a second.

"I was an only child of a single mother," Ann said. "Like you." Fear stabbed at her stomach. *Oh, baby, I'm sorry. Didn't mean to do this to you.* "I don't know about you, but I *hated* it."

Mer shrugged.

"I never wanted that for my child." Not much she could do about it, though, except do her best to make up for it. "I'm really glad she's going to have a sister. It would mean a lot to me if I knew she could count on you."

"She?"

"Oh, hell, I don't know. I can't keep calling the baby 'it,' can I?"

Mer's mouth twitched. "Ozzie. I'm going with Ozzie."

"Ozzie'll do for now." Ann debated about touching her. She wasn't a touchy-feely woman, didn't automatically reach for a hug or a comforting handclasp. She'd have to get over that, wouldn't she? Babies needed a lot of physical attention, a lot of cuddling.

But she didn't think she and Mer were quite there yet. "So. Can I count on you?"

Mer blinked hard, the spikes of mascara-gobbed eyelashes flapping. "Well, yeah, I guess so. If Ozzie's gonna have you and Dad as parents, the kid's gonna need me, isn't it?"

THIRTY-FOUR

August crawled by. Ann threw up regularly. She went to the doctor, got a due date—mid-April—and got sent home with vitamins, a sheaf of pamphlets, and an appointment for another checkup a month away. It didn't seem nearly enough. Wasn't she supposed to start getting ready? Why didn't anyone tell her what to *do*?

She spoke to Tom only once, a brief and strange conversation on his front steps in which she informed him of the results of her checkup, reciting the facts as unemotionally as if she was telling him about the city inspector's visit.

He'd asked her to marry him again, dutifully, angrily, which made it easier to turn him down again. It ticked her off that he even asked. This was hard enough; no reason he had to make it harder. Yet he was.

They'd been friends. They were having a baby together. And instead of growing closer, finding a comfortable and functional relationship as coparents—and wasn't that a nice politically correct term for it?—they were distinctly awkward with each other, like people who barely knew each other, whose first impressions weren't great, but who were forced to interact. Coworkers after a merger, former rivals after a trade.

But Ann and Mer were okay. They were both a little surprised by it. Mer's dad was still so damned pissed at her that Ann's house was a calm refuge. Ann had forgiven her, just that quick, just that easy. Mer still couldn't believe it. She wasn't sure why Ann remained clearly annoyed with her dad, and he flatly refused to talk about, or to, her.

Even the whole grounding wasn't as bad as it had been the first time. He let her take care of the puppies, let her go to Ann's once a week for dinner, allowed Josh to come and—if supervised—play chess. She couldn't beat him, not even close, but she'd beaten Boom the last two times she played him, and that was pretty good.

"Mer!" her dad hollered from downstairs.

"What?" she shouted back, just as loud, to make the point. He might be bigger than she was, but she really doubted he could outscream her.

"You left your cell down here! It's Cassie."

"Great." Just what she needed. Mom. Cassie hadn't called her in, oh, four weeks? Five?

"Stay," she told Coop, who was sprawled across the bed. As if he was going to move; he liked the bed, his huge head plopped square in the middle of a pillow, shedding fur all over the flowery quilt.

She clomped down the stairs. Dad was waiting for her at the bottom, holding the phone out, scowling. He did a lot of that.

"You think," he said, "that you could get a ring tone that doesn't have the word fuck in it?"

"Yeah, but what would be the fun in that?" She sprinted back up, shoved the door closed behind her, and clicked the lock.

"Hello?"

"Sweetheart!" Cassie chirped. "How are you?"

"Okay," she answered automatically. Obviously Tom hadn't said anything about the little episode at Ann's. Or her mom didn't care.

"I have news!" She was practically giggling, and Mer felt her stomach sink.

"If you're having a baby, too, I'm going to throw up."

"A baby? Of course I'm not having a baby." She paused for a second. "Too? If you're—"

"No. Just a neighbor."

"Oh." Cassie could be suspicious if she wanted to be. She just usually didn't bother, and she didn't now. "I'm getting married! Isn't that *great*? Oh, honey, I'm so happy."

"To who?"

"Howard, silly."

No wonder she sounded so happy. Howard had a bank account the size of Lake Michigan.

"That's great, Mom," she said automatically. And it probably was. At least she wouldn't have to listen to Cassie complain about how stingy Tom was anymore. And the old guy had to have a nice place.

"Thank you." She was darn near crowing. She'd gotten what she wanted, sort of, from Tom. But this time she was getting the guy down the aisle; marriage had to be a better deal than child support. "He wants to talk to you."

"Talk to me?" He'd never said more than "Hello" or "Nice to meet you" to her. What the heck were they going to talk about on the phone? "What—" But her mother was already gone.

"Hello!" Howard's voice was hearty, Santa Claus cheerful. "It's Howard."

"Yeah, I figured," she said. *Sheesh.* "Congratulations."

"Thank you. I just wanted to reassure you that I plan to take very good care of your mother."

"Yeah, okay." What was she supposed to say to that? "Thanks?"

"And to reinforce the point that you will be welcome any time. I have a lovely home up in Lake Forest. I've already selected a room for you. I hope you like it."

You had to give the guy points for trying. But Lake Forest? If she thought her dad's neighborhood was a little too scrubbed and polished, Lake Forest took that to a whole 'nother level. She'd probably get arrested every time she set foot on the street, just for dragging down the general class of the place.

"I have very exciting news," he was going on. "I talked to the people at Merrydale Academy. My daughters both went there, it's a magnificent school. And, despite your rather, um, adventurous academic history, they're willing to accept you on my say. It's a lovely place, Mercedes. My girls adored it."

"Merrydale Academy? Where the f—" She stopped, swallowing the curse. Saying that in front of Howard was like swearing in front of your kind old grandma. He didn't deserve that. But she was going to have to be seriously medicated to go to any school with *academy* in the name.

"Yes, well." He cleared his throat. "It's in Vermont. Quite isolated, of course, but lovely. The academics are superb. Your mother assured me you are quite fond of the outdoors."

"Yeah." The only outdoors she'd ever spent any time in was the space between her front stoop and the bus stop. Her brain spun like she'd just gotten up way too fast. "Can I talk to Mom?"

"Of course." He chuckled. "Welcome to the family."

"Yeah. Thanks," she mumbled, answering on autopilot.

She heard the murmur of voices through the phone, Cassie's thrilled giggle.

"Sweetheart!" she said. Her voice was high, cutting through the air like a whistle, and Mer had to hold the phone away from her ear before she burst a drum. "I know it's quite the rush. But this summer, we've had so much time to spend together, and it's been just wonderful."

"Mom—"

"The wedding'll be the last weekend in August," she tripped on, as if she hadn't heard a thing. "Then your plane to Vermont will be the next Monday, and we're off to Tuscany. I'm *so* excited."

"*Mom.*"

Cassie hesitated. When her voice came again, it was low and even. "This will be a fresh start for you, Mer. You'll be well looked after, have an opportunity to develop discipline and . . . What was that, honey? That the dean said?"

Howard's voice rumbled in the background. "Oh, yes. Character and intellectual rigor. This is the kind of opportunity that doesn't come along often, Mer. A whole new class of people to interact with. It's up to you to make the most of it."

Yeah, well, Cassie'd made the most of her opportunity, hadn't she? Got Howard in her clutches but good, without Mer around to muck things up.

Boarding school. You didn't have to be a genius to translate "character, discipline, and rigor." There'd be tutors, and monitors, and people watching over her at every turn. She'd be shoehorned into their mold, a nice, obedient Stepford girl, or else.

"Sure, Mom," she said. "Congrats again." She snapped the phone shut, hard enough to make Cooper raise his head and look at her.

"Such a good dog," she said, and buried her face in his neck.

———

She went down the ivy.

Dad, she figured rightly, wasn't Boom. Didn't have sisters or nieces and tended to take things at face value.

It was a perfect afternoon. There were a zillion people out on the golf course, with bare legs and caps, zooming around in carts. Kids wheeling up and down the street on bikes and scooters, running through sprinklers. People in their gardens, walking their dogs. Not too hot today, the sun mild, with just enough breeze to remind you that fall was coming, and you'd better enjoy it while you could.

Josh was playing; she heard him halfway down the block, something light and pretty that sounded like hummingbirds flying over the keys.

His house was white clapboard, with black shutters and deep green bushes and a bright red front door that stood open, letting the air in through the screen.

She poked her head in. "Anybody home?"

He looked up and grinned and slid right into Iron Maiden, his left hand thumping so loud on the low keys they seemed in danger of breaking.

She stepped in to listen for a while. He played classical mostly, stuff that put her to sleep even though she could recognize how hard it was to play. Sometimes it seemed impossible the way the music moved so fast, like Josh had more than ten fingers to work with.

But he played old school metal, too, which shouldn't have worked on the piano but he made sound okay. Nothing new, not ever. But Metallica and Judas Priest and even Ozzie.

He finished with a crash that rattled the pictures on the wall and spun on the bench.

"Hey!" he said. "Your dad let you out."

"Yeah." There was something nice about his living room. It was what she figured her dad's house was supposed to be but hadn't gotten to: soft couches with overstuffed cushions, shiny floors with rugs that felt good beneath your feet, a coffee table that his mom didn't mind if you put your feet up on, all kinds of pictures of their family hanging on walls the color of new moss. "Anybody home?"

"Nope," he said. "Em's got a dance competition this weekend. They're all in Duluth."

"And you didn't go?" she asked, pretending shock.

"Much as I love her, that's way too many little girls in tutus for me."

Em was his little sister, and so damned cute she rivaled the puppies. She was six and thought Josh had hung the moon. He pretty much felt the same way about her and had no problem at all letting people know it.

A little sister, she thought with a sudden pang. Maybe she'd have one, too, almost as cute.

Didn't matter, though. Wasn't as if she was going to be around the new baby. She'd be lucky if the ankle biter knew who she was.

"So they're gone? All weekend?"

"Yup."

Her dad wouldn't leave her alone for an hour without a guard.

She sat down next to Josh on the piano bench, and he slid over to make room.

He was such a good guy. Probably the nicest one she'd ever known, and damned if he didn't get cuter the longer she knew him.

She nudged her right hand on top of his.

Oh, why the hell not? She kissed him.

He didn't move. Didn't kiss her back. But her thumb was on his wrist, and she could feel his pulse start to go nuts.

"Why don't we go upstairs?" she suggested.

"Upstairs?" His eyes went wide. "Huh. Upstairs."

"Yeah. Upstairs."

"But I've never . . ."

"Yeah." She grinned. *So cute.* "I know."

"Well." His Adam's apple whipped up and down like a yo-yo. "Thanks. But no."

"What?" She couldn't have heard right.

"Thank you, but no." He'd regained his usual cool.

"You don't want me." Josh didn't want her. Her geek virgin friend didn't want her. "You gay?"

Instead of being insulted, he laughed. "No. You know I'm not gay."

Her cheeks burned. *"Shit."* The day was crappy enough to start out with; now it had slid right down into the sewer. She started to move away, ready to sprint for the door.

He slung his arm around her back, pressed her head down on his shoulder with his hand. It was warm there, and comfortable. Too bad he was a bastard.

"Now, hang on there. It has nothing to do with not wanting you, and you're not idiot enough to believe that, either. It's just, well, I've got a plan."

"A plan." She could maybe stay here. For a second. She could always holler at him later. Maybe throw a couple of things at him for good measure.

"Yup. See, I'm not the kind of guy you have wild flings with."

"But I just offered—"

"Hush," he said. "I'm the kind of guy you want after you've been through all the guys who break your heart, all the bad boys who aren't worth the time you spend on them. The one who might not have looked that interesting when you're twenty but who looks really, really great when you get all that out of your system. The one you marry."

The air rushed out of her in a giant whoosh. "Marry?"

"Now, don't freak out on me. It's a long time away, and you'll be allowed to make up your own mind. I won't drug you, or clobber you over the head, or anything like that." She heard the warmth in his voice, the absolute conviction. She didn't think she'd ever been that sure about anything in her entire life. "So I'll be here. To cheer you on, to let you cry on my shoulder, to be your friend. Until you figure out you can't live without me."

Okay, now she did really want to sleep with him. Must be some weird kind of reverse psychology, but it was working. She sighed and settled in. "Don't you think we could start the plan tomorrow?" she suggested. "After we . . . ?"

"Nope," he said. "Though you should probably go over there and sit on the couch before I change my mind."

"You're not going to change your mind," she said. "You never do."

"Exactly." He ran his free hand over the keys, a rapid slide of notes. "So what happened?"

"What do you mean, what happened?"

He picked out a light tune, slow and sweet. "It's what you do. Something ticks you off, and you go do something dumb before you stop and think about it. Figure this one had to be a doozy."

"You—" She tried to work up a good anger about that. Must be something to that "music soothes" thing. It just sounded like too much trouble. "My mom's getting married."

"That's nice," he said. "A sibling, and a stepdad. Pretty soon you'll have a decent-sized family."

The weird thing was, he actually meant it. All her friends back in Chicago couldn't stand their families and were counting down the days until they could be free of them. But Josh loved his family. Even the weird and grumpy old aunts and uncles his mom was forever making him drive around. "You're so strange."

"What a flatterer you are. Can't imagine how I resisted you." The music slowed, until he let the last note fade into the air. "Now. Since you tried to use me and all, I figure you owe me something. Just so I'll forgive you."

"Most guys like to be used."

"And your point?"

Yeah, he wasn't most guys. "So what do I owe you?"

"I want you to go to Homecoming with me."

"What?" She sat up. He didn't look like he was joking. "Homecoming? Me?"

"Yup."

"You don't want to bring me to Homecoming." She tried not to be flattered. "I'm, like, the anti-Homecoming."

"So?"

"It'd serve you right if I said yes. And wore leather."

"Leather?" he said. "Great!"

She was almost sorry she couldn't do it. She'd kind of like to see the faces on all the Barbie clones when she came in wearing Doc Martens and spikes. Maybe she'd get her tongue pierced for the occasion. "I'm not going to be here, though."

His smile was completely confident. "Second Saturday in October. I'll let you out of the football game, but the bonfire's required."

THIRTY-FIVE

"Mer ran away."

"What?" Ann let her back door close behind her and tugged the belt of her robe around her middle. "You don't look very panicked about it."

"Oh, I know where she is. She's at the bus station, and her bus doesn't leave for an hour."

"She *told* you?

"Nope. Josh did." Evening had just turned the corner into night. There were a couple of stars winking overhead, a few lights flickering through bedroom windows in the houses across the yard. "I knew I liked that boy."

Ann told her heart to settle down; it couldn't keep going nuts every time she saw Tom.

But her heart didn't pay attention.

She was carrying his baby. He'd asked her to marry him.

Okay, he was an idiot. He didn't listen. Didn't understand when he did.

But he had a right to be involved in his child's life. She was going to have to figure out a way to see him without her insides jumping around like a windup monkey.

"So get changed," he said. "There's time, but we gotta get moving."

"You want me to come?"

"Of course I want you to come," he said, as if it were perfectly obvious. "Look, I don't care if you go to the bus station in your jammies. And I'm pretty sure a fair number of the guys there won't, either. But you might."

"But—"

"I'm going to ask her to stay with me," he said. "But, in case she says no, I need you as a backup."

"You want me to ask her to move in with *me*?" She knew she was slow these days. Her brain seemed to be permanently set on low speed. It made Mary smile knowingly every time she mentioned it, which only made her worry.

Her mother, on the other hand, swore she'd never been as sharp as when she was pregnant. But then, she also claimed she hadn't thrown up once, either, and couldn't imagine why Ann was. Helpful, her mother.

But she still couldn't figure out what the heck Tom was talking about.

"A backup?"

"Not forever, of course. Just until I can smooth things out between us. I wouldn't ask you if it wasn't important," he said. "But I think there's a fair chance she'll refuse to come home with me. And she *likes* you."

"She likes you, too."

He shot her a look of disbelief.

"Besides," Ann said. "It's not a job requirement. That she likes you, I mean. Sometimes I don't like my mother."

"You don't like your mother?" He'd appeared less surprised when she'd told him she was pregnant.

"Sometimes I don't, no. Oh, I love her," she said. "Very much. But sometimes I don't like her."

He shook his head.

"So she doesn't have to like you. In fact, I think that's just part of the deal. If they like you *all* the time, you're probably doing it wrong."

"I must be the best father ever then." He looked her up and down. "So you coming?"

She was already untying her robe. "I'm coming."

The bus station had been recently remodeled. Its harsh lights were as bright as daylight, illuminating shiny pale linoleum floors, red plastic seats, plain white walls with blurry, fake-arsty photos of buses on the road and maps highlighting their routes.

At ten thirty, the place was half-full. A Somali woman in a bright orange hijab cuddled a baby. A group of teenaged boys clustered in one corner, bopping along with whatever junk their earbuds delivered directly to their brains. Two girls in pink velour sweatpants leaned against each other and dozed. A huge, dark man with shoulder-length braids had so many tattoos on his arms that it was hard to tell where the ink left off and his black leather wristbands began.

"There she is."

There was no missing the purple streaks. She sat with her back to them, her black collar tucked up high around her ears. She was flipping through a newspaper, sipping from a can of Red Bull.

They each took a chair on either side of her. She looked up briefly, then continued scanning the entertainment pages.

"Hey," Tom said. "You forgot something."

"Who?" Mer snorted and flipped a page. "You?"

"Nope." Tom crossed an ankle over the other knee and settled back. "Your dog."

"I didn't forget Cooper," she said. "What, you think I'm stupid? I got a hundred and thirty-two dollars, and I'm riding the bus. I wouldn't do that to him." She carefully folded up her paper, smoothing the top page. "I knew you'd take care of him."

They smelled the man before they saw him, shuffling by in a grimy trench coat, lank hair streaming from beneath a dark blue knit cap. Tom glared at him, sending him skittering back three quick steps. Ann dug in her pocket and handed him a five.

Mer laughed. "Doesn't that just sum you two up? Can't say Ozzie won't get balanced parenting."

A blare over the speaker announced an arrival. The doors flew open, and a stream of people stumbled through, blinking at the lights.

"So Josh told you, huh?" Mer asked. "I figured he would."

"Then why'd you run?"

"I figured he'd tell you I was heading to Chicago, too," she said. "Give you the choice. You could just call Mom, have her head me off at that end. Give you the easy way out."

"What, I'm gonna get rid of you now? When you can finally be useful?" Tom was trying for casual but wasn't quite making it. "We're gonna need a babysitter."

"I've never babysat in my life."

"That's okay," Ann put in. "Neither have I."

Mer gave her a long look. "You okay?"

"Yup. Although next time you want to run away, could you just run over to my house? It's past my bedtime."

"I'll think about it."

Tom's leg jiggled up and down, until he rested his fist on it to hold it still. "You ready to come home?"

Mer considered. She hadn't been lying about the one hundred and thirty-two dollars. The way she looked at it, her options were the streets, boarding school, or the suburbs.

She tried to pretend she didn't care. "I suppose. If it's okay with you."

Her dad's hand came down on her shoulder and, if she didn't know better, she would have thought his eyes got a little misty.

"It's okay with me," he said.

―――――――

Mer stayed. She went to Chicago for Cassie and Howard's wedding, which was quick and quiet, held in Howard's library and presided over by his old friend the judge. It was, surprisingly enough for Cassie, relatively modest, with the exception of the hefty emerald-cut diamond Howard slipped on her left hand.

His children, who were closer to Cassie's age than Mer's, were not happy. But he was. And, Mer thought, so was Cassie, and not just because she was moving into a house the size of a department store.

She tried high school. Even with Josh's encouragement, she made it all of two weeks before shifting to the alternative program.

Tom had been skeptical. The program allowed students to come and go on their own schedule, to work at their own pace. Most of the other students were just out of rehab or worked full-time and had to fit school around that. There were only four teachers, but they were always there. The expectations for the students were clear, and they weren't allowed to move on in the material before they'd mastered the last, and the consequences for screwing around were both straightforward and immediate. So far she hadn't been suspended. He was learning to take progress where he could.

He wasn't making any progress with Ann, though. Mostly, he figured, because he just couldn't keep his big mouth shut.

But it all seemed so obvious to him that he couldn't resist pointing it out. They were having a baby together. They got along pretty well. Her marriage was merely a technicality. Time to take care of the legalities and marry him. If they were going to do it before the baby came—which he much preferred—she had to get moving.

The last time he suggested it, she slammed the door in his face.

Fall snuck in and settled down. The leaves turned, almost overnight, a blaze of yellow and orange and red. Sprinkler systems were shut down for the winter all over the neighborhood, and autumn-themed decorations were starting to appear: a big bundle of cornstalks in front of one house, a pumpkin the size of a car beside another. The backside of a witch had been tacked onto a tree in front of the Michelsons', the end of her broom sticking out horizontally, so it looked like she'd just whammed right into the tree.

Funny, funny, he thought. Though he had to admit the MADD sign underneath was a nice touch.

"Dad?" Mer hollered from upstairs.

It wasn't that big a house. He didn't understand why she had to scream quite so loud instead of coming to find him. But he was too happy that she was calling him "Dad" to do much about it now. Manners weren't that high on his list yet.

"In the kitchen!" he yelled back, and started rummaging through the fridge.

Her feet battered the stairs.

"Dad, I . . . What are you looking for?"

"Food."

"There's all sorts of food in there. I went shopping."

"Yeah, but there's a lot of vegetables in here, Mer. I need *food.*"

She sighed and hustled him aside before burrowing in herself. She pulled out two containers of Tupperware, something wrapped in foil, a tiny jar of some fancy kind of mustard that she'd sworn was worth the ungodly price.

"Roast beef?" she asked him.

"Sure," he said, and settled himself on a chair. "On white bread."

"Sorry. It's all whole wheat." She laid two slices of meat on a thick slab of bread, started piling it with slices of tomato and lettuce and onion.

"You're kind of a pain to have around," he said.

"I know," she said cheerfully, then handed him a sandwich he might have to dislocate his jaw to fit in his mouth. Then, "I need a dress."

"A dress? You wear those?"

"No. Which is why we need to go shopping. I'm going to the dance with Josh."

He raised an eyebrow in midbite.

"Oh, not like that," she said. "We're just friends. And he said I could go in jeans and a T-shirt, if I wanted. But I don't want to embarrass him. His coach'll be there."

"I don't think Josh could ever be embarrassed by you," he said. "But sure. How much you think you'll need? I can drop you off at the mall as soon as I finish this."

"No. How the hell should I know what to buy? You have to come with me. You have to help me."

"Oh, no." Tom would do a lot of things for his daughter. But dress shopping was not one of them. "I'll pay. That's as far as I'm going to go. What the hell do I know about shopping?"

"You know when a woman looks good, don't you?"

"Big assumption there, Mer, that I want you to look good. I'd prefer you ugly as an old troll until I'm too old to notice that you're dating."

She sighed. "Please?"

Crap. She'd asked nicely. That should be rewarded, shouldn't it?

"I'll tell you what," he said. "You need a girl. We'll get Ann to help us." And she'd have to spend all afternoon with them, hanging around while Mer tried stuff on. She'd see what a good team they made, what they'd be like as a family.

And then he could propose to her again.

He wasn't a patient man. But he was persistent.

When he knocked on her door she opened it, frowning. "What?"

Yikes. Pregnancy, he'd discovered, was making her damned cranky.

His brothers had warned him. He didn't remember Cassie being anything but pleasant—of course, he hadn't lived next door to her, and she'd probably been trying to *get* him to marry her, instead of resisting—and so he hadn't believed them.

He was starting to think they'd understated things.

She was wearing a huge sweatshirt that came to her knees and had splotches of bleach all over the front. She'd made an attempt to tie her hair back, but mostly it was flying around like Medusa's snakes, and she had one of the puppies in her arms.

"Uh . . . well . . ." He shot Mer a worried glance. "We're, um . . ."

"Out with it."

"We need help," he said quickly. "If you don't mind. Though it's okay if you don't want to."

Her suspicious gaze slid from one to the other. "What is it?"

Mer, bless her, took pity on him. "I need a dress. For the Homecoming dance. I have no idea what to do."

"You think I do?" She looked down at herself. An old pair of khakis were tight on the thighs, and it looked like the puppies had decided her cheap rubber sandals made good chew toys.

"Oh." Mer reached over and gave the dog a scratch behind its ear. "Okay, then."

"No, no, of course I'll help." She stepped back and considered Mer seriously. "We're just going to have to call in the big guns, that's all."

"Great!" Tom rocked back on his heels, grinning. "I'll get the truck, and—"

"Oh, no," Ann said. "Girls only. Besides, you're going to be busy."

He was torn between jubilation that he didn't have to go shopping and disappointment that he wasn't going to get to spend the afternoon with her after all. "I am?"

"Yup." She shoved the puppy into his arms, and he automatically hung on. It squirmed wildly, feet scrambling in dangerous places. "They're ready to go. I gave one to Ashia, but the rest you're going to have to find homes for. Might as well move them over to your place before we get back."

"Move them over?" Puppies. At his house. "Now, I'm sure they're comfortable where they are. I've been looking for homes, I told you I would, but I don't want to pick just anyone. You know you wouldn't want that," he said. Reasonably, he thought.

"You need some incentive," she said. "Besides, you'd better

get used to being responsible for young things, don't you think?" She gave him what could only be called the evil eye. "We'll do the dress. And you—" She jabbed a finger in his direction, hard enough that he thought it would have made a hole if it had connected with his chest. "Take care of the puppies."

THIRTY-SIX

Mer went next door at three on the afternoon of the Homecoming dance. Tom'd needled her about that. How could it possibly take so long to get ready? She'd just smiled and tripped out.

He went over at six forty-five. Josh was already there, in a dark suit and tie, his hair damp, with a plastic corsage box in his hand.

He was standing in the kitchen, shifting from foot to foot, an untouched glass of cola on the island. It was the most nervous Tom had ever seen him.

He figured it was his duty to notch up that anxiety a little more. "Do I have to do the scary dad thing?" he asked. "Threaten you with bodily harm if you touch my daughter in any but the most respectful way?"

Oddly, that seemed to relax him. He stopped jiggling and grinned. "No, sir. We're just friends. Though it's not really a *just*, is it? We're friends."

"Uh-huh." He and Ann had been friends, too, and look what had happened there.

Ann came in just then, with Cleo clicking at her heels. "You all might as well sit down. Gonna be a few minutes."

"Aren't you needed up there?"

"Nope. I just get in the way." She turned for the fridge, and

Tom found himself studying her body, searching for signs of their baby in her. Was there a new curve to her belly, beneath her loose yoga pants and her long shirt? He thought her boobs were bigger.

It seemed like it should show. Something that huge and important should have more impact. Like the instant the egg implanted, a woman should look *pregnant*.

"You want something?" she asked.

"I'll take what he's got."

"Okay." She tossed him a can of Coke before pouring herself a glass of cranberry juice.

"How come he got a glass?"

"Because I like him better than you." But she was fighting a smile.

"Don't they all," he said. "I found a home for another puppy."

"Will I approve?"

She hadn't been kidding. She'd nixed the first home he'd found for a dog; good family, but the yard was too small. The rest she'd given the nod to, but only because he'd worked really hard to make sure she couldn't say no to them. One had gone to the farm, to his brother's family. No better place for a dog than that. One went to Lorraine's grandson, another to Leo and his brand-new fiancée.

"Boom's taking him."

"How'd you talk him into that?"

"Didn't have to. I just had him over for the football game on Sunday."

"You got him drunk and made him take a dog before he sobered up?"

He popped the top on his cola and took a long drink. "Nope. Well, he drank. Of course he drank. But he was dead sober. It was the girl. You know, the big chubby one?" The dog had feet that were half as big as her body and enough curiosity for a whole litter. "She just climbed up into his lap, poked around a little, and fell asleep for the whole afternoon. He was a goner."

"Good going, Nash."

Faint praise, that. Over a dog. And he was ridiculously pleased about it.

"Just one left," she went on.

"None left. We're keeping Zon."

"You think I'll approve of you as a puppy parent?" She hid her smile behind her glass. "Maybe Boom'll take both of 'em."

"Hey, I—"

The clunk of Josh's glass on marble interrupted him.

"Holy . . ."

Mer hovered in the doorway. She had her hands clasped in front of her waist, her eyes down. Mary hovered behind her, smiling proudly.

Her hair had been freshly purpled, the streaks deep and shiny, making the rest of her hair look like star-glossed midnight. Her makeup was pale, a smoky haze of violet above her eyes, a shiny gloss of peach on her mouth.

Her dress was simple, a long, sleek spill of deep-colored silk that hugged the curves that she usually kept well hidden.

There were hints of the usual Mer: a tangle of knotted cord around her wrist, twined with chunks of crystal and rock. Beads around her neck, jet black and long. Her fingernails were short and unpolished, her shoes simple black flats.

"I couldn't do the heels," she said. "I hope it's okay."

"Okay," Josh repeated, and Tom poked him in the ribs with his elbow.

"Just friends, huh?"

It seemed to bring the kid to his senses. "Yup. Just friends. I figure we've got another five years to go on that at least," he said. "But she doesn't make it easy." He walked forward, holding out the flowers. "You look beautiful."

"Oh, well." She blushed. And then she caught sight of all their faces and scowled. "Cut the shit. I *can* clean up, you know."

"There's my girl," Tom said.

"We'd better go." Josh put his hand on her back and guided her toward the door. "We've got to stop at my house first. Pictures, you know."

Damn it, Tom thought. He was supposed to be taking pictures, wasn't he?

"She'll make copies for you, too, Mr. Nash."

"That'd be great, Josh. Thanks."

He leaned over to Ann while the two of them made their way to the door. "What color's her dress?"

"Midnight blue," she whispered back.

"Never thought I'd be so fond of those damned tent-sized clothes she wears," he said. "But if I'd known she looked like that underneath, I would have had to lock her up."

"Maybe we'll have a boy," she said consolingly.

We. It hovered in the air between them. It had been her baby; it had been his baby. But it was their baby, a life they'd made together. They hadn't talked about it like that, planning the future, imagining what he might be when he grew up.

Mary cleared her throat. "I'd better get going."

"You did a beautiful job," Ann said. "I could never have done that. She looks amazing."

"Easy enough to do. She's a beautiful girl."

"Would you like to stay for dinner?"

With a thoughtful expression, Mary's gaze slid from Ann to Tom and back again. "Oh, thanks, but a few friends are coming over later. A bit of a housewarming."

Last week Mary had moved into a small but pleasant apartment two miles from Cedar Ridge. At first Ann had worried about that; the last thing Mary needed was to spend more time there. But she seemed happier. She'd started a knitting club at the home, which met twice a week, and sometimes volunteered to play piano for the sing-alongs.

"Is Henry coming?"

"Oh, well." She checked her bag, clicking open the top and peering in before snapping it shut again. "Yes, Henry's coming," she said primly. "Along with several others." Then she sailed out the door.

Tom was chuckling when he turned toward Ann. And then his smile faded. She was standing by the refrigerator, her hand on her belly, her eyes shiny with unshed tears.

She smiled back, but her mouth trembled.

They'd sent a kid off together. All dressed up and fancy. One of the markers of parenthood, just like bringing them home from the hospital for the first time, sending them off to their first day of school. Graduation, moving them into the dorm. All the giant footsteps that marked a life, the ones that parents were supposed to do together.

He and Cassie had never done that. Not once. It was one of the reasons he'd sworn never to do this again without being married. And he'd missed all those milestones for Mer before this one; hadn't seen her first steps, her first lost tooth, her first date. Only now did he realize how much he'd missed.

Were they going to do this together, he and Ann? He wanted that. The punch of longing for it was so strong that it staggered him. He wanted to be able to smile at her as their child passed another milestone, remember all the ones that had gone before, and dream of all the ones that were to come.

Almost as much as he wanted her.

He was beside her before he realized his feet had moved. She just kept looking up at him, smoke swirling in those great wide eyes.

Kissing her just seemed like the thing—the only thing—to do. He put his all into it. *I'll take care of you, I'll take care of the baby, we can have a life together, we should do this together.*

She was breathing hard when he pulled back, her hands fisted in his shirt.

"I—"

He knew a protest coming when he saw it, figured the most efficient way to stop it was to make sure she couldn't talk. He held her head in his hands, stroked the cords of her neck with his thumbs. Kissed her mouth, her temples, her jaw, all the while trying like hell to hold on to some thread of coherent thought. There was a goal here: to show her what they could be, *should* be.

She twisted her hands in the front of his shirt, caught between pulling him closer and pushing him away, keeping him right in that place between denial and surrender.

"I'm already pregnant," she murmured.

"Yeah." He moved his hands over her belly in reverent disbelief. "Seems a shame only to get one night out of the deal. People try and try for months, sometimes years on end."

"A shame," she said thoughtfully. And then she pulled him close and kissed him back, hard and hot.

"Let's go," he said. He grabbed her hand and headed up the stairs, heading for her bedroom.

She stopped at the entrance to her room, holding him in place, both of her hands wrapped around his. "Not in there."

"Hmm?" What? She had objections now?

"That was our room." She swallowed hard. "Our bed."

"Oh." *Shit*. He folded her in his arms, rocked her back and forth while she clung to him. She felt good there, like she belonged. Like he'd spent half his life holding her close or waiting to do so.

Then he felt her mouth against his collarbone, light as the brush of a feather, enough to rock him to his core. "That one, on the left. Guest room. We never used it."

He caught glimpses as they spun toward the bed. It wasn't dark yet, but the room was dim and gray, the shades closed. Simple: bed, chest, chair, in dark woods and creamy fabrics. Then he let it all go.

She pushed him back, climbed on top of him, her hair spilling down as she bent forward to kiss him, to shove her hands up his shirt and burrow against his skin.

But he didn't want fast. He wanted tender. Wanted to show her that he could be in it for the long haul, warm and sweet, beyond the first mad rush of heat.

He watched her. Watched her skin ripple as he skated his hand over her, watched her breath shudder in and out when he reached down, and down.

He didn't know if it was his imagination that made her different. Rounder, softer, warmer. He wanted that mark on her, to know that sheltering his child had changed her.

He tried to hold on to the details, to keep the greater goal in mind. Show her how it could be for them, if she'd just agree. But it all blurred together, as evening slid into night, as he slid into her. Breath, skin, heartbeat, pleasure. Ann.

"Marry me," he said as she went limp in his arms, drifting off into sleep. "Marry me."

Her eyes flew open. She rolled away and sat up, tucking the sheet high beneath her armpits, scraping her hair away from her face with a shaking hand. "Why'd you have to ask me now?"

Damn it. "It seemed like the appropriate time."

"It's not." She blew out a breath, focused on something across the room. Closing him out. "I didn't mean to give you the wrong idea, Tom. I can't. You know I can't."

"Yes, you can." The simmer of anger started slow and low. "I talked to a lawyer. It's not that complicated, though a little time-consuming. And since I'd prefer that it be done before the baby comes, we need to get going."

Her gaze arrowed. "You talked to a lawyer?"

"Yes. I wanted to be ready when you are."

"Damn it!" She sprang from the bed, naked and furious and gorgeous. "You think I wanted it like this, either? You know how I was raised. From the moment I was old enough to know I wanted kids, I knew I wanted a regular family. Mom, dad, picket fence, the whole thing, everything I never had. But I have no choice, Tom. And you're not helping."

"If you want me to pay attention, hon, you'd better cover up."

She glanced down, as if she'd forgotten she wasn't wearing clothes, and her lip curled. She pulled the comforter off the bed and whipped it around her shoulders, and he was sorry he'd said anything.

"If that's what you want, too, then you're just being obstinate."

"And you're being purposely obtuse."

The simmer was kicking into a boil. He stood up. Her eyes flicked down, and then up again, a cool and distant appraisal. Ouch.

"Damn it, Ann, this is stupid. We're having a baby together. We should get married."

"I . . . am . . . already . . . married," she said, as slowly as if she were trying to make herself understood to someone who was barely conscious.

"That can be taken care of easily enough," he said. "One way or the other."

She jerked back as if he'd struck her. And then she said, low and even and final, "If you think that about me, then you don't know me at all."

"I know you well enough to know that hanging on to some promise you made years ago, a promise that doesn't apply to the current circumstances, is just damned stubbornness." If he couldn't woo her with sex, he'd do it with logic. "Take the rampant sentimentality out of it and be practical. It's only sensible."

"Sensible," she said flatly. "Practical."

"Yes."

"I want you gone." She gathered the drooping sweep of the comforter around her. "And if you have one practical, sensible, smart cell left in your body—which I highly doubt—you'll do it fast. I'm awash in hormones. I'm pretty sure I'm not legally responsible for my actions."

Sometimes you faced a batter head on, threw a fastball right down the center and dared him to hit it. Sometimes, though, you just had to issue the walk and wait for the next opportunity if you wanted to pitch another day.

Tomorrow, he decided. He'd pitch again tomorrow.

"I'll go," he said, "but you have to help me find my shorts."

THIRTY-SEVEN

Saturday morning, a perfect fall day, with the air fresh and crisp, smelling of leaves and apples and the first fires of the season. Ann took a long, slow run—the doctor said she could keep it up, as long as she felt like it—with Cleo by her side. Old times, except for the fact that she'd thrown up twice before she went out, and that she'd slept with Tom last night.

Big mistake, she thought, as her feet hit the asphalt and Cleo panted beside her. She nodded at her neighbors: George Kozlowski picking up the morning paper, wrapped in a robe with a coffee cup in hand; Mr. Schneider out with his four-year-old, who was exploding the little piles of leaves as fast as his dad could rake them up; three moms, pushing strollers toward the park.

She shouldn't have done it. Not when she knew he wanted something that she just couldn't give. But it had seemed—not harmless, but forgivable; she was already pregnant, she had already broken one vow. She'd be huge before too long, and then a mother. By the next time she had a chance to have sex, she might be too old to care.

A mother. The thought burst into her brain at least a dozen times a day. She still had a hard time believing it was real. When would she start to believe? After the first ultrasound, when she saw her child on the screen in black-and-white? When she started to show, when the baby started to kick? Or maybe the first time they put him—or her—in her arms?

Maybe she was just afraid to believe it. So much could still go wrong; the fear was as strong as the shock. She'd wake up in the middle of the night and slide her hands over her belly, as if her touch could communicate through her flesh: *Keep safe, baby. Keep safe.*

But more and more, despite it all, what kept pushing up through it all was the joy.

She was having a baby. Perhaps the biggest dream of all, the one that had died the hardest. Maybe it never really had died; she'd just buried it deep and ignored it.

She couldn't quite surrender to the joy. It seemed to be tempting fate. Get too happy, ride too high, and you were just asking to be knocked back to earth. But she couldn't seem to help it. It kept growing, constant as the baby. Every day she woke up, still pregnant, a day closer to motherhood, and the joy curled its tendrils deep, taking hold.

She'd worked up a light sweat by the time she returned from her run. Her stamina was down, her wind short. She hadn't been running as much this summer.

Sighting home, Cleo raced ahead of her, shooting around the back of the house as she gave a happy bark.

Tom sat on the back stairs, elbows on his knees, hands loose between his legs. Cleo stuck her nose in his palm, wagged happily when he gave her a hearty rub.

"Hey," he said, and climbed to his feet.

"Hey." Her heart started to thump, hard and heavy. It didn't matter how much she told herself that she had to get over this ridiculous infatuation with him; she couldn't look at him without feeling like a girl, giddy and uncertain and alive. But there was nothing girlish about the remembrance of him in her bed, and how her skin tingled with the feel of him.

There wasn't a good solution here. She knew it. Her brain understood it. The rest of her, however, just kept hoping.

She ran her hand over her forehead, scraping back damp

strands of hair. Her skin was sticky, and her T-shirt clung to her back. She looked bad, and she knew it and tried very hard to believe that it didn't matter. What difference did it make if he liked how she looked or not?

She didn't believe it for a minute.

"You headed for the nursing home?" he asked.

"Cedar Ridge?" Why would he care? "That's the plan. You need me for something? Mer, or the dogs?"

"No." He shook his head and tucked his hands in the pockets of his black leather jacket. "I want to meet your husband."

That cured her of stray urges and fantasies but quick. "Meet my husband," she repeated slowly.

"Umm-hmm." He squinted up at the sky, as if there were something more to see there than clean blue. "If he's the reason we can't get married, I want to meet him."

"You do understand, don't you, that there's nothing *to* meet?"

"There must be something that's keeping you from marrying me."

"But . . ." There had to be a good reason that this was a really bad idea. Having your baby's father in the same room as your husband just seemed too Jerry Springerish to be the wise course of action.

But he wanted to know her, and apparently he thought that marrying her was the best plan. And there was a lot of her at Cedar Ridge. It had been her home as much as any place the last twelve years. It had been the center of her life. If Tom wanted to understand her, he had to understand her and John.

"Okay," she said.

"Huh. I thought I was going to have to work harder at talking you into that one."

"It's a public place. What, I'm going to call them and tell them to keep you out?"

"That's true." And supremely logical. But somehow that logical brain of hers had seemed to short-circuit lately, and all his excellent arguments just bounced off instead of finding their rightful place. So he hadn't expected her acquiescence now.

"Just let me go catch a shower," she said, and left him standing in the yard to wait for her.

They drove to Cedar Ridge in silence. Ann kept sneaking glances at him, trying to gauge what he was thinking, what he expected to get out of this visit. But he had his game face on, mouth set and brows low over his eyes. She never saw that expression much anymore, didn't think of him that way. When he came to her in her dreams, in her fantasies—something he did with depressing regularity, given that she should be getting him *out* of such things—he was laughing, or smiling at her with his eyes simmering with heat and promise.

She drove automatically. The car could probably pilot itself to Cedar Ridge, it had made this trek so often. Her usual parking spot was open, three slots to the left of the front door. The lot was almost always empty.

Cleo trotted ahead of them; she knew where they were going, too, and her tail was wagging in anticipation. People were never excited to come here, hesitating at the door, their steps slow down the hall. They moved fast on the way out, but never on the way in. But for Cleo, Cedar Ridge was about as good as it got.

The automatic glass doors whooshed open, and she snuck another peak at Tom. He seemed suddenly tall beside her, strong and almost overwhelmingly physical, as if entering a place where so many were frail and fading made his robust good health all the more noticeable.

She tried to see it through his eyes. It was so familiar to her now, and the first time she'd come here she'd been too lost to take it in. Those first weeks at Cedar Ridge were a blur; she hadn't been sleeping, hadn't been eating, and had been too much in shock to notice anything about her surroundings.

The facility was about as nice as such places got. They tried; it only took a glance to see that they tried. The lobby had deep wing chairs and plush carpets and prints of fields and farmhouses. The floors were clean, the walls freshly painted. There was a small, pretty chapel, a community room with a flat-screen TV and two card tables and a lot of plaid sofas.

But no matter how well kept the place was, it couldn't hide the fact that its residents were breaking down. People shuffled down the hall, with relatives or nurse's aides at their elbows. There were a half dozen wheelchairs arrayed in front of the television, tuned to a football game, and she didn't know if a single person had any idea whatsoever what was going on on the screen.

There were decorations in the hall, bright and cheerful cornucopias and pumpkins and cardboard turkeys. Orange streamers swooped in great loops along the ceiling, and paper gourds swung from the lights. But the people beneath were faded, their colors dulled.

"Okay," she said, pausing before the familiar door. JOHN MCCRARY, it said, ARCHITECT. As if that was all there was to him. "This is John's room. And he's . . ." She wanted to prep him somehow. Explain John's condition, make him understand that there was so much more to the man than what he'd see today.

But there was no easy way to do it, no way to make him *understand*.

So she just shoved the door open, allowing Cleo to rush through. She went to the bed immediately, sniffing around John's feet, the corner of the sheet that trailed over the side, making sure all was as it was supposed to be, before finding her spot in the corner and curling up.

Tom went first to the photos on the closet. He stood there a long time, taking them all in, the chronicles of a young man with many blessings and a lot of plans. Did he see a youth that wasn't much different than his? Ann wondered. Lots of sports, lots of friends, a family that loved him.

John had been good at a lot of things, swinging through life with the confidence of one who'd never considered that things wouldn't go his way, because he'd make them. It beamed from the pictures, in his big, open grin, the easy way he stood, his arms around his friends, around Ann, claiming a world that surely held only good things for him.

Tom held his fists at his side, his arms stiff. She saw him close his eyes briefly, sucking in a deep breath, before he turned for the bed.

Though she'd seen it a million times, it was still startling sometimes to see John there. That wasn't how he was in her head. In her head, even now, he was that boy in the pictures, the man she'd planned her life with, too damned alive to be anything else.

She made herself study him. If you didn't know it was the same man as in the pictures, she didn't think you would ever guess. He'd lost so much flesh that now it seemed that skin merely stretched over bones. His face hadn't wrinkled—no sun, no worries—and yet somehow he looked older, the skin tissue-thin and colorless, his mouth slightly open with an uneven twist to one side. His eyes, too, were never all the way shut, the irises popping back and forth in spastic motion.

She heard Tom's breathing accelerate, the air sucking in and out, as if he were struggling to get enough in. And then he simply turned and walked out.

She followed him, down the hall and across the lobby, rushing to keep up as his long strides ate up the yards at a speed that would have been running for anyone else, the people who were alert enough to notice glancing up in surprise as he hurried by.

He burst through the front doors, into the bright fall sunshine, and gulped great lungfuls of air. Then he leaned back against the rough brick wall with his face lifted to the sky and his eyes shut. "I'm changing my will," he said.

"What?"

"If I ever end up in that condition, whoever puts me out of my misery gets everything."

Red flashed behind her eyeballs. "How dare you." He didn't know her. Didn't know John, didn't know anything about how she'd gotten here.

Did he think she hadn't thought about it? Hadn't cried about it, hadn't run it through her brain a million times, trying to figure out what was right?

"How *dare* you," she sputtered. "Spend two minutes in that room and you think you have any idea what it's like?"

He opened his eyes and glared down at her. He was angry, and what right did he have to be angry?

She tried to put it aside. It wouldn't do any good for her to scream at him, would it? She tried to explain, struggling for the right words. "He breathes on his own. His heart beats on its own."

A muscle twitched in his jaw. "If you loved him, you wouldn't let him live like that."

"What do you want me to do? Starve him to death?" It was the only real option. And she couldn't do it. It niggled in her dreams, woke her up many a night. But it wasn't just like shutting off a machine, a machine that was keeping him alive. Food, water . . . They seemed such a basic right to her.

Intellectually she understood that others could make another decision. Sometimes she wished that she could.

But she couldn't.

"Who cares how you do it?" he said. "If it's me, shoot me."

And standing there now, next to Tom, it all burst through, twelve years of injustice and fury, boiling, seething, finding its way out.

"You have no idea," she said. "What I've been through. What *we've* been through, how many times I've thought this over. I struggle with it every day. Every *minute*. And you come in here and you think you know what's right?" Her voice was getting louder. "We said for better or worse. And goddamn it, this is the *worse*. But I'm still here, for him, because I know damned well he'd still be here for me. Till death do us part."

He knew *nothing*, she thought. A blown shoulder, feeling guilty about some slut he'd knocked up. He damn well *should* feel guilty; it shouldn't take a marriage license to make him a father.

You made a commitment, you were there. Period.

"You can be there," she told him. "For the appointments. For the baby. We'll work out a custody arrangement." She'd gotten control of her voice, making it low and deadly final. "But that's it. That's *it*."

And she left him there, standing alone in the parking lot, while she jammed the car into drive and took off. She glanced back, one quick peek in the rearview mirror. He stood tall, unmoving, all in black, once again the man she'd first met, the one who scowled down from the mound and dared the world to hit him, the one nobody knew, the one he wouldn't let anybody know.

And then she peeled out into the street and headed for home.

THIRTY-EIGHT

April 23, 3:30 a.m.

Ann was screaming.

She'd been in the hospital for seven hours and been screaming for a good hour and a half. Not nonstop, of course. Sometimes she moaned, sometimes she panted. A lot of the time, she swore bloody murder. Mostly at Tom.

He was pale, skin chalky and sweaty while he paced back and forth. He carefully averted his eyes every time they exposed a private area, looked a little more queasy every time Ann got another contraction, and generally made sure he didn't get too close. Mer figured he was afraid she was going to toss something at him.

Mer was on camera duty. She flitted around the edges of the room with a fixed and nervous grin on her face.

Judy had lit something in each corner of the room; candles, incense, some kind of leaves. She blew them out when one nurse or another told her she wasn't allowed to burn things in here, then lit them again as soon as they left. She hummed something soothing and swathed the lights in red fabric so the room took on a pink glow. Now she was at Ann's side, rubbing her with scented oils, urging her to breathe.

"Go with the experience," she told her, when Ann's fists twisted in the sheets, her face contorting as she bared her teeth like a pissed-off badger. "Calm, dear. Serene. Breathe in the lavender."

"I would breathe," Ann gritted out, "if this damn baby would just *get out of the way*."

"You need a focal point," Judy said, rummaging in her bag.

"If you bring out a voodoo doll or a serene goddess statue or something like that, I'm going to throw it at your head," Ann said. "Or better yet, have Tom do it."

"You think I don't know you better than that after all these years?" She drew out a basketball and balanced it carefully on the bedside tray. "There. Concentrate on that."

Ann stared at it as if Judy'd just pulled out a purple elephant. "You got me a basketball?"

"Of course." Judy spun it around so the black-marker scrawl faced her daughter.

"What's that on it?" Ann asked suspiciously.

"I had it signed. Tim . . . what's his name, Duncan? That's the one you like, isn't it?"

"That's the one," Ann said, and started to smile, until the next contraction had her grimacing again.

"You like Tim Duncan?" Tom vacillated between surprise and offense. "Tim *Duncan*?"

"Oh hush, dear," Judy said. "Not now. Ann, honey, you must focus now, and relax. You don't want to bring your baby into a harsh world. Soft, relaxed, loving. It should only hear love in your voice. Let it come, ride with the pain. The pain is your friend," she urged.

"The pain is not my fucking friend!" Ann snarled. "The pain *hurts*."

"It is natural," Judy went on in a singsong voice. "It is only in embracing it, in going through this passage, that we can find our full womanhood."

Ann grunted, closing her eyes. Her belly moved beneath the thin cotton, tightening, twisting. Sweat ran down her temples, splotched her ugly hospital gown at her armpits, and beneath her breasts.

When Tom edged toward the door, her eyes flew open and lasered in on him.

"You're not leaving."

"No, I—" He swallowed hard. "I thought maybe I could get you something. Some more ice. I'm a little thirsty. You thirsty?"

"You know damn well I can't drink anything!" She flung the words at him, as if they were knives and each one could hack into his flesh. "Get over here."

"What? I—" He knew he was going to piss her off. Every damn thing he did pissed her off.

"*Get over here.*"

"Okay." He sidled over, wary and careful as a guy approaching a dangerous animal. She grabbed his hand and squeezed, so hard the tips of his fingers turned white.

"That hurt?" she said sweetly.

"Uh . . . What answer do you want?"

"I want to know that it hurts," she said. "Because this isn't fair. Isn't fair that you get to stand over there, all comfortable and handsome, after I blew up to the size of a whale, and I haven't been able to sleep a whole night for three months, because *your* kid likes to kick me at four a.m., and I've got heartburn and my skin breaks out and I can't fit into any of my shoes, and now I've been here for seven effin' hours, and I'm still only at six centimeters. And it *hurts*."

"Okay, it hurts," he said obligingly.

"Good." The contraction eased off, and she relaxed back into the bed, gulping. "I don't care if I break your damn fingers. I don't care if they fall off. You're not to worry about it until it's all over, all right? I want you here, right beside me, hurting. If you gotta go to the can, I don't care. In fact, I hope you do. I hope you gotta go so bad it feels like your bladder is the size of a Macy's Thanksgiving balloon. I don't care if you're hungry. I hope you starve. I want you here, so I can squeeze your damned hand until you feel one percent of what I'm feeling." She sucked in a deep breath, blew it out on a howl. "Here it comes again!"

"Close your eyes, sweetheart," her mother said, in the sing-song voice of a yoga teacher. "You don't want your child to enter in anger. Visualize yourself in a pool, a warm pool that allows the pain to flow through you. It is a passage, a natural path to a new joy."

She gave it a shot. Two deep breaths, eyes closed, until the pain rippled through her belly like a vise. "I want drugs," she said.

"Oh, no." Judy rubbed her shoulder soothingly, until Ann reached up and knocked her hand away. "You want to experience this. To feel it, every second of bringing your child into the world. The pain is a gift, to sear this in your memory, to mark the beginning of life."

Ann waited until she could talk again, then gave her mother a dark look. "Did you take something before you got here?"

"Of course not," Judy said serenely.

"I don't know why," Ann said, "it's perfectly okay, even spiritual, for you to use chemicals for the freakin' fun of it, and I'm not supposed to take any when it feels like someone's tearing me open from the inside out?"

"But sweetheart—"

"Enough." Mary, who'd been sitting quietly in the corner, her fingers flying through a baby sweater, put aside her yarn and needles and stood up.

"Judy, exactly how long were you in labor with Ann?"

"Well, it was only three hours or so," she allowed. "But it's really not the actual quantity, it's the—"

"Yes, it is," Mary interrupted. "Now, you blow out whatever the hell it is you have smoking up the place. Then you sit over in that corner and shut up. Meditate if you want, call on the spirits, support your daughter in any way you want as long as it's quiet. And you don't say anything until she asks you. You don't *move* unless she asks you."

"But—"

From the outside, it didn't seem as if Mary's expression

changed. But Judy must have seen something there, something not to be argued with. Her mouth snapped shut, and she moved to pinch out the wide candle that burned in the corner above a cluster of wilting branches.

"Now." Mary turned to Tom.

"Yes, ma'am."

"You're doing okay. You just keep doing what she tells you, agree with everything she says, even if she says you're the biggest bastard ever to walk the earth, even if she says you go in tomorrow to get your balls cut off. Just keep quiet, nod, and whatever you do, don't faint."

"I'll try."

"Mer."

"Here."

Mer had faded into the corner, making herself small in the shadows. Her camera was aimed square at the bed. Ready to snap, making sure she didn't miss anything.

"You go out and find a doctor, a nurse. Fast. Tell them we need an anesthesiologist in here, and don't let them put you off. There's a window of opportunity here, and we're bumping up against it. If it's too late, we're not going to be happy."

She was out the hall and heading for anybody in scrubs before Mary had even finished speaking.

Mary turned toward the bed, placing her hand gently on Ann's clammy brow. "Now, dear," she said calmly, as if those orders had never come out of her mouth. "Let's have that baby, shall we?"

———

7:34 a.m.

The nurse yanked on her thin purple gloves with a snap that made Tom flinch. "Time to see how far along we are."

She guided Ann's feet into the stirrups, flipped the sheet out of the way, and started groping.

Tom couldn't pace. Ann still gripped onto his hand, keeping him near—and yes, his bladder was starting to ache, and yes, he could really have used a sandwich—but he needed to pace. So he started shifting, foot to foot. He didn't want to get any closer to her; he was afraid she was going to start squeezing something more delicate than his fingers, and they'd gone dead numb an hour ago. But for damn sure he didn't want to get any nearer to the end of the bed while the nurse was rooting around down there.

The nurse grinned. "Well, there we are. Let's have a baby."

"What? I'm at ten?" Ann asked in disbelief.

"Yup," the nurse said. "Ten."

Ann dropped her head back to the pillow. "I'm *finally* at ten. I was starting to think I was never going to get to ten."

"You're there now." The nurse shifted, felt around. "Next contraction, we'll try a push. I'll count, and you hold your breath and just keep pushing until I tell you to stop, and we'll have a baby in no time."

"A baby." Her head snapped up. "Wait. I don't think I'm ready. Let's just rest a little first."

"Little late for that, Ann," the nurse told her, smiling. She'd heard it all before.

"A baby." The room swam around Tom. A baby. She was having their baby.

Judy slid a chair under his butt just as he started to go down.

Mer, who'd been nodding off in the blue couch in the corner, suddenly sprang to attention. "We're having a baby?"

"Looks that way," the nurse said.

"'It's about time." Because Ann had banned her from taking a picture from either end for the last four hours, there hadn't been much for her to do. And it had been a lot more quiet in the room since the epidural kicked in.

Now she lifted her camera to her eye, popping around from position to position, trying to find the right one to snap the momentous event.

"All right," the nurse said.

Mer suddenly lowered her camera, her fierce gaze sliding from Ann to Tom and back again. "Just wait," she said.

"It doesn't really work that way, dear," the nurse told her.

"But it's not right," Mer said. "Dad, you're being stupid. The two of you have barely talked to each other the last seven months. That's my brother or sister in there, and I'm not letting them grow up like that. I'm just not."

"That's nice," the nurse said. "And I do appreciate you've got something to say, but you're just going to have to hang on a minute." She looked up at Ann. "Take a breath, Ann. Hold it in. Now *push*."

She counted through it, while Ann leaned forward and grimaced, her face turning red with the strain, as Tom's already pale face headed for bleached.

"Good push," the nurse said. "But it's a good-sized baby, I think. You rest for the next one, and we'll do it again. Same thing, only a little harder."

"*Harder?*" Ann goggled at her. "Maybe we should go have that cesarean after all."

The nurse patted her knee. "Let's just give this a good go first, hmm?"

"I was talking, here," Mer said. "Now. My Ozzie needs parents. Both of you. None of this back and forth between the two, trying to play one off the other, different rules at every place. *Parents*. Together. And so the both of you gotta get over this."

"Over this?" Tom's eyes were glassy, and he couldn't have gotten out of the chair if the fire alarm went off. "It's not the time, Mer."

"It's *exactly* the time," she said sternly. "Before it's too late. So she won't marry you. So what? You should be proud that she takes her vows seriously, that she's the kind of woman who sticks to her promises, no matter how bad it gets. That's the kind of woman you want raising your kid, right?"

He looked over to Ann, who was beet red, her hair plastered to her head, looking about as bad as it was possible for her to look, and his face softened. God, she was gorgeous. "Yeah."

"And you should tell her you love her."

"Oh, she knows that."

At Ann's surprise, he lifted his eyebrows.

"You didn't know that?"

"No," she said. "I didn't know that."

"You should have known that."

"And how was I supposed to know that?"

"Enough," Mer told them, and they shut up. "You really want to argue this out now? Dad, just tell her."

"I love you," he snapped out. And then, softer, warmer, "I love you."

"I love you, too."

"There you go," Mer said. "Don't know why you guys didn't figure that one out a long time ago. *We* knew. Didn't we, Mary?"

"From the first."

Ann sucked in a breath. "I think another one's coming again—"

"Then you'd better talk fast," Mer told her. "You, you got other responsibilities. We know that. But you got one here, too, and it's time for you to own up to it."

Ann gritted her teeth, gripped her hands tighter around Tom's and Mary's. And she nodded. "I don't know if it's enough for you," she said in a rush. "I can't go in front of a preacher. Not now. But I'm yours. Better or worse. You and the baby and Mer. Till death do us part."

"Till death do us part." Tom nodded, accepting.

"Okay, now that that's over with." The nurse settled herself between Ann's legs, until only her cap showed above the hammock of the sheets. "Whaddya say we get this baby out?"

THIRTY-NINE

Five years later

"Hey," Tom said. "I thought it was time we had a little chat."

The headstone was substantial but simple, a thick rectangle of polished granite, the letters deeply carved:

John Martin McCrary
Son, husband, friend, beloved

This was a nice cemetery, Tom thought, perched on a little hill thick with oak trees taking on their fall browns and reds. Far down the hill, you could catch the glitter of water where a tiny lake settled into the soft roll of land.

New grass, green and lush, had taken hold over the dirt, the shade of the new stuff just enough different from the growth surrounding it to mark the rectangle of the grave.

"I see your mom's been here." The flowers in the brass vase beside the marker were mums the color of spices, fresh enough that they had to have been put there within the last day. "She's doing okay, you know. We see her a lot. Got herself a little condo about a mile away. And a friend, too. Henry." He put his hand on the top of the stone. It was cold, but it felt solid. "She started a class at the community center. You know, the one you designed? For the girls. Who would have thought they wanted to knit? But they like it, and they like her, and she got some store to donate a truckload of yarn and needles. She's a lot tougher than she looks, that one. But then, you know that."

He went silent, listening to the whisper of the breeze through the trees, the impatient chatter of the birds. "We don't see your dad so much. He's down South a lot, golfing. Got his handicap down to seven."

It had been an infection that had taken John at last, swift and mysterious, unaffected by the antibiotics the doctors pumped in, and they'd never even identified where it started.

Tom tugged on his collar, stiff as a board. "Did she make you get all dressed up when you got married, too? Damned uncomfortable, this thing."

He pointed down the hill, where Boom, clad in classy black with matching sunglasses, was valiantly trying to keep Tom's son from tipping over a gravestone and ruining his minitux.

"See that one, down there? That's Johnnie. He's a wild one, you know. If we make it through the wedding without him wrecking the church, it's gonna be a miracle. Only person he ever behaves for is your mother. They're buds."

Boom, who'd finally solved the problem by scooping Johnnie up and tucking him under his arm, looked in Tom's direction and tapped his wristwatch.

"Just a minute," he called, then turned back to the grave. The stone was so highly polished he could see the sky reflected in it, drifting clouds and a tracery of the branches overhead. "Can't be late. Mer's got it in her head I'm gonna be late, and she's been nagging me about it for a week," he said. "We gave her your house to live in. Hope you don't mind. She's taking good care of it, and it's nice to have her next door. Ann redid my house . . . How'd you live with her when she was doing that? Man. You'd've thought what kind of plates we had over the outlets was gonna affect national security, she spent so much time mulling it over."

He smiled. But then, he could never help but smile when he thought of her. "Turned out great, though. And Mer, she actually graduated, if you can imagine, then went to cooking school. Me and Boom, we told her we'd stake her to a restaurant, soon as she's ready, but she says she needs a couple more years of experience first. And Lord, does she love her brother and sister."

With his forefinger, he moved aside the blanket that covered the face of the bundle he held in his left arm. "Oh, yeah. The sister. This here's Gracie." She was sleeping peacefully; she did that a lot, nothing like Johnnie, who'd hollered a good chunk of his first year of life. Her skin was like milk chocolate, her cheeks the kind of chubby that was made for pinching, and she had to be the most beautiful thing he'd ever seen. "The adoption was just finalized. One of my boys, he got his girlfriend pregnant, and they asked us to take her. Can you imagine? Us. Said they couldn't think of anyone better." The wonder of it still caught him sometimes. He'd look down at Gracie, at the smile she'd give him when he found her in the crib in the morning, awake and burbling, and he'd wonder how he'd ever lived without her. It was as if there'd been a place inside him all along, just waiting for her.

"So that just leaves Ann." His throat was thickening up already, and he wondered how he was going to get through the ceremony without bawling. Boom'd threatened to punch him if he started dripping. "She's good, John. Really good. Great, amazing, the best woman on earth. But then, you know that." He swallowed. "Thank you. Thank you for loving her well, for letting her love you back."

That was the wonder of it all. Loving one person didn't make you love another less. It let you love more.

He tucked Gracie up against his shoulder, where she fit like she'd been made to rest there, and turned toward the limo that sat beyond the line of graves, waiting for them.

"I'll take good care of her," he said.